Scott Anderson

Moonlight
Hotel

Scott Anderson is a war correspondent and a contributing writer at *The New York Times Magazine*. His work has also appeared in *Vanity Fair, Esquire, Harper's Magazine, Outside*, and many other publications. Over the years he has written from Beirut, Northern Ireland, Chechnya, Israel, Sudan, El Salvador, and a number of other war-torn areas. He is the author of the novel *Triage* and the nonfiction books *The 4 O'Clock Murders, The Man Who Tried to Save the World*, and, with his brother Jon Lee Anderson, *War Zones*. Anderson lives in upstate New York.

Also by Scott Anderson

The Man Who Tried to Save the World

Triage

The 4 O'Clock Murders

War Zones *(with Jon Lee Anderson)*

Inside the League *(with Jon Lee Anderson)*

Moonlight
Hotel

Moonlight Hotel

A Novel

Scott Anderson

Anchor Books
A Division of Random House, Inc.
New York

FIRST ANCHOR BOOKS EDITION, AUGUST 2007

The Library of Congress has cataloged the Doubleday edition as follows:
Anderson, Scott, 1959–
    Moonlight hotel : a novel / Scott Anderson.
        p.   cm.
    I. Title.
PS3551.N3945M66 2006
813'.54–dc22
2005051966

Anchor ISBN: 978-1-4000-9563-6

Book design by Maria Carella

www.anchorbooks.com

Printed in the United States of America
10 9 8 7 6 5 4 3 2 1

To the memory of my mother and father

Moonlight
Hotel

Prologue

He marked the days by their dawns. With each, he found he had lost a bit more of her during the night.

First to leave was the touch of her: the feel of her hand, the way she tousled his hair, kissed the nape of his neck. After this, it was her scent: the perfume she wore, the breath of her. By the fourth morning, he began to lose the sight of her. He tried to forestall this by concentrating on specific moments when they had been together but, try as he might, her likeness grew steadily more indistinct, a ghost floating ever farther away, and then, not even a ghost, just an absence where she had been. In this way, he lost her smile, the shape of her eyes, he lost the memory of the hopefulness with which she had gazed out at the world.

What stayed was her sound—her laugh, her sigh, the quiet way she sneezed—and it was a great comfort to him during those long days of waiting to still have these, to hear her again whenever he wished. But then even these started to go, one by one, drowned out by the other sounds in his mind or those coming from beyond the walls of his room. By dawn of the seventh day, he found she was gone completely, that he had nothing left of her to lose.

What made this somewhat ironic was that, judging by the

manner in which they kept him, David was not supposed to have any knowledge of the dawn—really any knowledge at all. His room had no window, its steel door was never opened, and the chute mechanism through which they passed him food had been designed to admit no light. But what those holding him had overlooked—or, perhaps, simply couldn't be bothered with—was the narrow band of light that seeped beneath the base of the door. This band was not more than an inch in width, but this was enough to tell David many things.

It was enough to tell him, for example, that his cell was on the top floor of the prison and facing its open courtyard; if he were on a lower floor, his room would be in shadow at sunrise and would fall back into it long before sunset, he would not see the tinges of gold and red in the late light. It told him his meals came at wildly irregular hours of the day and night. It told him the executions began at dawn.

With the first one, he had been caught unprepared. It had been on his third morning there, and he had been watching that band of darkest blue spread across the gap beneath his door, that cobalt blue which is the first sign of a dawning sky, when out in the courtyard he heard very different sounds from those he had grown accustomed to: a rhythmic tromping of feet, commands called out by a man with a lilting singsong voice. When the volley of gunshots came, the reverberation banged against the door of his cell so hard that he was momentarily deafened, he felt the echo in his jaw and teeth. After that first time, he learned death's cadence, he memorized that last call of the commander—a melodic, four-syllable tune—and then he covered his ears and gritted his teeth. On some mornings, this period passed quickly—five or six bangs upon the door, upon his ears and teeth, and then it was over—but on others it continued for hours, endless mornings of the same little killing song rising on the air.

During the rest of the time, David focused on remembering her, and on learning what he could from the other sounds afforded him. By listening to their footfalls, he was able to identify the different guards who regularly paced the corridor outside: there was the Shuffler, the Marcher, the Fat One. From beyond the prison walls, he sometimes heard a car horn or the call of a food vendor, and if it was painful to hear these things–they stirred a longing in him–they also told David there was a breeze floating over the city just then, that out there, normal life was continuing and those living it had a breeze upon their faces.

And on the dawn of that seventh morning, just as that band of dark blue began to spread beneath his door, David understood something else, the closest thing to a revelation he would experience during those long days of waiting. The sight and sound of her had not vanished in the sleep of his nights, but rather in all those hours he had spent watching that gap beneath his door, in all those other sounds he had listened to. He had been so intent on cheating the darkness and silence they meant for him that, in the end, there had been no place left for the barest memory of her.

This realization came at that moment when he heard strange footsteps coming along the corridor, when the shadow of two feet appeared beneath his door, and it struck him with such force that he didn't even have time to be startled by the clang of his opening door, by the sudden burst of early light that now bathed his face.

In the doorway stood Rustam. He was staring down at him, smiling his wry smile, but David was still so disoriented that what he focused on was the strip of white cloth Rustam held in both his hands, gripping it rather like a cook might grip a dishrag.

"So at last I find you, Mr. Richards," Rustam said in that soft, gentle voice of his. As he came across the room, he raised the blindfold. "I'm sorry."

Part One

One

She was leaning on the balcony railing, staring into the night, and David saw how her bare arms shone white, like marble or bone, from the lights of the house. She turned to look at him over her shoulder, tossing her blond hair as she did so. She smiled.

"You must have the best view in Kutar," she said.

David set their drinks on the railing, leaned like her, gazed out at what she saw. "One of them, I guess," he said.

They were on the back balcony of the house. The land fell away abruptly at that point on the ridgeline, giving the illusion at night that one was perched on the edge of a steep cliff. The airport and northern suburbs were below them, and then the desert began, a great darkness broken only by an occasional vehicle coming over the national highway and a few bright lights in the far distance. During his first weeks in Kutar, David had thought those lights were of isolated homes, homes he could never make out during the day, until his telescope arrived and he discovered they were stars low on the horizon. He looked to her and told her this.

She was very pretty in a wholesome, middle-America kind of way: striking eyes somewhere between blue and gray, a pleasant mouth, the emerald-green sheath dress suited her pale skin. He had forgotten her name. Julia, possibly, or maybe Janine.

She took a perfunctory sip from her drink, glanced at her wristwatch. "I should probably get going. Corinne will get worried."

David knew this was the time for him to say something–really, most anything would do. Instead he looked back out at the desert.

An upland breeze brought sounds from the northern suburbs: car horns, the rhythmic clang of metal, the whine of a truck laboring over Gowarshad Pass. From somewhere down the ridge came the baying of a wolf. David had heard the coastal range was home to great packs of wolves–the small, tan-colored sort one found in this part of the world–but he had yet to see one personally.

It was her green dress that he had first noticed at the party; even now, in what passed for early autumn in Kutar, most foreigners wore shades of white on account of the heat. Corinne, the wife of the political attaché, had waved David over and introduced her cousin, just in from Chicago for a visit, with a sly expression. Janine? Perhaps it was Jennifer.

At the balcony, he pointed into the dark, off to the east. "The sun comes up right over there. At first the desert is pink, then orange. Then it turns to gold." He lowered his arm, turned to her. "You should stay and watch the sunrise."

He saw the way her hand tightened on the railing, she gave a nervous little laugh. "I don't know," she said. "What would Corinne think?"

David smiled, as much to himself as to her. Corinne knew exactly what to think. Corinne would be far more surprised if her cousin from Chicago actually made the journey back down the mountain tonight. He didn't say this, though.

"You can call her," he said, "tell her you want to see the sunrise."

She reached for her glass again, but stopped, her lips quivering in an uncertain way. He leaned in to kiss her lightly on the jaw. "You should stay," he whispered.

He kissed her again, a bit lower this time, on her throat, and he felt her sharp intake of breath, her tensing. She smelled of gardenia and rose and something astringent, and she tilted her head back to make room for him.

By the bed, he watched her undress, felt a tug of something almost like sadness at the careful way she removed the green dress and draped it over a chairback.

Afterward, with her sleeping beside him, David gazed up at his bedroom ceiling and listened. There were the usual sounds of the night: the low thrum of the city, the odd creaks of the house; the wolf was quiet now. He felt her breath, hot and regular, on his neck.

He smiled in the dark, struck by the incongruous thought that her breaths on his throat were meant to serve a purpose, as if he were some inflatable object that needed air. With this thought, he considered kissing her—the top of her head was just an inch from his mouth, her hair brushed his lips—but he didn't want to wake her. Instead, after a time he moved out of her embrace, the warm breath on his throat was gone, because what had started out as a humorous image had become a bit unsettling, and he silently rose from the bed and went back outside. He looked to the east, as if for the first traces of dawn, even though he knew this was still a long way off.

The Monday morning staff meeting began at 10:30. David arrived a bit early, as was his habit, in order to claim a seat facing the windows and the embassy's inner courtyard. Though he couldn't see the courtyard garden from that vantage point—the conference room was on the third floor—some of the upper branches of the trees were visible, and he liked having them to gaze at when the meetings went long.

The others began filing in shortly after, singly or in pairs, and David said a few words of greeting to each. To his surprise, Bill Myerson sat directly across from him. David couldn't recall him ever sitting there before, and he wondered if it signified something. He nodded at Bill, then opened one of his file folders and pretended to scan its contents.

Ambassador Draper strode in precisely on time and made for his chair at the head of the table. Flipping to a blank page in his notebook, he took a silver pen from his shirt pocket, looked along the table with a knowing smile.

"Well," he said, "I just read over the NSA's situation report." He paused for effect. "No mention of us again."

There were polite chuckles at the ambassador's favorite—and at this point, somewhat tired—opening joke. Every Sunday, the National Security Agency cabled a classified report to all overseas missions listing any potential crises—military unrest, labor strikes, the failing health of a head of state—that might be cause for concern somewhere in the world that week. Over the course of a year, a particularly troubled country might garner dozens of such citations, but this was not the case with Kutar; before his own posting there, David had checked the NSA index and discovered the kingdom hadn't even been mentioned in nearly a decade.

"So let's do it," John Draper said, and turned to the man on his immediate right, the agricultural, commercial, and economic attaché, Lee Warren.

Because the American mission to Kutar was so small—nine officials, a support staff of some two dozen, the eight Marine Guards—all the traditional diplomatic portfolios were handled by a mere four attachés. This rarely caused problems. In Lee Warren's case, for example, Kutar had virtually no external commerce to speak of, its role in the global economy was largely theoretical, and for the attachés the consolidation held the benefit of making them eligible for a wider range of postings in the future.

As usual, Lee spoke for only a few minutes, and then it was the turn of Cheryl Thompson, the consular officer. Cheryl reported that her office had received 112 new visa applications during the previous week, but had processed 163—9 approvals, 154 rejections—as it tried to pare down the backlog. This brought an approving nod from the ambassador.

"Excellent," he said. "At this rate, we should be pretty well caught up by Christmas."

"I should think so," Cheryl replied.

It was, in fact, Kutar's very insignificance that had made Ambassador Draper's arrival six months earlier a bit puzzling. Not yet forty-five, his rise through the Foreign Service up to that point had been steady and swift, so there was considerable debate among the American legation as to why he had ended up there. Some speculated he was being groomed for a more sensitive post in the region, and thus "paying his dues," but at least as many suspected he had made an enemy of someone important at State and was suffering retribution. For his part, John Draper never let on that he was anything but thrilled to be in Kutar—which, of course, was itself the sign of a good diplomat.

In any event, David had taken a quick liking to Draper, as had most of the staff. Handsome, with the lanky frame of a former athlete, the ambassador exuded an energy and optimism that was refreshing. With his attractive wife, Susan, and their three polite children, the Drapers seemed the very essence of a diplomatic family—charming, earnest, easy with all kinds of people—the sort that could be relied upon to cast the United States in a positive light abroad. And even if the vigor he brought to the post seemed a tad excessive—the previous ambassador had found once-a-month staff meetings more than sufficient—David saw its benefit as a guard against the torpor of the place.

"And the king thinks he'll get everyone on board with it?" John Draper was following up on some issue raised by Harold Derwinski, the political attaché, the details of which David had missed.

"I'd say it's still in the talking phase," Harold replied. "There's liable to be some grumbling from the traditionalists, but it's got a lot of support with the technocrats."

"Good," the ambassador said, "let's keep on top of that."

As the meeting wore on, David looked to the tree branches beyond Bill Myerson's head. What passed for winter in Kutar–a misting rain, an ocean-borne wind–wouldn't start for at least another three months, and until then even the slenderest of limbs would barely move in the still air of the enclosed garden; the little leaves would wear their brown coats of dust. Beyond the tree branches and the embassy roof, he saw the top of the coastal ridge and the uppermost reaches of the poorer hillside neighborhoods of Laradan, cascades of white houses that from this distance looked rather like mottled snow. He knew he couldn't see his own home from the conference room–it was off to the right and blocked by an office building–but he looked in that direction anyway.

"Bill?" the ambassador called.

David turned to see Bill Myerson staring fixedly at him from across the table, his mind clearly far away.

"Bill? Anything?" The ambassador tried again.

This brought the deputy chief of mission back with a start. "Sorry, John. No, nothing." Bill reddened, stole an embarrassed glance at David, then looked back down the long table to John Draper. "Sorry," he muttered again.

The ambassador nodded, continued on. The speaking role finally fell to David, the foreign aid and development officer.

"Not much to report," he said, scanning the papers before him as if to make sure he wasn't overlooking something. "The piping has come in for the Farwan irrigation project, so that's getting

back up to speed. And there's going to be a ribbon-cutting ceremony for the new high school in Ansara Sunday after next; naturally, they'd love it if you could chopper in for it."

John Draper nodded. "Anything from the geologists?"

"I spoke with them on Thursday," David replied. "They said
they might be a few more weeks yet."

This brought a sigh of frustration from the ambassador. A
year ago, the U.S. Geological Survey had issued a report theorizing
that, based on rock-strata mappings, the northern mountains of
Kutar might conceal a large reservoir of water, an aquifer that, if
tapped, could make farming possible in that desolate region. A
team of American geologists had been sent into the mountains to
take water-table readings, but what was supposed to have been a
two-month mission was already well into its fourth.

"This thing is kind of dragging out, isn't it?" John Draper said.

David nodded. "It's just very rough terrain up there, and it's
all hard-rock."

" Hard-rock?"

"It slows down the drilling a lot. You're always having to replace the drill bits."

The ambassador pondered this with a frown. "I just don't like
the idea of those guys being stuck out there in the middle of
nowhere indefinitely." But then whatever worries he had seemed
to pass; he looked to David with a smile. "Still, it'd really be something for Kutar if it plays out, wouldn't it?"

What the ambassador didn't know, or perhaps chose to
ignore, was that the aquifer theory was but the latest in a long
series which had bestowed all manner of imagined riches on the
northern mountains over the years–gold, titanium, manganese,
there had even been talk of oil at one time–and that each had
ultimately proven to be wrong. Certainly the water theory looked
more promising than most of the previous ones, but the high
stack of disappointing geological reports David kept in his office
had served to temper his enthusiasm, had allowed him to at least

entertain the dispiriting notion that this impoverished region of Kutar might, in fact, already be living up to its full potential on the planet.

The Monday morning staff meeting didn't seem the place to bring this up, though. "Yes," David smiled back at the ambassador, "that really would be something."

As the gathering was breaking up, Harold Derwinski called their attention one last time. "Just a reminder about the reception at the Swiss ambassador's tonight." He shot a respectful glance at John Draper. "Now I know there've been a lot of these functions lately, we've all got busy lives, but the Swiss are pretty important allies, so it'd be nice to have a good turnout."

"Allies?" Stan Peterson cocked an eyebrow in mock surprise. "I thought this thing was to celebrate Swiss neutrality."

The ambassador chuckled. "I think you know what he means, Stan." He turned to the political attaché, gave a nod. "Good point, Harry. Thanks for the reminder."

———

The city of Laradan was ancient, although precisely how ancient had never been determined. For at least the first two thousand years of its existence, settlement had been confined to the bluff just above the harbor, and what had been created over that time was a sprawling warren of three- and four-story whitewashed buildings and winding alleys, churches and mosques and little plazas. It was for this area–the Old City–that Laradan was famous, to the extent that it was famous at all, and in which the few foreign tourists who found their way to Kutar concentrated their activities.

At the western end of the Old City was the palace compound, and then began the New City, an orderly grid of right-angle streets and Mediterranean-style office buildings constructed by the British in the 1880s and fronting on the half-moon of Serenity Bay. While there were now more modern and desirable business areas, the New City remained the site for most of the twenty-odd embassies in Kutar, including the American one, a vaguely Italianate manor house facing the bay. From the large, quartered windows of his office on the third floor, David had a view of the entire waterfront promenade that, on cool nights, served as the social hub of the city. Into the very late hours, thousands would stroll its three-mile length, from the central harbor on the eastern promontory of Serenity Bay clear along to the Moonlight Hotel, a once-grand old place on its western end, and then they would turn and stroll back again.

It had only been in the modern era, with the advent of water pumps, that Laradan began expanding into the foothills, and it was there that most of its 500,000 or so residents now lived. These neighborhoods ranged from the very poor and crowded–slums, really–on the slopes above the New City to the leafy compounds and fine homes of the Baktiar quarter above the Old City.

One peculiar aspect of Laradan was that most all of it looked the same, a five-year-old building virtually indistinguishable from one that had stood for five hundred. Perhaps this was due to the whitewash that the Kutarans slathered over everything, or to the dense housing and narrow streets that seemed to be their preference, but save for the more obvious accoutrements of the twentieth century, a medieval merchant suddenly risen from the dead and dropped into present-day Laradan would probably have felt quite at home. David had never before lived in a place with this aura of timelessness, and he found it quite appealing.

Along with this was the city's cosmopolitan nature. Being a port, all kinds of peoples had passed through over the centuries, and enough had stayed on to give it the feel of an exotic crossroads. In the oldest part of the Old City there still existed the Jewish and Armenian quarters. In enclaves of the central bazaar were clustered the shops of Lebanese jewelers and Indian tailors and East African spice merchants. From what David had observed, these various minorities coexisted quite easily with the majority population, although he suspected this tolerance stemmed more from Laradan's mercantile nature than from any especially enlightened views of its inhabitants; like port cities everywhere, this was a place where money held greater sway than God or politics, where harmony was largely a matter of self-interest.

But what David could never fully dispel, what, in fact, colored his judgment of the city and the country—even the development proposals that crossed his desk—were the views from the verandas of his home. Looking south from that acute point on the ridgeline, he could see a vast stretch of the coastal shelf, not just Laradan directly below, but the fields and orchards and villages that spread down the coast in either direction, that filled every last corner, it seemed, of the thin strip of habitable land between the mountains and the sea. By walking a few steps around the house to his other veranda, he could take in the meager sprawl of the northern suburbs, the scant patchworks of warehouses and working-class neighborhoods that huddled at the inland base of Gowarshad Pass, before the great desert began. With these views, framed as they were by the endless sea on one horizon, the endless desert on the other, David carried a constant awareness of the tenuousness of the lives being led down there, could never shake the idea that it would take very little—not a major cataclysm at all—to sweep it away. He did not believe he was being morbid in this. He believed anyone living with such views might harbor the same thought.

———

"Champagne, sir?" Behind his silver tray of glasses, the Swiss ambassador's houseboy wore a doleful look.

"Thank you." David took a glass and watched the servant shamble off across the mansion porch. He suspected the man's unhappiness stemmed from his Arabian Nights outfit—burgundy turban, glittering jacket, small upturned gold slippers—which had to be uncomfortable in the heat. It was also unclear how the motif tied in with Swiss Neutrality Day, except that ceremonial costumes were a rather recent innovation in Kutar and selection was limited;

much to the delight of British diplomats, the caterers at that year's Fourth of July party at the American embassy had shown up in pirate outfits.

From the porch, David looked over the lawn, scanned the clusters of guests dimly lit in the glow of lawn torches. He spotted Joanna—that was her name, he had learned—standing with Corinne and an older couple near one of the buffet tables. Joanna saw him, gave a wave, but David pretended to not notice, continued his sweeping gaze toward the swimming pool. And there was Diane. She stood with several others near the pumphouse, but she had already seen him, her face struck gold by torchlight as she stared at him, and David suspected she had positioned herself in such a way to watch the porch for his arrival. He took a sip from his champagne flute, started down the stairs.

A number of the guests nodded as he crossed the lawn, made way for him to join their circles of conversation—he really was quite popular within the diplomatic community—but David kept moving, smiling, raising a hand as if to suggest he had to find someone, would circle back by as soon as he could. He reached Corinne's side, gave her and Joanna polite pecks on the cheek. With a sinking heart, he saw they were talking to Nigel Mayhew and his wife.

A stoutish man in his mid-sixties who sported a fine white mustache, Nigel Mayhew was the sort of old-school British diplomat—a graduate of Eton and Oxford, he never failed to remind a listener—that one rarely actually encountered anymore. Even the navy-blue pinstriped suit and blue-and-red school tie that he invariably wore to such events seemed designed to conjure that earlier, better age when diplomacy was the province of soberminded, upper-class men such as himself.

"David, you know the Mayhews, don't you?" Corinne asked.

"Of course." David smiled. "How are you, Nigel, Sarah?"

The British First Secretary gave a quick, almost imperceptible nod. "Richards."

Of the many things David found annoying about Nigel Mayhew, he especially disliked his habit of addressing other men by their last names. As always, Sarah Mayhew, a doughty, plump woman in her sixties, said nothing, simply fixed David with a beatific smile.

"So Chicago, eh?" Nigel said, turning back to Joanna. "A cattle town, if memory serves, what first put it on the map."

Joanna gave David a hesitant glance. "Well, actually, more shipping and railroads. It was the transportation hub when the upper plains opened up to farming, and all the railroads led there."

"Of course." Nigel nodded vigorously. "Can't very well move cattle without railroads. And a rather windy place, too, as I recall."

Joanna smiled. "That's right. It's called the Windy City."

"Ah, yes." The British First Secretary looked positively triumphant. "I remember some mention of that back at Eton."

Just then Nicky Draper, the ambassador's seven-year-old son, darted by with two other young boys, and David seized the moment to call him over.

"Hi, Uncle David." The boy was wearing a little suit for the occasion—a plaid jacket, khaki shorts—but his socks and knees were already grass stained from whatever he and the other boys had been doing. David crouched down to his level.

"Whatcha up to, pal?"

Nicky shrugged. "Playing. Are we still going sailing on Saturday?"

David smiled. For some reason, the ambassador's son had taken an intense liking to him from their very first meeting. He was a sweet, sensitive boy but had been lonely in Kutar at the outset, and David had made a point of talking or playing with him for a few minutes whenever there was some function where children were invited. The previous month, he'd even taken Nicky on one of his weekend trips up-country, had let him ride on a camel while wearing a turban, and it was on that trip that the boy had first called him Uncle David.

"You still want to go sailing?" he asked.

Nicky nodded earnestly.

"Okay, then." David tousled the boy's hair and stood up, watched him immediately dash off to rejoin his friends. He saw Joanna smiling at him in an uncomfortably appraising way, but at least he had broken Nigel Mayhew's grip on the conversation. "So how was your day?" he asked her.

She talked of going to the bazaar with Corinne, the silk fabric she had bought there after much negotiation, their lunch at a quiet restaurant on the mountainside with its shaded terrace overlooking the city. David found he was only half listening to her, a smile frozen on his face, nodding at the appropriate moments.

He wanted to leave. He wanted to take Joanna up the hill to his home and stare out at the desert with her. He wanted to watch the slow, deliberate way she removed her clothes, to hear the funny little sigh she gave, a kind of verbal tic, when she first settled into his bed. But because even in Kutar there was a protocol to such things, he knew they couldn't leave, not yet; they had to at least stay through the fireworks and toasts.

The evening wore on, a slow circling of faces that had become too familiar, an interminable series of chats among people who seemed to have long since exhausted whatever had once been interesting to say to one another. Beyond the garden walls, the sounds of the city rose, but on that lantern-lit expanse of lawn David felt as if he were aboard some cruise ship stranded in the night, he and the others condemned to endlessly mingle, to pick at hors d'oeuvres, to sip champagne, voyagers caught in a doldrum, all soldiering on to make the best of an eternal wait. He didn't know how the others withstood it—the "real diplomats" who were wedded to the capital, who spent their days attending meetings and conferences and compiling reports, who spent most evenings at functions like this. At least as the foreign aid officer, David had an escape hatch: the field, his various projects scattered about the country.

At last there were the fireworks—a brief affair out by the swimming pool—and then there was the toast to Swiss pacifism, and it was then that he and Joanna finally could make their escape. As they crossed the lawn, David noticed the servants had taken advantage of the distraction out by the pool to cast off their small golden slippers. They seemed much happier now, padding about in their bare feet.

In the car, he told Musa, the embassy driver, to turn the air-conditioning up to full strength. He put a hand on Joanna's back, felt the dampness there, then ran a hand up her spine and made her shiver. They laughed together and she leaned into him, caressed his leg just above the knee. "You're terrible," she said, and there was a tenderness in her voice that gave David pause.

She was leaving in two days. He thought he would probably miss her.

He watched her face as he moved inside her. Her eyes were shut tight, her breath was coming in short gasps, and the red blush, almost a rash, had blossomed over her chest, and David knew she was near. She reached her hand for the pillow next to her, clenched a clump of it into her fist, the way she always did, and then the moaning came, more a whimper than a moan, soft and low, and David felt the tensing through her entire body and then the release of it, and afterward he watched her eyes flutter open, her breathing settle down, her lips curve into her smile, and he smiled back.

After a time, she reached for her pack of cigarettes on the bedside table, and he slowly rose from the bed. This seemed to be the unspoken signal between them, the cigarette, the moment when the spell was broken and he was free to move about. He stretched and wandered over to the window, casually pulled back the thin curtain. They had taken a room in one of the cheap merchant hotels in the Old City, near the central bazaar, but the streets outside were quiet and empty in the afternoon heat.

"So you're sleeping with her, aren't you?"

David turned. Diane was sitting against the headboard, the sheet pulled up around her breasts, her cigarette poised between two fingers as she studied him.

"Who?" he asked.

"Don't be coy, David; it doesn't suit you. Corinne's cousin, the blonde."

The room was small and still and the gray smoke hung in the air. "Her name is Joanna," he said. "And, yes, I was sleeping with her."

She arched an eyebrow. "Was?"

"She left for the States yesterday."

Diane shook her head, gave a quick laugh, but her eyes were hard, hurt. "How perfect for you. I'm curious, though; do you ask how long they're going to be around before you sleep with them? What's the cutoff? Ten days? Two weeks?"

He stifled a sigh, took up his trousers from the floor. She watched him dress.

"Sorry," she said after a while. "Kind of." She leaned over to stub out her cigarette in the ashtray. "I think Bill suspects something."

David looked at her. He had begun thinking that himself, especially since the Monday staff meeting, Bill sitting across from him, staring at him like that. But David also knew it was easy to imagine such things, especially when one already felt guilty. "Why?" he asked.

Diane was getting dressed herself now. She shrugged. "He's been pretty withdrawn lately, irritable. He's not the type to come out and ask, though."

David nodded. From what he knew of Bill Myerson, he sensed that his pride would keep him from confronting his wife until he was absolutely certain—maybe not even then.

Their affair had started seven or eight months ago, the culmination of a long flirtation that had finally slipped from control at some embassy garden party. Diane was in her mid-thirties, twelve years younger than Bill, unhappy and bored in Kutar. David didn't really have an excuse, except that Diane was pretty: tall, with olive skin, sharp features. In the hotel room, she finished dressing and stood with her arms folded over her chest, staring at the floor.

"It may not be that, though," she said softly. "There've been some other things going on with us."

The statement lingered between them. David knew she wanted him to ask, but Diane also knew he wouldn't. That was one of the tricky things with affairs–maintaining their limits, staying vigilant against lapses–and he was better at all that than she was.

She went to the bedside table, took another cigarette from her pack. "I'm going to Rome tomorrow. I'll be gone a few days."

She liked imparting information to him at the last minute. David figured it was her way of showing autonomy or resentment, but it never really bothered him; in the hotel room, he was just glad the conversation had moved on.

"That'll be nice." He smiled. "A shopping trip?"

Diane studied him again, eyes squinted against the smoke. At last, she gave a tired nod–"Yeah, something like that"–and turned to leave.

David started to follow her out, but at the threshold he happened to glance back at the rumpled bed they had just shared, the already-yellowing stain they had left there, and for no reason he could immediately identify, he closed his eyes and rested his temple against the edge of the open door–it was cool and rough against his skin–and all he heard was the quiet of the city from beyond the window and the clack of Diane's shoes as she descended the staircase, and he stayed like that until he heard the sound of her stop.

"David? Are you coming?" she called, and her question floated up through the stairwell with a slight echo.

The day ended like every other: bright and clear, a softening of the blanched white–of the houses, the sunstruck rocks–to gold, then to pink, and then there was that last wash of silver and blue. He had forgotten to tell Joanna about that, the silver blue, that briefest of moments just after the sun slipped behind the western peaks when the world lay suspended between day and night, between white and black, that magical instant of possibility–never more than a few minutes in the dry, clarified air of the desert–when there was no shadow or darkness or light, when everything was simply in between, murky, silver and blue and waiting. And then it passed and night came on, and with its passing came the realization that there was no magic, no real possibility, that all it meant was that even here, in one of the more forgotten corners of the universe, time was still marked.

Leaning against the railing of his southern veranda, David gazed down at the darkening city. He scanned the sea in hopes of spotting a passing ship, but all he could make out were the little fishing boats from the harbor, all close along the shoreline and heading in for the night, the ocean beyond empty and calm.

He pondered how he would remember this land, where it would fit into his thoughts. His tour there was almost over–it had been twenty-one months already–and he believed he would miss it. He liked the people, found them friendly and warm. He enjoyed the desert and the exoticism of the hill villages, the markets. Some of his projects, especially those in the northern mountains, were interesting. And, of course, there were the women. Not the local women–they were attractive, to be sure, but Kutar remained a conservative society and he'd been warned to stay clear–but the foreign ones who lived there or who happened to pass through. There was something about the place, maybe its remoteness or its monotony or even its very conservatism, that seemed to bring out the daring in a certain sort of woman, and during David's time here he had encountered a good number of them: secretaries, diplomats, visitors like Joanna, wives like Diane.

But as he stood there that evening, David believed what he would miss most of all was the view from his southern veranda at just these moments—not the simple beauty of it, but rather the feeling that came over him as night settled on the city. He could not readily explain this emotion, except that it was at these precise times when he most keenly felt the fragility of the world around him, of the lives being lived below, and it stirred in him a kind of tender protectiveness. It sounded terribly grandiose, he knew, but it was as if he were watching over a place that lay defenseless—to the night, to the surrounding sea and desert—and he was its protector.

Two

At the front of the sailboat, Paolo bore a worried expression. "You're certain this is safe?"

"Perfectly," David said, untying the mooring line. "I'm a good sailor."

"And if we get stranded out there?"

David looked past the port mouth to the open sea; wind riffled the water, there were even small whitecaps. "Trust me, that won't happen today."

"So you're saying there's too much wind. We could tip over."

David grinned at his friend as he pushed away from the pier. He was never sure if Paolo's fretfulness was genuine or something of an act—maybe a combination of the two. "You know," he called, "in some countries cowardice is considered a negative trait. Maybe you should try to be a bit more like Nicky here."

He cocked his chin at the boy sitting on the cross-seat of the boat in his life preserver. Paolo laughed at this; Nicky lit up with pride.

It was midmorning on Saturday, the fishermen's idle day, and David had arranged to rent one of the larger boats they used for open water. He was looking forward to the outing, as he hadn't sailed since coming to Kutar, and had decided to invite Paolo along at the last minute; he hadn't seen his friend in several weeks and he thought Nicky would like him.

He realized his mistake as soon as they cleared the port mouth. The boat was high-hulled to hold a good catch, but that also made it tippy in high wind, and the wind that day was unusually strong. The instant they rounded the harbor wall it hit them, heeled the boat to starboard, and they nearly went over before David could release the sail line. Nicky squealed with joy as they dropped back down.

"Let's do that again!" he shouted.

But David looked past the boy to Paolo; his friend had gone pale with fear. "Sorry," he called. "I was holding her too tight. Are you okay?"

Paolo glanced at the boy, then nodded, flipped a nonchalant hand in the air. "Yes, of course. But maybe we can try to be a bit more temperate."

David took up the sail line again, got the boat's feel, and settled into an easy course, one with just enough pitch to please Nicky. Paolo gradually relaxed, even seemed to enjoy himself as he pointed out different sights along the shoreline to Nicky. It was a spectacular day, clear and sunny as always, and from the water, the whitewashed city looked like some grand wedding cake as it ascended the foothills.

David had met Paolo Alfani shortly after his arrival, at a reception at the Italian embassy, and considered him the closest thing to a good friend that he had in Kutar. At their first meeting, he had naturally assumed the short, heavy-set Italian was a diplomat, and been surprised to learn he was an electrical-parts distributor, one of the very few Western businessmen living in Laradan. Over the subsequent months, David had found himself seeking out Paolo's companionship, partly because he genuinely enjoyed it, but also from a desire to escape the tight orbit of the diplomatic circle. Theirs was an easygoing friendship, one more entertaining than deep, and with an element of mutual benefit: David often invited Paolo along to embassy parties where he might make business contacts, while Paolo had introduced him to a different class of Laradanis than he usually encountered, to areas of the city he would not normally have gone.

They went out as far as Ambar Point, about five miles from the harbor, and then David turned about, found a soft tack line for the longer trip back. Paolo took off his shirt and sprawled out on the small bow deck to sun himself, and they settled into that easy quiet that comes with being at sea. The wind was more predictable on the open water, had lost the crosscuts of closer to shore, so after a while David looked to Nicky and patted the tiller seat beside him. The boy clambered back.

"You want to learn how to sail? Here." He placed the line in Nicky's hand, kept his own on it in case of a sudden gust. "Feel how it tugs? That's from the wind pushing on the sail. Now pull the rope in some and see what happens."

With both hands, Nicky pulled on the line and the boat picked up speed, pitched a bit higher out of the water. At the bow, Paolo lifted his head.

"Let's not go crazy there, little boy," he called.

David tried to explain the concept of tacking to Nicky, wasn't sure how much of it he grasped. He recalled from his own childhood that sailing couldn't be learned in the abstract; like riding a bicycle, one had to just try it, so he took Nicky through a tack, shifted him to the other side of the tiller seat.

"See how that works? When you're heading into the wind, you have to cut back and forth."

The boy nodded solemnly. "You have to zigzag."

"Exactly. That's one of the first really important things to learn about sailing." He nudged Nicky with his shoulder, grinned down at him. "You're a natural."

The boy smiled, leaned into his side.

David had never had such a close relationship with a child,

and though he liked it immensely, he sometimes found the responsibility a bit daunting. He was not used to being needed in this way, had no idea why the boy had chosen him.

After a time, he noticed Nicky was getting red—the Drapers were rather pale complected—so he let the boat drift while he rigged a tarpaulin above the cross-seat, had the boy sit in its shade. Back on the tiller, David charted a more aggressive tack line for the harbor, let his thoughts drift to the soothing sound of the water splashing in their wake.

"Oh, did I tell you?" Paolo called from the bow, propping up on his elbows and fairly shouting to be heard over the wind. "I'm getting my transfer at last."

"Really?" David called back. "Where to?"

"I'm not sure yet, but somewhere in Italy. I'm thinking of requesting Turin. Do you know it?"

David shook his head.

"The city isn't much, but it's close to the Alps, and I can teach the boys to ski. We'll see, but after three years here, I think they owe me."

"Absolutely," David called. "That's great news, Paolo."

Paolo's wife, Andreina, and their two young boys lived outside Rome, and David knew the separation was a constant frustration to his friend, one that came up often in their conversations. Andreina had been out to Kutar several times, the boys just once, and even with his company's liberal vacation policy, Paolo was only able to return home every four or five months. He had requested a transfer ages ago, but apparently no one else at the company was willing to live in Kutar.

"So they finally forced someone to take the position?" David asked.

"They had to," Paolo grinned. "I told them that if I wasn't out by Christmas, I would quit." He sat up, took a cigarette from his shirt pocket, and cupped his hands to light it against the wind. "And what about you? You're leaving soon, no?"

David nodded, started to answer, but then he saw Nicky's stricken look as he peered out from the shade.

"You're leaving?" the boy asked.

David cast a quick glance at Paolo, then shook his head. "Not anytime soon, pal. I'll be here for a long time yet." He gave the boy a reassuring smile, but it didn't work; clutching his sides, Nicky stared down into the boatwell, at the thin layer of grimy water sloshing there, and appeared to fight back tears. With a signal from David, Paolo slid off the bow deck, came back to where the boy sat.

They were still a long way from the harbor, and despite all the adults' efforts to cheer him, Nicky remained disconsolate. They fell into a heavy silence, David and Paolo staring across the sea at the whitewashed city, the boy not lifting his eyes from the brown water washing over his feet.

"Come here," David said finally. But Nicky just shook his head, didn't look up.

"Come back here." This time he spoke firmly, it was more an order than a request, and the obedient, well-disciplined boy got up from the cross-seat and started back. David patted the tiller seat beside him.

"You want to take the sheet again?" he asked. "That's what you call the rope in sailing, the sheet." The boy didn't respond, so David forced the rope into his hand, took his own away. "You're sailing us now. If you don't hold on to it, we'll just sit out here."

Nicky let the rope fall from his fingers. The boom swung out, the boat stalled in the waves, and David put his foot on the coil of sail line to stop it from going out altogether. He pulled it back in, recaught the wind, and again gave the line to Nicky. Again, the boy let go.

Without a word, David brought the rope in once more, but when he pressed it into Nicky's hand this time, he kept his own on top. Taking his other hand from the tiller, he put it around the boy's shoulder, gave him a quick kiss on the top of the head.

"Don't worry," he said, "I'm not going anywhere." He released his grip on the line, and this time the boy held on.

They stayed that way for a while, in the sun of the afternoon, Nicky clutching the rope, David working the tiller, as they charted a course toward shore.

———

"I don't know how to swim, you know," Paolo said, reaching for his beer glass. "I would have sunk like a stone out there."

David slumped back in his seat, incredulous. "Jesus, Paolo, why didn't you tell me? I would have at least gotten you a life preserver."

The Italian wagged a finger. "No, no. Better to be thought a coward than unaccomplished. And anyway, all these safety devices people are so fond of now—life preservers, the seat belt—they're tedious. One should just live. If you drive too fast, or capsize in a boat . . ." He gave a shrug of indifference.

David grinned, thought of the contrast between his friend's attitude now and when they'd been out on the water.

They had dropped Nicky off at the ambassador's residence and gone to a café bar on People's Struggle Boulevard, near Paolo's home. The sun was just beginning to fall behind the western rooftops, casting the nearly empty café in the heavy gold of last light, and the combination of beer and the day's sail had put David in a sleepy, peaceful mood. He would have been content to spend the evening there, talking with Paolo, but he knew he had to leave soon.

"There's a party tonight at the German embassy," he said. "You should come."

"German?" Paolo grimaced. "The hors d'oeuvres will be vile."

"They're running low on lightbulbs. It'll be a quick sale."

Paolo chuckled at this old joke between them. David knew very little about the worlds of commerce or technology, and when at their first meeting Paolo had said he was an electrical-parts distributor, David had asked if that meant lightbulbs and wall sockets.

"It doesn't sound like a good time," Paolo shook his head. "I think I will pass."

"Come on. We can protect each other."

Over the course of parties they'd attended together, they had worked out a series of signals to rescue one another from boring conversations.

Finally, Paolo relented. "But you owe me," he said. "Someday I will make you go to one of my sales conventions."

Outside, the streetlamps of the boulevard had just come on, the first of the night's moths and bats flitting about their glow.

Running along the spine of Baktiar Hill, People's Struggle Boulevard was the sole remnant of an ambitious modernization drive launched by the current king's grandfather during the so-called Era of Progress of the 1920s. Inspired by his visit to several Western European capitals, the king had drawn up plans for an elaborate network of broad, tree-lined avenues in Laradan, punctuated with grand monuments to figures from Kutar's history. It hadn't been long, however, before Britain, the kingdom's chief patron at the time, blanched at the project's cost and quietly scuttled the scheme. In a fit of pique, the king had changed the name of the one completed thoroughfare, Queen Victoria Street, to The People's Heroic Struggle Against Colonial Domination Boulevard, but the road was now universally referred to as either The People's Struggle, or, among the more caustic members of the diplomatic community, The Daily Struggle. It was part of the route David took most every day between his house on the ridge and the embassy, and despite the boulevard's lifelessness—the outdoor cafés and restaurants originally envisioned for its medians had never taken root, its sides were flanked by the drab high walls of government ministries—he was rather fond of the towering palms that had been planted along its length, the dark canopy and cooling shadow they formed against the sun.

They walked up the hill a couple of blocks and stopped on the corner of Paolo's street, watched the road for a taxi that would take David to his home.

"The car's coming for me at eight," he said. "Shall we swing by your place?"

Paolo gave a put-upon shrug, gazed up at a flickering street-lamp. "Oh, will I be pleased to see the last of this place, I can't tell you. Four more weeks and . . ." He fluttered a hand in the air.

David squeezed his friend's arm. "It really is great news, Paolo—and for your boys, too. They'll certainly be glad to have their father around."

"That part, I'm not so sure." Paolo shook his head, but did so with a tender smile. "They've become horribly spoiled under Andreina. I shall have to institute a new regime."

David laughed. It was impossible to imagine his friend as a disciplinarian; he would spoil his children worse than his wife.

There was little traffic on the boulevard; their wait extended.

"He's a sensitive boy, isn't he," Paolo said after a while, "that Nicky? And very attached to you."

David nodded. "I worry about him."

"Worry?" Paolo turned to him with a curious expression.

David suddenly felt embarrassed, wondered if this was an unusual reaction to have for a child who was not your own. He looked out at the road, scanned the few cars, but there wasn't a taxi to be seen.

———

Paolo's prediction about the hors d'oeuvres proved accurate, but that was the least of it. Perhaps in reaction to their nation's reputation for stiffness, the German legation to Kutar was forever coming up with self-consciously playful themes for their parties, and for this occasion they had settled on Polynesia: the drinks were in plastic tiki mugs with paper umbrellas, women were given leis of silk flowers, and a small band strolled through the embassy ballroom strumming ukuleles and crooning in fractured English. Given the spectacle, David found it vaguely comforting to see that another facet of the Germanic reputation, their fondness for uniformity, remained intact: every male member of the delegation, from the security guards on up to the ambassador, was clad in matching blue-and-white floral shirts.

"I'm sorry," David said, as they stood to one corner, "I should have looked at the invitation more closely." Paolo gave a sad sigh. David watched the band wander by, singing what may have been "White Christmas." "And where in the hell did they find the ukuleles?"

"Germans are very resourceful," Paolo muttered, before simply wandering away.

Standing by himself, David was just considering a similar search for refuge–perhaps the garden–when Nigel Mayhew bore down on him. The British First Secretary, once again in his pin-striped suit, was with his wife and a couple of middle-aged men from the British embassy whom David had only ever seen at these parties.

"Quite a show the Jerrys have put on, aye?" Nigel gazed admiringly about the room. "'Course, they always have had a flair for the creative."

The other men nodded in agreement. David looked around for Paolo, but he had vanished from sight.

"We were discussing the situation up-country," Nigel said, abruptly turned grave. "What's your take on it, Richards?"

Here was another annoying thing about the First Secretary. With fourteen years of service in Kutar, he regarded himself as the leading expert on the goings-on in the kingdom, the American delegation as woefully ignorant, and was forever seeking out new evidence to bolster his belief. On this occasion, as on most, David didn't disappoint. "I'm not sure I'm following you, Mayhew."

The Briton seemed taken aback. "But surely you've heard? The insurgents attacked another army garrison this morning. Not a particularly bloody affair–three or four dead from the sound of it–but that makes the third this month."

Despite all eyes upon him, David was unable to feign much concern. "Well," he said with a faint smile, "it *is* the twenty-eighth."

The joke fell flat. The other two men cast puzzled looks at Nigel.

"I do hope that isn't the attitude of everyone over at the American embassy," he murmured. "I'd hope that someone over there appreciates the gravity of the situation."

David's smile grew uncontrollably at this, because while it was inherently amusing to attach the word "gravity" to anything in Kutar, that was especially true with events in the northern highlands. The sad truth was that the sporadic fighting which occurred there was of scant interest even to the locals; as any of them would explain–and usually in voices heavy with boredom–there had always been trouble in the north, there always would be.

"It's been going on a long time," David shrugged, just seeking some way to extricate himself.

"Not like this. It's getting worse. The question is, how bad does it have to get before someone takes the initiative here, gets the two sides talking?"

This question was delivered with an air of challenge. Coming on top of the whole Polynesian thing, David wasn't in the mood.

"Good point," he replied. "Maybe you should ask London that."

"London?" Nigel frowned.

"Well, as I recall, the drawing of the border, the decision to throw two peoples together with nothing in common, that was done under the colonial administration, wasn't it? So who knows, maybe London feels a sense of responsibility about it. Seems worth a try, anyway."

David offered this in a pleasant, offhand way, and on Sarah Mayhew–married to the man who had written the definitive history on the British colonial era in Kutar—it produced the hint of a truly genuine smile.

Just as the first satisfying tinges of red began to rise on the First Secretary's face, David pretended to spot someone across the ballroom. "Pardon me," he said, and strode away before Nigel Mayhew could find the words to respond.

He went into the smaller reception room—a couple of groups in subdued conversation, no one he particularly wanted to speak with—and then passed along to the veranda, and there was Paolo, standing by the steps leading to the lawn and talking with an attractive woman David hadn't seen before. She was tall, with dark skin and long black hair—Italian or Spanish, he thought, possibly Jewish—and appeared to be in her late twenties. Paolo saw him at the threshold and motioned him over.

"Signorina Chalasani," Paolo said, "allow me to introduce my good friend, David Richards."

Her hand was thin, delicate in his, and as David looked into her eyes—they were upturned slightly and the darkest brown—he sensed she was appraising him.

"Oh yes, Mr. Richards," she said, with an air of amusement. "I've heard of you."

Her accent was English—upper class, public school—but tinged with something else. "Good things, I hope."

Her gaze was mischievous. "Mixed."

"Mixed?" Paolo laughed, a bit too heartily. "To be expected, I suppose. A man in David's position, he's bound to ruffle some feathers."

She glanced at Paolo, then back to David. "And what position is that?"

"I'm with the American embassy," he said. "The aid and development officer."

"Ah," she nodded. "The nice American come to help the poor little people of Kutar."

The sarcasm in her voice was unmistakable and, as attractive as she was, David was finding this woman unpleasant. "Something like that. And you, you're with an embassy here?"

She shook her head. "I'm a Kutaran. At least by heritage. I live in London, but I come back every few years to visit."

He recognized the name now. The Chalasanis were one of the old warlord clans of the north, had been quite powerful at one time. A branch of the family had emigrated to England at the turn of the century and built a financial empire, become wealthy from shipping and real estate.

"Any relation to Sir Hamid Chalasani?" David asked. He was referring to the reigning patriarch of the émigré clan, a tough old man in his eighties who had recently been knighted by the Queen.

She nodded. "My grandfather."

"I see," he smiled. "Well, I'd say the world has helped your particular family of little Kutarans quite enough already."

She laughed at this. "Touché."

They talked on for a few minutes, the three of them, and David felt his initial negative assessment of Amira Chalasani diminish. She still was not his type—he never got on well with aristocrats, and this woman was certainly that—but there was something undeniably intriguing about her. He also noticed she wasn't wearing a wedding ring. But perhaps most of all it was simply habit, what David did whenever he met a pretty single woman, that finally compelled him to make an overture.

"Since you'll be in town for a while," he said, as he and Paolo prepared to leave, "maybe you'd like to have dinner some night."

She got that amused look again. "No."

He waited for more—women always offered some reason for turning a man down, but with Amira Chalasani there was nothing. "No?" he finally repeated.

"No, thank you." With that she turned and started across the veranda for the reception room.

David watched her go, nonplussed. "What the hell is her problem, do you think?"

Next to him, Paolo shrugged.

"And what was that part about 'mixed,' that she'd heard mixed things about me?"

Paolo scratched at his neck, as if giving the question careful thought. "Hard to say. Perhaps your reputation as a whoremonger?"

David laughed. "Not a whoremonger, a womanizer. There's a big difference."

"Ah, but womanizer is such a boring word, so American. Whoremonger, it has cachet."

————————

The Monday morning staff meeting was even drearier than normal. Cheryl Thompson gave her usual rundown of visas applied for, visas denied, was pleased to report further progress in paring the application backlog. Lee Warren reported that Kutar's wheat crop was shaping up to be a bumper harvest—which was actually bad news, as it would cut into American imports—while Harold Derwinski, the political attaché, noted that the Magic Mosaic That Is America film festival, a traveling exhibition sponsored by the United States Information Agency, was opening at the cultural center in three weeks, and urged everyone to put out the word, as attendance at last year's festival had been disappointing.

"And don't forget to tell them that there'll be free refreshments," Harold concluded, as he handed out photocopies of the program schedule.

At a post-festival evaluation meeting held in this same room after last year's debacle—one group of Kutaran schoolchildren had grown so bored during a screening that they began crying en masse—David had proposed that perhaps they should show movies people might actually want to see but, looking over the upcoming roster, he saw this suggestion had failed to win any converts at USIA: a film entitled *I Dream of Freedom* chronicled a young Cuban girl's yearning for a better life in Miami, while *Hour of Power!* was touted as a fascinating, behind-the-scenes look at the work of the Rural Electrification Administration.

At least that week David had a bit of news regarding the geologists up north: they now estimated they would be wrapping up their fieldwork in two or three weeks.

"That's great," Ambassador Draper said. "I imagine those poor guys must be getting pretty stir-crazy up there."

"Yes sir, I'd imagine so," David said, but what he was really imagining was the day John Draper tired of these excruciating weekly staff meetings.

It appeared that Monday's ordeal was just about over when a thick Texas drawl came from down the table. "Well, I got a little something y'all should maybe be apprised of."

David peered down to see Colonel Allen B. Munn, the American military liaison to the Kutaran armed forces, sitting a few seats away. The colonel didn't usually attend the Monday meetings, and David hadn't noticed him come into the room.

"Seems an army garrison up north was attacked over the weekend," Munn said. "Three confirmed fatalities for the good guys, casualties unknown among the hostiles."

The colonel was a squat bullet of a man, his slightly bulging eyes given added severity by his very close crew cut, and there was something in his appearance and the wear of his crisply starched Marine uniform—every button and seam was clearly under strain—that belied his laconic manner, that had the effect of lending import, even menace, to whatever he said. It certainly had that effect on John Draper, who now studied Munn with alarm.

"Whereabouts?" he asked. "Anywhere near the geology team?"

With a grunt the colonel got to his feet, and crossed to the large map of Kutar that hung on the conference-room wall.

It was only at that moment that David realized he'd already heard mention of this incident—from Nigel Mayhew at the German party—but he had been so desperate to get away from the man that he hadn't even bothered to learn its location. Replaying that conversation in his mind, he deduced the attack had been on Saturday morning; he'd last spoken with the geologists on Friday.

With quiet but immense relief, he watched Munn tap the map beside Lashkhan, a small town in the far northern reaches of the country. David turned to the ambassador. "I shouldn't worry, sir," he said. "That's at least eighty miles from their camp."

But John Draper still looked worried. "Eighty miles isn't much."

David thought of how to respond without sounding condescending. "Up there eighty miles takes on a whole different meaning. There's no real roads to speak of, very hard to move around. There's also little communication between the different tribal factions, so even if there's trouble in one spot, it can be completely calm the next valley over. I'll get a message through to the team right now, but I'm sure everything is fine."

This mollified John Draper somewhat, but he continued to stare at the map.

"Seems to me these kinds of attacks are increasing."

"Yes, sir," Munn said. "Three of them this past month." The colonel drew up to his full height, which David guessed was right around the Marine Corps minimum of five foot six, and puffed out his chest so that he looked almost at attention. "I'm thinking we might want to go proactive here, Mr. Ambassador."

"Proactive?" John Draper frowned.

"Get ahead of the curve. Get this puppy leashed up before it bites someone." The ambassador still appeared confused, so Munn spelled it out: "Put out an alert, sir."

This drew dismayed looks around the conference table. To anyone with even a rudimentary knowledge of Kutar—and everyone in the room was at least as knowledgeable as Munn, who had arrived only three months earlier—it was hard to conceive of a worse possible response to events in the northern mountains than issuing a State Department alert. The fact was that the insurgency there, based largely along clan lines, had been going on sporadically for decades, and even if there had been a slight uptick in incidents recently, it was still nothing more than a minor nuisance to the Kutaran government. Should the outside world suddenly voice concern—let alone, put out an alert—it could easily be predicted that the few tourists and foreign investors who had begun finding their way to Kutar would instantly abandon it. That in turn might cause the king to overreact, maybe even launch a punitive strike into the north.

And certainly nothing underscored the absurdity of such a move more than the map at which they all stared. Kutar had a roughly rectangular shape, bound on the south by the sea and on the east and west by much larger neighbors, with most of its population clustered along the narrow coastal shelf. Beyond that first range of mountains was the great inland desert—a two-hundred-mile expanse of emptiness save for a few oasis towns—and it was only past the desert that the northern massif began. The town of Lashkhan was in the very back reaches of those mountains, near where the Kutaran frontier with its northern neighbor became a wavery, dotted line, never firmly demarcated for lack of interest or purpose. What all this meant was that, for the average Kutaran, events in a place like Lashkhan might as well have occurred in Tokyo or Detroit for as much as they affected their daily lives.

Lee Warren broke the quiet by shifting in his chair. "Maybe instead of putting out an alert, we should push for negotiations," he offered. "From everything I've heard, the insurgents really aren't asking for that much."

This drew thoughtful nods around the conference table, but Colonel Munn redrew their attention with a stage cough. "Interesting concept there, fella. Personally, I've never been a big fan of appeasement, though I know it's got its devotees." He turned back to John Draper. "I say we go bold here, Mr. Ambassador. We put out an alert, we're telling 'em, 'Let's get this mess cleaned up before someone gets hurt.' We're telling 'em America cares."

But David wasn't overly anxious about how the ambassador might finally respond to Colonel Munn's suggestion; he trusted in the profound pall that Kutar cast over nearly all who worked there. One of the first things he had noted upon his arrival was the abiding calm—even lassitude—of the diplomatic corps. In that initial blast of still, hot air which greeted the newcomer to Kutar, there seemed to be an almost instinctual understanding that here they had come to one of the last true backwaters on earth, a tabula rasa when it came to global or even regional significance. And even if John Draper was highly ambitious, even if he was a Foreign Service wunderkind aching to be noticed, David had faith that the man had taken stock of his surroundings.

"Well, I appreciate your concerns, Colonel," the ambassador said at last, "but I think that's probably premature."

Colonel Munn raised his hands and stepped away from the map, a gesture that, to David, appeared designed to register both resignation and dissent.

"On the other hand, it might get us into the NSA report," Stan Peterson said, and this brought laughter throughout the room.

Diane smiled and waved to Enrico Valladares, the Spanish chargé d'affaires, as he crossed the Casablanca dining room. Once he was out of sight, though, the smile left, she shook her head vehemently.

"This place drives me crazy," she said. "It's impossible to go anywhere without seeing someone you know."

That was true. In all of Laradan, there were only half a dozen or so restaurants the foreign community frequented, and the Casablanca, with its air-conditioned dining room and pleasant garden terrace, was especially popular at lunchtime. They had arranged to meet at three o'clock, when the other Americans would be gone—but, of course, that was when the southern Europeans liked to eat.

"What does it matter?" David said. "We're just two friends having lunch."

Diane gave him an icy glance, went back to picking at her plate.

"So," he asked after a few minutes of silence, "how was Rome?"

"Okay. Rainy."

He was growing irritated. Diane had asked to meet him, had made a big deal out of it, and so far she had barely said a word. He watched her spear a wedge of tomato with her fork, shake it off, spear it again.

"You know," he said, "if you don't want to arouse suspicion, we should at least talk. We look like we're fighting."

Diane turned up then, set her fork on the plate. "You're right. So I've decided I can't do this anymore. I'm ending this. Bill deserves better." She took up the cloth napkin in her fist and began kneading it. It reminded David of what she did with the pillow when they made love, and he watched her fingers. "I guess we reach a point—some of us, anyway—where we have to take stock of things, how we're living, treating those we care about. Our legacy, I guess."

"Legacy?" David smiled in spite of the situation. "Only old people talk about legacy."

Diane shrugged, smiled a bit herself. "I guess I feel old, then. Anyway, I'm not doing this anymore."

They stared at each other. David thought of what he might say to change her mind, but realized it wouldn't happen with words. It would take a gesture—grabbing her and kissing her, say—but he couldn't very well do that in the middle of the Casablanca dining room. But the more he thought about it, the longer he watched her, the less he was sure that he wanted to try, that maybe it would be a very indecent thing for him to do, because on

Diane's face was such a look of exhaustion that maybe the decent thing was to let her be. And so he said nothing, did nothing, and after a long time, Diane turned and gazed across the room. David saw the way her eyes flitted about, fixing on nothing in particular, and he knew she was giving her decision one last pass, one final review. A smile rose on her lips, and then she nodded once, sharply and to herself, and her expression became a genuinely happy one, exultant even, and Diane got up from the table and started purposefully for the restaurant door.

———————

There were times when David found the view of the city and the sea from his southern veranda almost too much to bear—too captivating or beautiful or busy—and it was at those times that he lingered on the northern veranda, when he found the emptiness of the desert soothing because there was so little to see. So was his mood that night, after his luncheon with Diane. He was alone, in an armchair he had brought out from the living room.

He spotted a red dot far out in the desert. From long experience, he knew it was the taillights of a truck heading north on the national highway, the same road he would be on in a few hours. John Draper, still a bit edgy about the geologist team and the recent fighting, had asked him to run up there to check on things and, in his mind's eye, David traced the long journey he had already made several times before: the hot drive across the desert, the slow, bone-jarring trek through the mountains. From the end of the highway in Erbil, it was six hours up pitted dirt tracks to the geologists' camp; if all went well, he could be there by late afternoon.

As the red dot dimmed into nothingness, David pondered what Diane had said at lunch. Not about ending their affair—he had halfway expected that, had even been considering doing it himself recently—but the part about legacy, of taking stock of how one lived. In his thirty-four years, David had never given it much thought, suspected that few people did. He simply went through the days, the years, trying to enjoy himself when he could, to have interest in what passed before his eyes, to not think too much of what had been left behind—certainly nothing so grand as "legacy."

This wasn't to say he didn't experience nostalgia. He did, but it tended to be of the fleeting kind. Because what David had discovered was that, at a certain point, remembering the good moments of the past became a kind of pain, that one could end up hoping for something or someone to return that never would. In any event, he had always been more given to looking ahead, not behind.

At about one in the morning, he sat forward in his armchair on the veranda, his attention drawn to an odd sight in the desert below. From the airport complex, a long line of trucks was making its way out to the national highway and turning north.

David knew that truckers often formed convoys for the night journey over the desert, but these usually consisted of four or five vehicles—certainly nothing like the fifty or sixty he now saw. Curious, he brought his telescope out from the living room and trained it on the scene.

They were military transport trucks, and in their open beds sat row after row of soldiers, swaying to the motion of the road, guns cradled between their knees. David slowly straightened, gazed down at the long ribbon of red lights with his naked eye, and all at once felt a terrible premonition.

Three

David recognized the lanky, stooped figure of Walter Jensen as soon as the Land Rover cleared the last rise to the camp. The old man was in front of the main tent, his hands tucked into his jean pockets, and he watched the approaching vehicle as if it were the most interesting thing he'd seen all day. David climbed down from the passenger seat, crossed the pebbled earth to shake his hand.

"The others are still out in the field," Walter said, "but figured I'd come in early to meet you. What's up?"

"Not much," David said, stretching his back from the jouncing of the journey. "Just working on my disability claim."

Walter chuckled. David gazed over the small camp—five tents, a latrine—set in the barren valley. It was a lonely spot, closed on all sides by jagged stone mountains that looked like broken eggshells and, although it was not yet four o'clock, the western cliffs were already in evening shadow.

The remoteness of the geologists' camp was a constant worry to the ambassador. Without a radio on-site, all messages in or out had to be relayed through the police station in Zilmaz, an hour away—which was how David had sent word that he was coming up. The arrangement didn't seem to bother the geologists, though; David had always suspected that limited contact with the embassy was their preference.

He'd left Laradan at dawn with Tehar, one of the embassy drivers. They'd made good time across the desert and stopped only twice en route, first at the police station in Erbil, the provincial capital, then at the much smaller garrison in Zilmaz, to ask about any new reports of fighting in the area. All appeared to be quiet; in fact, the Zilmaz police hadn't even heard of the latest incident in the far north. As for the military convoy David had seen heading up the national highway, no one seemed to know a thing about it.

He followed Walter to the main tent, and they sat across from each other at a large worktable in the center of the room, its surface covered with maps. David explained the reason for his visit. "So nothing like that going on around here?" he asked. "Tension in the air, armed men roaming about?"

Walter scratched at his ear and stared at the ground, slowly shook his head. He was a rangy man in his early seventies with rough-hewn features and the broad twang of the American West— a native of Utah, David remembered from an earlier conversation. "Nope, can't say we've had anything like that." He looked up. "But at this point, think we'd probably welcome the distraction."

David laughed. On the worktable he recognized the master map, an enormous topographical that Walter had shown him the last time he'd been up about a month ago. It was now marked with scores of handwritten notations: Xs and arrows and small circles, each with a cryptic series of numbers and letters penciled in alongside.

"Looks like you've been busy," he said.

"Yep." Walter Jensen leaned forward in his chair, yawned mightily. "And there's definitely water up here. Question is how much." He stared at his map for a moment. "An odd one. We're finding it up high. Usually a good sign—usually means you're talking a deep well–but we're coming in dry on the slopes. See here?" He pointed to an *X* near the center. "A positive reading at ninety-two hundred feet for water at seventy-three. You come down here a mile"–his finger slid to a nearby circle–"you're at seventy-five hundred, no reading at all." He tapped his finger, gave a little sigh. "Just can't find a table on this thing."

David sipped from his coffee. Listening to Walter Jensen, he was reminded of the peculiar, pared-down way that men from the American West spoke, as if each word came with a price tag.

"You think it's domes?" he asked. From some hydrology courses he'd taken in college, David knew a bit about water, enough to know it often moved or lay in unexpected ways. The common perception of an aquifer was of a subterranean lake, with a flat, steady waterline, and while that was true of some, others looked more like underground trees, branches and tributaries snaking off at odd angles, pushing out as a spring in one spot, plunging deep into the earth in another. And, of course, just finding water didn't mean you'd found an aquifer; in hard-rock, snow water could collect inside a mountain and, with nothing forcing it out, sit there for a million years.

"Could be," the chief geologist nodded. "Could be we got a bunch of domes on a bunch of different mountains. That's the deal, you pack up, go find something else to do. But if we can show they all connect in"–he swept his hand to encompass all the *X*s marked across the breadth of his map–"well, then you got a very significant resource here."

David glanced up. Walter's eyes were blue, slightly bloodshot; they bore the rigors of his outdoor life. "What about using fluorescence?"

The old man nodded. "Yep, fluorescence would make it a whole lot easier; pump a dye down a well, see if it shows up in the others. But you're talking sophisticated equipment, a major field mission–and I don't see Uncle Sam footing the bill for something like that out here." He gave a dry smile. "Short of that, you play your hunches, hope to find the Grand Canal, so to speak." His expression indicated the odds of this happening were slim. "But who knows? We'll give it a few more weeks, might get lucky."

David frowned. "Just what do you mean by a few more weeks, Walter? When we last talked, you said two or three."

The geologist scratched at his neck. "Yeah, maybe a bit more than that. Figure we've already put this much time in up here, might as well see it through."

David stifled a sigh, gazed around the main tent. It was an old army-issue hard frame, with a pallet floor and venting in the ceiling. In the far corner, the team's two camp helpers were preparing the evening meal, their chopping and clanging of pots sounding unusually loud in the quiet of the mountains.

He pondered the tremendous effort that had gone into establishing this camp, all the supplies trucked in, the planning involved–to say nothing of the deprivations imposed on the five scientists, half a world away from their families, the months they'd already spent climbing over rocks and drilling holes, all to make their Xs and circles and notations on Walter Jensen's map.

"Can I put a straight-up question to you?" he asked.

Walter shrugged. "My favorite kind."

"Why are you sticking with this so long? You're already nearly two months over schedule, and I can't believe"–David tried a smile, waved a hand around the tent–"it's for the hardship pay. I ask because the ambassador is getting nervous about you guys being up here, what with the increase in insurgent activity, and the last thing he wants to hear is that you're extending again."

The geologist nodded. "But you know what these projects are like. Never know what you're getting into until you're into it." He cocked his head toward outside. "You see it. Almost solid granite. Equipment getting chewed up, trucks always breaking down. A very inhospitable environment."

"That's kind of my point, Walter," David said quietly. "I mean, if it's this hard to find the aquifer, how hard is it going to be to tap into? You know the specs on this thing, so at this point, the kind of well you'd have to dig and the line you'd have to run, how would it ever be cost-effective?"

If the aquifer could be found, the second phase of the project called for pumping the water into one of the surrounding valleys, where there was set-aside funding for the development of three thousand hectares of farmland—modest, by any standards.

"Well, there's your first problem," Walter replied. "Go a fifty-mile radius from here, it's all rock. You can't grow a thing no matter how much water you put on it."

David stared at the old man in bewilderment. "Okay, now I'm really not following you."

Walter Jensen studied him for a long moment, a sly smile working at the corner of his mouth. "So let me ask *you* something straight up. Where's your loyalties on this?"

David didn't understand the question.

"About the only thing Kutar buys from the U.S. is food, right?" Walter said. "Obviously, the boys at USDA want to keep it that way, build on that, so they wouldn't take kindly to a project that might swing the numbers the other way, wouldn't you say?"

David still wasn't sure where this was going, how the U.S. Department of Agriculture figured in, but he grasped enough to know what was being asked of him. "My interest is in what helps this country."

"Okay." The geologist nodded, gazed over his map. "You ever notice that depression this side of Zulfiqar?"

David had, of course. Zulfiqar was an oasis town in the heart of the desert, and just above it the sand dunes abruptly stopped, the highway dropped down onto a pancake-flat plain that extended some eighty miles, all the way to the foothills of the northern mountains. It was the most tedious leg of the journey north, not a house or a tree to relieve the eye.

"Something about it piqued my interest," Walter said, "so a ways back, I had a couple of the guys go down and take some samples." He looked up at David then, slowly shook his head. "That's not sand. Half an inch down, that's solid sediment dirt. That was an inland sea at one time. So sure, you'd have to run a long line, but you get water down there, you can grow anything. You put enough water on it, you've got the next San Joaquin Valley. Fact, soil composition, climate range, it *is* the San Joaquin."

David sank back in his seat as he absorbed this. The San Joaquin Valley in central California had been regarded as little more than a wasteland until a massive water-diversion scheme in the 1930s, tapping into the snowpack of the Sierra Nevadas, had converted it into some of the richest farmland in America. For such a thing to be replicated in the Zulfiqar depression would profoundly transform the economy not only of northern Kutar but of the entire kingdom, would have a ripple effect throughout the region.

And as he considered this, David came to understand both Walter Jensen's question to him and why the geology team had been so peculiarly uncommunicative with the embassy. Because if it became generally known that Kutar sat on a potential agricultural gold mine—not some small-scale farming scheme that the United States could fund to foster goodwill, but a gold mine of possibly enormous proportions—then the American agricultural attaché to Kutar, Lee Warren, would have no choice but to relay that information to his superiors at the USDA. And since the USDA's primary overseas mandate was to protect the interests of American agribusiness—certainly not to help Third World countries become export competitors—one could be sure they'd waste no time in trying to scuttle the whole enterprise.

"So who all knows about this?" David asked.

"No one," Walter said. "The fellas here, of course, a couple of my buddies back at headquarters. My feeling's been, let's stay low on this, see if this aquifer actually exists first, then try to put together some kind of constituency."

"Constituency?"

The old man smiled. "That's why I decided to tell you—figured you might have some ideas. Maybe the State Department, some of the international development organizations, get things lined up before the USDA and Commerce and they can jump in and kill it." His smile eased away, he turned to stare out the tent flap at the valley. "You know, I've been working these backwater countries almost forty years now. Any kind of geological survey you can think of, I've probably done it, and every one that panned out, I've watched the multinationals either kill it—get Congress to slap on trade restrictions—or take over: come in, sprinkle some money around the capital, put the president's brother on the payroll, end of story." He looked to David. "Just once, I'd like to see one of these little countries get it over on the Union Carbides and Monsantos, keep it for themselves."

David nodded, appreciated that behind his twang and country-boy manner, Walter Jensen was a shrewd strategist, a man who grasped how the system might be worked against itself. "Well, count me in. If it plays out, anything I can do to help."

The other geologists returned just before sunset, and David hauled out the two cases of beer he had brought from the city, handed around some bottles. The other scientists were much younger than Walter Jensen, in their late twenties or early thirties, with the tans and scrubby beards of men used to working outdoors. If any had once been excited by being in such a remote, primitive place—and for at least two of them, David recalled, this was their first overseas assignment—that excitement had long since worn off, and the conversation soon moved away from water tables and rock strata to life back in the States, what they missed, what they had taken for granted until coming here. There was a chill in the night air, the feel of winter coming on. They built a bonfire behind the main tent and for a long time sat there in aluminum folding chairs, drinking beer, telling stories, watching the sparks dance up into the black sky. David thought of how pleasant it could be to spend time in the company of men with no women around to complicate things. Not for the fourteen weeks these men had just spent, but for one night it was quite nice.

The geologists began turning in around midnight. They'd set up cots for David and Tehar in the main tent, but David stayed out by the fire by himself for a while, staring at the burning wood, listening to its pop and hiss, the snores of the men around him. For a time he thought of his conversation with Walter, conjured images of orchards and miles of green fields, of the San Joaquin Valley magically set down in the heart of Kutar, but then he reminded himself this was all still theory, a speculation, and pushed it from his mind.

Instead he fell to remembering nights very much like this one, camping with his brother, Eddie. Even as kids, it was something they had shared–a love of being out under the stars, listening to the night sounds, even if it was only in their backyard–but what David remembered most were the real camping trips they had taken when they were a little older, when he was coming home a lot on college breaks. Eddie was still in high school then but having a hard time of it, and their parents had thought it would be a good idea for the two of them to spend time together. Depending on the season, they'd gone all over the place: down to Kentucky and West Virginia, up to Canada and the Adirondacks. One time, he remembered, they'd been coming back into Cleveland on a Sunday night from two days of canoeing in western Pennsylvania, Eddie getting broodier by the mile at the prospect of school the next day, and David had pulled into a gas station–"Fuck it; let's go back"–and he'd called their parents to say they weren't coming home just yet, that it might be a few days, and as they'd headed back toward the Allegheny River, Eddie had been the happiest seventeen-year-old kid alive, singing along to the car radio turned up full blast, using the dashboard as a drum.

"Maybe we should never go back," he had shouted over the music. "Maybe we should just keep going."

By the campfire, David tilted his head back to look at the stars, only to discover that, sitting within the pool of flamelight, he couldn't see them at all, he could barely distinguish the outlines of the nearest tents. He rose and walked a short distance, out into the true night. There he saw how the valley's stones and eggshell peaks gleamed white under a half-moon and a hundred thousand stars, that all around him was the sparkle of mica or crystal, and it was as if he had crossed over into a place of infinite radiance, a land that never went dark.

———

Ahead shone the lights of Zulfiqar oasis. They had been visible for the past hour, ever since they had started over the depression, but still appeared no closer.

He and Tehar had left the geologists' camp in early afternoon, so that dusk had already been closing when they dropped out of the mountains. Upon reaching the national highway at Erbil, Tehar had looked over and grinned, happy to at last take the Land Rover above second gear. They were racing and silent now, just empty night road before them.

David's initial excitement over Walter's revelation about the Zulfiqar depression had muted somewhat—reality, or at least pragmatism, settling in—but his gaze was still drawn to the plain that surrounded them. He now saw the small sagebrushlike plants dotting its surface, which shone silver in the moonlight. He tried to envision that land with water on it, the crops and trees that might grow there, what Walter Jensen already saw.

In the quiet of the car, it occurred to him that perhaps the most valuable gift the United States could bestow on a country like Kutar were men like Walter Jensen. Not so much for their fair-mindedness or pulling for the underdog—those traits were common enough in any culture—but rather for their abiding faith in the possible, that peculiarly American conviction that change and progress were always an option. It was a fundamentally different approach to life, and it represented a shock to the culture of fatalism that so suffused a place like Kutar. The northern aquifer might yet prove an illusion—certainly the prognosis couldn't be considered favorable at this late date—but it was American geologists who were doggedly trying to find it, just as it had been an old man from Utah who'd thought to scratch the surface of the Zulfiqar depression to see what lay beneath, something neither the Kutarans nor their British colonizers had apparently ever bothered to do. From what David had observed during his six years in the field, the world needed less resignation, more curiosity and tenacity, more men like Walter Jensen.

They climbed out of the plain, and all at once Zulfiqar was before them. It was a true oasis town, very much like David's childhood conception of one, and he was intrigued by the idea that its size—a quarter-mile across, maybe three thousand inhabitants—had probably not changed in a thousand years. He usually made a point of stopping briefly in Zulfiqar on his journeys to the north, found it a nice interlude between the coast and the mountains, and he saw the familiar faded sign of the Shakra Inn ahead. He looked at Tehar. "Are you hungry?"

The driver, a polite, quiet man in his early forties, gave a diffident shrug. "Maybe a little."

The inn was an old caravanserai that had been renovated for modern travelers, with dining rooms overlooking the inner courtyard where animals had once sheltered, the upper floor converted into a dozen hotel rooms. David and Tehar stepped into the lobby and, adhering to Kutaran custom, where restaurants were still separated by class—it was unthinkable, an insult to the establishment, that a driver would eat at the same table as his charge—stepped into their respective dining rooms.

Scattered about the main dining room were several groups of well-dressed Kutaran men—businessmen returning to Laradan, David assumed—and then he was quite surprised to see, in front of one of the windows overlooking the courtyard, a young Western woman sitting alone. She was reading a book, appeared to be in her mid-twenties, and David was quite certain he hadn't seen her before, that she wasn't a secretary or the daughter of some diplomat in the capital. He took a table near hers, said hello when she happened to glance up.

"Hello." She gave a perfunctory smile, turned back to her reading.

David had detected an accent–English, perhaps, or maybe Australian–but the single word wasn't enough for him to place it. He ordered a beer from the waiter, gazed around the room, found nothing to draw his attention more than the reading woman.

She was pretty in a tomboyish way, with short blond hair and the broad shoulders of a swimmer. Her clothes were those of a visitor to Kutar rather than one of its foreign residents: hiking shoes, blue jeans, a cotton T-shirt under a windbreaker. She felt his stare, peered at him over the top of her book. "Something wrong?"

"Sorry. It's just odd to see a woman here–I mean, a foreign woman traveling alone."

She eyed him cautiously as she reached for her beer bottle, took a sip. "How do you know I'm alone?"

David saw that his words could be interpreted as insinuating, and felt himself redden. This seemed to reassure the woman, for she gave an amused laugh. "That's okay. I'm alone."

Her name was Marisa and she was twenty-seven, from Sydney, Australia. She'd been traveling around the region for several months now, was vaguely bound for London. She had been on her way back to Laradan from a weeklong trek in the mountains, but had decided to hop off when the bus stopped in Zulfiqar.

"It looked like an interesting place," she said. "Kind of reminds me of some of the little towns in the Outback."

He smiled. "Except with camels."

She smiled back. "We have camels in Australia."

"Oh, right. Well, with more camels then."

Her smiled widened. "We have lots of camels." She was teasing him now, comfortable; she had set her book aside.

"Okay, so it's exactly like Australia; makes one wonder why you ever left home."

They laughed together, and David motioned for two more beers as the waiter passed by. He moved over to her table, took the seat beside her, and they fell into the kind of easy conversation that happens between travelers, about her wanderings, his job, what it was like to live in Kutar, what she planned to do when she at last reached London. At one point, the waiter delivered a message from Tehar, inquiring when they might be continuing their journey, and David sent word back that it might be awhile yet.

They became quite oblivious to their surroundings, ordered more beers as they chatted, until finally there came that moment when one of them noticed they were the last ones in the dining room, that they really had been talking for a long time, that the waiters were probably dying for them to leave so they could turn off the lights and go home. And then both seemed to appreciate their situation at the same instant—that they were all alone here in the heart of the desert, that they would never see each other again—and then words left them, and they looked into each other's eyes for just a little too long before turning away, staring down at their empty glasses on the table.

"So," Marisa said, her voice tentative, a fingernail scratching at the label of a bottle, "are you staying here tonight?"

And David felt a stab of something then, something so quick and sharp that it took him an instant to recognize it as pain. He looked to the window, into the courtyard where animals had once sheltered, and the lights there sparkled before his eyes.

He turned back to the girl. She was watching him with a puzzled expression.

"Yes," he said, "I'm staying the night."

———

A sound rose from the distance, a high shrill whistle, and David smiled in the dark. He recognized it as that of a truck approaching on the highway–specifically, of a heavy truck moving at a good speed–and he had always found it curious how similar this sound was to that of an ocean surf heard from far away. He listened as it dropped in pitch, became a rumble, and then the truck passed on the road outside and he heard the rattle of the windowpane, felt a slight tremor pass through the bed beneath him. He waited for the whistling sound to return as the truck receded down the highway, but instead there came another rumble, another tremor, and another after that.

In the hotel room, David frowned, looked at his watch in the faint light. It was not even 3:00 AM yet, a good two hours before the truckers normally started to move. He slipped from the bed and stepped to the window.

From the north, an open-bed military transport came into view, its headlights dimmed. As it sped by, he glimpsed a mound of oddly shaped plastic bundles in back, two soldiers standing and clutching the awning frame for balance. It was such a strange sight, so incongruous to whatever he had been thinking, that David couldn't immediately absorb its significance. Then another transport passed and in its bed he saw neat rows of men on stretchers, a soldier and a man in a white coat hovering above them.

He turned from the window, leaned against the wall. In the bed, the Australian girl still slept. She had thrown herself free of the covers, lay on her side. Her legs were extended in such a way that she appeared to be running, and her left foot rhythmically caressed the bedsheet–back and forth, back and forth–as she maneuvered her way through some dream.

An enormous map of Kutar had been tacked to the wall of the British cultural center ballroom, and Colonel Allen B. Munn stared up at its lines and color shadings and place-names as if studying a particularly inscrutable work of modern art. From their seats at the nearby conference table, his three counterparts, the military liaisons of Britain, France, and Germany, did likewise.

At last Munn gave a slow shake of his head, turned to face his audience. "Well, I'm not gonna sugarcoat this, ladies and gentlemen; any way you look at it, we've had some pretty suboptimal achievement trends eventuating these past seventy-two hours."

It was Monday afternoon, two and a half days since David had seen those first truckloads of battlefield casualties speeding past the Shakra Inn in Zulfiqar, but the pace of events since had made time feel suspended. After calling down to the embassy with the news, he and Tehar had raced back to the capital, and David had spent the next forty-eight hours working the telephones, calling any of his northern contacts he could think of—project managers, police commanders, mayors—in an attempt to monitor what was happening in the mountains. The news had just kept getting worse.

The magnitude of the weekend's disaster was already known to the forty or so diplomats gathered in the cultural center ballroom. At least in broad outline; there were still large and unsettling gaps in the story, and it was in hopes of filling them that the British ambassador had organized this meeting with the resident military liaisons. Shortly before 2:00 PM, the four officers had filed into the ballroom and, under the anxious gaze of the diplomats sitting in rows of folding metal chairs, somberly spread their papers and charts over the conference table at the front of the hall.

From what had been pieced together so far, it seemed that an infantry battalion had been dispatched from the capital on Wednesday night to conduct a search-and-destroy mission in the vicinity of Lashkhan, the remote northern town that had been the site of the most recent rebel attack. While this unit was undoubtedly the convoy David had seen from his veranda that night, it was still not known why the operation had been launched or even who had approved it. What was known was that, on midmorning of

Friday, the battalion had driven headlong into an ambush and been slaughtered; rumors were circulating that at least two hundred soldiers were dead, possibly three times that number.

But as bad as the ambush had been, far worse was the chain reaction it had sparked. As the battalion survivors fled south for their lives, they had been joined by other army units in the Lashkhan area, and then by others across the mountain range. By Saturday, soldiers and policemen throughout the north had begun abandoning their isolated garrisons as fast as they could and—along with mayors and municipal workers and anyone else who felt at risk—joining the stampede out. From the chartered plane sent to spirit them from their remote camp, the American geologists had reported seeing a flood of refugees—some in overladen buses and trucks, others on foot—on every road leading out of the mountains. Now, on Monday afternoon, there were rumors that the army's flight had finally been checked near the city of Erbil, but even if this were true, a glance at the map of Kutar revealed just how sweeping a catastrophe the weekend had brought: in a mere three days, and as the result of a single forty-five-minute battle, the rule of government had simply vanished from one-third of the nation.

"Disappointing?" Colonel Munn called from his spot beneath the map. "You bet. But on the bright side, it does look like we're locking on to stabilization mode." With a telescoping pointer, he tapped at the southern edge of the massif, at the foothill towns just above Erbil. "As of 1800 hours yesterday, the army started forming a defensive perimeter along this ridgeline here and, from everything we're hearing today, that line is holding firm."

Ambassador Draper sat a couple of rows in front of David, and he now raised his hand. "Let's back up a second, Colonel," he called. "Have we even determined who ordered this operation in the first place?"

Munn shifted on his feet, cast an uneasy glance at his fellow liaisons. "Uh, not yet, sir. It's a pretty murky situation we're dealing with here—a suboptimal information flow, as it were."

"And what of the king?" the ambassador asked. "Has anyone figured out his involvement?"

At this, all eyes turned to Nigel Mayhew, the British First Secretary, sitting in the first row of folding chairs. With fourteen years of service in Kutar, Nigel was both the senior member of the diplomatic community and the one with the most extensive contacts within the royal palace.

"I had an audience with the king on Thursday," he announced. "There wasn't even the hint that something like this was being contemplated. Since then, I've been in touch with every palace official I know, and they all appear to have been caught totally unawares." With a grave air, Nigel gazed over his diplomatic colleagues. "Either they're all lying—which I don't believe—or no one over there saw this coming."

This sparked a worried murmur through the room, for the silence emanating from the palace was already a source of deep concern. That silence had been understandable in the first hours of the crisis—obviously the king would be in no rush to take personal responsibility for a military operation that had proven a fiasco—but the continuing hush was leading to speculation that perhaps he'd played no role at all, that maybe what they were witnessing was a slow-motion coup by the generals. Nigel Mayhew's report certainly bolstered this theory.

At the front of the room, Colonel Munn scratched at his ear. "Yeah, well, it's starting to look like this thing might have outgrowthed from the Defense Ministry—not a conspiracy or anything like that, you understand, just a kind of . . . miscommunication."

"Miscommunication?" Ambassador Draper repeated.

"Well, a communicational lapse, if you will, one of those cross-cultural misunderstandings that have a way of happening around here from time to time."

It was as if someone had called for a moment of silence. Under the scrutinizing stare of forty diplomats, Munn scratched at his ear more vigorously. Watching the short, rotund man in his khaki uniform, David was reminded of a nervous rodent.

"Now, I could have it all wrong," Munn continued, "but what happened was, we"—he nodded at his fellow military liaisons at the conference table—"were having our usual monthly meeting with the high command over there at the ministry last week, and it seems possible—and, again, I'm just conjecturing here—but it seems possible that certain viewpoints or opinions might have been verbalized at that point in time that maybe the high command there misconstrued."

"What sort of viewpoints?" Ambassador Draper asked in a low, hard voice.

"I can't recall the specifics, of course, it was just one of those discussions where everyone was feeling pretty informal—you know, letting our hair down, conversing amongst ourselves the way military men do sometimes. We got to talking about the situation up north, the recent attacks up there, how sometimes it seems like maybe civilians don't fully appreciate the need for robust action to defend the democratic lifestyle and—"

"Check your briefing book, Colonel," Ambassador Draper said acidly. "Kutar does not have a democratic lifestyle."

Colonel Munn nodded, shifted on his feet again. "And it seems possible that one or the other of us might have verbalized something along those lines that maybe the high command there misconstrued . . ."

Ambassador Draper slumped back in his chair in disgust. "Let me get this straight, Colonel. You four are sitting around the Defense Ministry bullshitting with the generals, and one of you says, 'It's time to teach the insurgents a lesson, go up there and kick some butt.'"

"Well, I can't recall if the word 'butt' was used, sir, but—"

"So the generals think they've been given a green light by us, they get their blood up, and next thing you know, they've sent an infantry battalion charging up there. Is that it?"

At the front of the room, Colonel Munn cleared his throat. "Well I'd hate to speculate before all the facts are in, sir, but I'd say that's a scenario we can't completely rule out at this particular point in time." He cast a somewhat pleading look over at the conference table, but the other liaisons were all busily shuffling through their papers, studiously avoiding the baleful stares of their audience.

"In any event," Munn tried an upbeat tone, "I think we can all agree that the important thing now is to forward-look, and the good news is I think we're pretty close to putting this whole unfortunate episode behind us." He seemed suddenly refreshed, even cheerful. "As some of you already know, we've been getting a lot of input from the Pentagon these past couple of days, having a lot of consultations with the Alliance people in Brussels, and from all that, it looks like the Kutarans have come up with a pretty good counter-initiative. They're calling it Operation Chokechain, and to give you a little bit of orientation on that, I'm gonna hand this thing over to Major Smallwood here."

Colonel Munn hurried for the refuge of the conference table, as Major Smallwood rose from his seat. The British military liaison was a ruddy-cheeked, broad-shouldered man, and there was an air of ceremony in the way he took the pointer from Munn's hand, strode briskly to the command position beneath the map.

"Good afternoon," he called. "First off, let me emphasize that all matters pertaining to this operation should be considered of the utmost confidence. That means not to be shared with anyone outside this room. I do hope we can all agree to this at the outset."

The major paused, almost as if expecting some kind of group response. David glanced about the ballroom, made brief eye contact with several other members of the American embassy's newly formed Emergency Working Group on the Kutar Situation. In addition to himself and the ambassador, the group consisted of Bill Myerson and the political and legal attachés, and David assumed he'd only been included by virtue of having raised the first alarm with his telephone call from the Shakra Inn.

"Very well," Major Smallwood said. He turned to the map, pointed to the same foothill towns above Erbil that Munn had indicated. "Phase one of Operation Chokechain is to stabilize this forward line over the next few days—get the lads quieted down, reestablish supply lines and the chain of command. At the same time, the bulk of the Kutaran armed forces, along with their heavy weaponry, will be brought up from the coast and deployed here, in Erbil." He slid the pointer down to tap at the provincial capital. "Once all that is in place, everything's holding together nicely, we go to phase two: the forward line is vacated, the lads fall back to the secondary line in Erbil."

This brought looks of consternation around the room. None appeared more troubled than the French ambassador, a slight, frail man in his sixties. "You mean to abandon the front line?"

Major Smallwood nodded. "De-operationalize; that is correct, sir. The tactical goal of Chokechain is to instill overconfidence in the enemy, and to lure him onto terrain of the government's choosing."

Colonel Munn, unable to control his excitement, jumped up from his seat at the conference table. "The hostiles have had a free run so far, we let 'em think they still have it. We pull our boys off the ridgeline, they're gonna pursue. We get them down to where the land flattens out, where we've got troops and artillery dug in and waiting, and"—Munn made a yanking motion by his own neck—"chokechain. Those sons of bitches aren't gonna know what hit 'em."

"But to me, this seems very risky," the French ambassador persisted. "In Erbil, the desert will be at the army's back, there is nowhere to go if something goes wrong."

Munn stifled a sigh. "War is all about risk, monsieur. But calculated risk. And the operative word here—you just said it—is 'if.' 'If something goes wrong.' Because nothing's going wrong with this operation. It's based on classic military tacticals, what Napoleon used to sandbag the Germans at Austerlitz." He turned to the German officer seated on his right. "No offense there, Helmut."

The German liaison shrugged. "It was the Austrians."

From the audience, John Draper gave a disparaging laugh. "I'm sure it worked just swell at Austerlitz, Colonel, but you're talking about the Kutaran army here, not Napoleon's."

Munn lingered in the moment, a grin rising on his face. "Which is why Chokechain is being augmented," he said. "Operation Kindred Spirit." He slowly sat back down, turned to Major Smallwood. "Go ahead, Major, lay it on 'em."

Beneath the map, Smallwood set the pointer aside, crossed his arms over his chest. "Alliance headquarters has just authorized the deployment to Kutar of an elite unit of civic-action specialists—military advisers in laymen's terms. Their mandate is to advise and assist, on a strictly noncombatant basis, the government forces with their restoration initiatives in the north. Our understanding is that they will begin arriving here day after tomorrow."

The diplomats gathered in the ballroom were so stunned by this news that for a moment all they could do was gape at Major Smallwood. First the British ambassador, then the American and German, rose to their feet, looked at one another in disbelief.

"The king has approved this?" the British ambassador finally whispered.

At the front of the room, Major Smallwood hesitated, as if choosing his words with great care. "Of that I'm not certain, sir. I'm not certain how much the king is choosing to involve himself in day-to-day military affairs."

The British ambassador spun to Nigel Mayhew. "Contact the palace, Nigel. Tell them we want an audience with the king—myself and the other ambassadors—as soon as possible."

Nigel Mayhew nodded, started to his feet, but froze when Colonel Munn again leaped up from the table.

"Uh, sir, and just what would the agenda of this meeting be?"

The British ambassador gave Munn a withering stare. "To let the king know what's occurring in his own country. To urge him to take action before the killing gets worse."

"Well, absolutely." Munn nodded. "But we've got to be prudent about this, make sure it fits within the framework of Kindred Spirit."

David had never seen John Draper angry before, but he was angry now.

"Colonel," he called across the room, "let me explain something to you: I'm the American envoy here, and as the American envoy, I relay our policy in this country. Now until I hear otherwise from the State Department, our mission here is to try to end the fighting, not to build on the body count. Which is a diplomat's way of saying you can take your Operation Kindred Spirit and go fuck yourself." He looked to Nigel Mayhew. "Call the palace, Nigel."

But there was something in the way Munn leaned over the table on his fists, the command of his presence, which caused the British First Secretary to stay where he was. When Munn turned back to John Draper, it was with the hint of a smirk. "Allow me to point out, Mr. Ambassador," he said, in that slow, Texas drawl of his, "that Kindred Spirit is an Alliance operation approved by the joint military command in Brussels. It is, therefore, outside the purview of normal diplomatic channels, including our own State Department. One of the prices to be paid, I'm afraid, for strategic cooperation with our good European friends here." He straightened abruptly, gave a laconic grin. "Now I sure don't want to get into a pissing contest with anyone here—don't think any of us want that—because the really important thing right now is that we present a unified front, speak with one voice."

He stepped away from the table, walked slowly toward Major Smallwood and the map. Halfway there, however, he executed a dramatic pivot to face his audience.

"Why's that, you ask? Because it's starting to look like we got a very major problem on our hands here, folks, something a lot more serious than any of us could have even imagined three days ago."

A puzzled silence held the room, broken finally by John Draper. "What the hell are you talking about?"

The colonel clasped his hands behind his back. "Naturally I can't go into all the nitty-gritty in an open forum like this, but let me just say that various intelligence reports we're picking up strongly indicate the hostiles got a big helping hand with this thing, that they have come under the sway and influence of a third party."

"Third party?" the British ambassador repeated.

"Affirmative. An outside power, if you will."

"But that's absurd," the British ambassador replied. "Kutar has excellent relations with all its neighbors. Why should one of them—"

He was cut off by Munn's grim chuckle. "We're not talking the other kids in the sandbox here, Mr. Ambassador; we're talking the big kahuna. We're talking that empire of evil whose greatest enemies are God and the freedoms we all cherish."

"You're implying the Soviets are behind this, Colonel?" John Draper's voice had dropped to a cool whisper. "I really hope you know what you're talking about, because that's a very serious charge."

At the front of the room, Munn seemed just the slightest discomfited; he kneaded his hands behind his back. "Well like I said, I'd hate to speculate before all the facts are in. But sure as I'm standing here, I know that some ragtag bunch of desert inbreeds—and I don't intend that figure of speech to be ethnically demeaning in any way—didn't put this thing together on their own."

He broke his stance, continued his slow stroll toward Major Smallwood.

"Now, I'd like to go to something else we've all talked about these past couple of days, this business of maybe having a coup on our hands." He stopped again, pointedly looked at Ambassador Draper. "I'm a military man, sir. I know how military men think, and I'm telling you, the generals won't stand by on this one. If the king goes the appeasement route here, if he starts negotiating with the guys who've just killed a hundred or two hundred or five hundred of these generals' boys, well, you can be damned sure you'll have a coup." Munn gave a slow, deliberate gaze around the room. "The official policy of the Alliance to this crisis—as approved and directed by the joint military command this morning—is one of proactive nonengagement. That is, we are to assist the Kutaran armed forces in their peace-building initiatives against the anti-freedom forces in a noncombatant, consultative mode. We do not encourage the king to pursue a reckless diplomatic effort that has the potential of undermining his government and widening this conflict." He put his hands on his hips, rocked slightly on his heels. "Now, if we can just kind of look up the road a bit, I think maybe we can all see the virtues of this policy. After Chokechain, after the government's got the upper hand and is operating from a position of strength, that's the time for negotiation. And the fact that the Alliance helped bring that about through Kindred Spirit, that we came to the Kutaran people in their hour of need—well, that's bound to pay some long-term dividends. Until then, however, I strongly feel—and I think this is something we can all agree on—that we must proceed with extreme caution. Caution and prudence."

He looked to John Draper, waited for a response that didn't come. Instead, the ambassador sank slowly to his seat.

To David, the universe seemed to have taken on a surreal edge—a place where talk of peace was reckless and going to war was prudent—and afterward, it would strike him that it was right then, on that Monday afternoon in the British cultural center ballroom, that a coup had taken place, when the age of diplomacy ended and that of the generals began. And he would also come to understand how it happened, how it had happened so many times in so many other places before: with everything in such chaos, events occurring so rapidly, it was next to impossible to gain the time and clarity of thought to know what was the right thing to do, to find a way to resist, to really do much of anything at all.

———

David glanced at his desk clock again: 4:30 PM, 8:30 AM in Cleveland, his mother would have left for work by now. He reached for the telephone, punched in the code to access the government's international WATS line.

By now, he was quite certain that neither *The Plain Dealer* nor the CBS evening news had carried any mention of the weekend's events in Kutar; otherwise, his parents would have already called him. But wars befalling far-off foreigners was one thing, those involving American military advisers was another, and David knew it was now only a matter of time—and probably a very short time—before the crisis in Kutar came to the attention of the American media and, inevitably, into his parents' living room. It placed David in the awkward position of trying to forestall his parents' concerns to a situation they weren't yet aware of—and that was probably easiest done by talking to his father alone.

"Son?" He heard the surprise in his father's voice. "Aw, hell, you just missed your mother."

"Oh, damn." David tried to sound disappointed, wondered how well it conveyed over the scratchy international line. "I planned to call earlier, but got tied up with stuff."

"So, what's going on? You never phone at this time."

David usually called from his home and on the weekends. "Not much," he said. "Well, a little something. I figure you'll be hearing about it soon enough, so . . ."

The WATS line was supposed to be fairly secure, but David

avoided going into details anyway, simply mentioned that the rebels had taken a lot of territory and that Alliance military advisers were on their way to assist the government.

"Now hold on a second; whereabouts did you say the front line is?"

Over the phone line, David heard the rustle of paper, knew his father had retrieved his map of Kutar and was spreading it out on the kitchen table.

"Just above Erbil," David said. "You see there? About two-thirds of the way up?"

"Oh yeah, there it is." His father let out a soft whistle. "Damn, someone sure fucked up, didn't they?"

"Sure looks that way. But, like I said, the rebels don't really have anywhere to go from there. Even if they manage to take Erbil somehow, they've still got two hundred miles of desert in front of them before they get down here."

"Right," his father said. "And so what's the army planning on doing?"

This was something he definitely couldn't get into over the phone. "Oh, I don't know, Dad. I'm not in the loop on that kind of stuff."

"Yeah, well, I wouldn't worry. Once the Alliance boys get there, they'll sort it out in a hurry. Those guys aren't idiots, you know!"

David smiled to himself, fought the urge to tell his father that, actually, the guy running this operation was an idiot. Doing so, though, would have produced the opposite effect he intended with his call.

"No, I know they're not," he said instead. "And who knows, maybe this'll be a wake-up call to the government here, make them realize they need to deal with this northern problem once and for all." He scanned the walls of his office, tried to think of what more to say. "The main thing is I just don't want Mom to worry."

"Oh, don't sweat that." His father chuckled. "I'll move the front line up north about a hundred miles, hide the newspaper from her. It'll be fun; Christ knows I need another project around here."

David laughed. His father had retired six months ago after thirty-eight years at Dean Witter and was, by all accounts, going half crazy trying to fill his days.

"Well, I'd better go. Give my love to Mom."

"Will do. And all our love to you. I'm awfully proud of you, son."

David smiled; this had been his father's sign-off for as long as he could remember. "Thanks, Dad."

When he hung up, David went to stand in front of one of his office windows, gazed out at Serenity Bay. The water was calm—serene was the word that unavoidably came to mind—and on the horizon, a light-colored freighter was heading east, sending a thin funnel of black smoke into the late-afternoon sky. Directly below, a few couples were strolling along the promenade, a number sure to multiply as sunset neared.

Watching the strollers, David was struck by how in Kutar even crises seemed to be imbued with a certain lethargy. From what he had observed, the debacle in the north had scarcely made an impression upon the residents of Laradan, life was continuing very much as before.

He wasn't alone in this observation. At that afternoon's gathering at the British cultural center, several diplomats had commented on how, among the traditional bellwethers that indicated such things, there had yet to register even the hint of public alarm: food prices were staying stable in the local markets, which meant people weren't panic buying; there had been no surge in visa applications at any of the consulates.

Among the diplomats, most attributed this calm to simple ignorance; since the king had yet to make any public comment on the disaster, it had also gone unreported by every newspaper and radio station in the country. The problem with this theory, David knew, was that Kutarans had long since stopped looking to the government-controlled media for the truth about anything. Rather, they relied on a vast and remarkably accurate word-of-mouth grapevine, so that already it could be assumed most everyone had a fairly good idea of what had happened in the mountains, the casualties involved, where the line of government rule now stood. Given that, David wondered, how to explain the Laradanis' nonchalance.

Part of it, no doubt, came down to basic geography. The north was the far hinterlands, primitive and backward and cut off from the rest of the nation by the great desert. For those Kutarans living along the coast, the region barely registered in their consciousness, just didn't matter.

There was also the issue of history. There had always been some kind of trouble in the north, and even if the current unrest was exceptional in its scope—the rebels had never attacked so widely or successfully before—bad news from the region was in the normal course of things.

But David suspected something deeper at work, something also rooted in history, and this was the very complicated regard with which Kutarans held the West.

As in other former colonies around the world, this was a country that had yet to fully forge its own national identity, that still existed in a kind of thrall to its Western patrons. And who could blame it? Because ultimately what history told the Kutarans was that the West, having created the improbable concoction that was their nation, always stood ready to impose a temporary remedy when that mixture blew up.

Until the arrival of British colonizers in the middle of the nineteenth century, the true Kingdom of Kutar had consisted of little more than the city-state of Laradan, with the reigning monarch preserving the peace—and his throne—through a policy of noninterference with the surrounding clans. The British had put a quick stop to that easy arrangement. Maintaining that central authority was essential to the colony's long-term progress, they had first subdued the coastal chieftains to the will of their vassal-king, and then fashioned a wholly new nation by extending Kutar's borders all the way to the northern mountains. If not progress in the strict definition, this contrivance did at least succeed in creating a round-robin system of resentments among the inhabitants–northerner against southerner, tribe against tribe–which had the salutary effect, from Britain's standpoint, of making the Kutaran monarch wholly dependent on its soldiers and colonial administration to stay in power. While this ensured there could never be a serious internal threat to British hegemony, it also meant the country was likely to rip apart should they ever leave.

The day of reckoning came on June 1, 1952, when, at a solemn sunrise ceremony on the Laradan waterfront, the Union Jack was lowered for the last time and Kutar–hastily retrofitted as a parliamentary monarchy–was declared independent. Before setting out for the Royal Navy yacht waiting in Serenity Bay, the departing British governor bestowed a golden key–the symbolic key to the nation–upon Kutar's first democratically elected prime minister as the now-figurehead king, Abdul Rahman I, placidly looked on.

It may well have been the shortest-lived democracy in human history. Even before the Royal Navy yacht had raised its anchor from Serenity Bay, reports were coming in of rebellion throughout the north. Within hours, the unrest had spread to the poorer neighborhoods of Laradan as rival clans and political factions vied for power or revenge. Instead of celebration, the prime minister's Independence Day radio address that night was given over to a plea for calm as the country tumbled toward open civil war.

But as luck would have it–good or ill, depending on one's perspective–it seemed a couple of escape clauses had been built into the transition to popular rule. For one thing, the departing British had never quite got around to reforming the Kutaran military and, among its senior commanders, first loyalty rested not with some elected politician but with the man who had appointed them: the king. For another, the West had not truly cut Kutar loose. Rather, Great Britain's custodial duties had been handed off to its ally and successor in the region, the United States. In answer to urgent requests from the king and his generals, that same evening American troops deployed from their two small bases in Laradan—an airfield north of the city, and a naval refueling depot in Central Harbor—to take up positions in the capital and assist the king's soldiers in restoring order. Once that was done, the Americans were ferried north to quash the uprising there. Within the week peace was at hand, and on June 8—thereafter known as Kutaran Salvation Day, a national holiday—King Rahman I took to the airwaves to announce the creation of something called a "people's monarchy," a novel form of government that included the abolition of parliament, the casting into exile of the prime minister and other prominent Independence Day "conspirators," and the permanent imposition of martial law.

Certainly a great deal had changed in Kutar in the thirty-one years since the Independence Day upheavals—the average citizen enjoyed far more freedom now under the rule of King Rahman II than they had under his father, the American military bases had long since been shuttered—but the fundamental lessons of that time remained fixed in the Kutaran psyche. One was a constant awareness of the fragility of their nation, the belief that abrupt change was an invitation to chaos. Just as profound was the conviction that the West held the true reins of power in their country, that though the accents had changed, they remained just as much the wards of foreigners as on that day in 1848 when the first envoys and soldiers of the British crown had come ashore to proclaim themselves heralds of progress. And in that conviction and knotted history was the reason an American colonel could now step forward to seize the moment, to seduce a people into believing he had a plan to mend their country all over again.

And who, in all honesty, would not want to be seduced? In Colonel Munn's plan was boldness and simplicity. Forget the tediousness of peace talks or tinkering at the margins of a problem. Here was the opportunity to sweep it all away, to change the landscape forever with one brash, decisive stroke.

How appealing, David thought to himself as he stood by his office window that afternoon, how very American. In fact, how very much a man like Colonel Munn resembled a darker mirror image of a man like Walter Jensen.

Even thinking of Walter's name caused David to jolt slightly. It had been only four days since he and the old man had sat in the mess tent in the northern mountains, since he had first learned of the potential riches of the Zulfiqar depression. But now Walter Jensen and the other geologists were on their way home, that camp and the elusive aquifer upon which those riches depended were deep in rebel-held territory, and Kutar's future prosperity remained an open question, any answer now even further up the road.

How quickly the world could change, especially for the worse.

————

The following evening, King Rahman II, dressed in his ceremonial robe and sitting atop his throne, finally took to the airwaves to give a minimalist account of the "difficulties" in the north and to assure the populace that the situation was well in control. That this account was belied by developments along the coast—not just the convoys of soldiers leaving for up-country, but the steady trickle of northern refugees coming over Gowarshad Pass to settle in Laradan's parks and vacant lots—had little discernible effect on his subjects. Instead, the king's announcement that Western advisers were on their way seemed to allay any latent apprehensions among them.

That next afternoon, the Alliance military advisers arrived–"crisis support specialists" was their official designation, unsmiling, crew-cutted men with large duffel bags and aviator sunglasses–and were immediately ferried north. Over the subsequent days, David watched from the northern veranda of his home as a remarkable array of heavy weaponry–tanks, artillery pieces, howitzers–were loaded onto flatbeds at the army bases by the airport, and sent up the national highway.

At the front itself, however, all remained quiet. Since the army had formed its defensive line in the hills above Erbil, there had been no new reports of fighting–or even, for that matter, a sighting of the enemy. After a week, this enduring stillness began to feel a bit eerie.

Within the diplomatic community in Laradan, it also gave rise to the hope that perhaps the next, horrible chapter of the conflict could be avoided, and this hope was especially fervent among those privy to the details of Operation Chokechain. Maybe, they quietly conjectured, the rebels had caught wind of the trap awaiting them in Erbil and wisely decided to not push their luck. Whatever the cause, all agreed that each passing day of peacefulness strengthened the argument for negotiation, pushed the rationale for a bloody counteroffensive further away.

This was certainly the view of First Secretary Nigel Mayhew. In the days after the briefing by Colonel Munn, and with the tacit approval of the British ambassador, Mayhew's waking hours became a blur of hushed conversations and semi-clandestine meetings–at the palace, in the living rooms of private homes, in teahouses tucked away in forgotten corners of the Old City–as he single-handedly tried to fashion a settlement that might avert the next round of killing. That this effort ran counter to Alliance policy did not concern him; frankly, it was part of the allure.

In his more private moments, Nigel Mayhew recalled the

many instances over the centuries in which an ordinary Britisher such as himself—not a prince or a general, but a subaltern or a sea captain or a junior diplomat—had come face-to-face with an improbable destiny, and had, through ingenuity or bluff or sheer will, flouted the order of the day to change history. The little city of Laradan might seem a frail vehicle to cart such ambition, but surely so had Rorke's Drift, so had Lucknow. It was here, quite suddenly, at the sunset of a respectable if unremarkable career, that Nigel Mayhew imagined he might, in some modest way, place his name alongside those of British legend, those fellow countrymen who, through the ages, had found themselves at the confluence of desperate events and not flinched, had instead steered them to a more desirous outcome.

In contrast to Nigel's labors, this period of peacefulness cast Amira Chalasani into a kind of paralysis. Having at last dispensed with her social obligations in Laradan, she had just been preparing to leave for her family's village in the north when the rout in the mountains came—and even though that village was below the battleline, still firmly in government hands, something now held her back from making the journey. She couldn't put her finger on what that something was; in fact, she seemed quite determined to leave the issue unexamined. Instead, from her penthouse suite at the Excelsior Hotel, the finest hotel in Laradan, Amira spent her time telephoning officials she knew in the various ministries for any new reports from the north, her family back in England for advice on whom she might contact next. Her days settled into a dreary pattern: by each afternoon, the battery of telephone calls that had consumed her morning had finally reassured her, she was thoroughly resolved to set off the following day, but when that day came, she would awaken to a new cascade of doubts, and the tedious process would start over again.

This was very unlike her—she had always taken pride in being an intrepid sort—but when Amira tried to analyze what held her, all that came was "blackness." That was it. What lay past the desert, what was happening in the mountains, was simply blackness, and nothing in her experience could prepare for what she might meet there. It would be like walking through a tunnel or a strange house in total darkness—and perhaps this is why she left the matter unexamined, because once these analogies occurred to her, she would have recognized the true source of her fear, what, above all else, she didn't wish to consider: that the land she believed she knew was, in truth, quite alien to her. And this was too much. This was alarmist. Surely some news would come down, somebody would say something in one of these telephone calls that would lend a perspective. Until then, Amira could only wait, either for insight or for an emboldening of her heart.

For Paolo Alfani, this time of waiting brought a more fully realized revelation, a somewhat philosophical one.

At the age of forty-two, the businessman saw that his entire life had been about order: creating it, harnessing it, prospering from it. It was devotion to order that had enabled him to make something of himself, to attend university, to rise through the ranks of his company—even, paradoxically, the reason he was still in Kutar.

In his three years in Laradan, he had taken his company's grotesquely disorganized regional office and transformed it into a model of efficiency. This hadn't been an exercise in ego, a manager's desire to put his stamp on things; the improvements Paolo had implemented were reflected in sales, with his company now the leading electrical-parts importer in Kutar. At the risk of sounding boastful, no wonder the head office had taken so long to act on his transfer request.

But what was the precise opposite of order? Well, chaos, of course. And what could possibly induce more chaos than war? It sounded cold-blooded put this way—and Paolo Alfani would never have given voice to it for fear of being misunderstood—but along with the horror and suffering that war caused, it was also rather like a giant puzzle. The normal ways of doing things were shattered, systems collapsed. Confronted with chaos on such a scale, a man devoted to order could either throw up his hands in defeat or see in it the greatest challenge of his life. Paolo certainly didn't wish for this war to worsen, but if it did, this little country would be in desperate need of people like him.

David recognized her, but couldn't immediately recall from where. Then she noticed him, came to his table.

"Amira Chalasani," she said, extending her hand. "But I'm sorry, I've forgotten your name."

"David Richards," he said, half standing. He offered the seat across from him, but she remained standing, saw the slight confusion in his eyes.

"We met at the German party, remember? With your Italian friend?"

David remembered then. And at the same instant, he remembered that she had been snide to him, had rebuffed him, and this was enough to compel him to offer the seat again. "Please," he said. "I'd enjoy the company."

Amira hesitated, glanced about the crowded dining room before relenting.

"I'm surprised to see you here," she said. "This part of town is not popular with the diplomatic community."

It was a Friday night, the end of an intensely busy week, and David had wandered into the Old City and chosen the restaurant quite by chance. He'd been leafing through an out-of-date *Time* magazine when she walked in.

"That's why I came here," he replied. "After these past two weeks, the last people I want to see are other diplomats."

She smiled. "I imagine it's been rather hectic for you."

He nodded. They talked briefly about the situation in the

north, but David was very relieved when their conversation moved on, to the changes Amira had noticed in Laradan since her last visit four years ago, to how Kutar compared to other places David had been posted; even their discussion about the beastly heat of recent days, of when it might end, was a welcome respite. He enjoyed watching her speak, the way her dark eyes flitted about the room, came to rest on him for a moment, then moved on, and he was watching her so intently that he only half caught the mention of her upcoming trip to the north.

"I'm sorry," he said. "To where again?"

"Chalasan, my ancestral village. I've been putting it off forever, but now I'm finally doing it; I leave in the morning."

"Chalasan," he repeated, scanning his mental map of Kutar, trying to place it.

"I'm sure you've never been there. It's very small and out of the way, in a valley just above Erbil."

David stared at her. He had heard nothing new about Operation Chokechain for several days but assumed it was still going forward, and he tried to think of how to warn her, how much he could say. "I wouldn't do that, if I were you," he whispered at last.

"No, Chalasan is fine." Amira smiled again. "Believe me, I've talked to just about everyone in the Interior Ministry at this point. They all say it's calm there, the front line is a good twenty miles away."

He gazed into his wineglass on the table. She was not making this easy. He slowly looked up. "Front lines have a way of changing. You should wait a little longer."

She returned his stare. "You know something."

He gave the barest nod. "And I've already told you more than I should."

Amira slumped back in her chair in disgust. "Americans." She made the word sound like an epithet. "How is it that the Americans know more about what's happening in my country than I do, than anyone at the ministries?"

David felt a surge of annoyance. He had just compromised his position to warn this woman, and this was how she repaid him. He summoned forth his memories of the German party, the irritation he'd felt with her then, and it added to his pique. "Your country? I thought your country was England."

She seemed taken aback, blinked rapidly. He had meant to wound with the comment, and was pleased that he had. But then Amira broke into a grin. "You're still mad at me from the party, aren't you? What was it I said again?"

"Something about the big American come to help the poor little people of Kutar."

"That's right." She laughed. "And that offended you?"

He shrugged. "A bit. It's not like I'm getting rich being over here. And coming from a member of the oligarchy that just got up and walked out of this place, yes, I found it kind of offensive."

"Oligarchy?" She laughed again. "Oh, you are mad at me!"

David found himself smiling back in spite of himself. Amira leaned over the table, placed a hand on his.

"I'm sorry, it was very rude of me. How can I make it up to you?"

He looked at her hand, her eyes, and all at once his indignation vanished. "You can have dinner with me some night."

She slowly drew her hand away, and David watched a coolness come over her. "I just did," she said.

She reached for her shoulder bag, brought out her wallet. He brushed her money back.

"No, please, let the oligarchy pay."

He laughed. "Put it away."

But when she rose to leave, David watched the way she slipped the bag over her shoulder, how she flipped her hair from her face, and he suddenly didn't want to be left alone there with his old *Time* magazine. "Don't go."

Amira looked down at him, and David felt stripped, forlorn in her stare.

"To the north, I mean. Don't go up there."

She studied him with the same amused smile he remembered from the German party. "Good night," she said, and turned to go.

————

Although built upon Napoleonic models of warfare, certain lessons of military history seemed to have been insufficiently considered in the planning of operations Chokechain and Kindred Spirit.

Perhaps the most obvious was that excessive secrecy on the battlefield can have unintended consequences, that soldiers abruptly ordered to withdraw from a secure position for no discernible reason tend to become confused and fearful in roughly the same ratio as their enemy is emboldened. Perhaps another was that even an elite team of foreign military advisers might have difficulty implementing the Austerlitz gambit–a strategy in which both surprise and concealment are crucial–upon a desert landscape that doesn't readily allow for either. And it appeared that another old lesson of men at war had been overlooked, a very basic one: much like the elemental law of physics which holds that an object, once in motion, tends to stay in motion, so it has long been observed that a soldier, once running for his life, has a tendency to keep running.

Having only recently calmed down from their escape from the mountains, the Kutaran troops holding the forward line above Erbil viewed the strange order to abandon their positions initially with disbelief, and then with alarm. In their first retreat, the mountainous landscape had at least offered some protection from their pursuers–ridgelines and forests and stone outcroppings–but they all knew that beyond Erbil lay nothing but open desert, that out there was death itself. Within an hour into the withdrawal, order began to fray and then it collapsed, soldiers throwing off packs and weapons and anything else that might slow their descent. By the time they reached Erbil, they were a terrified mob, each man out for himself, and as they swept through the lines of their entrenched comrades, their hysteria became infectious. At first, only individual reserve soldiers joined their flight, but then it was whole companies, whole battalions, all efforts by their officers to stem the tide proving futile–and then, when masses of rebels appeared on the hillsides above, the officers joined the race out as well. It did not end until the last soldier was free of Erbil, until the last straggler had stumbled into the oasis town of Zulfiqar, the new frontier of government control, ninety miles away. Probably fewer shots had been fired in this rout than in the first one, but the toll on the Kutaran military was far more staggering; abandoned in the trenches in Erbil or stranded in the gypsum patches of the Zulfiqar depression was an enormous share–perhaps half, perhaps more, no one really knew–of the nation's heavy weaponry.

The next day, another meeting of the diplomatic community was held in the ballroom of the British cultural center. Standing beneath the map of Kutar, Colonel Allen B. Munn announced that, in light of its "non-positive success ratios," Operation Kindred Spirit was now adjudged "complete." In its place, Alliance headquarters had just approved a new mission, Operation Stalwart Friend, with two more units of military advisers on their way to the kingdom to assist in the campaign against the rebels–or, as they were now officially designated in Alliance memoranda, "the anti-freedom forces." That same evening, the State Department issued an urgent advisory against travel to Kutar and, in light of the rapidly deteriorating security situation, ordered the evacuation of all American citizens and nonessential embassy personnel. Other legations quickly followed suit. Shortly after, the first chartered commercial plane touched down at Kutar National Airport to disgorge several dozen Western journalists coming to cover the war, and to take away the families, the secretaries, the businessmen, and the tourists who had suddenly found themselves in a country tearing apart.

The task of organizing the evacuation fell to the German

legation, and they did so in methodical fashion. Each foreign national was to register with his or her embassy, there to be assigned a place on one of the daily flights and told to go to the German embassy on the specified date for the bus convoy to the airport. Each adult was allowed to bring two suitcases, each child one, and promptly at three o'clock every afternoon for the next week, the buses would pull out of the embassy gates with their security escorts for the forty-five-minute journey through the city and over Gowarshad Pass.

To make sure all went smoothly, David accompanied the con voy on the first day of the evacuation. He noticed that, at the crowds of curious gathered along the streets, at the soldiers beside their checkpoints, the departing children smiled and waved, but that the adults tended to stare straight ahead, as if there was a shame in what they were doing, as if they couldn't bring themselves to look upon those they were leaving.

"So you're essential personnel?" his father asked.

David chuckled into the receiver. "For the time being, anyway."

"That's my boy!"

"Now, Jim, stop it." His mother was on the kitchen extension, exasperation in her voice. "You really want our son to stay in a war zone?"

"Oh, hell, nothing's gonna happen to him," his father said. "The front line's two hundred miles away—and besides, they've got that Colonel Munn there."

David lurched forward in his office chair, bewildered. "What did you say?"

"Sorry, son, I was explaining to your mother."

"No, I know, but did you say something about Munn?"

"That's his name, isn't it?" his father asked. "The guy running the show over there?"

David kneaded his forehead with his fingertips, still confused. "Well, yeah, but how do you know about him?"

"You kidding?" His father laughed. "He's all over the news, can't turn on the television without seeing him. He seems like quite a guy, a real go-getter. I bet he's even more impressive in person, huh?"

David closed his eyes, rubbed his temple more forcefully. He very much wanted to disabuse his father of whatever he'd been hearing–to tell him that Munn was the fool who had caused all this–but when he opened his eyes, David saw Bill Myerson standing in his office doorway. He instinctively glanced past Bill's shoulder, to the open area beyond, but to what purpose he wouldn't have been able to say.

"Look, I have to go," David said into the receiver, "but I'll call again soon, okay? Love to you both." He hung up, half rose from his chair as Bill came into the room.

"Sorry to interrupt," he said. "I just wanted to speak with you for a minute."

"Sure, sure." David forced a weak smile, motioned to the armchair across the desk, but instead the deputy chief of mission wandered over to one of the tall windows to gaze out at the promenade.

"Nice view from here," he muttered. "I'm on the other side of the building, you know, so I don't see the sea at all."

"Yes, I know," David said. "I've never really understood that."

Bill turned to him with a frown. "Hmm?"

"Well, usually senior people have the best views. It's odd that you and the ambassador are on the street side."

Bill nodded distractedly, as if he hadn't really listened, and looked back out.

This was agonizing. David wished the man would just confront him.

"You know Diane is leaving today, right?"

David studied the DCM's profile, trying to gauge where this

might be going. "Yes, I heard that. I think maybe I saw her name on the manifest."

"And that I'm leaving on Friday, that I've resigned?"

"No," David whispered, genuinely surprised, "I didn't know that. What . . . ?"

Bill nodded to his reflection in the glass. "Taking an early retirement. I just told John last night, imagine he'll make a general announcement soon. He'll probably make Stan acting DCM until . . ." He smiled slightly, turned to David. "Well, until anyone can figure out what's going to happen in this place."

His smile eased away, and he stared at David for a long moment. "I don't know how much you know about it, but Diane had a pretty bad health scare here recently. She finally got some tests done in Rome—it turns out it's nothing, thank God—but . . . well, it's caused us to kind of reappraise things, I guess. She's always wanted to have kids, so that's what we're going to do. Adopt. She's on her way to Thailand now, to the Cambodian refugee camps, you know?" His smile returned, less tentative than before. "I'll join her as soon as I can, figure if I don't, she'll end up adopting a whole village."

David laughed softly. "That's wonderful, Bill. I'm very happy for both of you."

The DCM nodded, looked down to David's paper-strewn desk. "Anyway, I wanted to tell you that. She's had a hard time here—I'm sure you know that—and your friendship has meant a lot to her. I imagine she'd like to say goodbye."

David felt rooted to the spot, couldn't think of what to say, and before he could, Bill Myerson started for the open door.

"Watch yourself here," he called over his shoulder. "I think it's going to get worse."

———

He found Diane on the German embassy lawn, perched awkwardly atop the larger of her two suitcases, surrounded by other women and their luggage. She wore a pale-yellow sundress, diamond earrings he hadn't seen before, and she looked very pretty sitting there, much as she had in the easy first days of their affair.

"Hard to believe you're essential personnel," she said, smiling.

David grinned. "Desperate times." He continued to gaze down at her. "Bill told me you're on your way to Thailand."

Diane grimaced, stared off at the children scampering over the great lawn, giddy at the adventure that had befallen them. "Yeah, well, I'm starting to rethink the idea. They're fine when they're little, but this whole walking-talking-runny-nose thing . . ."

David laughed. "What are you planning to get? Have you decided?"

"Maybe siblings, a boy and a girl. Maybe more. Bill is saying no more than two, but I've got a head start on him. Anyway, he won't be able to resist when he sees them. They're such beautiful children, you know?"

David nodded, looked across the lawn. At the front gate, the first of the convoy buses was just pulling into the parking lot. "Why didn't you tell me about Rome?"

Diane gave an improbable chuckle, shook her head. "That I thought I was dying? That I thought I was spending my last days on earth in this place? You really wanted to hear that?" She smiled up at him again, more tenderly than before. "It was an affair, remember? It's what you're good at. Stay with what you're good at."

Just before six that evening, the plane carrying Diane and some 280 other foreign nationals taxied away from Laradan's main terminal and accelerated down the tarmac. From his northern veranda, David briefly lost sight of the plane against the backdrop of rock and sand, but then it rose onto the horizon, arcing up into a hot blue sky, banking west.

Four

"You ever wonder why so many consular officers are black women?"

At the poolside table, David looked up from his book. Cheryl Thompson was staring off in the direction of the changing rooms, her bare legs propped on an empty patio chair, but she now turned to him. He eyed her warily, shrugged.

"Funny, I've never actually noticed that."

He had, of course; the pattern was so consistent as to be impossible to not notice. In fact, a black woman had been the consular chief–the embassy official in charge of granting or denying visas–at all three of David's foreign postings, but he was reluctant to say this.

"A lot of people think it's a kind of mafia," Cheryl said. "You know, one of us got into a position of authority, then started looking out for all the other black women. But that's not true. It's because we resent foreigners. We remember how hard it was for us or our parents to make it, so we resent the idea of foreigners just coming over to the States and having an easy time of it." She smiled. "You have some nice white man from Minnesota, life's always been good, he's going to let everyone in."

David thought about this for a moment. "But why just women? Why not black men?"

"Oh, that part *is* a mafia," Cheryl said, and they laughed together.

It was a Saturday afternoon, and they were on the patio of the Officers Club, a walled compound of two or three acres shaded by leafy trees up on Baktiar Hill. Its proper name was the Foreign Residents Leisure Center, but it had originally been built as a clubhouse for British officers during the colonial era, and it was for this that it was still known.

It was a peculiar place, although popular with diplomatic families on the weekends. Along with the pool area and gardens, it consisted of a cluster of incongruous Tudor-style buildings connected by cobblestoned walkways: a bar and a billiard room, a banquet hall, a seldom-visited library. On the walls of the main lobby were framed photographs of what it had all looked like in the 1880s—enormous leather couches and armchairs, Victorian reading lamps, fine china and silver in the banquet room—but a radical renovation in the early 1960s had ushered in a Caribbean motif. Cast out was the heavy furniture, replaced with rattan and wicker; the poolside snack bar now wore a little thatched roof and faux-reed façade, and old calypso records, scratchy and warped from overuse, played on the sound system.

"Why do you think John kept his kids here?" Cheryl asked.

David looked up from his book again, to the empty pool beside them. On Saturday afternoons in the past, it would have been a thrashing mass of children, but now, a week since the evacuation had concluded, all the foreign children in Laradan were gone. Not quite all; at the last minute, John Draper and some of the other ambassadors had decided to have their own kids stay on.

"I think he wanted to make a statement," David replied. "You know, that everything's going to work out, the government will prevail—a symbolic gesture kind of thing."

Cheryl nodded. "I wish he'd have let me make a symbolic

gesture. I would've kept my boys here." She looked dour for a moment, then smiled. "But I guess only ambassadors are allowed to do that, right? I'll have to check the State Department handbook, look up 'symbolic gestures.'"

David set his book aside. "Okay, here's one. I'm a thirty-two-year-old doctor, just out of medical school, single, perfect health. My specialty is . . . I don't know, something that there's a shortage of in the States, and I'm willing to go anywhere–North Dakota, Appalachia, you name it–in exchange for a work visa."

This was a game they had begun playing, David assuming the role of an applicant in Cheryl's consular office, but he had yet to find a persona that met her high standards. She now gazed off, bobbled her head slowly, as if giving his case careful thought.

"Denied," she said at last. "You look good on paper, but there's something off-putting in your manner."

"My manner?"

"Something a bit smarmy. And the single thing, that bothers me. The fact that you went into pediatrics, it probably means you're a pedophile."

"Pediatrics? I didn't say anything about pediatrics."

"Denied. You're also argumentative."

David laughed, slumped back in his chair in defeat.

His newfound friendship with Cheryl Thompson was one of the more unlikely outgrowths of the current crisis. They had arrived in Kutar at nearly the same time but, prior to the past couple of weeks, their dealings with each other had consisted of greetings in hallways, perhaps a few words about the weather. David had always found Cheryl stiff, even severe–he couldn't recall ever hearing her laugh–and had attributed it to the difficulties she undoubtedly faced in trying to negotiate Kutar, a place where few people had ever encountered a black woman in a position of authority. It came as a surprise, therefore, when, one morning during the evacuation, she had suddenly appeared at the threshold of his office, said maybe it was time they got to know each other. They had developed something of a ritual since then, stopping by each other's office in the lull of midafternoons, chatting for a few minutes about whatever came to mind. With her husband and two little boys now gone, it seemed Cheryl desired simple human contact, and through their talks, David had discovered a different side to her: warm, funny in a caustic kind of way. Before, if he'd walked out on the patio of the Officers Club and seen Cheryl Thompson sitting alone, it never would have occurred to him to join her; on that Saturday afternoon, it would have felt strange to sit anywhere else.

Their relationship typified the changes that had taken place throughout the embassy since the evacuation. Among those Americans who remained—with Bill Myerson's departure, there were now just five officials, a few assistants, the Marine Guards—an esprit de corps had developed, and along with it, a collapsing of formality. Everyone was on a first-name basis now, even the Marine Guards who had stowed away their black dress uniforms in favor of combat fatigues, who now moved about the embassy compound with assault rifles on their shoulders. Over the past two weeks, David had learned more about his colleagues' personal lives—about summer cabins in Maine and failed first marriages and unfinished novels, about emotionally withdrawn children and ghastly in-laws—than he had in the previous twenty-two months.

This new conviviality was evident among the other foreigners who remained in Laradan as well, and it went on display whenever there was a gathering of the diplomatic community—which was often. David had assumed that, in light of the crisis, the usually thick calendar of parties and receptions would be trimmed, but he had been mistaken. Instead the various legations appeared to be scouring the record books to come up with something else to honor or celebrate most every night; in David's estimation, the most resourceful thus far had been the Norwegians' commemoration of Zambian Independence Day.

But if the purpose of these parties was to distract from their collective isolation, they tended to have the opposite effect. With nearly all the wives and children gone, the embassies stripped down to their most essential members—which almost invariably meant middle-aged men—there was a dreariness to these gatherings that no amount of alcohol or strangely clad servants could quite dispel. It was at such times that David was most grateful for the presence of Cheryl Thompson and the few other women diplomats, most from northern European countries, who had stayed on.

By contrast, the crisis seemed to have had an energizing effect on the residents of Laradan—understandable, perhaps, in a city normally so dull that a minor traffic accident could keep hundreds of onlookers enthralled for hours. To be sure, the military disaster in Erbil had generated much greater concern than the previous one, but this was offset by a fascination with the changes that this disaster had brought. In each of the capital's half-dozen parks, tent camps had been erected for those northern refugees coming in over Gowarshad Pass, and for the Westernized Laradanis, the opportunity to stroll these camps and observe the inhabitants in their colorful traditional dress was rather like visiting some vast ethnographical zoo.

At least as exotic was the swarm of foreign journalists and relief workers who had descended upon the kingdom. The relief workers seemed to fall rather quickly from view—David imagined them stacking boxes somewhere or roaming the city in search of warehouse space—but the journalists were a different story. For the first few days, they had been everywhere: massed out in front of the palace, at the daily Defense Ministry briefings, shuttling up to the front line at Zulfiqar in rented Land Rovers. Some had even shown up at the nightly diplomatic parties, but they tended to be a rather pushy and socially inept lot, driven by an urgency that neither Kutar nor the foreign legations could satisfy, and their attendance at these affairs had quickly dwindled out of mutual annoyance. Already, David had heard, some were packing up and moving on, dispirited by the peaceful stasis now entering its third week.

In truth, this wait was wearing on him as well: the wait for the rebels to attack Zulfiqar, for the rumored army counterattack into the north, the interminable wait for something, anything, to happen. David knew there were others playing an active role in events, but he was not among them. Instead he had spent these past days in the grip of helplessness, poring over the files of development projects that had now ground to a halt, preparing status reports for Washington in which the words "unknown" and "suspended" figured prominently.

After a time, Cheryl rose from the poolside table, yawned as she stretched. "Well, I think I'll take off. I've got one of the embassy cars. Want a lift home?"

David glanced at his watch. "I would, except I'm supposed to meet Nigel Mayhew here."

Cheryl winced. "Nigel Mayhew?"

"I don't know, he wants to talk to me about something." He looked up at her, grinned. "All right, here's one: I'm a senior British diplomat, a graduate of Eton–"

"Denied!" Laughing, Cheryl grabbed her towel, gave a little wave goodbye, and started for the changing rooms. David watched her go. He noticed that she had a very nice figure. A familiar thought came to him—more like a set of speculations—but he pushed them from his mind.

Nigel Mayhew, clad in his requisite navy-blue suit, arrived a few minutes after two. Spotting David, he hurried around the pool.

"Sorry to be late, Richards," he said, sinking heavily into a seat. He looked especially florid in the harsh midday light, and rivulets of sweat trickled down his neck.

"Mad dogs and Englishmen, huh?" David teased, but the man didn't seem to get the joke. "The heat," he explained. "Your suit."

"Oh yes, right." Nigel gave a perfunctory chuckle. "Kipling, wasn't it? Yes, well, when one is First Secretary . . ." He took in David's shorts and T-shirt. "Still, do trust I haven't kept you from anything important."

David smiled. "Nothing too important. What's up?"

Nigel cast a careful gaze around the patio. No one was within earshot, but he leaned closer anyway. "I'd like to put a question to you first, if I may. Colonel Munn, what's your opinion of him?"

"Off the record?"

"Off the record."

"I think he's an imbecile. I suspect the other military liaisons are imbeciles, too, except they don't have speaking parts."

Nigel nodded. "And Ambassador Draper? What's his take on the colonel, do you think?"

Now it was David who glanced around the patio, for this was getting on thinner ice. "Well, I'm not John's confidant, but I think it's pretty clear he despises him."

Nigel nodded again. "I ask because I've just come from a meeting at the palace, several of the top ministers. As I'm sure you know, there's been quite a few of these meetings lately, but . . ." He hesitated, studied David's face. "You're familiar with the '78 accords, I assume?"

David was, of course. Under pressure from Western governments and human rights organizations, in 1978 King Rahman II had acceded to the reestablishment of the national parliament, and the creation of an autonomous provincial council system. The reforms had been intended to defuse a growing insurgency in the north at the time, but once international attention had turned elsewhere, the king had stripped the parliament of any real authority and made the provincial councils subordinate to his appointed governors, most of them royal relatives or retired generals.

"I think we're quite close to a settlement here," Nigel said. "Basically it means getting the palace to live up to the '78 terms: a scaling down of the military garrisons in the north, restructuring the parliament and regional councils so they actually have some power. There's still a lot of details to work out, but after Erbil, the ministers realize they have to do something."

David stared off across the pool.

It wasn't as if he were hearing all this for the first time. In recent days, there had been a lot of quiet talk in Laradan–among diplomats, local businessmen–that in the current situation might be found the solution to Kutar's northern problem. After all, this was an artificial nation, the product of some colonial cartographer's blithe hand in joining two very different peoples–the easygoing coastal dwellers astride one of the world's great trading routes, the taciturn mountain tribesmen tucked away in one of its most forgotten corners–into an unnatural union. And since the current battle lines neatly traced that divide, so the reasoning went, what better time to work out a new arrangement? What was surprising, though, was hearing that foreign diplomats were actively urging this course on the palace and finding a receptive audience.

"And the rebels have agreed to it?" he asked.

Nigel shrugged. "In principle. You know, all the northerners have ever really wanted is to be left alone, to run things up there as they see fit. If this goes through and the government lives up to its word, they get that."

"And the king?"

The First Secretary arched an eyebrow. "Well, that's where it gets tricky. As I said, most of the ministers are on board, but before we take it to the king, we need to have . . . what's that expression you Americans have, 'our chickens on the line'?"

"Ducks in a row."

Nigel nodded. "He's not a bad sort, you know, the king. Much more given to co-opting his enemies than killing them but, like mandarins everywhere, he'll only give ground when he absolutely has to. Now naturally we expect to take the lead on this, Kutar being a former British colony, but we both feel–myself and the ambassador–that the king must be convinced we speak for the diplomatic community at large. Otherwise, he can simply turn to his army commanders and let them take over." The First Secretary paused, stroked one tip of his white mustache. "And maybe even a greater concern is how the Alliance people here will react."

All at once, David saw exactly where this was going. As the commanding officer of the sixty or seventy Alliance advisers who had been brought in for Operation Stalwart Friend, Colonel Munn was now essentially running the war. And while he'd used his new-found prominence to freeze out the diplomatic community—since the fiasco in Erbil, he'd given no further briefings, and he'd apparently even avoided meeting with Ambassador Draper on several occasions—the mission objective of Stalwart Friend made clear what he was planning: a resolution to the Kutar crisis was to be achieved solely through "optimized civic engagement," or victory on the battlefield.

"I have it on good authority," Nigel said, "that the counter-offensive is to start next weekend. Well, that would rather queer a peace settlement, wouldn't it?"

David gazed down at his hands, picked at a fingernail. "And you're telling me this because . . . ?"

"Because when we meet with the king, the ambassador and myself, we need to have an American in the room. As I said, we'll take the lead, but without an American at least sitting in, lending moral support, it doesn't work."

David looked up, slowly shook his head. "But there's no way, Nigel. With Stalwart Friend, there's no way Ambassador Draper can . . ."

He trailed off before the First Secretary's spreading grin.

"Which is why I've come to you, old boy." Nigel leaned closer. "Absolutely right. Under Stalwart Friend, Draper can't offi-cially involve himself in anything that countermands it. For the same reason, it's pointless for myself or the ambassador to ap-proach Draper directly; it would just place him in an impossible position." He folded his hands together on the table, massaged a thumb. "So, what we thought is that perhaps he could hear mention of the plan through unofficial means—from one of his own people, for example—and on the basis of that, he might choose to make a . . . well, an unofficial overture."

"Unofficial overture?"

Nigel shrugged. "Not himself in the room, but perhaps a subordinate. It's not ideal, of course, but probably the best we can hope for under the circumstances."

David gazed off, pondered whether even being the bearer of this message could bring repercussions. He finally nodded. "Okay. I'll pass it along. I can't promise anything, obviously, but I'll pass it along."

"Excellent. That's all I ask."

They rose together, walked toward the main clubhouse building.

"And when do you think you might speak to him?" Nigel asked. "Not to put a rush on things, but if the offensive is coming next weekend, we haven't much time."

"I'll try to corner him at the party tonight."

The First Secretary brightened at this. "Oh, yes, I'd quite forgotten. A film festival, isn't it?"

David grinned. "Don't get your hopes up."

Somehow, the USIA's traveling film exhibition, The Magic Mosaic That Is America, had found its way on board the transport plane bringing in the most recent wave of Alliance military advisers. Ambassador Draper, feeling that public screenings would be inappropriate in the current atmosphere, had decided instead to use the films as a pretext for another diplomatic party.

"I'll try to come by for it," Nigel said, "but I've another whole round of meetings this afternoon. Still an awful lot to be hashed out . . ." They were in the lobby now and he drew up, grew thoughtful as he scanned the old photographs lining the walls.

"You know, it's very difficult to compete with you people," he muttered after a time. "The Kutarans, there's something rather childlike about them—I know that must sound condescending, but it's true. We Brits, we're like their father figure: responsible, steady–a bit overbearing, no doubt, the ones who tell them to do their homework, eat their vegetables–but I think deep down they know we have their best interests at heart." He looked to David then. "But you Americans, you're the favorite uncle. Exciting, dynamic, you sweep in, let them eat candy, take them on adventures, they want to be like you. It makes it very hard to compete." He grew more somber. "The problem is, there's a great difference between a father and an uncle. We genuinely care what happens to them. I'm not at all sure you people do."

David, who had been following the analogy in good cheer, felt instantly defensive. At the very least, Nigel's vision of things ignored the many times in history when the British hadn't had the Kutarans' best interests at heart–never mind that it was that same legacy of British paternalism, so richly conveyed in Nigel's words, which lay at the core of the mess they were dealing with now.

But David had no stomach for an argument just then. "That's not true," he said simply. "We do care about them."

"Really?" The First Secretary gave him a faintly apologetic smile. "Maybe so. Maybe I've misjudged you. I suppose we'll see, won't we?"

————

That same evening, David met up with Paolo Alfani at the Hotel Excelsior bar. The Italian businessman had missed the general evacuation–there had been too many loose ends to tie up, he explained, impossible to shut down his office so quickly–and he had busied himself these past days with trying to help some of the relief agencies sort out their operations in the city.

"They really are a remarkable bunch," he said, with a weary shake of his head. "Very nice people–the best of intentions, of course–but the incompetence defies belief. Yesterday I watched a pallet come off one of the relief planes, and do you know what it was? Tinned ham. Two tons of tinned ham. You would think that someone might have learned beforehand that very few Kutarans eat pork. Another group is looking for any Baptist refugees who need assistance, but when I tell them the nearest Baptist is probably three thousand kilometers away, they look upon me as a Satanist."

David laughed. "Maybe you should put those two groups together. I'm pretty sure Baptists eat ham."

Paolo shook his head again, gazed around the bar. It was a cozy, wood-paneled place, fairly empty in normal times, but the influx of journalists had changed that; on this evening, they filled most of the tables and the lower half of the bar. "And how goes the war effort? All well with Munn and his Starboard Friend?"

David grinned. "Stalwart Friend, I believe it's called. It means strong, loyal."

"Ah. And it's to start next weekend, no? That's what everyone is saying."

"That's what I'm hearing, too."

It occurred to David that if the offensive launch time was such common knowledge in the streets of Laradan, surely the rebels were aware of it as well. On the other hand, perhaps it was this knowledge that had led them to accept Nigel Mayhew's secret mediation efforts.

He toyed with his glass of beer on the tabletop. He was curious to get Paolo's take on his conversation with Nigel, but knew he couldn't ask directly. "But there's some talk of trying to reach a settlement beforehand."

"Really?" The businessman appeared surprised.

David shrugged. "A rumor I heard."

"Yes, well, rumors. You can hear rumors about almost anything in Laradan just now." Paolo took a cigarette from his shirt pocket, lit it. "And anyway, why would the rebels agree to a settlement? Think of it from their perspective. Twice now the army has come for them, and twice they've sent it running. They've taken over a third of the country, most of its heavy weapons, and they've barely fired a shot. No, I would think that, with your Colonel Munn running things on this side, the rebels must feel they have both God and good luck on theirs." He glanced toward the bar entrance, abruptly straightened. "Ah look, it's Miss Chalasani."

David turned to see Amira Chalasani crossing the hotel lobby just beyond. "No, wait, don't–"

But he was too late; Paolo had already jumped up from the table, started in her direction. "Signorina Chalasani?" he called. "Paolo Alfani–from the German party, remember? I'm here with David Richards. Please, will you join us for a drink?"

In the brightly lit lobby, Amira hesitated, but then smiled. "Well, thank you. Yes, that would be nice."

Out of politeness, David stood, extended his hand as she approached.

"And you remember David, I'm sure," Paolo said.

Amira took his hand. "Yes. In fact, we had dinner together one night down in the Old City."

"Oh, is that so?" The businessman arched a sly eyebrow, glanced between them as he tried to read the situation. "So perhaps this is not such a coincidental meeting . . ."

Amira laughed. "Sorry to disappoint, Mr. Alfani, but I'm staying at this hotel."

"Ah."

The waiter came by, and Amira ordered a glass of red wine. For some minutes, Paolo sustained the conversation, chatting about various things, but the tension between the other two became ever more apparent and awkward. At the end of a fairly long story about a misplaced shipment of generators, Paolo took the opportunity to leap to his feet. "Well, if you'll excuse me a moment, I must go to the toilet. But please, continue your conversation, I'll just try to catch up when I get back."

David and Amira chuckled sheepishly at this, turned to watch him go.

"Poor man," she said, "I think he's feeling rather confused."

She looked down to her wineglass, gripped it by the stem. David studied her. She was wearing a white blouse, and in the dim light of the bar it appeared almost incandescent against her dark features.

"So I came in because I wanted to apologize to you," she said finally. "It seems to be a pattern we've established."

"What for this time?"

"For getting angry at you that night when you told me not to go north." Amira glanced up at him then, tried to smile, but it was very fragile; she turned back to her glass. "I realize it was unfair of me. And, of course, Erbil fell just after that, so if I had been up there then . . ."

"Apology accepted." This brought no change in her manner, so David repeated it. "Apology accepted."

"Thank you."

David looked across the room, noticed a group of Kutaran businessmen at a nearby table. They seemed very much at ease sitting there with their whiskeys, had assumed those languorous poses, rather perfected in this part of the world, that suggested they might not stir again for many hours.

"So what have you been doing all this time?" he asked. "I haven't seen you at any of the embassy parties."

This instantly lifted Amira's mood; she laughed. "No, I've managed to escape most of those, thank God. Actually, I've been looking for my family."

"Your family?"

"My relatives from up north. Among the refugees, you know?"

David nodded. In recent days, the flow of refugees coming over Gowarshad Pass had begun to slow, but there were already tens of thousands settled in the parks and vacant lots of Laradan. "Any luck?"

Amira shook her head.

"I'm sorry."

"Not your fault." Her gaze settled on the same group of Ku-taran businessmen David had noticed. "Such a stupid place for a war," she said with sudden intensity. "That's what I can't get over. With just a few changes, a few small concessions . . ." She turned to him. "Have you wondered why everyone has stayed so placid through all this? It's not because they're confident. It's because they've given up. All they want is for this to be over—inde-pendence for the north, autonomy, whatever, they don't care. They just want it to end, but they know it's not going to. This is just one more round, one more slaughter." She slowly shook her head again. "It's like watching someone you love dying for a stupid reason—cigarettes or drugs."

As he watched her, David fell to reconsidering his own, far more involved, explanation for the calm that had held Laradan these past weeks. Perhaps Amira was right. Perhaps more than anything else, it was simple resignation. And as his thoughts turned this way, David felt a deeper appreciation for what Nigel Mayhew was trying to do: not merely to avert the killing planned for the days ahead, but to bring about actual change, to crack the apathy that gripped this place.

"I think it will end," he said softly, almost as if to himself.

"Really?" Amira looked at him in that bemused, appraising way of hers. "Are you just trying to make me feel better, or is this another American secret?"

David grinned. "Maybe we should leave it a mystery; we wouldn't want another apology from you at our next meeting." He glanced at his watch: it was already past nine, the ambassador's party would be in full swing. He noticed Paolo tentatively lingering a short distance away and waved him back over, got to his feet.

"I'm sorry to rush off," he told Amira, "but I need to be some-where."

Leaving the taxi at the curb, David flashed his embassy ID at the guard and passed through the open gates of the ambassador's residence. The circular drive was filled with black sedans, and their idle drivers sat together in groups around the lawn, smoking cigarettes and talking in low voices.

Susan Draper met him in the foyer, gave him a kiss on the cheek. "Your timing is impeccable; the film festival ended ten minutes ago."

Susan was an attractive woman, but the strain of the past weeks showed in the fret lines around her eyes, a new tautness to her mouth. She'd put on a sequined black cocktail dress for the party, but the effect was more poignant than alluring. David heard laughter, loud voices, coming from the direction of the reception room.

"How was it?"

"Just dreadful," she sighed. "We watched a Hopi woman make cornmeal, and a blind boy go to Yale. John finally had to turn the projector off; they're all just drinking now."

David chuckled and they started down the hall together, but Susan caught his arm.

"Oh, can I ask you a favor first? It's Nicky. He's been pretty blue these past few days, and he's so fond of you. Would you mind talking with him for a minute?"

David hoped his frustration didn't show; all he wanted to do was speak with the ambassador and then go home. "Sure. Where is he?"

"Up in his room. I managed to get him down here for a while, but . . ."

David climbed the stairs to the second floor. He heard the girls playing in their room, continued down the hall to Nicky's. The door was open, and the boy sat on the edge of his bed in his little suit, flipping through a book.

"Hey, pal. Whatcha doing?"

Nicky glanced up, then returned to the book. "Hi."

David sat alongside him. "What are you doing up here all by yourself? Don't you want to come down to the party?"

He shook his head. "It's really boring."

"Yeah, well, the movies are over now. Now they're all just eating ice cream and chocolate. Wouldn't you like some ice cream?" This was a gamble—ice cream, always a rarity in Kutar, had pretty much disappeared since the crisis—but it didn't pay off in any event; Nicky registered no interest, flipped another page in the book. David nudged him with his shoulder. "Come on, tell Uncle David. What's going on in that pointy little head of yours?"

This brought the glimmer of a smile, one Nicky tried his best to cover up. "I miss my friends," he said. "They've all gone away."

David scratched his knuckles along the boy's back. "Yeah, I know. It's hard, isn't it? But it's not like all your friends have left. I'm still here. Talit is still here." Talit was the son of the ambassador's gardener, and David had often seen the two boys playing in the yard. "Talit's your friend, isn't he?"

Nicky nodded. "But what about all the other ones? Daddy says they're coming back soon, but . . ." He looked up. "Is that true?"

David nodded. "Yes, that's true. They'll be back here before you know it. And then school's going to start up and"—he nudged Nicky with his shoulder again—"hey, have you been doing your homework?"

The boy grinned, shook his head hard.

"Well, you better, because if you haven't done your homework when school starts again, the teacher'll be mad. She'll beat you. She'll beat you with a stick." Nicky was giggling now, and David rose from the bed. "So you want to stay up here and do your homework?"

"No." He giggled louder.

"You want to come down to the party?"

"No. I want you to read me a book."

David stifled a sigh. He was not at all in the mood to read a children's book. Still, he returned to the edge of the bed. "Which book?"

Nicky handed him the one he was holding, *James and the Giant Peach.*

Too much text, David thought to himself. "That's a stupid book. Get a different one."

"You're stupid!" Nicky shouted happily.

"Well, you're stupidest. Get a different one."

The boy had just bounded over to his bookshelf in the corner when Susan Draper appeared in the doorway, looked tenderly at her son. "What is it, Nicky? You want to read a book? I'll read a book with you. Uncle David needs to go downstairs."

David rose from the bed, gave the disappointed little boy a tap with his foot. "Sorry, pal, next time. Next time we'll even read one of your stupid books."

"You're stupid!" Nicky shouted again.

"I'll be right back, honey," Susan said, then walked with David down the hall. They passed the closed door of the girls' room—one of them was singing along to a pop song—and Susan abruptly stopped, turned to him as if in anger. "We never should have left the kids here," she whispered vehemently. "I told John that, but he was adamant."

It was an unusual confidence, but such confidences were becoming commonplace in Laradan now. "I wouldn't worry, Susan," David offered. "Even if Stalwart Friend comes off, it's not like there'll be any fighting down here."

"That's not what I'm worried about. Where are they going to take the bodies, the wounded? The only hospitals are down here, and if this battle is as big as everyone's predicting . . ." She trailed off, appeared close to tears. "I don't want my kids seeing all that. Can you imagine Nicky, as sensitive as he is?" She searched David's face for a moment, then turned, hurried back toward her son's room. "I'm sorry, you don't need this. Go have some fun."

In the reception hall, the party was going strong, perhaps a hundred guests milling about the elegant room. David looked around for Nigel Mayhew but didn't see him, assumed his meetings had run late. In a corner, John Draper was amiably chatting with a couple of senior Japanese diplomats, and David waited for a break in their conversation before asking to speak with the ambassador in private. They went down the long corridor to the library.

"Want the good stuff?" the ambassador called as David closed the double doors behind them. At the far end of the room, John Draper held up a decanter of whiskey from the liquor service.

"No thanks," David said. "I'm all right."

John poured a measure into his empty tumbler, took a sip. Across the distance between them, he studied David with an odd expression, a touch of wariness. "So, what's up?"

David told of his meeting with Nigel Mayhew at the Officers Club, the secret peace talks under way. For a long time afterward, John Draper merely gazed out a window at the darkened lawn, rhythmically flexed the muscles in his jaw. Watching him, David was struck by how drawn the ambassador had become in recent days, how his once-genial, handsome face had taken on a perpetual scowl.

"That son of a bitch," John muttered finally. The words seemed to jog him from his dark reverie, he turned to David. "Sorry. I was thinking about . . . something else." He peered into his glass, swirled the ice cubes. "That'd be great, I hope the Brits can pull it off. But Nigel's right; I can't officially know about it."

David nodded. "Well, there's a bit more to it than that. They want an American in the room. When they go to the king, they want to have an American there."

Without a moment's consideration, John Draper shook his head. "Impossible. If I were to go into the palace with this, it'd–"

"But it doesn't have to be you," David interrupted. "It could be Stan or–"

The ambassador shook his head even more forcefully. "No fucking way. There's something you've got to appreciate here,

David. This goddamned Stalwart Friend, it's been cleared all the way to the White House. If any of us work against it, it's—hell, I don't know what it is, treason maybe. So unfortunately, you're going to have to tell Mayhew that we wish them the best of luck, we're pulling for them, but they have to carry this on their own. I'm sorry, but that's the way it is." He started for the door, had just gripped the handle when David came alongside.

"But what if you didn't know about it?" he asked. "What if someone on the staff just took it upon themselves to go to the meeting, never informed you?"

John Draper gave a dry chuckle. "Someone from the embassy meets with the king, and the ambassador doesn't know about it?"

David shrugged. "It happens. Someone's ambitious, they see it as their moment to shine."

Still gripping the door handle, John let out a sigh. "Oh, Christ." He then took his hand away, stepped back into the room. "Have a seat. It looks like I have to fill you in on a little something."

David settled onto the couch in the middle of the room, watched in silence as the ambassador paced along the bank of windows. At last he stopped, studied David with that same vaguely wary expression as when they'd first come into the library.

"So here's the deal," he said. "I don't know about Mayhew's plan, and you sure as hell don't know about this." He took another sip from his drink. "A numbered FEO came in from the National Security Advisor a few days ago. Do you know what that is?"

David shook his head.

"FEO: for eyes only. Not to be distributed or disseminated in any way, to be destroyed immediately after receipt. Numbered, because it's going to a very small group of people and they can trace it back if it's ever leaked. This one only went to five: myself, the Secretary . . ." The ambassador seemed to think better of continuing in this vein, trailed off with a shrug. "Bottom line: not only are we barred from supporting any peace negotiations here, I'm under explicit instructions to oppose them."

"What?" David was too surprised to formulate anything more. "What?"

John Draper nodded. "The people of Kutar are to be sacrificed to a higher purpose—namely, proving to the world that the Alliance is a viable force, that its members can work together to win a war. That wasn't the wording, of course, but that's what it comes down to."

"But why? It makes no—"

"It's Munn. That was my son-of-a-bitch comment earlier. Obviously Munn caught wind of what Mayhew's been up to. He can't very well stop the Brits from trying to broker a peace deal, but he can go one better and put us in opposition to it, and that's exactly what he's done. Also, why he's moved up the launch date. He's scrambling to make sure nothing derails his little Armageddon in the desert. So that's the real reason why I can't know about any of this, because once I do, I'm supposed to lobby against it. So, I'm sorry. I don't envy how you explain it to Mayhew—naturally, there can't be any mention of this—but the upshot is that no one goes into that meeting: not me, not Stan, and not you." He managed a small, bitter smile. "We're all just ornaments here now, David. The Pentagon has trumped State, and when that happens, a colonel trumps an ambassador, and there's not a fucking thing we can do about it." He raised his glass as if to drink from it again, but then paused, gazed speculatively at the closed double doors. "But who knows? Maybe the Brits don't need us at the palace as much as they think. They've still got an awful lot of clout here."

They walked in silence together down the long hall toward the reception room. Halfway there, though, the significance of something the ambassador had said dawned on David, and he drew up.

"The launch date," he said quietly. "You said it's been

changed. Nigel's under the impression they have until next week-end to put this together . . ."

The ambassador simply stared back at him, his eyes revealing nothing. But then David heard a light tinkling and glanced down to see that John was tapping his wedding ring against his glass, that he was strumming three of his fingers along its side.

Three days. Not a week until the onset of Stalwart Friend, but three days.

"Well," the ambassador said, "I should get back to my guests."

From the reception hall came the distant sound of laughter.

———————

The conversation went about as well as David had expected—which was to say not well at all. It wasn't helped by the fact that he could offer Nigel Mayhew little by way of reasons; basically, it was just, We can't get involved; good luck; you're on your own. Throughout, the First Secretary listened in stony silence, his lips pursed in disgust.

"So I take it this is what you mean by caring for the Kutarans," he said when David had finished. In the next moment, though, he softened. "I know it's not your doing, Richards. A pretty big blow is all."

"I know."

Not trusting his home telephone, David had risen very early that morning and come down to the British embassy—a fine old mansion a few blocks from the American one—while the rest of the city was just starting to stir. There, he'd had the duty officer put a call through to Nigel, asking him to come into the office as soon as possible. It was not even eight yet; they had the building almost to themselves on this Sunday morning.

"And no explanation why?" Nigel asked. "Nothing?"

David shook his head.

In his small, cluttered office, Nigel sighed, stared into space. At last he slapped his knees, rose to his feet. "Well, I do appreciate the effort, Richards, and I suppose we just soldier on as best we can. Still a chance we can pull it off. Not a good one, I suspect, but a chance."

David looked out the window behind Nigel's desk. The whitewashed city was losing its gold tinge of early morning, becoming the color of blanched bone.

"There's something else," he said. "It's Wednesday."

He turned to see the First Secretary squinting at him, puzzled. David cocked his head toward the window, in the direction of the coastal range and, beyond that, the war's front lines. As he grasped David's meaning, Nigel went pale, sank back into his seat.

"My God," he muttered, "you people really are determined to have this, aren't you?"

———————

David went out onto his northern veranda and settled into the armchair there. It was very late, he was exhausted, but he knew he wouldn't sleep yet.

A light wind blew, whistled in his ears, so that only the occasional fragment of recognizable sound came to him—the sputtering of a car's blown muffler, the barking of a dog somewhere in the darkness—before the wind shifted and the whistle returned.

In the past, and especially on a breezy night like this, the lights of the suburbs and airport shone steady in the clear air. That had changed. Now, with the constant activity at the army bases, the flow of military transports along the national highway, the air below had taken on a permanent murk. It was only beyond, out in the blackened desert, that clarity returned. David stared into the black. It was Monday night. In just over thirty hours, Operation Stalwart Friend would commence.

At Ambassador Draper's request, he had spent most of that day in Zulfiqar—or Base Camp Liberty as it was now designated in Alliance memoranda—to conduct an independent assessment of the front, although just what he was meant to assess David wasn't exactly sure. It was his fourth trip up since the inception of Stalwart Friend, and each time he'd found the oasis town less recognizable: more soldiers and tent camps and weaponry spreading over the landscape, its homes and palm trees cloaked in an ever-thickening coat of dust from the transport trucks shuttling in ever-more supplies.

On that day, though, David had sensed a very different spirit among the troops. Where on his earlier visits they had been portraits in listlessness, they now seemed possessed of a kind of skittish energy, a flush of vitality: men on the eve of battle.

This charged mood had been evident among the Alliance military advisers and Western journalists as well. The Shakra Inn was now the army's forward command center, and David had sat in on Colonel Munn's daily press briefing. The Texan's drawl seemed to have grown broader, his military bearing more pronounced, in front of the television cameras, and he'd developed a penchant for complicated backwoods aphorisms—"The anti-freedoms got to be more nervous than a fourteen-point stag on the first day of huntin' season," was one David recalled—which the attending journalists greatly enjoyed.

He had also gleaned in his private talks with several Alliance advisers that Stalwart Friend was to be far more devastating—"corrective," was the word the military men favored—than Munn had previously let on, not a counterjab designed to bring the rebels to the negotiating table in a weakened state, but a blow so crippling as to make negotiation unnecessary. Simultaneous with a predawn artillery bombardment of Erbil, ground forces were to sweep around either side of the city to close in behind. In this way, the rebels who had massed in Erbil—a classic defensive blunder confirmed by aerial photographs—could be surrounded and annihilated, the rebel movement decapitated once and for all. While not going into these details, Colonel Munn had provided a hint of what was coming at the conclusion of that day's press briefing.

"You want to fix a problem," he'd told the assembled journalists and officers, "sometimes you need glue, sometimes you need thread, and sometimes you need a hammer. Well, fasten your seat belts, folks, cuz it's hammer time in ole Kutar."

A cheer had gone up in the room, a current of bloodlust so palpable that it had carried on the air like a smell, like a taste.

But even at that late hour, David had clung to a last hope. That same day, Nigel Mayhew and the British ambassador were finally presenting their peace proposal to the king. Upon racing back to Laradan that afternoon—and even before briefing John Draper on his findings in Zulfiqar—David had sought out Nigel at the British embassy.

But the meeting at the palace had been a debacle. Buoyed by his generals—and, no doubt, Colonel Munn—the king had tolerated his British visitors and their talk of peace for all of five minutes before summarily stalking out of the royal reception hall. It meant there would be no eleventh-hour reprieve. There was now absolutely nothing standing in the way of the slaughter scheduled to begin in just thirty hours.

Sitting on his veranda that night, David thought of all the people he had once known and worked with out past the desert, up in the mountains. What would become of them before this was over? And what of his development projects there: the irrigation schemes he had overseen, the clinics built, the orchards planted? Would they survive or would all be in ruins? And what of Kutar itself? How many generations would it take to heal the wounds of Stalwart Friend?

The briefest flash of light caught the corner of his eye. It had come from somewhere along the eastern ridgeline, in a spot David could not recall ever having seen a light before. He stared in that direction for several minutes, but there was nothing more. He was just deciding he had imagined it, was about to turn away, when he saw it again: a quick white burst, like a flashlight being turned on for a split second, or a piece of glass catching the glow of the moon in just such a way. A moment later, the wind shifted, long enough for David to hear the soft clanking of metal, a few muffled voices, and then there was a brighter light, an explosion of light, and then there was a whooshing, tearing sound in the air. And he was still sitting there, trying to make sense of it, when there was a pop in the sky above him, when the night over the eastern ridgeline ended in the ghostly green wash of an aerial flare, and then an instant later came another pop and night ended over the western ridgeline as well. So mesmerizing was this light that it took David some time to notice the sound: a high, steady rattle, rather like that of ice being shaken in a metal cup, the sound that machine guns make.

Five

There had been occasions when David, like most people, had idly pondered what he might grab if forced to flee a burning home. His wallet, of course. His better suits. As many of those small objects of sentimental value which a person carries through life as he had time for. But when it actually happened to him—not a fire to outrun, but a war—David, like most people, forgot all those things. Instead, once the initial disbelief passed and he grasped what was occurring, he came in from the veranda and took a quick look around his living room, alien now in the green glow of the aerial flares that still burned overhead, and he went to his bookshelf and took down his album of photographs and walked out the front door. He didn't even consider what else he should have taken until he was probably a mile away, until he noticed the odd assortment of things others were carrying: radios, blankets, baby strollers, a surprising number of umbrellas. Those fleeing formed an unusual procession down the mountainside, one that steadily grew in length—dazed families in hastily thrown-on clothes or still in pajamas—and to David it seemed they could be divided into two groups by the objects they held: those who'd been quick-witted enough to grab something useful, and those who'd been in such shock that it had only dawned on them at the last moment that they might not return, who had snatched up umbrellas or hats or whatever else stood near their front doors. He walked the entire nine miles to the embassy, was the last staff member to reach it.

And across the breadth of Laradan that night, those other foreigners who had remained in a country at war now awoke to discover the war had come for them.

For Paolo Alfani, watching the explosions along the ridgeline from the roof of his Baktiar Hill home, there was the feeling of being a part of something both horrible and grand. It was as if he stood at the edge of an abyss, that awful and ecstatic sensation that comes with knowing a single step one way means perfect safety, a single step the other way oblivion. He now saw that choosing was not a simple matter, that in the human soul there is a yearning for both.

To Nigel Mayhew, holding and comforting his wife as they sat on the floor of their downstairs bathroom, all was ruin. Ruin of all his labors of the past weeks–his Pax Mayhew, as he and Sarah had jokingly called it–but also ruin of his most cherished conceits. He had believed that he knew this place intimately, understood its people and their ways maybe better than his own. On this night, he saw this was not true, that behind the diffident face they had always shown him lay a fury.

For Amira Chalasani, watching the cascade of tracer bullets and artillery shells lighting up Gowarshad Pass from her Hotel Excelsior balcony, there came the throat-catching shock of recognition. It was exactly this, she thought to herself, that had held her paralyzed in Laradan these past weeks, what had awaited her in the north. This didn't come to her in a literal way, these were not the images of nightmares actually endured, but rather in a kind of clairvoyance of the heart.

And for most everyone who happened to be in Laradan that

night, whether they were foreigners or natives, whether they were ten years old or ninety, there would at some point in those long hours come a fleeting and strange thought. Gazing upon the star-bursts of light streaking above their heads, at the pools and fingers of fire spreading over the hills that cradled them, they would think to themselves: how beautiful this world's pain can be made to look, how festive.

With dawn the extent of the night's calamity was laid bare: the en-tire coastal ridgeline above Laradan, from the summit of Gowar-shad Pass to all points east and west, now lay in rebel hands. But it had been more than a military disaster. Perhaps more shattering to the morale of those trapped below had been the attackers' as-tounding daring.

Even as Colonel Munn and his advisers had pored over their aerial maps showing the enemy fortifications in Erbil, choosing those sites to be "pacificationalized" in Stalwart Friend, the rebels had evidently slipped away from that city. Sweeping far out to ei-ther side of the government's line, they had then somehow man-aged to cross two hundred miles of empty desert undetected until they reached the landward side of the coastal mountain range. There they had climbed to the high ground and closed their circle, leaving the massed army in Zulfiqar on one side, the nearly de-fenseless city on the other. The aerial flares the rebels had fired over Gowarshad Pass were the first indication they were there.

But as bad as the situation was—and from nearly any perspec-tive, it was very bad—it could actually have been worse. That it was not was almost solely due to the courage and quick thinking of the capital-region army commander, a certain General Hassan Kalima. Swiftly organizing whatever reserve troops remained in Laradan and at the bases out by the airport, the general had led a bloody as-sault up Gowarshad Pass and held the road for a crucial few hours, long enough for the soldiers in Zulfiqar to scramble back across the desert and into the city. Now, in the gauzy, smoke-filled light of day, the Kutaran army was once again digging trenches and laying minefields, but this time at the upper edges of Laradan's hillside neighborhoods, in the very shadow of the enemy-held ridge.

But even as the residents struggled to absorb the magnitude of their situation that morning, a quiet began to settle on the capital, such an odd quiet that, by afternoon, it was almost possible to imagine nothing had happened at all. The small fires smoldering on the heights looked very much like the rubbish-dump fires that had always burned there, the occasional soft crackle of gunfire that echoed down registered like any of those other random, errant sounds that naturally float over a city.

That evening, there was an impromptu meeting of the diplomatic community at the American embassy, a chance for everyone to compare notes and discuss what might come next. At this gathering, David detected a curious tone of relief, of looking on the bright side. Thank God this time, he heard several remark, the army had shown the presence of mind to destroy most of its remaining heavy weaponry rather than let it fall into rebel hands; following behind the soldiers in their retreat from Zulfiqar, demolition teams were reported to have blown up great quantities of abandoned materiel, along with all twelve airplanes of the Kutaran Air Force out at the air base. And at least now the enemy would be in for a "fair fight," the army couldn't fall back or be outmaneuvered again, if only because there was no place left to fall back to. And then, of course, there had been the valiant stand put up by the reserve troops on Gowarshad Pass, an action that had undoubtedly saved the capital and showed that the soldiers had some fight in them yet.

In light of the continuing quiet along the ridge, John Draper allowed his staff to return to their homes that night, with instructions that they immediately make for the embassy if the shooting renewed. This was not an option for David; from what he could determine, his home was now either behind enemy lines or in no-man's-land. John invited him to stay at the ambassador's residence, but David chose to remain at the embassy and to sleep that night, as he had at other critical junctures of the crisis, on the couch in his office.

The following morning, he was at his desk when Stan Peterson, the acting deputy chief of mission, stopped by.

"There's a meeting at the British cultural center at noon," he said. "Apparently, Munn's going to make some announcement."

"His retirement?" David smiled.

Stan laughed. "Or maybe that he's really been working for the rebels all along."

With everything he had to do, David thought to give the meeting a pass, but as the hour drew nearer, he changed his mind. Perhaps it was mere morbid curiosity, but he was intrigued to see just how Colonel Munn might explain this latest debacle.

From the conference table in the cultural center ballroom, Colonel Allen B. Munn gazed across at the great map of Kutar and slowly shook his head.

"Well, much as I hate to admit it," he said, "you really gotta hand it to those yahoos. Someone up there's been reading their military history. Classic encirclement. Just what Giap pulled on the Frenchies at Dien Bien Phu." He turned to the French military liaison seated on his left. "No offense there, Jean-Claude."

The Frenchman gave a dispirited shrug.

"Maybe they're just a lot smarter than the guys running things on this side," John Draper called. He was leaning against the side wall of the room, his arms folded over his chest, and his look was one of angry derision.

Munn didn't seem to notice. "I'm gonna have to nonconcur

with you on that one, sir," he replied. "I've gotten to know most of the senior commanders over the course of this thing, and I can assure you, they're a pretty capable bunch."

Word had gone out to all the remaining legations that this was to be an important meeting but, due to both the depletion of their ranks from the evacuation and the press of events in Laradan that day, only about twenty diplomats had shown up at the cultural center. It made for a more intimate spectacle as Colonel Munn rose from his chair and strode somberly toward the map, his head bent, his hands clasped behind his back.

To David, there was a suspiciously cinematic quality to these mannerisms, as if the colonel were seeking to restore his battle-tarnished image by emulating the demeanor—the ruminative pacing, the furrowed brow—of actor-colonels in Hollywood films. But maybe it was more than that. Over the past weeks, Munn had developed something of a cult following among the foreign journalists gathered at the front in Zulfiqar, and that adoration had only reached new heights amid the latest fiasco. For ensuring they were protected during the mad dash back across the desert, for delivering them all safely into the capital, a grateful press corps was singing the colonel's praises to the outside world. From his parents in Cleveland, David had learned that dramatic footage of the retreat from Zulfiqar had been repeatedly shown on all the networks, and within this gripping tale, the American public was apparently finding its newest hero in the diminutive figure of Colonel Allen B. Munn.

"I'm telling you, son," his father had said on the phone that morning, "that guy could run for president. And with his foreign policy experience, he'd be tough to beat."

Beneath the map, Munn suddenly stopped, pivoted to face his audience.

"Now I got too much respect for you people to try and softball this thing, so allow me to be blunt: in analyzing the non-positive success ratios we got going on around here, it appears that errors in judgment may have occurred." He paused for the briefest instant, as if to convey regret. "But I didn't call y'all up here so we can sit around and play the blame game–know none of us have time for that. Fact of the matter is, we got a lot more urgent matters to discuss." He drew a folded sheet of paper from his breast pocket, nodded toward his military colleagues at the conference table. "Lieutenant Colonel Debray there is gonna hand out copies of this, but it's pretty short, so I'll go ahead and read it." He carefully unfolded the sheet of paper, gazed at it for a moment. "'Effective immediately, all embassies will close. All foreigners will leave Kutar.'" He looked up. "That's it. It came down from the anti-freedom forces this morning."

The news passed like an electric charge among the diplomats; there were startled murmurs, astonished looks. Copies were snatched from the French liaison's hands as he circulated through the room, and David stared at his copy as if the act of staring might yield something more.

"Effective immediately, all embassies will close. All foreigners will leave Kutar." That was all. No signature, no date, just eleven words rendered in careful block letters on an unlined piece of paper.

At the front of the room, Munn returned the paper to his pocket, cleared his throat to regain the group's attention. "Now in light of this correspondence and the non-positives we got transpiring on the ground, Alliance headquarters has just conducted a reappraisal of our mission objectives." He clasped his hands behind his back again, appeared to be standing at semiattention. "As of 1800 hours today, Operation Stalwart Friend will officially conclude, to be succeeded by Operation Resolute Ally."

"Oh, fuck," Stan Peterson called. "Is this where we drop a hydrogen bomb on them?"

This sparked bitter laughter through the room, which Munn

and the other military liaisons endured with wounded forbearance. When quiet returned, Munn looked toward the conference table. "Major, you wanna do the honors here?"

Major Smallwood sprang to his feet, snapped open a thin manila folder before him. "As per mission requirements of Alliance operation appellated Resolute Ally," he read in a crisp, clear voice, "HMS *Gloucester*, destroyer Monmouth class, is hereby instructed to initiate destinal progress at full speed for city of Laradan, Kingdom of Kutar, with said vessel projectioned to eventuate contact at 2100 hours Thursday. At 0800 hours Friday, personnel extraction will commencify from Pier 4, Central Harbor, city of Laradan, Kingdom of Kutar."

From their bewildered expressions, it appeared most of the nonnative English speakers in the room hadn't a clue what had just been said. But Ambassador Draper did; he pushed away from the side wall, advanced slowly on Major Smallwood.

"Extraction?" he muttered. "You mean we're leaving?"

"We are deoperationalizing, that is correct, sir," Colonel Munn replied.

Amid a new round of shocked murmurs, the British ambassador rose to his feet; already a pale man, he had gone white and trembled with anger. "Do you have any idea the message this sends to the people here? That we're going to just walk away from a mess that we—excuse me, that *you* four—created?"

Munn got his wounded look again. "We're all pretty tired here, sir, but I don't think that's any cause for personal invective." He gazed about the room. "Fact of the matter is, between this note"—he tapped at his breast pocket—"and the suboptimals we got developing, we've had to do some pretty quick rethinking here, and that's what Operation Resolute Ally is all about. Now, on an official level, we continue to have full confidence in the king and his government to defuse this crisis, and we will continue to lend him all the moral support at our disposal—that's all very clearly laid out in the mission statement. On an unofficial level, however—and

I'd appreciate it if this analysis could be kept amongst ourselves—this place is finished."

"What?" The British ambassador seemed to buckle slightly. "Finished?"

"That is correct, sir." Colonel Munn turned to the others. "We're hitting siege mode here, folks, and since the army has been divested of its heavy weapons, there ain't no way it can break a siege. On the other hand, when the anti-freedoms get *their* heavy weapons here—all that stuff they captured up in Erbil—and put it on that ridge, well, hold on to your popcorn, Nelly, cuz this ride's gonna get bumpy. They've got 110 millimeters, which means there isn't a spot in this city they can't hit. That's the reason for Resolute Ally. We gotta redeploy on out of here before those guns arrive."

"But we're diplomats, for God's sake," the British ambassador protested. "Embassies are neutral ground, sovereign territory."

Munn gave a dry chuckle. "Yeah, well, I'm sure that's how it works in England, Mr. Ambassador, but this isn't exactly the Queen's rules we got going on here. My personal feeling is that when you're about to be overrun by a bunch of gun-toting aborigines—and I don't mean any cultural disrespect by that term—the prudent thing is to get the hell on out of their way."

There was a long silence in the room. It didn't end until Colonel Munn, returning to the conference table, took up his sheaf of file folders and tapped them lightly against the table. Tucking the folders under his arm, he looked out at the diplomats with an expression suddenly gone soft. "Now if I can speak from the heart for a moment here, folks," he said, "let me just say that no one is more nongratified than myself by this adverse trend of events. But if it's any consolation, I think we all need to remember that, at the end of the day, this wasn't our fight, that we came in here to do good but our good just wasn't good enough—and there's probably a very valuable learning experience in there for us all." He turned as if to go, but then stopped. "One more thing: this is a foreigners-only evacuation. No exceptions. For that reason, you are advised to be circumspect about the operational parameters of Resolute Ally when conversing with the nationals, and to limit your good-byes to those you deem absolutely necessary. Last thing we wanna do is cause any undue panic around here."

———————

In the modern age, the act of fleeing a war has been complicated by the proliferation of paper. Those who harbor any hope of re-turn must remember to take their passports, their identity cards, the titles to their land, for if these papers are lost, a person risks falling into limbo, stateless and landless, for the rest of their lives.

Equally important are those papers to be destroyed. These might include records of military service or union membership, letters or books or even magazines; it might include almost any-thing that could suggest to those who find them that their owner is unreliable, a dissident, an enemy.

If all this paper creates a burden for a fleeing individual, it creates a far greater one for a fleeing institution—an embassy, for example. In the sheer mass of papers to be found in such a place lies an almost infinite potential for leaving behind something dan-gerous to someone.

Faced with the prospect that Laradan might soon fall, Am-bassador Draper ordered his staff to destroy any document that might incriminate a Kutaran national in the eyes of the rebels. In theory, this meant sorting through one's files to identify those which posed a risk, but this was unworkable in practice for two reasons: with only a day and a half until the evacuation, there was simply no time to be methodical and, since no one knew the rebels' intentions, no one could guess what might be incriminating. What this meant, then, was that everything had to be destroyed.

Returning to the American embassy after the meeting with Munn, each staff member went to his or her office and simply grabbed up as many folders from their file cabinets as they could manage. These they carried out of the building to the parking lot, to the bonfire the Marine Guards had built there, and then they went back to their offices to gather up more. Into the fire went every record of David's development projects around the country, all the bills and requisition forms and status reports that told the story of farm tools distributed or kilns built, and when he was finished with his own office, he went into those of his previously departed colleagues and continued the process there. After a while, it became routine, mindless.

The only objects that gave David pause were the personal items left behind by those who had gone out in the first evacuation. After all, back then everyone had assumed their departure was temporary, that they'd return in a few weeks, and remaining on desks and walls were photographs of children and parents, the artwork of nieces. As it turned out, other staffers working their way through the embassy had faced this same dilemma, so that by the time David asked John Draper for guidance, an answer had already come down: this was a personnel-only evacuation, one suitcase to each evacuee, if it didn't fit in that suitcase, it stayed or went into the fire.

Into that evening, the burning went on. At one point, David decided to take a brief break.

"Okay, here's one," he said, poking his head through the door of Cheryl Thompson's office. "I'm a professor of women's studies, black women's studies . . ."

He stopped. Cheryl was at her desk, she tried to give him a smile, but David saw that tears were coursing down her cheeks. He walked into the room. "What's wrong?"

Cheryl shook her head violently, the tears came harder, and she motioned to the stack of file folders on the desk before her. There were thirty or so, and David slowly took up the top one, opened it. Paper-clipped to the cover page was a color photograph of an olive-skinned man in his early twenties with a broad, happy grin. He closed the folder, returned it to the pile. "Approvals?"

Cheryl nodded. She lay a hand atop the stack, flicked their

edge with a fingernail. "All the crap we make them do. Standing in lines for hours, filling out endless forms, 'come back next week,' 'come back in three months.' And for what? What happens to them now?"

David leaned over and squeezed Cheryl's hand, gently lifted it from the stack.

"It'll be all right," he said. "They'll be all right."

Then he carefully picked up the folders and carried them from the room. It was a very small load, he could have easily managed one twice its size, but out of a kind of respect, David didn't take anything else as he made his way out to the fire.

———

Colonel Munn's warning to be circumspect about the nature of Operation Resolute Ally proved pointless. With bonfires rising from behind the walls of every embassy compound in the New City, it wasn't long before the average Kutaran figured out precisely what was happening. By that first evening, the front gate of the American embassy was lined with locals, some merely watching the activity within in curiosity, others trying to draw one of the Americans' attention, claiming they had visas or green cards or relatives living in the United States, insistently fluttering pieces of paper through the gate's grillwork. On Thursday morning, as the burning resumed, the crowd outside continued to swell. Their entreaties became more urgent now, the Americans inside more assiduous in ignoring them.

Most troubling for David and the other Americans was the demeanor of the local staff who remained with them in the compound, the drivers and guards and secretaries who assisted with the burning and dutifully performed whatever task was asked of them. These workers still had no idea of the plans for them, if they were to be included in the evacuation, and not one of them asked. Then again, they may have felt the answer was obvious in the way none of the Americans would look them in the eye. In the years ahead, many of those who were at the embassy in Laradan at the end would recall this as the most emotionally difficult aspect of their departure.

The second evacuation was to be conducted much like the first, but with certain modifications. Those leaving–about four hundred foreign nationals by best estimate, once all the journalists and relief workers were included–were to be at the British cultural center at 6:30 on Friday morning, and would then depart for the harbor in a convoy of buses. Given the charged atmosphere in Laradan, the potential for acts of hostility by the native population, security was to be much tighter this time, the guards from the various embassies reinforced with local police.

The evacuation would not, in fact, mean a complete end to the foreign presence in Kutar. David heard that Nigel Mayhew had chosen to remain behind–a last, brave representative of the Crown–and there were reports that several journalists were considering it as well. Apparently the British First Secretary was in the process of moving his office to rooms at the Moonlight Hotel; by virtue of its location on a promontory of Serenity Bay, the hotel was one of the farthest buildings from the ridgeline and, thus, considered one of the safer spots in the city.

Late on Thursday afternoon, as David brought yet another stack of papers out to the bonfire, one of the Marine Guards approached him, pointed a thumb over his shoulder at the front gate. "There's a guy out there says he's a friend of yours."

"Ignore him," David said, throwing the stack onto the fire. "Everyone wants to be my friend right now."

"But he's not a national. Says he's Italian; Paolo something."

David had quite forgotten about Paolo in the chaos of the last days. He followed the Marine to the gate, saw his friend waving from the middle of the crowd that was now eight-or ten-deep. "Any way to let him in?" he asked.

"Not a chance," the Marine said. "I open that a crack, and it'd be a flood in here."

Stepping close to the gate, David beckoned Paolo forward, watched him squeeze through the throng. Ignoring the arms grasping for him, the calls for his attention, David shook his friend's hand through the grillwork, gave an incredulous grin. "What the hell are you doing here?"

"I just came to say goodbye."

"Goodbye?" David laughed. "Christ, Paolo, I'm leaving too. We'll be on that damned boat together for at least two days."

Paolo smiled, looked over at the bonfire, and it was then that David noticed something odd about his friend. He was pale, looked very tired, but also strangely energized, his eyes wide and darting. He turned back to David.

"I'm staying," he said. "I don't know why."

For a moment, David merely stared at him, trying to make sense of his words. Looking into Paolo's feverish eyes, he wondered if the businessman might be narcotized or delirious from some illness. "What the hell are you talking about? It's–"

But Paolo took David's hand again, patted it as if to silence him. "No, no, it is all right, I've already decided. You're busy, don't worry yourself, it's already decided. So safe journey, eh? I hope we meet again some day." With that, he turned to go.

"Paolo, wait." David pressed against the gate, grabbed for his friend's shirt, but the Italian was already beyond reach, maneuvering his way out of the crowd. David watched him recede, briefly considered going after him. But then, whether borne of an awareness of all he still had to do or simply of his own exhaustion, David, too, turned away from the gate, started back for the building and another stack of papers, and he did not think of Paolo Alfani any more.

———

At his office window, David scanned the dark sea. It was nearly eight, the British destroyer was scheduled to come into view about now, but across that vast expanse of water was nothing but the play of moonlight. Directly below, the lights of the promenade shone. In normal times, the stone walk would have been crowded with strollers at that hour, the calls of candy and nut sellers rising above the sound of the surf, but on that night there was no one. It was as if the city were already abandoned.

He heard a light rapping and turned to see John Draper leaning against the door frame, watching him.

"How's it going?"

"Okay," David replied. He glanced about his office. Other than his photo album on one corner of the desk, it was stripped bare. "Just thinking how strange it's been, how quickly it all fell apart."

"Yeah, well, we've got Munn to thank for that." The ambassador pushed off the door frame. "If you've got a minute, I'd like to talk to you."

"Sure."

But rather than come in, John turned and started down the hall toward his own office. David followed.

They walked the corridor without speaking. The open rooms they passed had been purged of anything to suggest people had once worked there.

In the ambassador's suite, John Draper led the way to the couch-and-armchair arrangement in the far corner. On the carpet next to the coffee table was a canvas mailbag containing several dozen bulky manila envelopes.

"For the local staff," the ambassador explained as he settled onto the couch, motioned David to an armchair. "Three thousand dollars each. I took it out of the general op fund. We have more than four million bucks in there, and I figured we might as well give some of it to the people who've been good to us."

David nodded. Due to the primitive nature of the Kutaran banking system—checks and bank drafts were still something of a novelty in the kingdom, virtually all daily transactions were done in cash—the embassy kept a large amount of dollars in a vault in the communications room to cover its general operating costs, as well as whatever on-site expenses arose on David's various development projects.

"Well," John muttered, "it's the very least we can do." He sighed, sat back on the couch, and for a long time merely stared into space. In the silence, it occurred to David that the ambassador hadn't once looked in his direction since they'd entered the room.

"So, a couple of things," John finally said. "First off, State has decided they'd like someone to stay here. I imagine you've heard that Nigel Mayhew is staying on for the Brits—I don't know about any of the other embassies—but the consensus is that if we pull out of here completely, then we have absolutely no leverage with either side, and that could be a problem down the road however this thing plays out." He now glanced over at David. "Naturally, given the potential danger, this is only a request, not a directive, and it's completely voluntary. Absolutely no repercussions if someone declines—although, obviously, accepting means scoring major brownie points with State career-wise."

He waited for David to nod.

"In talking this over with Stan, we both felt you'd be the best choice. You get along well with the people here and, with all your projects up north, you probably have a better feel for that region than anyone else. You also already have a functioning relationship with Mayhew, which could be important—I imagine we'll be staking out a joint Anglo-American position as all this progresses, so having the two guys in the field working off the same page would be a definite plus."

The ambassador fell silent again, and David took this as his cue. "Well, thank you for the confidence," he said. "I'm fine with staying. In fact, it would be . . ."

He trailed off under John's thin smile, the slow shake of his head. "Not so fast. I figured you'd say that, but not so fast."

The ambassador took up a manila envelope from the couch cushion next to him, handed it across to David. "It's a CIA analysis on the rebels, just came in this evening. It's the first one they've done because . . . well, because no one gave a shit before. They could be completely off base with this—they usually are—but before you agree to anything, I want you to read it." He leaned back, rested his head against the wall to stare up at his office chandelier.

David wasn't sure if he was meant to read it right there, but then the ambassador spoke again: "Because if they're not off base, if they're even halfway accurate, then those guys up on the ridge look like a very scary bunch. None of the Soviet-involvement bullshit that Munn was trying to peddle there for a while, but apparently there's a lot of pseudo-mystical crap in their literature— the avenging-angel-come-to-purify-the-corrupted sort of thing." John Draper's gaze floated down from the ceiling until it came to rest on David again. "I want you to read it yourself but, in a nut-shell, they're saying that it's possible—not saying probable, because no one has that much of a handle on them—but it's possible we could be headed for a Khmer Rouge kind of situation here."

"Jesus Christ," David whispered. He stared down at the sealed envelope in his hands, but then his eyes were drawn to the side, to the half-filled mailbag on the carpet. The ambassador seemed to read his thoughts.

"I know. It's a fucking disgrace, but what can we do now?" He cocked his chin at the bag. "I figure, with the money maybe they can buy a ticket out for themselves and their families. An awful lot of people are streaming out of here, you know. Boats leaving all the time."

This was true. David had heard that Central Harbor was utter pandemonium as those trying to flee Laradan vied for a spot on one of the departing boats. But he'd also heard that those spots were now going for more than $1,000 apiece—and climbing higher all the time—which meant that, with their $3,000 packets, the thirty-four locals who worked at the American embassy might be able to get themselves and part of their families out but not all; some of their family members would have to stay behind. So why not give them $10,000 each? For that matter, why not empty the embassy account and make it $100,000? But it wasn't David's place to say these things to the ambassador.

John yawned, lightly slapped the cushion next to him. "So read the report, think about it. But like I said, absolutely no repercussions if you choose to decline."

David nodded.

From down the hall came the murmur of voices, footsteps. A Marine Guard poked his head through the open door of the ambassador's suite. "Sir? It's eight o'clock. The nationals are gathering in the conference room."

A pained grimace passed over John Draper's face, he rose to his feet. "Okay." He looked at the Marine, pointed to the mailbag by the coffee table. "You mind carrying this down for me?"

The soldier came across the room, cinched the bag shut, and hoisted it to his shoulder. The three of them left the suite and started down the hall toward the conference room, but halfway there, John Draper abruptly stopped, turned to David.

"Say, why don't you stay up at the residence tonight? It's got to be more comfortable than that couch of yours, and I know Nicky would love to see you."

Perhaps it was the beseeching look in the ambassador's eyes, but for some reason, David found this invitation more burdensome than any of the demands that had been placed on him these past weeks. He shook his head. "Thanks, but I think I'll stay here. I'll come down with the Marines in the morning."

As was protocol, a contingent of Marine Guards would remain on duty at the embassy until the last moment. In the morning, they would take down the American flag, lock the front gate, and meet the bus convoy at the harbor.

John Draper nodded, continued down the hall. David followed as far as the threshold to the conference room.

"Hello, everyone," the ambassador called to the thirty-four people gathered there as he stepped inside, flashing them the smile that had once seemed so warm, so all-American, but which now looked a bit ghostly.

———

"So, what are you thinking?" his father asked softly.

David smiled into the telephone receiver. "I don't know. That's why I called you."

A long silence, only the sound of their breathing passing along the line.

"Well, you know what your mother would say."

"Yeah."

"But she's not here right now."

"No, I know."

Another silence.

After recounting his conversation with the ambassador, David had told his father a little of what was in the CIA report, though not the most dire parts. He didn't have to. His father knew how to read between the lines, could tell there was more just from the tone in David's voice.

At the other end of the line, his father let out a long exhale of air. "'My two boys. My two boys.' You have any idea what it's like to say that for eighteen years and, all of a sudden, it's not true anymore, you've got to constantly correct yourself?" A groan. "Well, Christ, what am I saying? Of course you know. Probably worse than me."

At his desk, David closed his eyes. He had known the conversation would go this way; it was inevitable.

"The thing is," his father continued, "after Eddie, I don't know what would happen to your mother if something were to happen to you." A low chuckle, hollow and grim. "Well, actually, I do know."

At his desk, David nodded. "Just say the word, Dad, and I'll come home."

A new sound over the telephone line, a kind of rhythmic tapping, and it wasn't until his father spoke again, his voice suddenly high and constricted, that David realized it was the sound of sobbing.

"But Eddie didn't die for nothing," his father managed. "I refuse to believe that. I fucking refuse to believe that."

"I know, Dad. I know."

"He died for his country. He died for all of us. It wasn't for nothing."

"I know," David said, his voice going now, too, tears slipping down his cheeks.

"Because the United States doesn't do that. It doesn't send its boys off to die for nothing, and it doesn't walk away, it doesn't abandon its friends. I refuse to believe that. I will never believe that."

"Yeah," David whispered, unable to manage anything more.

Three months out of high school, unhappy and unmoored, Eddie had gotten into a barroom fight and beaten a man nearly half to death. On a deal that set aside a felony count, he'd joined the Marines. He'd been killed in Quang Tri Province on April 21, 1970, his twenty-fourth day in Vietnam, his eighth day in the field, from a single sniper shot that passed clean through his helmet just forward of his right ear. According to people who knew about such things, he probably never even knew what hit him, he had probably been dead before he hit the ground.

"You know who I blame, don't you?"

David desperately shook his head. "Oh, Dad, let's not do this again. Not now."

It was an argument they'd been having for thirteen years now, and if David didn't acquiesce, if he let his father get up a head of steam, the list became endless: the peaceniks, the cowards in Congress, Gene McCarthy, and Jane Fonda.

"No, I know," his father said, contrite, tired. "My point is, we're a people of honor. I truly believe that. We stand by our commitments. We don't abandon our friends. That's what Eddie's dying meant."

To David, it had always seemed his brother's death meant pretty much the opposite, but that was just another way back to the same argument. "Yeah," he acquiesced.

Another long quiet on the telephone, broken by a loud sniff from his father. "Well, it's coming on lunchtime here; your mother should be home soon."

"Yeah," David said.

A softness returned to his father's voice. "So what do you think you'll do?"

David gazed out his office window. On the far western sea, he now saw a small cluster of red-and-white lights, presumed them to be the British destroyer making its approach to Laradan. "I think you know what I'm going to do, Dad."

"Yeah." A brief silence, and then his father started to cry again. "I'm awfully proud of you, son."

David and the Marines who'd stayed at the embassy reached the harbor before the evacuation convoy. They waited near the end of the quay with the British sailors, pointed out to them the spot on the coastal range that marked the front line. One noticed the photo album under David's arm and gave him a puzzled look.

"That's your personal effects?"

David smiled, cocked his chin at the ridgeline. "Everything else is up there."

Around 7:30 AM, the buses came through the gates of Central Harbor and stopped at the base of the pier, perhaps three hundred yards away. Those leaving started along the stone walk in small groups. Colonel Munn was in his field uniform, half a dozen television cameras recording his determined stride, and David was reminded of MacArthur coming ashore in the Philippines.

"Let me just say," Munn addressed the cameras as he passed, "that in no way does this mean the end of our commitment to the people of Kutar, only its non-continuance. I can't stress that enough."

After a time, David spotted the ambassador and his family. John and Susan had donned black for the occasion, stared somberly ahead, while the girls, Jessica and Samantha, wore matching blue sundresses. Nicky, in his little suit, held his mother's hand, looked frightened by the Marine Guards who walked alongside the family, their assault rifles raised, fingers resting on triggers.

They came to the end of the pier, to where David waited beside the gangway to the launch. The embassy flag had been folded into a triangle and, along with the silver ring of keys to the compound, placed in a plastic sheath. The Marine Guards now lined up in parade formation and saluted as their commander solemnly placed the bundle in the ambassador's hands. John Draper blinked back tears as he stepped over to David, wrapped his arms about him in a hug.

"You're sure you want to do this?" he asked in a ragged voice.

"I'm sure," David replied. "It'll be fine."

Breaking his embrace, John pressed the sheathed flag and keys into David's hand, ushered his family forward. David kissed Susan and the girls, then knelt down to the boy.

"How're you doing, pal?"

"Okay."

He brushed the boy's hair back and smiled. "You're going on a big ship. It'll be fun."

Nicky gazed over the water, at the destroyer riding at anchor, and seemed unconvinced of this. He looked up at David. "Will I come back?"

David leaned in to kiss the boy on the forehead. "No, Nicky, you won't," he whispered. "You'll never come back here."

When the last launch pulled away, David stood for a while at the end of the quay, watched as it made its way toward the ship on the horizon. Then he turned and, with his photo album and his flag, began the long, lonely walk to the Moonlight Hotel.

Part Two

Six

Sir John Sedgwick was not well traveled, but he could read a map as well as the next man. Sitting in his London office in the winter of 1886 with his atlases, his gaze had roamed over the vast reaches of the earth, both its grand and insignificant places, until he came to the obscure little kingdom of Kutar and there he stopped, there he saw a land of bountiful promise.

With the completion of the Suez Canal linking the Mediterranean and Red seas the previous decade, an entire axis of international commerce had shifted. Just like that, the Orient was six thousand miles closer to Europe than it had been before. The terrible passage around Africa's Cape of Good Hope was being consigned to history, already becoming a bit of maritime lore. The new Silk Road to the East lay through the Mediterranean—no longer the "bathtub" of geography's creation—down the Suez and along the northern waters of the Indian Ocean. Upon this route, a thousand ships sailed, cities prospered, fortunes were to be made.

But Sir John Sedgwick was not interested in trade and shipping—these matters he relegated to his underlings at Sedgwick Holdings Ltd—he was interested in hotels, and what he noticed upon his maps was a singular lack of suitable accommodation on this great new watercourse of the world. There were any number of magnificent hotels along the Mediterranean shore, and India and the Far East were well appointed, but it was that middle stretch, those four thousand miles between Shepheards in Cairo and the Taj Palace in Bombay, where the traveling gentleman of 1886 still faced the dreary choice of staying in some tradesmen's hostel or remaining upon the ship which carried him. By happy coincidence, however, Great Britain had for some years been in possession of a small coastal kingdom named Kutar, and in his office that day, Sir Sedgwick discovered this colony lay very near the midpoint of that inhospitable void.

That spring, Sir Sedgwick dispatched an agent and an architect to Laradan, the capital of Kutar, with orders to procure a site where he might build a hotel worthy of this new golden age of travel. His emissaries found just such a place, a rocky promontory of some eight acres at one end of the quaintly named Serenity Bay. Construction began that autumn, with a team of British managers overseeing a veritable army of local laborers and Indian artisans hired on for the project.

At the time, Great Britain was experiencing one of its periodic fascinations with Indian design, and if not a panderer to fashion, Sir Sedgwick was not wholly oblivious to it either. For his hotel on the shores of Laradan, he opted for a particularly exuberant blend of the Imperial and Oriental, the solid utility of the Georgians complemented by the graceful curves and lavish ornamentation of the Moghuls. That this fusion might be an aesthetic error would be a judgment of hindsight; in Sir Sedgwick's day, his five-story creation of austere gray façades joined to cupolas and arches and domes of red sandstone was deemed bold and inventive. In a fanciful gesture, perhaps inspired by the name of the bay upon which it sat, he called his colossus the Moonlight Hotel.

Whatever its exterior confusions, within the place was a splendor. The vast lobby was a much more successful blending of East and West, its marble floors and leather couches and standing lamps capturing the warm clubbiness of the London Savoy, while its enormous potted plants and ceiling fans and slatted breezeway doors evoked the light airiness of the Galle Face in Colombo. For the first-time visitor to that hall, it was hard to decide what was more striking, the elaborate belting apparatus that linked all thirty-two of the overhead fans and turned them as one—according to the hotel's promotional literature, it was the second-largest fan-belt system in the hostelry world, bested only by the Mount Nelson in Cape Town—or the massive stone fireplace built into its western wall. This structure was large enough for a dozen men to stand within its hearth and, located in a city where temperatures rarely dropped below sixty degrees, all the more impressive for its lack of discernible purpose.

At the far end of the lobby was the formal dining room and, off to one side, those salons which the affluent traveler of the 1880s expected in a deluxe hotel: a games room, a ladies' lounge, a library, a bar. In these rooms, Sir Sedgwick had wisely dispensed with the East-West conceit. Whether dining in the restaurant or lingering over the billiards table, the Moonlight guest might detect nothing in his immediate surroundings to suggest he was any-where but in one of the Continent's finest hotels.

Just beyond the receptionist's desk, a grand staircase led up to the first floor of guest rooms, and here, too, the visitor couldn't help but be awed by Sir Sedgwick's extravagance. From the inlaid parquet floors with their intricate floral patterns, to the Tiffany-style lamps and gilt bathroom fittings, it appeared the British in-dustrialist had spared no expense in building his palace by the sea—and, indeed, he had not.

But most remarkable from an engineering standpoint was what had been achieved with the grounds. Through the liberal use of dynamite, and the picks and shovels of hundreds of laborers, the barren promontory upon which the hotel sat was transformed into a luxuriant garden. Hauling away countless tons of stone, the workers planed out the slopes for flower beds and lawns and tennis courts, brought in soil and sod and thirty-foot-tall palm trees, and then cut an underground aqueduct from the city's reservoir to keep all of it nourished. On the side of the hotel facing the open sea, the rock was quarried out to fashion a large swimming pool surrounded by a shaded patio, and it was another indication of Sir Sedgwick's ambition that this pool was filled not with seawater, as was the custom of the age, but rather with the same mountain spring water which flowed into the city's cisterns.

No wonder, then, that on the day of the grand opening in the spring of 1889, the King of Kutar himself stood alongside Sir Sedgwick, out from London on his private yacht, for the cutting of the ceremonial ribbon. To be a part of this gala event, colonial administrators had journeyed from as far as India and Aden, and all Laradan, it seemed, had set aside their daily tasks to line the city's streets and watch the dignitaries pass. What the uninvited could only glimpse through the hotel's wrought-iron gates was the path of white crushed gravel that led the guests past the flower gardens and towering palms. What they could not see at all—but had undoubtedly heard a great deal about in recent months—was the ornate water fountain with its bronze egrets and lolling cherubs situated at the end of that drive, the wide marble staircase that led to the building's gilded doors and the fabled lobby beyond. For those who crowded the waterfront promenade that night to watch the celebratory fireworks over Serenity Bay, the revelry surpassed even that which had accompanied the coronation of King Gamil VI seven years earlier. Perhaps this was due to the hopeful sentiment the event inspired. That coronation had been tradition; this was modernity, this was the heralding of a brighter future for a humble land.

But it is an old maxim of history that most truly epic blunders take time to reach full blossom—and so it was with Sir Sedgwick's. For the first several years, the luxury passenger ships plying the India route did stop at Laradan, and most every guest agreed that the Moonlight was one of the finest hotels they'd ever beheld.

Even then, however, it was clear Sir Sedgwick had overlooked some important details on that day in London when he had first gazed upon his maps.

For one thing, Laradan was not Cairo, nor was it Bombay. While passing ships might be enticed to briefly lay anchor, there was nothing about that modest city—no ancient ruins or great bazaars—to cause either the businessman or the touring traveler to linger for very long. Instead of the weeklong bookings enjoyed by Shepheards in Cairo, stays at the Moonlight tended to be for a night or two.

And while Kutar was indeed a jewel in the still-expanding British Crown, it was a gem of decidedly lesser value, more an amethyst, say, than a sapphire. With few natural resources worth exploiting and far removed from any theater of strategic concern, the kingdom was, frankly, a backwater, its colonial administrators drawn from the lower schools, its colonial garrison from the lesser regiments. In practical terms, this meant that those Britishers residing in Laradan who might patronize the hotel—and given the meager volume of travelers, such a local patronage was essential to filling the restaurant and bar and generally keeping the place busy—tended to derive from what could be considered the Empire's "second tier," or even its third: military officers with the touch of the lout about them, civil administrators serving out disappointing careers rather than building on distinguished ones. For Sir Sedgwick, fretting over his ledgers in London, this translated not only into unpaid bar bills and careless damage to the furnishings but, given the libertine sexual mores of his clientele, a staggering number of financial compensations to the families of despoiled cleaning girls, bellboys, and pool wallahs.

But if Sir Sedgwick's hotel was a drain on his fortune, it was initially more of a slow bleed than a hemorrhage; it took the crash of 1893 to achieve that. As that great economic calamity deepened and spread across the globe, the British tycoon was forced to close the Moonlight's doors for several years, keeping on only a skeleton staff to maintain it. No sooner had he begun to recover from that disaster–and already "recover" was a relative term to mean the loss of money at a less rapid rate–than the depression of 1905 struck. When Sir Sedgwick passed away a few years later, his heirs wasted no time in putting the Moonlight up for sale, and it was a measure of how severe a financial burden the place had become that, upon receiving a bid that was one-quarter of what had been spent on its construction, the heirs not only leaped at the offer, but considered their good fortune almost larcenous.

Within a short time, so would the man who'd made the offer. Just as this second owner had nursed the hotel back to near solvency, partially achieved by shuttering the upper two floors of rooms, there came the First World War and, with it, a collapse of maritime trade throughout the region. From then on developed a pattern of such eerily bad luck that the succession of increasingly desperate men who came into possession of the Moonlight could be excused for regarding world events as something of a conspiracy against them. Each new owner struggled toward profitability, a glimmer of promise finally twinkled at the bottom of the money pit, only to have a new catastrophe from afar come down upon them: another international depression in the 1930s, then another world war, then the collapse of the British Empire, and, finally, the death of the passenger ship at the hands of the passenger plane. Each new owner would come to curse the place, would pare the staff down further, close off more wings of rooms, until finally their spirit was broken and they, in turn, would sell it for a fraction of what they had paid.

And now the cycle was repeating itself once more. In the mid-1970s, the Moonlight had been taken over by a French hotel consortium and, with the gradual rise in tourism to Kutar, the absentee owners had recently decided on an ambitious renovation of the long-closed second floor of rooms. That renovation had just begun when the civil war reached Laradan. Scattered through those upper rooms, there now stood idle table saws, crates of imported wallpaper, and modern light fixtures, all the tools and trappings of a renaissance that undoubtedly would now be forestalled for many years to come.

As might be expected, this ill-fated history engendered a sense both of fatalism and of humor among those few Laradanis who looked to the Moonlight for their livelihood. So it was that, on the morning of the foreigners' evacuation at the harbor, Arkadi Hafizullah, the hotel manager, instantly effected a sardonic grin at the sight of the young Western man who appeared in the lobby, as if already they shared some private joke.

As the man neared the reception desk, Arkadi saw that he was not as young as he'd initially thought–perhaps thirty-five or so–although this was just a guess; despite his long exposure to them, the hotel manager had always found Westerners to look oddly alike, quite impossible to determine much about them at first glance. What made this man stand out, beyond the obvious peculiar timing of his arrival, was that he was rather disheveled. His khaki pants and white shirt were wrinkled and stained, and in his left arm he carried a strangely shaped piece of cloth and an oversize book of some sort.

"I'm David Richards," the young man said, "from the American embassy. I called last night to reserve a room."

"Oh yes, of course." Arkadi hoped his surprise didn't register on his face; he had been expecting someone older and more distinguished looking–certainly someone better dressed. Turning, he made a show of gazing over the vast pigeonhole board behind the reception desk, at the row upon row of keys that dangled there, that, in some cases, had dangled there undisturbed for seventy years. "A bit short notice," Arkadi said in his British-inflected English, "but I think we should be able to squeeze you in."

The manager often joked with new arrivals, because he'd found that a willingness for humor was usually a good indicator of how easy or difficult a guest would be. He was gratified when David Richards chuckled good-naturedly–he had a quick, friendly smile. Out of habit, Arkadi glanced to the hotel entrance for sign of a porter, but there was no one. "And your luggage," he asked, "it's coming later?"

"This is all I have." David Richards indicated the things he held. "I don't have anything else."

Arkadi now saw that the cloth was a folded American flag, the book an album for photographs. He gave a quick nod, felt slightly embarrassed at having elicited this information. "If you give me your sizes," he whispered, "I can send someone to the bazaar."

From across the counter, David studied the manager's face. He was middle-aged with handsome, broad features, and his graying hair and charcoal-gray suit lent him the air of a successful businessman. "Thank you," he said. "I'd appreciate that."

Arkadi led the way up the staircase to the rooms on the second floor. During his twenty-two years at the Moonlight, he'd become a good judge of character; he instinctively liked this American, and so he selected for him one of the better suites, on the side of the hotel facing the swimming pool and the open sea. At the door, he stood aside to allow his newest guest to enter first.

David crossed the threshold and stopped. The room was far grander than any he had stayed in before. In the morning light, sun rays seeped through the thinly curtained windows to cast the floor's floral design in a shiny glow. At one end, French doors led onto a balcony. He turned to the manager. "It's wonderful. Thank you."

David wasn't sure if he should tip the man—considering the contrast in their wardrobes, it seemed almost crass to do so—but before he could decide, Arkadi reached over to touch his shoulder.

"I'm very glad you're here," he said softly. "I'm glad that not everyone left us." Without waiting for a reply—rather as if to avert one—the manager then quickly backed out the door and closed it.

Alone in the room, David set his album and flag on the desk, and went out onto the balcony. The pool and patio were directly below him, and at the far end of the lawn, a delicate Moghul-style gazebo overlooked the bay. He saw no sign of any other guests. He scanned the horizon for the British destroyer, but the ship had passed from view.

He glanced at his watch. It was only midmorning, but it had already felt like a very long day, and David wasn't sure what to do with the rest of it.

There was a knock on the door. David expected to find a bell-boy or maid come to perform one of those inscrutable rituals that accompany one's arrival at a fine hotel, but instead it was Nigel Mayhew.

"Ah, Richards." The First Secretary beamed. "I'd heard rumors an American might be staying on. Can't say I'm surprised it's you."

David smiled, ushered him in. "Yeah, well, foolish minds think alike."

Nigel stepped to the center of the room, looked about appreciatively. "Very nice. Nicer than mine, in fact. My design"—he tapped his foot at the inlaid-wood pattern on the floor—"is warped. It's supposed to be a carnation, I think, but I'm constantly tripping over it." He wheeled in David's direction. "And have you met the others?"

"Others?"

"The other guests. Four of them, from what I understand. This Chalasani woman, just moved over from the Excelsior—quite delightful—and, oh, that little Italian chap with the white suits, a friend of yours, Pablo something or other. Don't know about the other two, but I thought perhaps we should arrange a get-together this afternoon, a chance for everyone to meet."

David nodded. "That sounds good."

"And at some point, I think you and I should sit down and work out a strategy for how to proceed here. An awful lot of ground to cover, just the two of us, so I'd suggest a kind of division of labor."

David nodded again. "Let's do that."

Nigel had been pacing the floor as he spoke, but he now drew up to peer at David, as if suddenly noticing the contrast in their moods. "But what's wrong, old boy?"

David shrugged. "I don't know; a bit of self-recrimination, I guess. I just keep thinking how different everything would be if your peace talks had come off, if we'd come on board like you asked."

Across the distance between them, Nigel nodded. "Yes, well, as I said before, Richards, not your fault. And in any event, I'd say there's a good chance it wouldn't have made any difference, that the whole thing was a bit of a ruse." He began to pace again, slower than before. "Think of it. The rebels stormed the ridge–what was it, eight, nine hours?–after the king had rejected negotiations, and they certainly didn't cover the distance from Erbil in that time. They'd been moving into place for days–weeks, probably–even while they were talking to me about a settlement. So who knows? Perhaps they would have stood down if the king had relented, or perhaps they'd have attacked anyway." He stopped, looked to David with a speculative smile. "That said, both sides might be ready to sing a different tune now. The advantage goes to the rebels, of course, they have the heights and the guns, but the army has mined the entire perimeter of the city, so the rebels would face tremendous losses in a ground assault. With this kind of stalemate it could be that both sides will see the benefit of negotiation."

"Or the rebels could just decide to bomb the city into submission."

The First Secretary nodded. "Yes. Or that."

David looked away, his gaze coming to rest on his photo album on the desk.

After his meeting with Ambassador Draper the previous evening, David had returned to his own office to read the sixteen-page CIA analysis on the rebel forces, or the Kutaran People's Liberation Army, as they now called themselves, and for no particular reason he could identify now–maybe he'd felt the report could be important down the road, or maybe he'd just been too tired to make another trip out to the bonfire–he'd slipped the document between the album covers rather than destroy it.

Like every State Department official sent abroad, David had a high security clearance, but he had long since forgotten the exacting regulations that attached to each of the various levels of classified information. Standing in the hotel room with Nigel, he specifically had no idea what rules might apply to sharing a top-secret report–as the CIA analysis was designated, each page stamped to that effect in bold red letters–with a colleague from a foreign government. The prudent course was to wait and ask Washington for guidance, but David had been with State long enough to know how that would play out: it would take a week to get an answer, and that answer would be "no," because at State, the default answer was always no.

Against this was the cold reality of the situation. They were a team now, he and Nigel, the last two Western diplomats in a city under siege, and what one knew, the other should, as well. David crossed to the desk, took the report from his photo album.

"The ambassador gave it to me last night," he said, handing it to Nigel. "Read page six."

The First Secretary quickly scanned the first pages, came to the sixth, and then read more closely. All at once, he jolted, looked at David in disbelief.

"Good Lord. They're comparing the rebels to the Khmer Rouge?"

David nodded. "A lot of qualifiers. They're very careful to hedge their bets, but some of the things they've pulled out of the KPLA literature, their leaders' speeches–you'll see, it's in the later pages–is pretty disturbing."

Nigel read on, his frown deepening with each paragraph. At

last, he came to the end, slowly flipped the last page over. "Rather a nasty picture they paint, isn't it?" He stared across the room, his eyes roamed the bare white wall. "But I think they're wrong. I daresay you could go through the writings of any of these insurgent groups and patch together something quite ominous. I just don't see this sort of bloodlust in the Kutarans." He turned to David, forced a faint smile. "And, of course, we must bear in mind the source. Not to be disparaging, I'm sure there's many fine men and women over at the CIA, but my personal experience with those chaps is that, when it comes to predictions, one might have better success putting a chimp in front of a Ouija board."

They laughed together, but then Nigel took up the report in his hand, turned again to its sixth page, and as he reread the passage outlining the similarities between the Kutaran insurgents and the Cambodians who had slaughtered more than a million of their countrymen, his humor slipped away, worry settled into his eyes.

"Still," he said quietly, handing the pages back to David, "I think we might want to keep this very much to ourselves for the time being. Hard to see what would be gained by floating it about." The First Secretary glanced at his watch, started for the door. "Have to get over to the palace. As for meeting the others, how does three o'clock suit you? Down in the lobby?"

"That'd be fine."

Nigel opened the door, but didn't step through immediately. Instead he turned to David with a tender expression. "I'm very pleased you stayed, Richards. Of all the Americans they could have left here, I'm very glad it was you."

David grinned. "Damning with faint praise, are we, Mayhew?" But then he appreciated that this was probably as close as the First Secretary could come to heartfelt, and he extended his hand. "Thank you, Nigel. Coming from you, that means a lot."

They gathered around the large mahogany table at the far end of the lobby, overlooking the patio and the pool. There were six of them. In addition to the three people David already knew–Paolo, Nigel, and Amira–were two he had never seen before: a dark-featured man of about his own age, and a thin, elderly woman wearing an elaborate gown and an extraordinary amount of jewelry. Befitting his leadership role in organizing the meeting, Nigel assumed the command position at the table's head.

"Considering all other hotels in the city have closed," he began, "I'd rather suspect this is the lot of us. And since we may be cooped up here for quite some time, I thought it a good idea we get acquainted."

The First Secretary then briefly outlined his mission in Kutar–to keep the British Foreign Office apprised of developments, to relay whatever diplomatic initiatives might be forthcoming toward resolving the crisis–before seeming to focus his attention on the two women at the table.

"It may also hearten you to know," he continued, "of my own rather extensive experience in the region. Fact is, I have been a student of Kutar for quite some time–dating back to my days at Oxford, if truth be told–and during my fourteen years of service here, I have developed something of a rapport with the king and most of his top ministers. I only mention this by way of assuring you that, should matters with these hooligans up on the ridge take a nasty turn, I shall do my utmost to ensure your continued safety." He paused long enough to take in the grateful nods of the women, before turning to David. "And now perhaps my American colleague, Mr. Richards, would like to say a few words."

David kept his remarks brief, simply mentioned that he had been the foreign aid and development officer at the American embassy, and had stayed on at the behest of his government.

The introductions continued down the table, and with each, there inevitably came an accounting of why they had chosen to remain. Paolo Alfani described the nature of his business in Kutar, and offered that he had stayed to see to the welfare of his company's local employees. Amira Chalasani explained she had been making one of her periodic visits to her ancestral homeland when the war started, and that she had remained out of concern for her relatives stranded in the north.

Naturally David was most interested in the statements of those who were strangers to him. As he had suspected, the dark-featured man turned out to be a journalist, an American named Stewart McBride. For the past several years, he had been reporting from the region for one of the larger wire services.

"And I stayed," Stewart McBride said with a slow shrug, as if the reason should be self-evident, "because, well, this is the most interesting story to come out of this area in a long time." He glanced around at the others. "I mean, what happens in these parts doesn't exactly keep the rest of the world awake at night."

The comment caused Nigel to bristle slightly. "True for the moment, perhaps, but let's just hope it remains that way." He turned to the elderly woman on his right. "Madame?"

The old lady reflexively placed a hand on the enormous diamond pendant that hung about her neck. Given the thick layers of powder and rouge that masked her thin face, David found it difficult to gauge her age—perhaps seventy, perhaps fifteen years further along—but she was still limber enough to sit very straight-backed, to raise her chin to an imperious angle. "I," she said, in the hard, throaty accent of Central Europe, "am the Contessa di Timisoara."

Nigel leaned to her elbow. "Timisoara? Afraid I'm not familiar with that house, madame; might I guess Moravia?"

The old lady tilted her head toward him, a gesture of forgiveness. "Romanian, sir. My great-uncle was the king of Romania." As she gazed over the others, a bitter light came into her eyes. "Until the Reds took over, of course. From those murderers, we were forced to flee for our lives—all of us—left with nothing but the clothes on our backs." Her bejeweled fingers twisted at the diamond pendant more vigorously.

Nigel Mayhew patted her other hand in sympathy. "Dreadfully sorry to stir all that up, Contessa. And you've found yourself here, because . . . ?"

"Because after that, they came for us again, my husband and I. There we were, living quite peacefully in our little pied-à-terre on Hyde Park, thinking our days of persecution were over, and suddenly, there they were again—like Bucharest 1944 all over."

Nigel gave a skeptical frown. "The Reds came for you in London?"

The old lady nodded. "Indeed. Their local collaborators, masquerading as government officials—of course, it was a Labour government at the time, so anything is possible. Well, thank God we'd had the presence of mind to store a few of our little keepsakes in Switzerland and so, with the help of some kindhearted bankers, we managed to find asylum there. But a ghastly country, if any of you know it, absolutely teeming with Swiss in the off-season, so when we heard about this place"—she gave a dismissive flip of her hand to indicate the Moonlight lobby—"we thought, 'Well, how much worse can it be?'" She laughed grimly. "That was sixteen years ago."

"I see," the First Secretary replied. "And your husband now . . . ?"

A wistful light came into the Contessa's eyes. "Martyred, sir. The dearest man the world has known, and he sacrificed himself for me." She looked at the others. "Because, you see, he knew the Reds would eventually come for us here, too, so he said, 'I will go on, I will live as a fugitive from them. At least that way, you will be safe here.' And that is the last I saw of him, the last I've ever heard."

David studied the old lady. It was a confusing tale, and a bit improbable in spots, but it didn't seem the time to press for details. "And you didn't join the evacuation because . . . ?"

The Contessa fixed him with a baleful stare. "Because I refuse to run from them any more." She wagged a finger. "No! Twice I've lost my home to these . . ." She turned to Nigel. "What was the word you used, ambassador?"

Nigel chuckled with delight. "I'm afraid you've promoted me, dear lady, but in any event, I believe the word was hooligans."

"That's it, hooligans." She struck a pose of defiance. "Twice these hooligans have run me off, and I refuse to let them do so again."

"Well put, Contessa," Nigel said. "Most eloquent." He looked along the table to the others. "And I suppose the one saving grace is that all of us here are holding European passports—European or American. Whatever happens in the days ahead, I should certainly think that has to account for something."

When the gathering in the lobby ended, David decided to take a walk through Laradan; the quiet on the ridgeline had persisted, and he hoped the stroll would give him some sense of the city's mood. Passing through the little metal gate just down from the gazebo, he stepped out onto the oceanfront promenade. The bay water was remarkably still that afternoon, but on the open sea beyond were small waves that glinted like ice.

The most immediate effect of the foreigners' evacuation that morning had been to spur a frantic last exodus of the local population. As the British navy launches had shuttled between the destroyer and the pier, an eclectic armada of refugee-laden vessels—coastal freighters, yachts, fishing trawlers—had streamed out of Central Harbor for parts unknown. Now, however, the last of those ships had passed over the horizon, and the port area had settled into the uneasy torpor which held elsewhere in Laradan. Normally busy streets were all but deserted, shopkeepers peered furtively from darkened interiors, and the few pedestrians out hurried along in the shadows of buildings, as if their city had been transformed into an enormous game of musical chairs and the music was about to stop. And from the ridgeline there came nothing but the occasional soft crack of a gunshot—no movement, no clouds of dust to suggest men or machines were being maneuvered into place, no indication at all of the fate being planned for those below.

As David walked, it occurred to him that Nigel had overlooked something in his comforting talk in the lobby about their relative immunity. Perhaps this would prove true for the six foreigners residing at the Moonlight, but with them there was the hotel manager, Arkadi Hafizullah, and his skeleton staff of four local employees—a cook, a valet, a cleaning woman, and a gardener—along with their various children. For all these people, David realized, the situation was both simpler and more frightening. For them, as for the few Kutarans he passed in the city that afternoon, there would be no brooding over possible immunity because they knew they had none, no soul searching over why they had remained because they had never been given a choice to do otherwise.

When he returned from his walk, David found a neat stack of new clothes at the foot of his bed, the purchases made for him at the bazaar by the Moonlight valet. Finally rid of the stained shirt and trousers he had worn for several days, he showered and changed into new ones, then decided to explore the hotel a little.

Wandering up the grand staircase, past the upper floors of shuttered rooms, he came to a smaller metal staircase and, at the top of it, a door leading onto the roof. He had to pry on the handle for a moment—the wood was warped from disuse—but finally the door sprang open.

If the rooftop had ever been a spot for guests to gather, it had been many years ago. Here and there about the whitewashed expanse were old piles of debris, stacks of construction material for repair projects long since completed or abandoned. In a utility shed, he found a jumble of discarded armchairs. Dusting one off, he carried it out to near the roof railing and sat to watch the sun set over the city.

This view of Laradan was not at all like the one he had known from his house on the ridge. From up there, the city had been a white, sprawling thing, and it had reminded David at times of some aquatic animal—an octopus, perhaps—clinging to its narrow perch between the mountains and the sea. From this lower vantage point, he saw that what dominated the city's skyline were the turquoise domes of the royal palace, the minarets and steeples of its mosques and churches. Along with the hillside neighborhoods climbing the slopes of the coastal range, it gave Laradan a very different feel in spite of the day's events: a place in defiance of its surroundings rather than helpless to them.

"Ah, so it's you."

David turned to see Amira Chalasani standing a short distance behind him. He rose, startled, even a bit embarrassed that she had found him there, and it showed on his face.

"I'm sorry," she said, "would you prefer to be alone?" She pointed a thumb over her shoulder at the rooftop door. "I followed your footprints."

"No, it's okay." He tried to recover, motioned her to the chair. "Please, I'll get another. My footprints?"

"In the dust on the staircase. I don't think anyone has been above the third floor in years, but I saw this one set of footprints and . . ." She gave him a hesitant smile. "But I think you want to be alone, no?"

"No. Please."

When he returned from the utility shed, Amira was standing by the railing, looking out at the city. David set the second chair close to the first. "A beautiful view, isn't it?" he called.

She nodded without turning around. "It used to be."

He sat and watched her from behind. Her head tilted slightly, and he knew she was gazing up at the ridgeline. She looked very small and fragile just then, her body framed against the wall of mountains, and David felt a kind of pity for her.

Amira's hands fell from the railing, she came back toward him. "What do you think the rebels are waiting for?"

"I don't know. Maybe for when their artillery gets here or . . . I really don't know."

She settled into the chair next to his and they stared at the mountains together. From that vantage point, Gowarshad Pass appeared as a neat V-shaped notch in the ridge, and David could make out his old house on the rock outcropping just above it. He thought of pointing it out to her.

"Nigel told me how you tried to help with the peace talks," she said. "That's what you were hinting at, wasn't it, that night we met at the Excelsior?"

David nodded. "The problem was the Alliance. They'd already decided there wouldn't be any talks, that the only solution was a military one." He laughed lightly, cocked his chin at the ridge. "We see how well that turned out."

Amira smiled. "Is that why you stayed? Out of a kind of penance?"

David's eyes traveled over the city. The sun was slipping toward the western peaks, the whitewashed city was softening to gold. Here and there, windows were catching the sun's last light at such an angle that they shone a brilliant fiery orange, as if the buildings which held them were burning. He shook his head.

"Not penance. Hope, I guess. The only logical way out of this now is through diplomacy, negotiation. I'd like to be a part of that."

She studied him. "And you believe that will happen?"

"Who knows? All we can do is work toward that, but . . . I don't know."

In the quiet between them, Amira looked out over the railing. A lone frond of a palm tree just beyond the roof caught the barest suggestion of a breeze, waved back and forth against the stillness.

"I had a strange experience a few days ago," she said after a while. "I've been volunteering with the refugee office at the Interior Ministry, and one of the groups I was helping with is from this small village in the far north. They had all come down together–very conservative, you know–and they'd been settled together in this little park up on Baktiar Hill. But this one morning I went to check on them and they were gone, no one knew where. I spent most of the day looking for them, and finally I found them. They had moved out to the eastern industrial zone, to this parking lot of a factory. They had all their tents up, spread over the asphalt, and the smoke from the factory was coming right down on top of them." She turned to David. "I asked why they had moved, and do you know what they said? They said they felt ashamed being in that park, surrounded by all those nice houses, and where they were now, no one saw them in their disgrace. Plus, the asphalt kept the dust down. I tried to reason with them. I told them the smoke was bad for the children, that being way out there, none of the social services people could help them, but no matter what I said, they wouldn't change their minds. And the truth is, they seemed much happier there." She searched David's face. "It's very odd, isn't it? To choose smoke and asphalt over grass and trees? But it made me think about this idea we're all raised with, that people are fundamentally the same the world over. I don't believe it's true. I think people are fundamentally different the world over, how they view things, what's important to them." She smiled. "So I guess that's all a long way of saying I don't think this will end in the way we imagine. However this ends, I think it will be in a way that none of us Westerners can predict; we won't even see it coming."

———

When Amira left, David returned to watching the city. Shadow was spreading over the valley now, the sun's glow only shone in the windows of a few buildings on the uppermost slopes, and the western sky was slipping to red, the eastern to dark blue.

Sitting there, he reconsidered her question as to why he had stayed, and he saw that perhaps she had been on to something, perhaps there was an element of penance to it. Because all at once it was very important to him to be seen as the representative of a moral nation, one that did not walk away from its obligations and friends.

At this, David chuckled to himself. What a bizarre thing to find yourself alone on a rooftop in a foreign land, and suddenly discover that you're a patriot.

Seven

"Please don't misunderstand me, signore," the Contessa said, casting her gaze in Paolo's direction. "I have nothing against Italians on an individual basis. But surely even you would agree that, as a race, they leave much to be desired."

Paolo, reddening with anger, was unable even to find the words to respond—and this was a mistake; with the Contessa, one had to be quick, one had to counterstrike, or matters only became worse. This was especially true in the mornings, for it was almost as if the old lady strategized in her bed at night over how to be most effectively wounding at the next breakfast.

She looked to the others at the lobby table. "It really is rather remarkable, don't you find? The same people who gave us the Renaissance, and for the past five hundred years, what? The Vespa? Some old popes?" She cut off any interruption with a raised hand. "Ah, but that's not completely fair. There was, of course, Mussolini."

"Mussolini?!" Paolo half rose from his chair in outrage.

The Contessa ignored him. "A controversial figure, I grant you, but at least he tried to instill some backbone in those people.

Naturally they hated him for it, turned on him the instant they had the chance."

"Are you aware, Contessa," Stewart McBride cut in, "that it was Mussolini who invented fascism?"

The Contessa gave a condescending chuckle. "Yes, dear boy. And if memory serves, it was your Wright brothers who invented the airplane, but we don't blame them for every plane that crashes, now do we?"

It had been five days since the evacuation at the harbor. By collective decision, the Moonlight residents had made the mahogany table in the lobby their permanent dining area—it was felt the hotel's cavernous dining hall would induce gloom in such a small group—and while David had agreed with the choice, he also saw that the setting accentuated the sameness of their days and conversations. Already there was the forming of alliances among them, the development of both friendships and aversions. Certainly the most flagrant in this regard was the Contessa. Toward Nigel Mayhew she displayed a kind of rapt adoration, while for Paolo Alfani she harbored a dislike that was as virulent as it was mysterious. Toward the rest, she seemed to have settled on a policy of staunch indifference; from what David could tell, she had yet to even learn their names.

At the breakfast table, he caught her eye. "In the interests of harmony, Contessa, maybe we should avoid political discussions, ethnic slurs, that sort of thing."

The old lady considered this with a scowl, looked to Nigel as if for a second opinion.

"Not a bad idea there, Richards," the First Secretary said. "Don't want to get on each other's nerves cooped up in this place."

The Contessa gave a sharp nod. "An excellent point, Ambassador. Harmony is essential in these situations."

What made all this sniping especially wearying was the lack of any discernible change in the situation elsewhere. With still no move by the rebels on the ridge, their guns quiet, a kind of paralysis had taken hold in Laradan, conjecture and worry filling the void of action. Not that David's days accurately reflected this. Each morning he set off for another round of meetings in the city—with government ministers and business leaders, with officers along the front—and in between these meetings were consultations with State Department officials back in Washington over the embassy's secure telephone line. Each evening he and Nigel convened back at the hotel to compare notes but, thus far, all their conversations had been the same: Washington and London were waiting, the army and palace were waiting, everyone was simply quiet and waiting for some move by those on the ridge. This was preferable to pitched battle, obviously, but the sense of being engaged in busywork cast its own pall over David.

Increasingly this pall appeared to be taking hold of everyone at the hotel. With the exception of the Contessa, all the others had found some purpose in staying on in the city—Amira had her volunteer work in the refugee camps; Paolo, with his fluency in the local language, had taken to acting as Stewart McBride's interpreter as the journalist roamed Laradan in search of compelling stories—but David noticed that, each morning, they seemed to linger at the lobby table a bit longer, to contemplate the new day with a little less enthusiasm. On that morning, it was Amira who finally stirred; glancing at her watch, she sighed, rose to her feet.

"Well, I suppose I should get going," she said without conviction.

But at that moment, there came the sound of grinding gravel from out in the hotel drive, the urgent slamming of car doors, and then a bald, middle-aged Kutaran military officer strode into the lobby trailed by two young aides. David recognized him as General Hassan Kalima, the hero of the defense of Laradan and recently promoted to army chief of staff, and he knew from the general's brisk walk, the hard set of his face, that this was not to be a social call.

For his part, Nigel seemed more alarmed at being caught out of his usual suit and tie; with no appointments scheduled for that morning, he had come down to the lobby in casual slacks and a sports shirt.

"Why General Kalima," he called, struggling to his feet, "what a pleasant surprise." As the general approached, Nigel made a series of helpless gestures at his own attire. "Do forgive my appearance—afraid we're all becoming a bit informal around here in the mornings—but please, do join us." His hands fluttered away from his chest to indicate the empty chair beside his own.

But General Kalima was clearly not interested in Nigel's wardrobe or in sitting for a chat; stopping a few feet from the table, he squared his shoulders—he was an imposing man, and exceptionally tall for a Kutaran—and fixed the First Secretary with the same dour expression he had worn since coming through the door. "May I speak with you in private for a moment?"

"Why yes, yes, of course." Nigel cast one last unhappy glance at his sports shirt, then hurried over, followed the general and his aides a short distance across the lobby. From the table, the others watched their huddled conversation.

"Something has happened," Paolo said softly, as if to himself.

"Whatever it is, this is highly improper," the Contessa said. "One can't just have these sorts of people barging in here unannounced."

Before she could carry her complaint further, General Kalima turned and strode away with the same vigor that had marked his entrance. In his wake, Nigel came slowly back toward the table. He was clutching a sheet of paper, looked pale, and David rose, went to his side.

"What is it?"

Nigel handed him the paper. "Just came down from the rebels," he muttered.

It was a poor photocopy—presumably the army had kept the

original—but the message was legible enough: "Mr. Mayhew is instructed to come to Gowarshad Pass at noon today."

David looked up to see that the older man appeared quite stricken. Nigel took the paper back but, apparently forgetting his own preference for discretion in such matters, numbly passed it into the outstretched hand of Stewart McBride. In silence, the note made its way around the table.

"What are you going to do?" David asked.

The First Secretary shrugged. "I'm not sure. Obviously, there's no time to get guidance from London—it's five in the morning there—and, as General Kalima said, there's no way to guarantee my security . . ."

"Don't go, Nigel," Paolo urged.

The Contessa swiftly turned on him. "Of course he's not going, you silly little man! Do you take the ambassador for a fool?" She looked at the others, her eyes aflame. "This is an old trick with these people: send word you want to talk peace, lure the leader out into the open and, next thing you know"—she snapped her fingers— "they've put his head on a stick." She glared at Paolo again. "Oh yes, don't tell me about these hoodlums, signore; I could write you a book on them."

It wasn't clear if Nigel heard any of this. With the note finally returned to his hand, he stared across the lobby as if lost in deepest thought. "If you'll excuse me," he said at last, "I think I shall return to my room"—and he started for the staircase rather like a man walking in his sleep.

———

He had placed Sarah's photograph beside the desk lamp, and Nigel now sat before it to stare at her image. The photograph was from their thirty-fifth wedding anniversary; he had it in a nice silver frame, and Sarah looked absolutely exquisite in the black silk gown he had bought for the occasion, in the diamond necklace and earrings he had given her on her previous birthday.

"Oh, Sarah," he whispered, "what have I done to us this time?"

It was always a source of amazement to others, whenever Nigel thought to mention it, that in their forty-one years of marriage, he and Sarah had never been apart for longer than a week at a time. It was all the more remarkable given his profession, of course, but Nigel had decided on that one-week limit as a young man, even before their marriage, and he had not departed from it: if asked to take a trip of greater duration, he brought Sarah along, and if that was impossible, he simply didn't go.

Because if Nigel Mayhew was an ambitious man, and he was, and if he occasionally succumbed to thoughts of his own indispensability, which he did, he had also never lost sight of the fact that there was at least one thing in his life, one person, that was more important than career or even duty.

In his hotel room, he allowed himself a thin smile.

No doubt there'd been times when Sarah had regretted that policy of his, he thought. Some of the places he'd dragged her to, the ghastly conditions she'd endured. But never once had she complained. All she'd ever wanted was what he wanted: to have each other, to be together wherever fate might take them.

And now, in their forty-first year together, he had broken with that. By deciding to stay in this wretched place, by putting her on that ship, Nigel had thrown aside the one vow that had always been his guide.

At his desk, he turned to stare out the curtained window, at the gauzy glare of the morning sea beyond.

He couldn't very well have let Sarah stay, obviously—which only begged the question of why he had. As for an answer to this, Nigel wasn't sure he fully grasped it himself.

Yes, the call of duty, the conviction that this peaceable little land shouldn't be forsaken, but perhaps something more philosophical as well.

Because it is a shocking thing, at the age of sixty-four, to discover that every understanding you've come to about a place and its people is in error, that all the wisdoms and truths gathered over a lifetime of studying and observing are shown to be false. And, frankly, Nigel didn't know if he could have faced that at his age, if he could have returned to England, gone into retirement, and merely pushed it all from his mind. Maybe as a younger man but not now, not when there was no time to recover, to create a new order or explanation of things. He had stayed because he needed to know why this had happened, what angry force raged up there in the mountains, to arrive at an answer if only to his own satisfaction.

But he'd really done it this time. He was not at all a superstitious man—at least, he'd never been before—but sitting there at his desk that morning, staring at the slip of paper he'd been given, the photograph of Sarah in her black dress, Nigel Mayhew couldn't help but feel that here was a kind of divine retribution, a punishment for his search. And why not? The bibles of the world were filled with stories of men damned for their curiosity.

He reached for the photograph, took it into his hands, traced a light finger along the length of her. "I love you so much," he said. "I miss you so much."

————

Leaving the others in the lobby, David went out the French doors to stand at the edge of the swimming pool. The water was very clear and still, and it suddenly puzzled him why, despite the heat, he hadn't gone for a swim since arriving at the hotel. To his knowledge, none of the others had either.

He thought of Nigel up in his room, staring at the rebels' note, weighing his decision—even though David was quite sure what that decision would be.

But as he stood there, David realized the note had roused something in him he had tried very hard to quell these past days, a quiet annoyance with the subordinate role he was playing to Nigel

Mayhew. He had constantly reminded himself this was only natural—after all, the First Secretary was much higher ranking and, Kutar being a former colony, it was to be expected a Briton would assume the lead diplomatic role—but it still nettled somewhat that it was Nigel who went to meetings at the palace with the king and his senior commanders, while David busied himself with junior ministers and colonels. Now, with the note from the ridge, it seemed the pattern was extending to the rebels too.

A slight breeze came over the bluff, just enough to riffle the pool's surface, and David looked up at the enveloping trees, their swaying fronds, as he pondered what to do. In fact, there was little to ponder; peevishness combined with a sense of honor left only one option.

Shortly after eleven, Nigel came downstairs. He had changed into one of his navy-blue suits, put on his red-and-white Oxford tie.

"Right then, off I go," he called to the others in a voice straining for cheeriness. "Shan't be too long, I'd imagine."

"Surely not to the ridge, Ambassador?" The Contessa was alarmed.

"The call of duty, madame, the call of duty."

David rose from the table. "I'm going with you."

The First Secretary drew up, gave a quick nod. "Much obliged, Richards, but afraid that won't do; the note doesn't say anything about my bringing an entourage."

"I don't care what the note says. We're in this together, and I'm not letting you go up there alone."

Nigel stared at David, and a smile slowly spread beneath his white mustache. He gave another sharp nod. "Very well. Suspect I'd rather enjoy the company."

His gratitude turned to dismay, however, when he caught sight of David's khaki trousers, his wrinkled white shirt, as he came across the lobby. "But surely you're not going dressed like that."

The soldiers at the forward checkpoint didn't speak, simply stared after them with a respectful somberness, as if watching men walk to the gallows. In their own silence, David and Nigel started up the Gowarshad Pass road toward the first hairpin.

David's legs felt rubbery, his shoulders were hunched. He tried to will himself to calm, to look up and take note of their surroundings, but found he couldn't do this, that all he could do was stare at the asphalt just beyond his feet. He was tensed for a sound, the clicking of a rifle bolt, a gunshot, but there was only that of the wind and their own ragged breathing.

They reached the first hairpin, rounded it, and started for the second. David attempted to distract himself by recalling how many turns there were to the top of the pass. He certainly knew, the hundreds of times he'd driven it these past two years, but right then he couldn't remember at all.

"You nervous?" he whispered finally.

"Me?" Nigel whispered back. "Heavens, no. An officer of the Crown—surely even these ruffians have respect for that."

In spite of the situation—maybe because of it—David chuckled, and then Nigel did too. "Well, all right, Richards," he said. "If we're going to get all modern here, yes, I'm a bit nervous."

They had just rounded the third hairpin when a young man leaped down from a cleft in the rocks. They both jumped slightly, and the young man seemed amused by this. He was in his mid-twenties and dressed in casual clothes, alone and unarmed by all appearances, and he came toward them with two white, letter-sized envelopes in his hand. Nigel took the envelopes with shaking fingers.

"Now see here, we want some answers," he said, trying for an air of authority his voice couldn't deliver. "Just what the devil is going on here?"

But the young man didn't speak, continued to stare at them with that same amused expression, and then he turned on his heels and started slowly up the road.

"Hang on a moment," the First Secretary called, finding a bit more timber in his voice, but the young man kept on.

Alone on the road, they looked at the envelopes. Both were addressed to Mr. Nigel Mayhew.

———————

The British embassy smelled of dust and rotting plants. As he followed Nigel down the third-floor corridor to the secure communications room, David glanced through open doors to the empty offices within. The British diplomats hadn't been nearly as thorough in their purging as the Americans; files were strewn over desks and floors, charts and posters remained tacked to walls.

"Quite a mess you people left here," he teased. "We cleaned our place out completely."

"Yes, well, you people have rather more secrets to keep, don't you?"

From the communications room, they relayed the contents of the rebels' notes to the British Foreign Ministry and the State Department, then went down the hall to the ambassador's office, a pleasant, airy room with a view toward the palace. There they settled into armchairs, reread the messages they had already read untold times.

As with the previous notes from the rebels—the one delivered by General Kalima that morning, the earlier one sent to Colonel Munn—these two had been written in block lettering so precise that, at first glance, they appeared to have been printed rather than done by hand. General Kalima had, of course, taken possession of the originals, and the poor quality of the photocopies he'd given them had the effect of lending their contents an even greater aura of cold-bloodedness.

The first note read:

The Moonlight Hotel is declared neutral territory. This only applies to the guests and staff members now there. No one else will be allowed entry, and the current authorities in Laradan will be responsible for enforcing this. This neutrality does not extend, except for the diplomats Mr. Mayhew and Mr. Richards, beyond the hotel premises.

As with the earlier communiqués, this one bore no signature, no indication at all of who might have produced it. The second note was much longer—longer, in fact, than all the others combined.

Arrange for an unarmed merchant ship of less than 17,000 tons. It can bring into Laradan those relief supplies listed below and nothing else. This ship will appear from the south-southwest at 7:00 AM this Friday, November 4, and will dock at Pier 4, Slip 3 of the Central Harbor at 10:00 AM. With the exception of the mooring team (two men), no one onshore will approach within two hundred meters of the ship. The ship's crew will unload the cargo, placing it in open view on the pier, and at 1:00 PM the ship will depart by the same course. At 1:30 PM, dockworkers will retrieve the cargo, this task to be completed and the pier cleared by 4:00 PM. So long as these instructions are followed precisely, the ship will be permitted to return to Laradan each Friday with those supplies that we will specify. Mr. Mayhew will return to Gowarshad Road at noon of each Saturday to receive further directives.

Below this was a handwritten list of the goods the rebels would allow to be brought in, and what had immediately caught David's eye was that it neatly matched the very items now running in short supply in Laradan: tents and water purification kits, specific medicines and tools. What it meant, quite plainly, was that the rebels had the city wired, they had eyes and ears everywhere, and it produced in David the sensation that they were now living as if on the slide of some vast microscope, observed by a force that knew their every weakness.

"Well, I'd say that rather scuttles the CIA's theory, wouldn't you?" Nigel said, cheerily tossing his copies onto the ambassador's desk. "These chaps certainly wouldn't be looking to us for help if they intended a bloodbath."

From his armchair, David studied the First Secretary. He had attributed Nigel's good mood since coming down from Gowarshad Pass to simple relief, but he now saw it had a deeper source— one he didn't quite grasp. "I'm not sure I'm following you here."

"Think of it, old boy," Nigel said with a trace of exasperation. "By declaring the hotel neutral ground, the KPLA is essentially recognizing our diplomatic status, they don't want any harm to come to us—which must mean they intend to make use of us in the future."

"Then why did they order all foreign diplomats to leave?" David replied. "Remember, we're here in defiance of that order, so maybe they just want to avoid any complications that would come from killing us, they're trying to minimize the chances of that happening."

Nigel considered this, a flicker of doubt passed over his face, but then he adamantly shook his head. "But why arrange for these regular meetings up on the road then? And why this business with the relief ship? Don't you see? It's really quite clever what they're doing." He leaned forward to take up his copies of the notes, fluttered them in the air. "The Kutaran government can't afford a fraction of these supplies, and the KPLA knows that. They'll have to come from us—from Western governments and relief agencies— and, for humanitarian reasons alone, they know we'll provide it. So, you see, in a roundabout manner—and not least, in a manner they can control—these chaps are inviting the outside world back in here."

David stared down at the notes in his hand. He wanted to be convinced of Nigel's assessment, but something stood in the way. "But why? That's what I don't get. Why invite it back in when you've just finished kicking it out?"

The First Secretary shrugged. "A change in tactics? A power struggle in which cooler heads prevailed? I'm not sure you can always parse out a clear-cut logic with these groups." A smile spread beneath his mustache. "In any event, I think this is one of those situations in which you . . . what's that American expression?–'don't examine the crotch of a gift horse'?"

David laughed. "Don't look a gift horse in the mouth. Examining the crotch, that must be a British thing."

Nigel ignored the gibe by glancing at his watch, abruptly rising to his feet. "Well, suspect it'll be some time yet before we get any word from London or Washington–might not even be today. In the meantime, perhaps we should head back to the hotel, give the others the good news."

David nodded, rose as well, but as they left the ambassador's office, he still felt a lingering note of dissonance, something somewhere was not quite right.

"Pretty fucking weird, isn't it?" Stewart McBride said, pointing with his cigarette to the ornate entranceway fountain, water splashing over its cherubs and egrets. "Like something you'd see in Vienna or on someone's front lawn in New Jersey." He turned, extended his hand to David. "We haven't really had much of a chance to get to know each other. Guess we've been keeping to different schedules."

It was an odd gesture–after all, they'd shared nearly every meal together for the past five days–but David shook the journalist's hand anyway. "I guess so. In its own way, this place manages to keep you pretty busy."

If mutually agreed to, this explanation for their very limited interaction was a rather bald fiction. In truth, Stewart McBride had spent his days scouring Laradan for news, and had concluded–rightly, thus far–that David didn't have any. For his part, David was imbued with that institutional wariness of journalists which eventually takes hold in all government officials. As for divining a motive behind Stewart's sudden friendliness, that was easy: for once, David did have news; by going to Gowarshad Pass, he *was* that day's news.

Upon returning from the British embassy, he and Nigel had found the others still gathered at the lobby table. The notes from the rebels had met with an ebullient reaction, and the mood had been such that David chose not to intrude upon it with his own nagging doubt. He had noticed Stewart McBride staring fixedly at him from across the table, however, and when he'd gone outside, the journalist had quickly followed.

"So what do you make of it all?" Stewart asked, still gazing at the gaudy fountain.

David cautiously studied him in profile. "Hard to know what to make of it exactly. It certainly seems like a positive development, though."

The journalist exhaled heavily, sent twin streams of smoke out his nose. "Yeah."

The longer they stood there, the more awkward the silence between them became. David looked down the gravel road, flanked by two perfectly symmetrical rows of palm trees, that led to the hotel's front gate. He had left the lobby with plans to stroll through the city, to mull over the day's events without the distraction of the others, but he now considered that having a companion might be preferable. "I was going to take a walk. You want to come along?"

"Sure." Stewart dropped the cigarette to the gravel, crushed it with his shoe.

They passed along the drive and out the front gate.

"So whereabouts in the States are you from?" the journalist asked as they walked.

"Cleveland. You?"

"Philly."

David smiled. "The City of Brotherly Love."

Stewart chuckled dryly. "Yeah. One of the dumber slogans a city's ever come up with. Just about the time they picked it, the race riots started."

Laradan, usually fairly quiet at that afternoon hour, was surprisingly busy—its streets clogged with vehicles, its stores crowded with shoppers—and it occurred to David that word of the rebels' directive must have leaked out, that after so many days of tense waiting, the news had engendered both relief and celebration among the residents.

"So, you're CIA?" Stewart asked after a time.

David grinned, shook his head. "Foreign aid officer."

"Yeah, you said that the other day, but I figured it was bullshit."

"Afraid not. I don't think Kutar rates enough for the CIA to leave someone here." He saw Stewart scrutinizing him. "You're not convinced."

The reporter shrugged. "Time will tell, I guess. Every CIA guy I've met in this region has been a fucking moron, so if you turn out to be one, I'll get suspicious."

David laughed. "Pretty high bar you're setting. And even if all CIA agents are morons, it doesn't necessarily follow that all morons are CIA agents."

"Good point. Sometimes they're Marine colonels."

As they strolled, they fell into easier conversation, one that centered on their experiences of the past several weeks.

Stewart had been part of the horde of journalists that flew into Kutar just after the first military fiasco in Erbil, and he had stayed on to witness the second, the rebel encirclement of the capital. On that occasion, he had been reporting from the frontline town of Zulfiqar–Colonel Munn's much vaunted "oasis of steel"– and had joined in the mad scramble back to Laradan.

"At one time, that would have gotten Munn court-martialed," he said, "but not anymore. The difference is television. For some reason, the TV cameras love that little shit. So now the Pentagon will appoint a committee to look into what happened here, and in six months they'll come out with a report saying, 'What do you know? The television guys were right all along, Munn really is an all-American hero.' Then they'll promote him, give him a medal for valor or good penmanship or something, and send him out to talk at high schools, maybe put him in some of their TV ads."

David laughed again. Despite his initial caution, he found he was taking a quick liking to Stewart McBride.

They came to a small square a few blocks from the American embassy, several competing cafés set among its shade trees. Every table was taken by groups of men–talking, smoking, playing cards. The ridgeline was visible over the rooftops on the far side of the square and, as Stewart stared at it, his mood grew more serious.

"So what happened up there?" he asked. "Other than giving you the notes, did the rebels say anything?"

An hour earlier, David might have tried to deflect the question, or at least limit his answer, but he saw no reason to now. "It was rebel, singular–a young guy, probably mid-twenties, and he didn't say a word. Nigel tried to talk to him, but he just handed over the notes and walked away."

The journalist nodded, cocked his chin at the ridge. "Did you know they've brought their artillery up? They started putting them in place this morning. You can just make out the tops of the barrels if you have a telescope or a good pair of binoculars." He took another cigarette from his shirt pocket and lit it. "Also, Pier 4, where they want this relief ship to come in? It's the most exposed pier in the entire harbor. The ridge is only three miles away at that point, and Pier 4 runs straight-perpendicular to it. They can line-sight their artillery ahead of time and blast that ship to pieces if they want."

David waited until Stewart turned to him. "You think that's what they're planning?"

Stewart shook his head. "No. Why go through all this bull-shit just to blow up a ship. No, there's something else going on here." He pulled on his cigarette and took a slow look around the square. "You know, I've covered maybe half a dozen wars in this region. There's a style to them, a kind of brute efficiency: a quick strike by one ethnic group against another, a government decides to smash some political movement, and they do it and then it's all over, everything gets patched up, like it never happened. But this one doesn't fit. There's something strange, slow motion about it." He rolled the cigarette between his fingers. "And this relief-ship deal, what's that about? As smart as those fuckers are up there, you've got to ask yourself why, what's in it for them?" He studied David. "You've been asking yourself that, too, haven't you?"

David now fully understood why Stewart had followed him from the lobby, but he wasn't yet ready to confide all in the jour-nalist. He gave a shrug. "Public relations?"

"Aimed at who? You trying to charm these people?" Stewart waved a hand over the cafés. "Hell, you've already got your boot on their throats, what do you need to charm them for? The West? You just finished chasing all the Westerners out of here, so who cares what they think? See what I mean? It doesn't add up."

His eyes clouded in concentration, the journalist gazed across the crowded square again. "I can't put my finger on how," he muttered, "those fuckers are way ahead of me on this one, but I think that ship is a Trojan horse."

David felt a slight prickling on his neck, because this was the precise phrase—unmoored, the reason staying out of reach—that had run through his mind all day.

————————

Amira took the squalling child into her arms, pulled the blanket back. The baby's cheek was hot to her touch, his dark hair matted with sweat, but he calmed quickly to her gentle rocking. She watched his eyes flutter, finally close, and she leaned down to return him to the outstretched hands of his mother.

"I think he's just overheated," she told the woman, stumbling through what she remembered of the northeastern dialect. "Leave the blanket loose and keep him in the shade. If he's still hot in a few hours, take him to the doctors."

The mother thanked her, and Amira moved on along the line of refugee tents.

She had no medical training, couldn't honestly tell the difference between a merely uncomfortable infant and a fevered one, but the doctors in their field tent at the corner of Independence Park were so overwhelmed that Amira wanted to spare them from minor problems if she could. This was a task for which she was uniquely suited. To her fellow Kutarans, Amira Chalasani might look like one of them, but her manner, her speech, her style of dress gave her away as an outsider, and in giving her away, conferred the automatic deference Kutarans showed to all foreigners, bestowed authority as she made her "doctor's rounds."

In any event, the overheated-baby theory was a logical one; for some reason, mothers in Kutar always overdressed their infants, swaddled them in blankets even in the heat of summer.

In the two days since the rebel communiqué about the relief ship, the initial euphoria it had spurred among the refugees had settled into a kind of tempered hope. All were waiting to learn what the outside world's response would be, if the ship would come after all, and as she toured the camps, Amira was besieged by the same questions: Was there any news? What did she think the West would do? To each questioner, she gave the same answer: there was no news, she couldn't even guess how the outside might respond.

She was probably being overly cautious in this. From their lengthy discussions with Washington and London, both David and Nigel sounded increasingly confident that the plan would go forward, but with no definite confirmation, it seemed risky to raise expectations that might still be dashed.

Amira came to a section of the camp she had visited several times before, a small enclave that housed an entire village from the central highlands. Despite the chaos of their flight, these neighbors had found each other in the strange city, and in Independence Park they had created a facsimile of their old home: areas had been set aside for children to play, clothes hung from communal lines strung between trees, and the women were gathered in a circle in front of their tents, chatting amiably as they cleaned or cooked, much as, several weeks earlier, they had gathered at their village well. As Amira approached, the women smiled, waved her over.

There was no reliable estimate of how many refugees had come into Laradan–perhaps a hundred thousand, perhaps double that–because many had quickly moved into the homes of relatives or friends. Those who remained–and here, Amira had heard numbers ranging from sixty to ninety thousand–were spread between the main tent camp in Independence Park and a dozen or so smaller ones scattered across the city's open land. The biggest influx had come with those first military setbacks in the north, the mass flight this had sparked across the region; after that, the rebel advance had been so rapid there had been little time for people to flee even if they had wanted to. Now, with the KPLA on the ridge above Laradan, it was as if a wall had been built across the country, separating those Kutarans gathered on the narrow coastal strip from all those beyond.

Except this was not entirely true. As with any such wall, this one had its cracks–an old goat trail, an unguarded cleft–and even now, handfuls of refugees were finding these cracks to slip into the city. For Amira, these last intrepid stragglers represented both hope and torment.

Her home village, in the Altafaram valley just north of Erbil, had passed into the rebel zone on the same day as the army's stunning collapse in that city. Since then, she had received no word from anyone there. So, as she made her rounds through Independence Park and the other tent camps, Amira had a kind of hidden agenda. Along with offering what aid or advice she could, she was also ever alert for the sound of the Altafaram dialect, for a familiar face, anxious to find anyone who might know what had become of the people of Chalasan.

In their circle, the women from the highland village implored Amira to sit, to eat, to have a glass of water, displaying that vaguely desperate hospitality common to the poor the world over. With the elaborate language that marked such exchanges in Kutar, Amira politely declined their various offers, gave the same answers to their questions about the relief ship that she'd already given a dozen times that day.

A short distance away from the chatting women, she noticed the men of the village sitting in loose clusters under the trees. They appeared utterly bereft there, not talking, just smoking cigarettes or staring without interest at the activity around them. Against the backdrop of Laradan, it reminded Amira of how traditional the roles of men and women were in northern Kutar, the women the home builders, the men the gatherers, how quickly the men might wither when their tasks were taken from them. When she moved on, the women all waved, wished her health and good luck, but the men studiously ignored her, as if they were ashamed to be seen there.

After a time, she circled back toward the medical tent, kept an eye out for any problems that warranted being reported to the camp's maintenance office: standing water, an overflowing latrine. Amira was impressed, frankly, by how well the government was handling the refugee crisis in the absence of any foreign relief workers. She realized this sounded elitist, but it was also a fact: that roving bands of disaster experts had long experience dealing with such human calamities, the Kutaran government had none, and yet it had taken to the task with something close to efficiency, delivering food and water to the tent cities, erecting field clinics, seeing that the latrine pits at the camps' edges were regularly emptied. The one great shortage at the moment was shelter, but with the misting rains of winter still weeks away, the newly homeless could at least survive in the open air or under their strung tarpaulins so long as they found shade during the heat of the day. What's more, if the relief ship did come, that issue might soon be resolved; in their communiqué, the rebels had listed one thousand field tents among the items they would allow in.

"Miss Chalasani?" Amira turned to see a young man in green hospital scrubs, one of the orderlies from the medical tent. "You're looking for people from Altafaram, yes?"

"Yes," she replied, hearing the hushed excitement in her voice.

The young man pointed over his shoulder. "Two just came into the clinic. They came over the mountains this morning."

Amira half ran toward the medical tent, leaving the orderly to catch up.

———

David was late returning to the hotel that night, his calls back and forth to Washington on the embassy's secure line having carried on well after dark. With the exception of Amira, he found all the other Moonlight residents gathered at the lobby table.

"Ah, Richards," Nigel called at his approach. "We've just been discussing the news. And it seems the palace has asked Mr. Alfani here"—he pointed to Paolo—"to oversee the entire operation down at the harbor."

"Well, as it should be." David smiled at his friend. "Organization is your strong suit, after all."

That afternoon, the Red Cross headquarters in Geneva had announced that a merchant vessel of 16,000 tons, the SS *Esmeralda*, had been chartered in Palumbo, the principal port of Kutar's western neighbor and a mere three hundred miles down the coast, for the purpose of providing the beleaguered city of Laradan with those relief supplies approved by the rebels. A vast consortium of Western relief groups and governmental agencies were now working feverishly to collect those supplies and to airlift them to Palumbo in time for the ship's sailing. The barrage of phone calls David had fielded from Washington that evening had largely dealt with delineating what the American government's official role in the humanitarian operation would be, and how he might best explain this role to the government of Kutar.

"Well, if you ask me," the Contessa said, "it's all a trick."

"A trick, madame?" Nigel leaned to her elbow.

"Absolutely. It's how the Reds always work. Stay low for a time, lull everyone to sleep, and then"—she snapped her fingers—"out with the knives."

David glanced across the table to see Stewart McBride staring at him. The journalist wore a smirk, but had also lifted an eyebrow, as if to say, "The old broad might be crazy, but she's also right." David looked away, because while the Contessa was surely in error about the KPLA's political orientation, it was still an unsettling experience to hear one's own quiet doubts given voice by her.

"Actually there's quite of history of these sorts of magnanimous gestures by the northern tribes," Nigel said. "Why, back in the 1870s—"

He was interrupted by the Contessa's mirthful laugh. "Ah, Mr. Ambassador, this talk of tribes, such an imagination; you really are quite the storyteller! Yes, it's definitely the Reds, of that we can be assured." She looked around with a disconcerting smile. "And let me tell you something else about these people. They do not stop. They will keep on and on until this city and everyone in it is laid to waste. Rape, torture, skinning alive, these are their hobbies." She dabbed her mouth with a napkin, let out a resigned sigh. "Well, live and learn, I suppose."

All at once, David couldn't listen to this conversation any longer; he turned to Paolo. "Amira isn't back yet?"

"She came in a while ago, but said she wasn't feeling well." The businessman cast a pointed glance at the Contessa. "Perhaps it was the company."

———————

Amira was sitting on the edge of her bed, barefoot but still dressed in her clothes of the day. David watched her stare at the inlaid design by her feet—a rose flower, from the look of it.

"We missed you downstairs," he said.

She nodded. "Thanks. I guess I just wasn't much in the mood." She looked up, forced a smile. "But I hear the relief ship's coming. That's great news, isn't it?"

David nodded. He had knocked on her door and Amira had invited him in. Now he took the chair by her desk and glanced about the room: a neat stack of books stood on the dresser in the far corner, a shorter one of magazines. "Did something happen today?"

Amira's smile slipped away, she bobbled her head. "Not really. Well, sort of, I suppose."

He waited, and her sadness seemed to deepen.

"A couple came over the mountains this morning from the Altafaram valley, from a village about eight miles below Chalasan. They'd spent the past two weeks crossing the desert, were absolutely shattered. I asked them if they knew anything about Chalasan, if they'd crossed paths with anyone from there, but . . ." Her gaze floated over the room, found nothing to focus on. "It's the same story we're hearing from all the ones coming over now, you know? The ones fleeing now have reason to be fearful—like this couple from Hagera, their two sons are in the military—so they avoided contact with everyone. They hid during the day, walked at night, so they actually have no idea what's happening, what the rebels are doing." She looked to David then, searched his face. "It's incredible when you think of it; two weeks crossing rebel territory and they don't know anything. They might as well have been on the moon."

David nodded. To a degree he would not have imagined possible beforehand, there was virtually no hard information coming out about what might be taking place in the KPLA-held areas. This was understandable among the first great influx of refugees—they had fled ahead of the rebel advance, prior to any actual contact with them—but it seemed the later arrivals had assiduously avoided all contact as well. Some had recounted stories of massacres and firing squads, but closer questioning invariably revealed they were repeating rumors overheard instead of atrocities personally witnessed, that they had fled in anticipation of terrible events rather than their actual experience.

"The other problem," Amira said, "is that Chalasan is at the very top of the valley, where the road dead-ends, so it's not a place that anyone passes through even in normal times. Which also means there was no chance for escape. As soon as the KPLA reached the mouth of the valley, they were trapped up there."

She went silent, stared across her room, at its ornate brocaded wallpaper, its gilt fittings. She appeared close to tears, but David couldn't think of what to do or say to comfort her.

"You know, I lived there for a couple of years when I was young," she said at last. "The typical émigré's story; my father didn't want me to forget the homeland, so he sent me back. I lived with my great-aunt. Zahra, my grandfather's youngest sister. She must be in her seventies now. She taught me how to sew, to cook, how to milk the sheep"—Amira smiled to herself—"all those things a proper Kutaran woman should know how to do. But she was so sweet to me, Zahra, so kind. I remember when I was leaving to go back to England, she cried and cried—we both did, because for two years, we'd been like mother and . . ." She turned to David again. "Well, this is something that I think is very difficult for most Westerners to understand, but they're all related to me, every last person in that village—a third cousin, an aunt's uncle's aunt, it becomes quite impossible to keep track—and since this started, I've had this fantasy. One day, they'd all come over the mountain together and I'd be here to meet them. I'd bring them to the hotel. I'd wire my grandfather for the money—he would send it instantly, as much as was needed—and we would all just stay here for as long as it lasted. The Contessa would love that, wouldn't she? Five hundred primitives running around the place?"

She blinked rapidly, the tears seemed very close, but then Amira shook her head violently, transformed in that odd, instantaneous way of hers. "Ah, the poor little oligarch feeling sorry for herself," she said with a grin. "It's all so tragic, isn't it?"

David smiled back. "Oligarchs have feelings, too."

She laughed and reared up from the bed, went to the dresser. "Would you like a drink?" She held up a bottle of whiskey. "It's the last of my duty-free. Single malt, of course."

"Of course. Yes, that would be nice."

She poured some into glasses for them, returned to the edge of the bed. She took a sip of the scotch, blanched slightly at its strength. "Anyway, enough on all this. Let's talk about something else."

And so they did. Not of the war, not of the tragedy that had come to consume their days, but of more pleasant times. David told amusing anecdotes about the diplomats who had once worked and lived in Kutar, stories from his previous foreign postings. She told of growing up as a child of privilege in the stately preserves of Sussex, of the reception where she had first met the Queen of England and been surprised by how petite she was. And eventually there came that moment that David knew well, when their glasses were empty and a silence had held too long between them, when Amira stared down at the design by her bare feet and he watched her, and then there came that next moment when she turned slowly up to him.

"Well," she said, "it's getting late."

And looking into her eyes, David wasn't at all sure if she expected him to make an overture, what her reaction might be if he did. But in the next instant, he realized this was actually not something he wanted to do.

"Yes, it is," he said, and rose from the chair. "I'm sorry for your day. I hope you get better news soon." He set his empty glass on the desk and headed toward the door.

"David?" She called in a soft voice, waited until he turned. "The relief ship coming—it *is* a good thing, isn't it?"

One hand on the doorknob, David hesitated. "I think so." He tried for more conviction. "I don't see why it wouldn't be."

He went along the hall to his own room, walked out onto the balcony. Some of the others in the hotel were still awake—light spilled onto the balconies to either side of his—but beyond there was only darkness, the sea's night surf coming to him as a whisper. At one time, David might have been soothed by this, but now he felt closed in by the blackness before him, the velvet hush of the sea. He left his balcony, his room, made for the staircase and the old chair he had set out upon the roof.

———

At the stroke of midnight of November 4, David finally unraveled the apprehensions that had troubled him ever since the day he had first read the rebels' communiqués, finally saw the awful trap they had walked into. But then, at that precise moment, so did everyone else in Laradan.

At seven that morning, the SS *Esmeralda* had appeared on the south-southwest horizon, its progress toward Pier 4, Slip 3 of Central Harbor watched by thousands of onlookers gathered along the oceanfront promenade. Immediately upon docking, the ship's cranes had swung into action, hoisting the various pallets and crates from the ship's holds to place them on the wharf. At 1:30 PM, half an hour after the *Esmeralda* had slipped from its berth to make for the open sea, dock stevedores under the supervision of Paolo Alfani began shuttling this cargo down the long wharf and into the harbor's main warehouse.

Among those who observed the operation from the harbormaster's office–various Kutaran government ministers, most all the foreign residents of the Moonlight Hotel–there had been a general feeling of relief, for the entire undertaking had gone off like clockwork, could not have more faithfully followed the rebels' rigorous instructions, which meant, of course, that the way was clear for the ship to return the following week with more supplies.

It was only later that night, while sitting on the Moonlight's roof, that David began to grasp the subtler import of all this. What he and everyone else involved in the operation had been compelled to overlook was that their good fortune–the new tents being distributed to Laradan's refugees, the fresh medicines replenishing the hospitals' pharmacies–had only come about because the rebels had ordained it, that the price for this good fortune was having scrupulously submitted to the dictates of their enemy.

Perhaps the psychological effect of this would have been reason enough for the rebels to devise the plan. After all, the sight of that ship returning each week laden with goods and always leaving empty would serve to constantly remind the city residents not only of their utter dependency on those on the ridge, but that they now lived in a place from which there was no escape. But sitting on the hotel roof, David at last appreciated the even more cunning motive behind the scheme.

Having placed Laradan in a stranglehold, the rebels had now provided it with a tenuous lifeline. And having so recently compelled the outside world to abandon the city, they had invited it back in just enough to make it that lifeline's guardian. Now those on the ridge could do whatever they wished, because any threat of retaliation from the outside meant that line could be cut instantly, the onus of causing Laradan to starve falling on those enlisted to keep it alive. A Trojan horse, David had thought to himself these past days, but on that night, he saw it was more akin to a hostage situation, the relief ship the weapon that would hold everyone in thrall.

In fact, some of this began to dawn on David a little before midnight—perhaps ten minutes before the hour—when there came a series of soft popping sounds over the coastal ridgeline and Laradan was suddenly aglow in the green bath of aerial flares. This illumination lasted long enough for those below to look to the skies, to gaze up at these unnatural stars and make one last prayer against what fate might hold for them.

Then, just as the bells of St. Bartholomew's church in the Old City began their midnight tolling, almost as if the bells themselves had summoned it, the ridgeline exploded in sound and smoke and a thousand streaks of red-and-orange flame. At long last, death was coming for the people of Laradan. At long last, their terrible time of waiting, of hope and prayer, had passed.

Eight

For most people, any conception of what happens when an artillery shell explodes is likely to be based on certain war movies they have seen. In this regard, the citizens of the city of Laradan were no different.

Typically in such movies, a shell explodes on open ground and anyone unlucky enough to be standing nearby is flung—or somersaulted, or cartwheeled, depending on the desired cinematic effect—to their death. Whatever limited realism this depiction might have to what occurs on a conventional battlefield, a wholly different dynamic takes place when a shell explodes in a city, as the people of Laradan were to learn on that night the rebel guns opened up.

It comes down to physics. What movies cannot render is that, often, the most lethal aspect of an explosion is not the scattering of projectiles in its blast, but the tremendous shock wave that blast releases. And whereas this shock wave rapidly weakens over the open ground of a traditional battlefield, the canyonlike structure of a city provides both channels for it to travel and an amplifying effect as it caroms off surrounding walls and buildings. This wave, too, will gradually weaken as it moves away from the source, but its exponentially more concentrated force will inflict far greater damage. It is also likely to leave behind clearly delineated, concentric circles of destruction. Much like reading the growth rings of a tree, a seasoned observer examining these circles can quite easily determine the explosion's precise epicenter, even if no obvious physical evidence–a crater, for example–is left behind.

In the immediate blast area, the ground will be swept perfectly clean. Naturally the size of this epicenter will depend on the explosion's magnitude–given the range of ordnance most commonly used by modern armies, it might extend anywhere from fifteen to eighty feet–but within this area, there will not be a scrap of paper or a nugget of loose asphalt, and anyone unlucky enough to have been standing there was not flung or somersaulted to their death, but vaporized: not a tooth, not a patch of clothing or a shoelace, they have simply turned to mist.

Moving past the epicenter, one will begin to come across small bits of debris, including scraps of flesh, but initially these will be so minute and degraded as to be unrecognizable. A little farther out and these scraps will become larger, but distinguishing them from mere detritus will still be difficult because human bodies break apart in unpredictable ways, and the parts here will be blackened with scorch marks, encrusted with dirt and gravel, so as to be easy to mistake for clumps of singed fabric or even twisted fragments of metal.

Beyond this ring, the human remains will start to take on recognizable form. At first, these are likely to be mostly detached limbs and torsos, some still clothed, but most naked or bare to their underwear, their outer garments having been shredded or burned away in the initial blast. In this area, there may also be a number of bodies without heads. This is because the head is the heaviest part of the human body, as well as its most delicately attached, and in the tremendous concussion of an artillery blast, it often severs at the top vertebrae of the spinal column. It is not at all uncommon in such situations to come across three or four heads lined up against a street curb or the side of a building some distance away from the explosion, the heads having rolled until coming to an obstacle to halt their momentum. In this section, one will also begin to come across the first of the survivors, most grievously wounded, and since many of them will still be conscious and pleading for a help that is beyond the ability of anyone to give them, it is usually this area that is the most upsetting to the eyewitness.

At a certain point away from the epicenter—anywhere from sixty to three hundred feet, again depending on the explosion's magnitude—it will appear one has reached the outer edge of destruction, but this will probably not be true. Depending on the trajectory of the shell and the architectural peculiarities of the city, shock waves are likely to have traveled through the surrounding buildings and alleyways, and there one is liable to find a number of more dead with no visible wounds upon them. These will be people who have essentially been crushed, their internal organs bursting from the tremendous split-second force to which they were exposed, and it is not at all abnormal to find these victims still sitting upright in chairs, as if they are merely napping or gazing meditatively into space.

But as ghastly as all this is, those who fall direct victim to an artillery shell's blast and shock wave normally represent only a portion of those killed when a city is bombarded. Many more are felled by glass shards from blown-out windows; these are like thousands of jagged daggers streaking out in all directions, sometimes with enough velocity to pierce metal or concrete or pass clean through a human chest. Others die from having buildings topple on them. And then there are the fires which so often accompany bombardments. While more advanced armies have developed firebombs that literally suck the oxygen out of a targeted area, quickly exterminating all within, the more common form of death in such circumstances is the protracted ordeal of carbon-monoxide poisoning as the building around the victim slowly burns. And then, of course, there are those who linger for a time, who don't succumb to their wounds until the next day or the one after that. Of all these ways to die, the people of Laradan were about to gain a terrible education.

While the rebel gunners on the ridge clearly had specific targets in mind that night, the very close range from which they were firing ensured these objectives were soon accomplished. So many shells landed amid the telecommunications complex atop Baktiar Hill, for example, that within the hour, all three of its transmission towers were toppled, the various buildings in the compound burning beyond salvage. Considerable attention was also paid to Laradan's main bus station, as well as to the government ministries that lined People's Struggle Boulevard. The results in this last sector apparently disappointed—built by the British in a blocky, late-Edwardian style, the buildings' solidness didn't lend to spectacular ruin—for the artillery batteries soon abandoned that district in favor of the rest of the city.

Here they let loose without design. A concentrated cluster of shells might abruptly tear into one corner of Laradan, followed by a single explosion a quarter-mile away, followed by another cluster a quarter-mile beyond that, and caught in these showers of fire and steel might be any manner of things: the stacked-in homes of a hillside neighborhood, a downtown office building, a traffic circle, a small shop that made wedding gowns.

What this meant for the people of Laradan was that safety lay nowhere that night, that death could find them just as easily in wherever they might flee to as in the place where they stood. Some residents sought refuge in the basements of their houses or apartment buildings, carting down blankets and mattresses, food and candles and children's toys; some of these died when their buildings collapsed or burned above them. Others hurried down streets in whatever direction they imagined protection might be found, jostling and colliding with those who imagined it was to be found in the opposite direction. A man survived because he turned a corner just as the street behind him was struck. A woman died because she turned a corner and ran straight to that spot where the next shell was to land. In short, this was a war like any other, in that what separated the living from the dead could be attributed to luck or fate or the divine, in that what could be said about the difference was either a very great deal or nothing at all.

Then, at precisely six that morning, the guns on the ridge fell silent as one, and there rose over Laradan that odd duet which plays in a stricken place: the smothering quiet, the pierces of noise. Across the city, now cloaked in a thick shroud of smoke and dust, there came the wail of sirens, of people in pain and mourning, the deep shuddering gasp that buildings make when they fall, and it was a time of flames lashing against a receding night, of pillars of black climbing toward a million dimming stars, an endlessly dying dark that finally surrendered to a dawn of such radiant and careless beauty that those below could almost believe the earth itself was taking note of their torment, had chosen this day to either comfort or mock them.

It was one of those flimsy plastic bags given out at the markets, the kind that tear very easily, and it performed lazy loops on the wind, like a languishing kite. David's eye was drawn to it by its erratic flight, by the bright-red color of its stenciled design, but then the bag settled to earth, scudded across the ground by his feet, and he saw that the red was not a design but a spattering of still-wet blood.

He had never been in a war before, but on those occasions when he had tried to imagine it, David had always assumed the experience would teach him a great many things; this was certainly the reputation that war enjoyed. So far, however, on his first true day of war, he could only identify two very small and distinct areas in which his knowledge had been expanded.

One had to do with paper. In all the books he had read, in all the movies he had seen, David couldn't recall any reference to the sheer masses of paper that war sets loose, that it might flutter through the sky amid the smoke and dust like confetti, that it might spread so thickly over the ground that it resembled a blotchy blanket of snow. Letters, accounting ledgers, children's schoolwork, pages torn from magazines, the paper was all around him as he walked through Laradan that day. It skipped along in the gutters. It waved at him from ruins. It clutched at his ankles.

His second area of education had to do with blood. He now knew that blood exposed to sunlight turned dark purple, nearly black, very quickly. He now knew that if blood were allowed to pool in the open air, it would coagulate and puff up until it resembled so much spilled pudding or insulation foam, and he had already learned before seeing the shopping bag looping through the air that blood on plastic can take a very long time to dry, that without a surface to absorb into, it might stay wet and red for many hours. Perhaps the oddest bit of knowledge he'd picked up in this sphere was that it was bees, even more than flies, that were attracted to blood. David had never previously seen enough bees in Laradan to take notice of them, but the bees were everywhere that day, great, frenzied swarms.

Beyond this, though, war was teaching him very little, and he wondered if this had been Eddie's experience in Vietnam as well. His brother had only been in the field eight days before he died, but in that time, had he seen things like this, had he been shocked by how little he learned from it?

Following the rebels' prior instructions, Nigel had set out for Gowarshad Pass at noon, and David had again accompanied him. There they had been met by the same rebel messenger as before. Once again, the young man had not uttered a word, had given no indication that he understood English or even the local language, before handing over another plain white envelope and walking away.

Back in the embassy car, Nigel had begun urgently listing

what they now must do, what needed to be communicated to the palace, to their own governments, to the others at the hotel, and David had stared out at the ruins they passed, at the soldiers and children and housewives scrabbling with picks and shovels and bare hands, and all at once he'd been unable to listen to the First Secretary for another minute. He told the driver to stop and, without explanation, had stepped out into the heat and burned dust of that day and begun to walk.

He did so with no particular destination in mind. He only knew he couldn't return to the hotel just then, couldn't sit in a conference room at the palace or the defense ministry and gaze at the stunned, haggard faces that would gaze back at his, and so he walked in the manner of the lost, past cars turned to blackened husks and buildings settled to powder. The longer he walked, the more helpless he felt, and this became something of a torment—how he envied Nigel his sense of purpose—and so he looked into the eyes of those he passed, into their deep and hollow stares, and he tried to derive some comfort in the awareness that they felt helpless, too. He turned onto Feroze Street. Where the Sarvanya orphanage had been, he saw a new patch of sky, a view toward the mountains that had not existed before.

By late afternoon, he found himself at the edge of Independence Park, at that corner where the medical tent stood.

To accommodate the number of wounded still being brought in, a section of the lawn had been cordoned off with rope, and David watched the doctors and nurses picking their way through the injured there. He saw Amira among them. She was in a green hospital gown and the bloodstains upon it were deep purple, the color of plums. This was a color of blood David hadn't yet seen, and he wondered if it was a trick of the waning light or the result of some protective coating on the gown.

He leaned against a tree a short distance away and watched Amira move among the wounded, stooping down to comfort an old man, stroking the head of a young child. What a peculiar sight she was there in her plum-speckled gown, gracefully threading her way amid all those torn, pained bodies, and it occurred to David that she was like an angel set down in their midst. He didn't believe this was a strange thought to have. He believed it would have occurred to anyone who had walked the streets of Laradan that day and come to this spot.

———

They gathered that evening in the lobby. Nigel produced a photocopy of the latest note from the rebels, and it passed from hand to hand in silence.

It began much like its predecessor. The SS *Esmeralda* would be allowed to return to Laradan that coming Friday, at the same hour and charting the same course as previously. Following was a list of those relief supplies that would be permitted on this voyage, and it was a source of bitter amusement to those in the lobby that the rebels had included a number of medical items designed to treat just the sorts of traumatic injuries their bombardment had caused: antibiotics, coagulant drugs to stem blood loss.

For the first time, however, the KPLA had spelled out their demands for ending the war: unconditional surrender of the royal government—and this was followed by a lengthy postscript:

Until hostilities cease, and so long as all procedures are faithfully observed, a diplomatic pouch consisting of one standard-size mailbag will be allowed to go out on the *Esmeralda*, and the same delivered upon her return. This pouch shall be for the exclusive use of official correspondence of the current regime in Laradan, and of those foreigners residing at the Moonlight Hotel. Mr. Nigel Mayhew shall be solely responsible for its contents, and any violation of its intended use will result in the immediate termination of this arrangement. The captain of the *Esmeralda* will personally retrieve and deliver these mail pouches, this exchange to take place at the harbormaster's office at Friday noon. A copy of these instructions, as well as the list of supplies permitted on the next voyage, has been transmitted to our agents in Palumbo for dissemination to the relevant authorities and agencies.

"But why all this about the mail?" Amira asked. "They give their terms for ending the war in one sentence, and spend an entire paragraph on this mail pouch."

Nigel glanced at David, gave the others a thin smile. "Because, as those rotters up there surely know, that pouch is now our only means of contact to the outside."

Laradan's telephone system had gone out during the night—a result of the rebels' meticulous shelling of the various switching stations—but throughout that day, there had been growing concern voiced over the toppling of the broadcast towers on Baktiar Hill. The most dire rumor held that, along with shutting down the national television company and most radio stations, their destruction had meant the severing of all communication links to the outside world. For some of those at the lobby table, Nigel's words were the first confirmation that this was, in fact, the case.

"But surely there is an auxiliary system," Paolo said. "At the Defense Ministry, the palace?"

The First Secretary shook his head. "It was all linked to the broadcasting towers. The same for shortwave radio transmission. Remember, this is a rather poor country."

"What about a satellite hookup?" Stewart asked, looking to David. "There's got to be a sat phone at the embassy."

David shook his head. "All the advanced communication gear was taken out in the last evacuation—they were worried about it falling into rebel hands. I've been making my calls to Washington over a secure line, but that's dead now, too, so I assume it was linked through the towers."

Nigel nodded. "Same at the British embassy."

Stewart slumped back, shook his head in disgust. "Christ, the biggest scoop of my life, and I can't even fucking file."

Across the table, Amira's eyes narrowed as she contemplated this. "So does that mean the rest of the world doesn't even know what's happened here?"

"Quite possibly," Nigel replied. "Perhaps some initial reports went out before the towers came down, but it's possible no word went out at all."

A troubled quiet settled over them. For everyone there, feeling a part of the global community was so taken for granted it was rarely considered, and much of that stemmed from the ease of modern communication, the assuredness that one could telephone or send a telex halfway around the world at a moment's notice. Now being in Laradan was like having been cast onto a furthermost frontier, a place where one might simply be swallowed up with no one being the wiser.

From his position at the head of the table, Nigel lightly cleared his throat. "Well, not an ideal arrangement, obviously, but it appears we must"–he glanced at David–"what's that cowboy expression you chaps use, 'play those cards with which we have been provided'?"

"Close enough," David said.

Nigel nodded, looked to the others. "Naturally, Richards and I intend to take advantage of this mail pouch to send comprehensive reports to our governments–as well as request that we be given satellite phones–and I'm sure McBride here will want to send out a lengthy dispatch. For the rest of you, by all means take this opportunity to notify your loved ones." His gaze lingered on Amira and the Contessa. "At the same time, we should understand that nothing is likely to improve here anytime soon. From my discussions at the palace today, it's clear the government has no intention of surrendering, and there's no reason to think the KPLA will lessen their demands–which means they might resume shelling the city at any time, or even launch a ground assault. And we must remember that we've six more days before the ship returns and our reports even go out. For these reasons, I feel it's my duty to urge each of you to leave. There are still a few fishing boats in the harbor that can be hired, and while this might be a dangerous journey—and, no doubt, quite dear—it remains an option." He paused. "For now. I think we can all foresee that within a very short time—a matter of days at most—others will have this same idea, and the last of those boats will be gone."

The First Secretary suddenly seemed to realize he had directed this exclusively to the women and, as if to amend himself, glanced at the other men. "This applies to all of us; nothing to be gained for any of us to come a-cropper in this place."

Over the course of that very long day, the residents of the Moonlight Hotel had traversed the stricken city seeking those places where their help might be most needed—and they had discovered it was most needed everywhere: at field hospitals and relief centers, amid the ruins of fallen buildings. Even the Contessa had made a contribution of sorts, visiting with the terrified families gathered along the oceanfront promenade, her blithe manner and terse words of sympathy producing a peculiarly calming effect. Some of them had been horrified, stunned to their core, by the things they had seen, and now, sitting around the mahogany table—exhausted, some still coated in the dust of their labors, some marked with small cuts and mottling bruises—they looked to one another in response to Nigel's words.

But if the horrors of that day had brought feelings of fear and impotence, they had also provoked more powerful emotions: a kinship borne of shared sorrow, a sense of being needed, desperately so—and, not least, that hard resolve which is forged in deepest anger.

Since, despite his late addendum, the First Secretary's advice had clearly been directed at the women, it was upon them that gazes ultimately settled.

Amira shook her head. "Thank you, Nigel, but I'm not leaving."

All turned to the Contessa.

"Absolutely not," she declared in a strong voice. "This time, we do not run. This time, we stand up to the savages."

It was unclear if the old lady was invoking the royal "we," as was her wont, or if she had chosen to speak for all of them, but the effect was the same. Around the table came smiles, soft laughter. Even Nigel seemed to think better of his counsel now.

"Well, bravo, Contessa," he said, "bravo. We'll teach these bloody vandals a lesson yet."

As the assembly was breaking up, Nigel caught David's eye, motioned for him to follow him out the French doors.

On the poolside terrace, bits of ash skittered along the flag-stones, the air carried the smell of burning. Nigel clasped his hands behind his back as he gazed into the night.

"Just wanted to touch base with you about these reports of ours. Have you given thought to what you'll tell the State Department?"

David shrugged, puzzled by the question. "Well, exactly what's happened."

Nigel nodded, turned to him. "And how do you think they'll react?"

He fought the urge to shrug again. "I don't know, but they'll certainly do something. They're not going to let this stand."

"Armed intervention? The Alliance back in here?"

"Maybe. I mean, after all, Kutar's an ally, and the KPLA has just shelled a civilian population. There's going to be some kind of response."

"Because that's really the only option now, isn't it? Armed intervention. Hopefully not headed up by that cretin Munn again, but anything short of that is pretty pointless, wouldn't you say?"

David studied the First Secretary, felt there was a subtext

here that he wasn't picking up on. "Why? What are you going to tell London?"

Nigel smiled. "The same, of course. But it doesn't matter what I tell London; London will do what Washington tells it to do. Now I'm not supposed to say that, obviously. I'm supposed to say that Great Britain has an independent foreign policy and, what with Kutar being a member of the Commonwealth, we will come to its aid regardless of the American response. But we both know that isn't true. We both know this will be decided in Washington, and my concern is that, having left this place once, the easiest course now is for them to do nothing." He gave David a look of sympathy. "Sorry, old boy. I know it places quite the burden on your shoulders."

Once again, David stared at the sheet of paper he had placed to one side of his desk, at the single sentence he had written there: "Dear Mom and Dad: By the time this reaches you, you'll probably have some idea of what has happened here."

With a sigh of frustration, he turned back to the paper he had placed in his typewriter, the beginning of his report to the State Department entitled "Urgent—Crisis Worsening in Kingdom of Kutar":

> *Dear Mr. Secretary:*
>
> *Between the hours of midnight and 6:00 AM today, Saturday, November 5, the Kutaran People's Liberation Army (KPLA) insurgents laying siege to the city of Laradan, Kingdom of Kutar, conducted an intensive bombardment of the city. Along with total destruction of the communications system, and extensive damage to government and transportation facilities, there was indiscriminate shelling of residential and business areas at nearly all points, resulting in massive loss of life and property damage. According to initial figures of the Government of Kutar (GOK), the confirmed*

casualty toll as of 6:00 PM today is approximately 1700 dead and
more than 5000 wounded, with the overwhelming majority in
both categories being civilians. In light of the high number of col-
lapsed buildings and lack of any reliable instrument to tabulate the
missing, GOK cautions these figures should be regarded as conser-
vative and subject to upward revision.

It had been nearly an hour since David had written that
single paragraph. His intention was to give a detailed, hour-by-
hour account of events in Laradan, a narrative he might add to in
the days ahead as circumstances warranted, but as he sat there, his
fingers poised over the typewriter keys, no further words came.
His earlier attempt to write his parents had, obviously, been even
less successful.

David told himself it was because the events were still too
fresh in his mind, or because he was simply exhausted, but he
knew it was more than that. Instead, it was the very things he
wished to tell that paralyzed him. Because what words were there
to describe what he had seen, what he had smelled in the air and
felt beneath his feet? Those words existed, of course, but his mind
seemed unwilling to find them.

He stared at the salutation he had typed, "Dear Mr. Secretary." How to appeal to this man he had never met? All he knew
about the Secretary of State was what he had read in newspapers
or heard from others—that he was personable, that he had a facile
mind. What were the words that might touch his heart? Did they
exist? If so, were they words that gave some sense of what Laradan
had been like that day, those graphic descriptions that had already
been penned about a thousand other battlefields in a thousand
other wars? Or would it be best to continue in the same flat tone
as his first paragraph, using facts and figures to tell of a city's
ruin, much as he had once reported on crop yields or electric
generation?

David raised his fingers over the typewriter keys again. He

recalled the Secretary had children, and this caused him to think of the Sarvanya orphanage on Feroze Street. "At approximately 1:30 PM local time," he composed in his mind, "I turned onto Feroze Street . . ." Again, though, the words seemed inadequate, his fingers over the keys remained still. His eyes traveled back to the letter he had started to his parents: "By the time this reaches you, you'll probably have some idea of what has happened here."

And what to say there? Well, assure them that he was fine, of course, but what after that? Surely not specific details of what he had seen, so what then? Talk about the weather? Describe the other guests at the hotel? Ask after Aunt Jane's bad back, or how the Cleveland Browns were doing? It was in just this way, sitting in his hotel room that night, that David began to have an intimation of that wall which rises up between those who know war and those who don't, between one's own life before war and after.

"I'm sorry," he muttered, as if to the pages before him, and he rose from the desk and went out onto his balcony.

The guns on the ridge were silent, as they had been since morning. In the portion of the city visible from that vantage point, David saw that several fires still burned, orange pools and pillars of gray smoke in the night. A breeze rustled through the shrubbery below, making it sound as if a light rain were falling, and on the sea was the glitter of moonbeams.

His eye was drawn to a small glow down by the gazebo which, after a moment, he recognized as that of a lit cigarette. David assumed it was one of the soldiers who now patrolled the perimeter of the hotel—perhaps the man had snuck through the back gate for the chance to smoke in peace—but then the cigarette burned brighter as it was inhaled, and he saw in the glow that it was Amira.

He felt her gaze as he came down the lawn and he stopped a short distance away, perhaps ten feet from the gazebo steps. Amira was sitting on the far side of the structure, her back to the sea, and although she wore the same white summer dress as earlier in the evening, the moonlight now gave it a spectral, indistinct quality, as if she weren't really there, and David was struck by the same thought he'd had watching her in Independence Park that afternoon, that she was like an angel set down in the darkness.

"I saw you from the balcony," he called. "But maybe you want to be alone."

Amira shook her head, and in the faint light he saw the whiteness of her teeth as she smiled. "No. Actually, I'd like the company."

He climbed the two steps to the gazebo, noticed the cigarette butts by her feet. "I didn't know you smoked."

"I don't, really," she said. "Peer pressure. I spent all day with the doctors and nurses down at Independence Park, and it's like a smoking marathon with them." She kicked the butts into a little pile with her sandal. "You're up late."

He glanced at the hotel, at his own room on the second floor, and saw he had left his lights on. "I've been trying to start my report to the State Department, but I seem to have writer's block. It's a hard thing to put into words, you know?"

She nodded. "I was trying to write my parents."

He crossed the open deck, the old wood moaning under his step, and leaned against a post. In the moon shadow, the gazebo cast its outline upon the lawn, delicate Moghul arches and trellises spread over the grass.

From that point on the lawn, there was a view down the entire length of the oceanfront promenade, all the way to Central Harbor. Along the stone walk small fires burned, illuminating the faces and bodies of some of those who had taken refuge there. David felt Amira come alongside, looking out at what he saw.

"What did your parents feel about you staying here?"

"Kind of mixed, I suppose." She leaned forward to place her elbows on the gazebo railing, peered down at the grass. "Worried, of course, but I think my father has secretly been rather proud; family–the extended family, you know?–it's very important to him." Down the promenade there came the sound of a child crying, the calming voice of its mother. "Well," Amira said, softer, "I suspect that'll change after today."

She straightened and turned her back to the view. "And what about with you, your family?"

David shrugged. "Similar, actually. My father's quite conservative, so the whole call-to-duty thing, that plays big with him. I don't think he realizes my staying was basically a matter of me drawing the short straw." He smiled. "My mother, she never wanted me to leave Cleveland in the first place."

An easy silence lingered between them. After a time, the wind shifted, and there came the scent of flowers and smoke. David leaned off the gazebo railing, turned his back to the city as well.

"Tell me about your village," he said.

"How's that?"

"Your village in the north. Tell me about it."

"What do you want to know?"

"Whatever you want to tell." He cocked his head toward the city. "Better than talking about that."

Amira crossed her arms over her chest, gazed across the hotel lawn, silvery in the moonlight. "Well, as I mentioned, it's the last village in the valley. The road in follows the river, you pass maybe seven or eight other villages. You go up about twenty miles, slowly climbing the whole time, the valley gets narrower, and then, at the very end of the road, the mountains all around, there's Chalasan. The hills surrounding it are terraced for the fields and orchards, and everything is very green–I suppose because you're so high, nearly to the snowline–but it's not good soil, very rocky, so everyone also has sheep and goats which they take up into the mountains. A stream flows through the middle of town, and all the houses–there's maybe a hundred or so–they're packed close together along its banks. And everything is made of stone: stone houses, a little stone mosque, stone alleyways, the square. It's really very pretty. The stream is fast-flowing, so wherever you are, even way up in the fields, you can hear it running. In the square there is a fountain, some benches under the trees where the old men sit."

She laughed suddenly, turned to him. "And then there's the house my great-grandfather built. He was a warlord, did you know?"

David grinned. "Yes, I did. 'The Scourge of the Altafaram,' I believe he was called."

"That's right." Her laugh grew more forceful. "Well, apparently he picked up a book somewhere about European nobility and how they lived—you know, the English manor houses, the French châteaus—and he decided that's how he should live also. But there must not have been any photographs or drawings in the book, because the house—it's absolutely massive—it came out very strange, just this crazy mix of different styles. And he built this tower. You know the kind of round turret towers you see in Germany and Switzerland? Well, he had to have one of those, too. It's forty, maybe fifty feet high. It's bizarre. When you come up the valley, it's just there, like some apparition."

She looked so radiant in her laughter, in her happiness, that David almost could not bear to look at her.

"But I really do love it up there," she said, with a gentle shake of her head. "I think about it all the time. I've practically covered my office walls with pictures of it."

"Your office?" David asked in surprise.

"Yes, my office in London. What, you thought I just played all the time?"

"I guess I just assumed, what with you being here this long . . ."

Amira nodded. "I'm a graphic designer. It's very project-oriented work—I do museums, art galleries—so I can set my own schedule, take a lot of time away if I want. Not that I'd planned being away this long." She smiled. "I'm appalled you thought I was just some Sloanie."

David laughed. "Not a Sloanie. More the ladies-luncheon type, heading up the local charity board."

"Well, I must admit, there's a lot of that too. Also benefit balls, sometimes two or three a week–the Chelsea Children's Hospital, the Battersea women's shelter, the Royal Hedgehog Preservation Society, the list is endless. God knows how much of my family's money I give away each year."

"Ah, the swarthy oligarch come to help the poor little English."

Amira laughed, reached over to playfully swat his arm. "Will you stop with that? Honestly, you're like a broken record with that."

They fell into a quiet, long enough to detect other sounds in the night: from the hotel grounds the soft clacking of palm fronds brushing against each other, and from beyond that odd high pitch which rises over a tranquil sea that is not really a sound but the lack of it.

"But, you know," she said, "I've often thought what it would be like to bring my friends here, what they'd make of it. They'd love this hotel, of course, but going up to Chalasan . . ." She chuckled. "I've threatened Kenneth with the idea for so long now, I imagine he's secretly quite relieved the war has come along to prevent it."

"Kenneth?"

"My boyfriend."

"Ah." David nodded.

The quiet between them seemed a bit pregnant now, and Amira moved to end it. "Anyway, why is it that whenever we talk, I'm the one who does it all?"

"That's not true."

"It is true. You've never told me anything about yourself."

"I told you I was from Cleveland. If you'd ever been there, you'd know that just about sums it up."

"But I've heard Cleveland's a wonderful city."

David shook his head. "I think you're confusing it with San Francisco."

"And what of your family? Brothers? Sisters?"

David hesitated for the briefest instant but then fell back to the reply he'd perfected over thirteen years, the easiest one. "No siblings. An only child."

There came a flash of light somewhere in the New City, and they turned in time to see a billow of fire and smoke shoot into the sky. Shortly after, the low rumble from the collapsed building reached them, like distant thunder.

"My God," Amira whispered, "how is this going to end?"

David thought of some of his favorite places in Laradan—the spice market, the little Protestant church on Javidan Square—and wondered what had become of them.

"I think you should go home, Amira," he said gently. "Like Nigel suggested tonight in the lobby. There's still time, but the last of the boats will fill up fast." He turned, saw she wore a quizzical expression. "Don't get me wrong. I admire everything you're doing here with the refugees, your bravery—we all do—but this is only going to get worse now, probably a lot worse."

Amira brought out another cigarette, lit it. "But I always knew it was going to get worse. Didn't you?" She exhaled a plume of smoke and it hung in the heavy air, a little gray cloud in the night. "Bravery. You know, I've been hearing that word all my life, but what does it actually mean? What does it mean to you?"

David didn't answer, just watched her.

"I thought you were brave for going up to the ridge with Nigel that first time. You didn't have to do that—in fact, we all talked about it after you left, how brave you were for doing that. But what is bravery, really?" She waved her hand at the city. "Before this, I always thought of it as a kind of selflessness, but now I think it's just the opposite. I think it's the selfishness of deciding what you can or can't live with. When you went up to the ridge with Nigel, was it out of bravery or because you wouldn't be able to live with yourself if something happened to him?" Her manner grew more tender as she looked at him. "I appreciate you worrying about me, David, I truly do, but I can't leave here now. I wouldn't be able to live with myself if I did."

He nodded, tried a contrite smile. "Okay. Sorry I brought it up."

Placing her cigarette on the gazebo railing, she motioned for his hands. "Let me see your cuts."

He had his shirtsleeves rolled up, and the cuts ran from his fingers all the way up his forearms, a lacework of irregular, narrow slices. Taking both of his hands by the wrists, Amira leaned close, studied the wounds in the weak light.

"I noticed them when we were all in the lobby. From digging in the ruins?"

David nodded. She moved up his right arm to gently poke around the deepest cut, a jagged slice through the flesh just below his elbow. It was still a bit painful, and he inhaled sharply at her prodding.

"Sorry. From corrugated metal probably; we've been seeing a lot of those. You should get a tetanus shot." She looked up into his face. Her eyes shone in the moonlight. "Do you remember where you got it?"

There had been a large crowd gathered before the Sarvanya orphanage on Feroze Street. Someone said they had heard voices from inside, and David had joined the men scrabbling through the rubble. He didn't feel the cuts at the time, it didn't even register that the blood dripping from his fingers might be his own.

"Probably on Feroze Street, over in the New City."

"Oh, Jesus, I heard about that: The orphanage, right?"

He nodded.

"I'm sorry," Amira whispered, and she caressed his arm, his cuts there, with a soft hand.

And at that instant, David remembered another night just like this one, standing in the moonlight with another woman with beautiful eyes, a woman in an emerald-green dress named Joanna. He remembered leaning against a railing to look out at the world with her, and he remembered moving close to kiss her neck, her jaw, he had felt the pulse of her on his lips. And that night had been such a short time ago, it had been an eternity ago, and standing there with Amira, David felt an amazement at all that had been lost to him so quickly.

Part of him wanted to kiss her the way he had kissed Joanna, to feel again that magical way one body might yield to another. But another part of him was afraid that maybe this was no longer possible, that never again would he feel the touch of a woman against his skin and think of it as anything other than comfort—and that was the last thing he wanted, that was the last thing he deserved.

He gently withdrew his hand from hers. "I should probably get back to my report."

Amira nodded, but there was sadness in her face. "You're not alone in this, you know? All of us here, we feel a kind of guilt."

In spite of the situation, David gave an incredulous chuckle. "You? What in the world do you have to feel guilty about?"

She shrugged. "For living while they die. For losing someone that should have been saved."

For a moment, he simply stared at her. Then he leaned forward to kiss her lightly on the cheek. "I'm sorry," he said.

Stepping down from the gazebo, David walked over the moonstruck lawn toward the hotel, and as he walked, he tried to put all other thoughts from his mind and to concentrate on the duty before him.

"At approximately 1:30 PM local time," he composed in his head, "I turned onto Feroze Street . . ."

By late Monday morning, some fifty-two hours after the bombardment had ended, the diggers working the collapsed apartment building on Halas Street at last penetrated to the basement rooms. There they discovered what appeared to be an extended family, but none of them were alive. Handing his shovel and gloves over to the young man acting as the site coordinator, David started down the street in the direction of the harbor.

He found Paolo in the warehouse that stood at the base of Pier 4, in the small, glass-enclosed office he had made his own. The businessman was poring over a sheaf of papers, making notations in the margins, but he seemed grateful for the interruption.

"Come in, come in, my friend," he said, sliding the papers to one side. "So you have found my little domain."

"It's not that difficult." David smiled as he took the folding metal chair across the desk. "It seems everyone down here knows you."

"Yes, well, the white suit, I rather stand out, don't I?"

It was more than that, of course. Apparently concluding that placing a foreigner in charge might limit the opportunities for pilferage, the Ministry of Social Welfare had made Paolo the de facto overseer of the relief operation at the harbor, the keeper of the keys to the warehouses. While this had undoubtedly engendered resentment among local officials, the decision had been thoroughly vindicated by the first voyage of the *Esmeralda*. With his proficiency in storage keeping and inventory, Paolo had ensured that all the incoming relief supplies were off the pier and securely warehoused long before the rebel-imposed deadline. Seeing that they remained secure, however, required constant vigilance, and in the three days since their delivery, the businessman had practically lived at the harbor, only returning to the Moonlight for meals and the occasional nap.

"So to what do I owe the honor of this visit?" Paolo asked, casting his arms wide.

David shrugged. "We miss you at the hotel. I wanted to see how you're doing."

"Yes, well, you've come to the hub, where it all happens." He pointed to two stacks of papers on the desk. "Here we have supply requests that lack proper authorization, and over here we have properly authorized requests for supplies that don't exist. You see? It really is the perfect job for a bureaucrat." Paolo chuckled, leaned back in his chair. "And how is it in the city today?"

"Better. The last of the fires are being put out. Still a lot of digging going on, though."

"And survivors?"

David shook his head. "Not many. Very few make it beyond forty-eight hours, and we're past that now."

Paolo sighed, gazed out the inner office windows to the warehouse floor. "It's very cowardly of me, I know, but I just don't want to see it. I never want to see things like that. From the hotel, straight along the promenade to here, to my boxes and crates." He gave an apologetic smile. "It's much easier that way."

"It's not cowardly at all." David turned to the windows as well. Extending across the concrete floor were stacked pallets of cardboard boxes, a small mountain of fifty-pound rice sacks. At the warehouse entrance, three harbor policemen sat on stools, middle-aged men in threadbare blue uniforms cradling old bolt-actions between their legs. "Your bodyguards?"

Paolo grinned. "The harbormaster has given me twenty of them, but I'm a little suspicious because they're all the oldest ones and I don't think their guns work. Still, it has its pleasing aspects. For one thing, they insist on saluting me. I've told them this isn't necessary, but it's a long habit with them, and already I'm growing quite fond of it." His smile eased away, his eyes grew thoughtful. "But it is nice to feel that I'm helping in some way, you know? Before, just standing by waiting, helpless, it was very frustrating, so to be able to do even a small thing . . ."

David nodded. "But it's not a small thing. It's a huge thing. If you weren't here, all this stuff would probably be in some general's basement by now."

His friend gave a shrug of modesty.

Their attention was drawn to a burst of movement by the warehouse entrance, the three lolling guards leaping up as one to accost an approaching man in a white robe. As if in anger, one snatched a slip of pink paper from the robed man's hand, and all three huddled to examine it, glancing between it and the visitor with equal distrust. Finally one of the guards barked a command, briskly led the man inside to the threshold of Paolo's office. After a quick exchange in the local language which David couldn't quite follow, Paolo placed the pink paper onto one of his stacks, pointed the men to a back corner of the warehouse.

"From one of the hospitals," he explained. "Apparently they are in urgent need of sterile bandages." As he watched the men recede into the warehouse, Paolo's face settled into a frown. "A difficult situation, no? The guards, they very much enjoy the power this job gives them, and I sit on top of the pyramid, the foreigner that everyone must come to with their bits of paper." He looked to David. "If this goes on too long, I think someone shall put a bullet in the back of my head."

Paolo smiled when he said this, but his eyes betrayed a certain worry.

———

Amira felt the explosions more than heard them. They registered as slight tremors that traveled up through her chair.

It was Wednesday night, and for the past several hours, the rebels had been shelling the city again. It was the first time they had done so since the initial bombardment, and in no way did the two compare. Instead of the frenzy of that first barrage, this one had a lazy, desultory quality–maybe half a dozen explosions in succession, then silence, followed by another set fifteen minutes later–as if the only purpose was to remind everyone they were still there, or to give their men something to do. At her hotel room desk, Amira was almost able to put it from her mind completely.

After great struggle, she had finally found a suitable form for writing her family and friends, and on the desk beside her was an impressive stack of those letters she had completed and which would go out on the *Esmeralda* in two days' time. The key, she had discovered, was brevity and falsehoods.

In each letter, whether to members of her family or to her friends, Amira had taken pains to downplay the effect of the bombardment–"not nearly so bad as you may have heard"–and to stress that, at the hotel, she was on neutral ground and far removed from where the fighting was taking place. She knew this wouldn't be wholly convincing to her family, familiar as they were with Laradan's small size, so with them, she had added a further layer of untruths. "All here feel the situation will soon resolve itself, either through foreign intervention or negotiations, which apparently are already under way. Should this not prove the case, I will, of course, arrange safe passage out–an option always available."

The only letter where she had managed a bit more than this was the one to Kenneth, her boyfriend. It had been nearly two months now since they had said goodbye at Heathrow Airport, and whatever longing Amira had felt for him had been alleviated these past weeks by their frequent telephone conversations. With that outlet now severed, she found she missed him a great deal. She had not written him in an overtly intimate way–after all, these letters were going out in a diplomatic pouch, who knew who might read them before they were delivered–but she had tried to convey her feelings given these constraints.

"I miss you terribly," she had written, "and I do hope you

understand why I've chosen to stay on here a while longer. But not very much longer, I promise."

But as she thought of it, Amira realized part of her was grateful that their long, chatty telephone calls were no longer possible. So much had changed with the bombardment–in Laradan, in her–and Amira didn't think she could bear hearing Kenneth tell of the latest comings and goings in London, of Terence's movie premiere or Nicole's latest romantic disaster, nor could she bear to tell him what it was really like here, what her daily life had become, the things she had seen. Theirs was an easy relationship, fun and light, and it would have been unfair to suddenly try to propel it to a new place. Maybe later, when they were back together, but not over the distance of five thousand miles, not while they dwelt in two such very different worlds.

A particularly powerful tremor passed through her chair, one that lasted for several seconds, and shortly after, Amira heard the cascade of sound, a series of low rumbles that grew louder and deeper as they overlapped and built on each other. Then quiet, a more abrupt quiet than she would have thought possible, and in this silence, she pondered what the unusual violence of those previous few seconds might indicate. Did it mean those shells had landed closer to the hotel than any before, or had the rebels fired more powerful shells? Or did it indicate nothing more than that the wind had shifted, because if there was one thing recent experience had taught Amira, it was the utter unreliability of sound, the completely mysterious way it could move and bend and change in the air. One could not help listening to it, trying to divine clues from it, and the futility of that brought a special kind of terror to being in Laradan now.

Sitting in the quiet, she recalled her conversation with David at the gazebo a few nights earlier, how he had urged her to leave, and this caused Amira to think of Fatima, the Moonlight cleaning girl.

Well, not actually a "girl" at all, but rather a woman precisely her age—twenty-nine—with a husband and two young boys. The family lived in the servants quarters at the back of the hotel, and Amira had often seen the father playing with the boys in that far corner of the garden. Earlier that evening, Fatima had come into the room with fresh towels.

From their previous conversations, Amira had learned that Fatima was originally from the northern town of Jawalar, and that her extended family had joined the exodus to Laradan in the early days of the war. Most of those relatives were now settled in one of the smaller parks in the western suburbs, and every day since the bombardment, Amira had asked after their welfare.

"Thanks to God, they are safe," had always been Fatima's cheerful reply. She had repeated the phrase that evening but, with the shelling resumed, its echoes passing through the room as she spoke, the cleaning woman had been unable to muster much conviction, she had seemed delicate and frightened.

At her desk, Amira now imagined how easy it might be to change Fatima's life. According to Paolo, there were still a handful of fishing boats in Central Harbor but, even at three thousand dollars a head, filling up quickly for the last passage out. Twelve thousand dollars for Fatima and her family, more money than the cleaning woman and her husband would ever see, but mere pennies to Amira, and she considered how effortlessly she might send this sweet woman and her family sailing off to a new life.

But not so effortless, in fact, because what new life would await them? A refugee camp somewhere? Four more lost exiles to join the millions already lost around the globe? And, of course, this was not truly a family of four; it didn't work that way in Kutar. There were grandparents, aunts and uncles, all those relatives who had come over the mountain from Jawalar. This was a family of dozens, maybe hundreds, and then these families tied into others until . . . Well, once you started down this road, you could just keep going.

It was so much easier for Amira. She had money. She was

one of the English Chalasanis. She had escaped before she was even born, and amid all the reassuring lies she had penned in her letters, she had also written one uncomfortable truth: for her, there would always be a way out. If there was one last seat on one last boat and that fare was a thousand times three thousand dollars, escape was "an option always available."

Maybe this was why she had reacted so strongly when David had suggested it.

Another violent shaking of her chair, another cascade of thunderclaps. Amira thought of leaving her room, of escaping the noise, but couldn't imagine where it was that she might go.

The noon whistle sounded, and David stepped over to the large picture window of the harbormaster's office to join Stewart McBride and the cluster of Kutaran government officials monitoring the activity along Pier 4. Or, rather, watching for some suggestion of activity. The ship's cranes had finished setting her cargo out on the dock some time ago, a gangway had been lowered from the *Esmeralda*'s midship and, per the rebels' instructions, it was at noon that the ship's captain was to disembark to collect the mail pouch. As the last shrill notes of the whistle died away, however, there was no sign of him—indeed, of anyone—on the freighter deck.

"Is he coming?" Nigel called from the far side of the office.

"Not yet," David called back.

With a disgusted shake of his head, the First Secretary went back to shoving the last of the envelopes into the heavy canvas mailbag.

All that morning, various Kutaran government cars had pulled to a stop before the Central Harbor administration building, and a steady procession of officials—junior ministers, military officers, palace courtiers—had trooped up to the harbormaster's office on the third floor. Each had carried a packet of some kind—plain

manila envelopes, others adorned with ribbons and sealing wax—
and these they had placed on the growing mound of such packets
on the harbormaster's desk under Nigel's watchful eye. From the
six-page master list that the First Secretary had compiled, it was
clear the Kutaran government was casting its appeals for help far
and wide: along with thick envelopes to its overseas legations were
others addressed to foreign heads of state and ministers, human
rights organizations and religious figures.

"Richards? Anything?" Nigel called from across the room
again.

David turned from the picture window, shook his head.
Swearing under his breath, Nigel stormed across the floor to join
him, his anger so palpable that several Kutaran officials scrambled
to get out of his way.

"Just where is this damned fool?" he hissed, staring out at the
empty wharf. "Doesn't he understand we've a deadline here?"

At very long last, a portly figure in a white naval suit emerged
from the *Esmeralda*'s pilothouse, shambled over to the head of the
gangway. There, he drew up to execute a great yawning stretch,
before casting a disinterested eye over his surroundings—gazing
this way and that along the deserted wharf—while absently
scratching at his groin.

"What in the devil . . . ?" Nigel muttered, but finally the man—
presumably the ship's captain—began a slow saunter down the
gangway. "Right," Nigel said, starting back across the room, "let's
get the pouch sealed up."

David knew that the intricate protocols governing the diplomatic pouch dated back to medieval times, but he didn't realize
that the process still involved an element of pageantry. The First
Secretary obviously did. By the harbormaster's desk, he reached
into his suit pocket to bring out a thin wafer of tin and a silver tool
that looked rather like a ticket punch. Tying off the nylon draw-
string of the now-bulging mailbag, he folded the wafer over the

cord just below the knot, then squeezed it with the seal press. When he was done, the tin bore a surprisingly detailed impression of the British coat of arms.

"Very impressive," Stewart McBride said, peering close. "You can even see the tongue hanging out the cat's mouth."

"Hardly a cat, McBride; the lion of St. George."

Stewart straightened with an earnest-seeming frown. "Yeah, I've always wondered about that; why a lion when there's no lions in England?"

Nigel eyed the journalist, tried to determine if he was joking or simply ignorant; with Americans, it was often hard to tell. "I'll lend you *The History of the English-Speaking Peoples*, volume two, I believe it is; he explains it in some detail." He lifted the mailbag an inch or two off the table. "Oof. Let's hope that chap has a strong back."

Presently, the *Esmeralda*'s captain appeared in the doorway of the harbormaster's office. He was a slovenly, corpulent man—a Greek by the name of Dimitrios Terezios, according to lading papers David had seen—and his short walk down the pier had left him panting for air, new patches of perspiration spreading over his already soiled and salt-encrusted uniform. His most arresting feature, however, was his eyes. Small and dark and closely set in a jowly face, they gave him the manner of someone perpetually aggrieved and prone to violence.

Perhaps this was why Nigel, in spite of his earlier anger, fixed the man with a determinedly pleasant smile. "Well, we're all very pleased you were able to make it, captain." He patted the side of the mailbag. "I'm afraid it's rather heavy, but I'm sure we can bend the rules enough to provide you with a handcart."

His breath finally calming, Dimitrios Terezios ran the tip of his tongue over his thick lips, took a long, slow look around the office. He appeared to be searching for just the right words in reply. "Fuck that," he managed at last.

Nigel frowned. "I beg your pardon?"

"Fuck that. I'm not pushing a cart. You want that on the ship, get yourself a couple of dockhands."

The First Secretary cast a quick, nervous glance at David, turned back to the captain. "Now see here, chap, I'm afraid that's really out of the question. The rebels have made it very clear that it is you, and you alone, who is being permitted out on the wharf." He tried another tentative smile. "And, as I'm sure you can appreciate, we're really not in a position to argue with them given the circumstances."

Dimitrios nodded. "Well, that's swell. But maybe what you don't appreciate is there's a higher principle at stake here–namely, that I'm a ship captain, and not some fucking dock monkey. You want to get that shit on board, you get yourself a cart and some dockhands, and have them haul it out there."

Nigel's patience was gone now, he raised his voice. "But that is utterly out of the question, man. The rebels were absolutely explicit . . ." He trailed off as the captain advanced on him.

"Let me give you some advice here, pal. I spent twenty years working the docks of Brooklyn, met people from all over the world–crossroads of the universe, right?–and you know what it taught me? It taught me that you try to play nice with these people, you play by their rules, they'll give it to you straight up the ass every time. Buddhists, Hindus, Muslims, they're all the same. You gotta stand up to them, tell 'em to fuck off every chance you get. It's the only thing they respect. You get what I'm saying here?" Oblivious to the dark stares of the Kutarans in the room, Dimitrios turned to David. "Moral values, in other words. Now I realize you guys've got your balls in a wringer here, but that doesn't mean you've got to give up your moral values. Because that's the only thing standing between us and the law of the jungle. You see what I'm saying here?" Receiving no reply, the captain wheeled and started from the room. "Tell the dockhands to put the bag at the foot of the gangway, I'll send a couple of my boys down to collect it."

As he watched the *Esmeralda*'s captain descend the staircase, Nigel slowly shook his head in disgust. "Our fate resting in the hands of a Greek; how much worse can this get, Richards?"

———

That night, David was passing the entrance to the hotel bar when he heard his name shouted. Looking in, he saw Stewart and Paolo at one of the back tables, the journalist urgently beckoning him with a raised hand.

"Excellent," Stewart called at his approach, "I need a drinking companion." He motioned to Paolo. "I'm afraid the Europeans just don't cut it on that front."

Paolo smiled at David. "I told him that in Italy we don't drink to get drunk."

"See what I mean?" Stewart wagged a finger. "'It's vital that a man get drunk at regular intervals in his life.' Socrates said that. Or maybe it was Emerson."

A third-full bottle of bourbon stood on the table and, judging by the slight wobble of his head, it was the journalist who had done it the most damage. Amin, the hotel valet who doubled as the bartender, was instantly at David's elbow.

"Just a beer, please, Amin."

"And another shot glass," Stewart said.

David slid into a chair. "So, what's the celebration?"

"Filing," Stewart replied. "It's an old journalistic tradition that whenever you file a long article, you get falling-down drunk. One of the more enticing features of the profession, frankly."

Amin returned with David's beer and a shot glass, which Stewart immediately filled.

"Nearly six thousand words," he continued. "That's not what they'll run, of course–I'll be lucky to see two thousand–but still a lot better than what I usually get on this beat. Haiku, I think is the technical term. If I was paid by the word out here, I would've starved to death a long time ago, as much as anyone gives a rat's ass about this region." He raised his glass in toast. "To the working class."

David sipped from his glass, set it back down.

"But that will change now, no?" Paolo turned to David. "With all the appeals the government has sent out, and once your report gets to Washington–"

He was cut off by Stewart's merry laugh; he clasped a hand down on Paolo's shoulder. "Hmm, sounds like our Italian friend here has been dipping into the harder stuff." He dropped his hand, shook his head. "Sorry, but all that doesn't mean a goddamn thing, nothing's going to change." He looked to David. "Isn't that right?"

David felt the stirrings of irritation with the journalist–maybe it was just defensiveness–but he covered it with a shrug, a smile. "I don't know about that."

"Really?" Stewart hunched over the table, glanced between the two of them. "Ask yourself this: Why are the rebels letting the palace send stuff out in the diplomatic pouch? That's pretty weird, isn't it? Letting them tell the outside how bad it is here, letting them beg for help? It doesn't make sense, unless you figure it's part of their plan."

"Their plan?" Paolo frowned.

But Stewart was looking intently into David's eyes and, suddenly, he didn't seem drunk at all. "To get everyone's hopes up, to let them believe someone might actually save them. This way, every week, everyone gets their hearts broken all over again."

He heard her footsteps, the light approach of them on the roof, and David turned to watch her settle into the armchair beside his.

"Thought I might find you up here," Amira said.

He grinned. "I guess I'm pretty predictable."

She nodded. "Like my old cat. Whenever I couldn't find her, she would be on the top of the living room bookcase. I never could figure out how she got up there–let alone why."

"Because she wanted to see out. The same with me." David glanced past the railing at the lights of the city, then back to her. "You think it's strange?"

"No. Kind of reassuring, really, like we have our own personal sentry up here, watching over us. We should put you on salary."

David laughed, settled his head against the chair back.

The rebel shelling of earlier that night had stopped—at least for the time being—and across the breadth of Laradan, perhaps a dozen fires burned. In the quiet, it was almost possible to imagine them as marking something festive, bonfires to celebrate an autumn harvest or a saint's day. For a long time, they sat in their chairs and watched the flames.

"What do you think Washington will do when they get your report?" Amira finally asked, but then immediately caught herself. "Sorry. You're probably sick of being asked that."

David smiled. "Not as sick as asking it myself." His smile eased. "I don't know, but they'll do something. I can't imagine them just letting this go on. The problem is, it may take some time."

Amira nodded, stared up at the sky. She noticed the air was slightly humid that night, the moon and stars had lost some of their desert brilliance, the first signs of the approaching fogs of winter. "You know, I haven't cried once since this started. Not that I'm naturally the weepy sort, but it does seem strange to me that with all that's happened . . ." She turned to him. "But maybe that's the reason. Because I know it's not going to end anytime soon, that it's too early for crying."

David nodded. Amira's gaze traveled down to his bare forearms perched on the armrests. It was hard to be sure in the weak light, but his cuts appeared to be healing, most little more than scratches now.

"Why do you come to the medical tent?" she asked softly. "I

saw you there this afternoon. You were leaning against that tree, just like yesterday and the day before."

David looked away, as if in embarrassment. "I don't know. I guess maybe I find it comforting to see a place where there's some . . . well, where someone's helping them, I guess."

"You don't think you're helping them?"

He vehemently shook his head. "No. I don't think I'm doing a fucking thing here."

All at once, she felt very sorry for him. "But that's not true, David." She motioned to his hands. "You've been helping rescue people in the ruins, you've been–"

"They've all been dead. Everyone we've brought out, they've been dead."

Amira bit her lip, as if to stave off a grief that had just flooded into her from nowhere. "Well, maybe with your report, then," she whispered. "When your report reaches Washington."

David nodded, and he realized that he needed to cling to this hope even more than her, perhaps more than anyone else in the city. "Yes," he said. "Maybe then."

In the end, he had not written about the Sarvanya orphanage on Feroze Street. He had not told the Secretary of how they had carried the children from those ruins, the neat rows they had made on the sidewalk of their small, broken bodies. He had not tried to describe crawling into a lost corner of that shattered building to find a little girl lying there, a little girl warmed by a shaft of sunlight slanting down from where a roof had been, a little girl sleeping the sleep of an angel in a children's picture book, so still and peaceful beneath her blanket of baby-powder dust that, right up until the moment he reached for her, David could almost imagine death to be a gentle thing.

Instead, he had continued his report in the same terse manner as he had started, and it was only in his very last sentence that he had slipped somewhat. "If I may close on a more personal note," he had written to the Secretary, "I would like to tell you that the people here look to us for their salvation."

From a far corner of the city there came a sudden towering of sparks against the night, a small, brilliant-orange mushroom cloud as a burning building collapsed in on itself.

On the rooftop, David became aware of a muffled, whimpering sound, and when he turned, he saw that Amira was crying into her hands, her anguish shuddering through her chest. He leaned over to lightly stroke her back with his hand, and he felt the dull pain of his own slowly healing wounds.

Nine

"The priesthood?" Amira was astonished. "You're joking, surely."

"I know, pretty fucking weird, isn't it?" Stewart grinned. "But, no, when I was a teenager, that was the plan. I was going to go to seminary, come out, and start spreading the Good News. And man, did I have the fire. Anyone came near me, they got a sermon. Even my parents got sick of it."

"So what happened?" the Contessa asked.

Stewart chuckled. "Oh, not a very original story, I'm afraid, Contessa. I started getting laid."

Without Nigel Mayhew's censorious presence, the old lady allowed herself to join in the laughter around the table.

It was Friday, the day of the *Esmeralda*'s return, and for most everyone at the Moonlight, anticipation of the event had made for a largely sleepless night. Now, with the crown of dawn just beginning to spread above the eastern mountains, all the hotel residents save Nigel had been gathered at the lobby table for some time.

"But seriously," Amira asked, "what changed your mind?"

Stewart cupped his hands around his mug of coffee, tapped

his fingers against it. "I think I just realized it wasn't for me, the best way to try to change things—help people, I guess."

"So you chose journalism instead?" The Contessa blanched. "Good Lord, man, whoever was advising you?"

Stewart grinned, turned back to Amira. "I just couldn't see what contribution I'd be making. I mean, sure, maybe to my own congregation, helping them with their problems or whatever, but on a larger scale, making a difference in the world."

Amira nodded. "And you feel you can do that as a journalist?"

Stewart shrugged. "I used to." He looked toward the windows and the swimming pool. "I used to think so."

If any of those at the lobby table had been pressed to describe their hopes at the *Esmeralda*'s return, they probably would have given a guarded reply. To play it safe, they might have said that all they wished for was a general sense of what the future held, some indication that the outside was moved by their plight—in essence, a sign that they were not beyond the conscience of a world they had once been a part of.

This element of caution would have been far less evident among the local population; in one of those paradoxes common to people living in war, a grinding sense of despair had somehow mutated in recent days into a fervent optimism.

In the two weeks since that massive inaugural bombardment, the war's effects had become increasingly pronounced in Laradan. Due to damage to the electrical grid, there were now rolling blackouts across the city, and there was growing talk that water would soon be rationed as well. Fish, once a staple of the Laradani diet, had vanished from the markets as the last of the fishing boats had slipped off with their far more lucrative cargoes of refugees. Other goods were becoming scarce and very dear, and this seemed especially true of those everyday items one never thought of in normal times: flashlight batteries, soap, toothpaste. Along with all this and the intermittent shelling, snipers on the ridge had taken to picking off the occasional random victim in the city's streets, a handful of them every day. In each of these ways, the residents of Laradan felt life's steady constriction.

But against this was the promise of the *Esmeralda*'s return. Every Laradani knew of the appeals the king had sent out on that ship, and to most it seemed inconceivable that the world, once informed, would not take steps to ease their suffering. As that week of waiting had worn on, this belief had given way to a kind of self-perpetuating mania. In recent days, each lull in the shelling had sent fanciful rumors racing through the city–that the rebels were running out of ammunition, that many of their gun crews, having sickened of such gratuitous slaughter, were refusing to open fire– and each successive dispelling of these rumors, in the form of another round of shelling, seemed only to spur more elaborate and unlikely tales. On Wednesday, a story had spread that American fighter jets were on their way to bomb the rebel gun emplacements, and into that evening thousands of Laradanis had lined the promenade to scan the horizons for the first glimpse of their foreign saviors. When those fighters failed to appear, the residents returned to their homes, not disheartened but convinced it could only mean the Americans were planning something even more ambitious; after all, so many reports, so many people, they couldn't all be wrong.

"Personally, I've always been a great supporter of religion," the Contessa said, laying a hand on Stewart's arm. "Trusting in God, upholding the faith, it's the key to civilization, isn't it?"

The journalist nodded. "A lot of people think so. But I had no idea you were religious, Contessa."

"Oh, not me," the old lady recoiled. "No, I mean for the peasants. Nothing better to keep them busy." She looked to the others with a wistful expression. "Why, I remember when I was a girl, my father would take us children to visit the peasant churches on the high holidays. It was something of a family tradition, you see?

Well, we went to the most dreadful little places—dark and smelly, the priest some illiterate bumpkin—but how happy they all were! All those hours of kneeling and chanting and circling about, those people loved that sort of thing. And do you know? It was just what they needed, it kept them out of mischief." She shook her head sadly. "It's when they got too much time on their hands that all our troubles started."

David arched an eyebrow. "Funny, I never realized that keeping the peasants busy was the purpose of religion."

"Well, of course it is, dear boy," the old lady chuckled. "Everyone knows that."

"I thought it was about the salvation of man, helping the suffering."

The Contessa sighed, looked to Stewart. "You were a man of faith once, you explain it to him."

A jaunty whistle announced the approach of Nigel Mayhew. He was clad in one of his navy-blue suits and seemed in fine spirits as he came across the lobby.

"Morning, all." He cocked his head toward the windows. "I've been watching from my balcony. She's just come into view."

As one, those at the table rose and hurried outside, descended to a point on the promontory that afforded an unobstructed view of the western horizon. In the far distance, a tiny dark object rode the ocean, a wisp of black smoke curled into the sky; at last, the *Esmeralda* had returned.

———

To escape both the stifling heat and the attention of the others in the crowded harbormaster's office, David didn't wait for the full sorting of the mail pile. Instead, the moment he spotted the manila envelope with its official emblem, he snatched it up and made for the stairwell. It was quite a bit cooler there, and he sat on a step to unfasten the envelope's metal clasps. The letter was on heavy bond and bore the signature of the Undersecretary of State.

Dear Mr. Richards:

I wish to sincerely thank you for your comprehensive report of November 10 regarding the current situation in Kingdom of Kutar. As you are no doubt aware, this administration has long been an outspoken champion of the principle that a nation's welfare is best insured by the peaceful coexistence of its citizens, and that intra-national strife–such as that described in your report of November 10–can only be counterproductive to a nation's long-term political, economic, and social stability. For these reasons, we are deeply concerned by the situation you describe in Kingdom of Kutar, and feel strongly that a cessation of hostilities there is not only desirable but necessary.

In furtherance of this goal, it is our judgment that the Government of Kutar (GOK) should continue to prosecute their military initiatives against the Kutaran People's Liberation Army (KPLA) until such time as a successful resolution of hostilities has been achieved. In amplification of this policy, please find enclosed personal communications from the Secretary to His Majesty King Abdul Rahman II, which we ask you to deliver to His Majesty or his assigned representatives at the earliest convenience.

I also wish to inform you that I have forwarded your request for a telephonic "scrambler" to the State Department's Office of Mission Security, Communication, and Intelligence, which is tasked to act upon such matters, with instructions that they consider your request as of the highest priority.

Finally, I am pleased to report that the contribution of the United States government to the current relief effort for the city of Laradan has totaled more than $4 million, complementing some $14 million from private American donor organizations, a level of assistance which I am sure will serve to remind the Kutaran people of the long-standing American tradition of generosity to those in need, as well as of our very strong commitment to their continuing welfare.

Once again, I thank you for your report of November 10, and

for the ongoing service you are performing for your country. The Secretary has asked me to personally assure you that we are all deeply concerned by the situation you have described, and that it is our firm intention to continue to monitor events in Kingdom of Kutar very closely. In the meantime, should you require further clarification of United States policy on this matter, or if there are new developments in Kingdom of Kutar which you feel should be brought to our attention, please do not hesitate to contact my office at any time.

David lowered the paper, stared at the stained stairwell wall before him in disbelief.

As a guard against disappointment, he had constantly played worst-case scenarios in his mind over the past week, but this letter was so much worse than anything he had entertained, than anything he had prepared for. Not a policy, not even the hint that some kind of American response might be forthcoming at some unspecified time in the future—at the very least, David had expected that. Instead, the "principle" that war was a bad thing, that it would behoove the Kutaran government to win it.

Staring at the wall, David turned his thoughts back on himself. Had he been naïve? Deluded? Had he honestly expected Washington to be so outraged by events in Kutar, so stirred by his report, that it would swiftly make plans to come to its defense? No, in all honesty, he had not. But he had also not expected his government to be so indifferent toward a friend and ally as to offer absolutely nothing and call it a policy.

"So what's the word, old boy?"

David turned to see Nigel standing at the top of the landing. "It's bad."

"How bad?"

David rose. "So bad that bad would be a huge improvement." He climbed partway up the stairs to pass the letter into Nigel's hand. As the First Secretary read, David leaned against the stair-well wall, gazed down at his feet.

After a time, Nigel grunted. "Four million in relief aid; that's about what the Pentagon spends for a screwdriver, isn't it?"

David gave a bitter chuckle. "For a flathead maybe; I think a Phillips runs around six."

At last Nigel lowered the letter in his hand. "Well, I'd say it rather explains my letter from the Foreign Office: 'deep concern, great disappointment that such a thing should befall a Common-wealth member, all best wishes.' Remember how I said London would follow Washington's lead on this?"

Through the open door of the harbormaster's office came a low hum of voices, the muted conversation of the thirty or forty Kutaran officials gathered there. David knew just from the tone carrying on the air, but he felt compelled to ask anyway; he mo-tioned toward the room. "And what are they hearing?"

"Outrage," Nigel replied. "Expressions of concern–that seems to be particularly popular. Some of the human rights groups are vowing action–protests, condemnations in parliaments, that sort of thing–but as far as anything concrete, anything from for-eign governments . . ." He flicked the edge of the Undersecretary's letter with a fingernail. "Of course, everyone rather had their hopes pinned on this."

David thought of the scene in that office, the generals and ministers and palace officials who had been expectantly gathered there for hours, waiting to learn of the world's response to their pleas, now waiting for him, their last–and, all along, greatest–hope to return from the stairwell.

"I can't go back in there, Nigel," he whispered. "I just can't face them."

For a long moment the First Secretary impassively stared at him from the top of the landing. Then he took the three steps down to David's level, leaned against the staircase railing to face him.

"Listen to me, old boy," he said in a low, measured voice. "America is the only chance this place has. I'm sorry it's like that, but we all knew that would be the case. So you must make a choice now. You either play it safe here, be the diplomat, or you get angry–maybe angrier than you've ever been."

David looked into the older man's eyes.

"We have forty minutes before the ship leaves," Nigel continued. "Along with your report, you can send out a response to this." He fluttered the letter in his hand. "You can tell them that they're betraying this country, that what they're advocating is impossible and they know it. You can tell them that their policy is, in effect, a lie." A sly smile spread beneath his mustache. "We can both do it, you to State, me to the Foreign Office. We can burn our bridges together."

As David considered this, a smile slowly rose to his lips, as well. He nodded. "All right. Let's do it."

When they returned to the harbormaster's office, all conversation instantly stopped, all turned to David in a kind of dread anticipation. But David avoided their gazes, followed Nigel to where Dimitrios Terezios waited for the outgoing mailbag to be sealed. Nigel took the ship's captain aside.

"Seems something rather unexpected has come up," he said. "We can send the pouch on ahead now, but would it be possible for you to wait a bit, to carry something else out for us?"

If Dimitrios weighed this request at all, it was only for the split second it took to shake his head. "No fucking way."

"But it's vitally important," Nigel pressed. "The future of this country may be at stake."

The effect of this plea was to make the *Esmeralda*'s captain's gesture of refusal even more forceful. "That's swell. But like I said before, pal, I'm a captain, I don't carry stuff. It's against the maritime code."

"What's the Red Cross paying you to make this run, Captain?" David interceded. "I know it's a lot, and if this city falls, all that ends." He watched Dimitrios's beady eyes narrow as he took this in. "All we're asking is for you to carry out a few sheets of paper, two letter envelopes, that's all."

The captain studied him with suspicion, finally issued a put-upon sigh. "Make it snappy; we have to push off at one."

Collaring a harbormaster official, Nigel quickly arranged to take over the shipping clerks' office on the second floor, away from the others, and there he and David settled at adjacent desks.

"Give them the what for, Richards," the older man prodded. "Shame the bloody bastards."

David took up his pen, stared at the blank sheet of paper before him. But there was no time to stare; he began to write:

> *Dear Mr. Undersecretary:*
>
> *I have received your letter of November 14. In it, you state the administration's position that an end to this conflict is to be achieved by the Kutaran government breaking the KPLA siege of Laradan. I must inform you that, given the government's lack of weaponry and disadvantaged situation, this option is utterly unrealistic. As a result, the administration's position on this matter cannot be said to constitute a policy, but rather the absence of one.*
>
> *As the acting American representative to Kutar, what I am asking for is clear guidance on what I should advise the government. Is American or Alliance assistance likely to be forthcoming in the near future? If not, should the government enter into negotiations with the KPLA forces, since this is the only practical alternative left to them?*
>
> *Please excuse my bluntness in this letter. It is made necessary both by the fact that I have very few minutes to write, and by the current situation in Laradan. As detailed in my accompanying report, since my last correspondence of a week ago, the continuing shelling of the city has resulted in the deaths of approximately eight hundred more residents, almost all of them civilians. In light of this, I feel strongly that we must be forthright with the Kutaran people*

as to what level of aid, if any, they can expect from us so that they might plan for their future or bring this killing to an end. To do anything less is to perpetuate a disservice to a nation we once considered a friend, and to call into question our own sense of national honor.

Very sincerely yours,
David Richards

——————

They decided to walk back to the hotel together, along the promenade. A soft breeze whispered off the water, bringing the scent of brine.

"So," Amira asked, "were you surprised?"

Walking alongside, David nodded.

The burst of resolve he had displayed in the harbormaster's office, the angry words he had penned, had only briefly lifted his spirits. Now he felt perhaps an even deeper sense of numbness than upon first reading the letter from the Undersecretary. It reminded him of that incredulity which can take hold some hours after witnessing a terrible accident—"Did I really see that?" "Did that actually happen?"—with the difference in this situation that the proof was tangible, it was in the State Department envelope he carried.

"Maybe I was naïve," he said, "but I thought at the very least they'd offer some vague promise, a veiled threat to the rebels. As it is, I can't say I'm looking forward to this meeting with the king."

He and Nigel were to be at the royal palace at 4:30 PM. While David had seen King Rahman II at a number of official ceremonies during the previous two years, had even shaken his hand on occasion, he'd never had a personal audience with him, and the news he bore that day seemed a particularly poor introduction.

"It's not your fault, you know?" Amira said. "He can't blame you."

David nodded. "Except I'm the American representative here so, ultimately, I am to blame."

They passed several refugee families that had chosen to make the stone walk their new home, their few possessions stacked in neat piles along its verge. With a bit of imagination, one could almost mistake them for the fruit and candy sellers who had once lined the promenade.

Attempting to shift his mood, David pointed to the bulging plastic bag Amira carried. "You seem to have a lot of friends."

She glanced down at the bag, smiled. "Yes, I suppose I do."

At the harbormaster's office, with everything else going on, Amira only had time to skim several of the letters—the ones from Kenneth and her parents, naturally, those from her two sisters—and there were probably thirty others in the plastic bag she had found to carry them all. She was looking forward to spending the afternoon with them, hoped they might provide some solace from the disappointment of the day.

"And what of you?" She motioned to his own plastic bag. "News from home?"

David nodded. "A couple of letters from my parents that I saw, a lot from friends, but I haven't even opened any of them yet." He gave a dry chuckle. "Funny, I was so desperate for news all week, but now . . ."

Amira nodded too.

Far out to sea, the *Esmeralda* was a small dark dot as it made for the distant port of Palumbo. Along the promenade, a number of people leaned against the railing, mutely watched the disappearing ship.

They were about a mile from the hotel when they heard the shell. It made a ripping, shuddering sound in the air, and then it exploded maybe two hundred yards away, among the trees of the riverfront park. As the plume of dust and debris billowed, the refugees living in that area began scattering in all directions across the grass—from that distance, they looked rather like insects or mice whose nest had just been disturbed—and then there was another explosion, much closer, so close that the concussion hit David and Amira like a slap to the head, left them dizzy and deaf.

"What do we do?" Amira shouted, but her voice came to David as soft as velvet.

He grabbed her hand, urgently looked around for someplace to shelter. But there was no place for them; whatever protective nooks or crevices there were along the promenade were already taken by those who now lived there, and so he clutched Amira's hand tighter and they started to run down the exposed stone walk. And even as they ran, David knew this was the worst thing to do, that the next explosion might just as easily come in the spot they were running toward as in the one where they had stood, that out in the open like this, a shell landing anywhere nearby would cut them down, that the safest thing was to stop and lie flat upon the stones. But find someone who will lie out in the open during an artillery barrage, and so they ran, tripped over huddled families, crashed into others running like them, kept running until their breaths were ragged and the blood throbbed in their deafened ears.

And then it stopped. Ten, maybe twelve, shells had come down on that small corner of the city, and then the gunners six miles away had decided to knock off for the afternoon, or to break for coffee, or to turn their attention elsewhere, and it was as if a tropical squall had swept across the stones and now it had passed. The runners stopped, the huddled rose to their feet, and amid the trees of the riverfront park, people began to gingerly approach those still-smoldering places where the shells had landed, to inspect the newly cratered ground and fallen trees and shredded tents.

David and Amira drew up on the promenade, and he pulled the hair from her face. From somewhere in the distance came the siren of an ambulance, but on their deadened ears it sounded cheery and light, like a cuckoo clock. "Are you all right?" he asked.

She nodded, even though her whole body trembled. They

continued on toward the hotel at a normal pace, and it was not until they were nearly to the Moonlight gate that Amira realized that she still held her plastic bag of mail in one hand, that she still clutched David's hand with the other.

———————

The king was a surprisingly small and delicate man, and somehow the vestments he wore for official meetings—the elaborate tunic robe, the high, bejeweled turban—seemed only to exaggerate his diminutive stature. This detail had been obscured, no doubt deliberately, on the previous occasions when David had seen the king, but in the grand Council of State chamber, with his courtiers and ministers arrayed along the conference tables to either side of his throne, the middle-aged Abdul Rahman II looked like some boy-king, his slippered feet barely touching the carpeted floor.

By palace tradition, David and Nigel sat side by side in armless chairs at the foot of the royal carpet, waited as the letters from the American Secretary of State and the British Foreign Minister passed from the Court Vizier to the Chief Minister, and only then to the king. David was sure King Rahman already knew every detail of the letters, their contents relayed by those court advisers who had been at the harbormaster's office, and the element of theater as he now read through the pages added to the tense silence of the room.

At last the king looked up, airily handed the letters off to an aide standing at his side. When he focused his attention on David, so did every other official in the room.

"So the American government advises us to take the ridge and end the siege," he said pleasantly. "Is that about the sum of it, Mr. . . . ?"

"Richards," David replied. "David Richards."

"Mr. Richards. Naturally I'm curious how they propose we do this. Their letter to me didn't go into specifics. Perhaps they did with you?"

David shook his head. "No, Your Majesty. They didn't."

"I see." The king briefly glanced along his rows of ministers, before returning to David. "So in other words, in response to our appeals, the extent of assistance the Americans are offering is the counsel that we win the war. Would you say that's an accurate assessment, Mr. Richards?"

The king said this in the same offhand manner, but David sensed the sarcastic tone was about to give way to something more heated.

"If you will, Your Majesty," he replied, "I don't think the State Department fully appreciates the seriousness of this crisis and—"

"No, it seems they don't." King Rahman cut him off, his voice now rising. "And whose fault is that, would you say, Mr. Richards? Could it be the fault of the envoy they left here, a failure on his part to accurately describe the situation?"

David managed a thin smile. "That's certainly possible, Your Majesty, but if I can—"

Nigel tried to come to David's rescue. "If it pleases, Your Majesty, let me say that both Mr. Richards and myself sent very strongly worded messages back to our governments this morning. I should certainly think that once London more fully understands the gravity—"

The king raised a hand, and Nigel immediately fell silent. "Thank you, Mr. Mayhew, but with all respect to the British government, I think we both know it is the United States which will decide matters here, so I'm rather more interested in what the American envoy might have to say."

Even from royalty, this slight was too much for the First Secretary; he straightened in his chair, jutted his chin. "I'm afraid I shall have to disagree with you there, Your Majesty. Great Britain has always maintained a foreign policy independent of its allies, especially when it pertains to members of the Commonwealth. I think I can safely say . . ."

But Nigel fell quiet again, this time under the weight of the king's slow, almost mournful, shake of his head. "Please, Nigel," he said softly. "We've known each other too long, and the situation is too grave." He returned his attention to David. "So what of it, Mr. Richards? How do we go about convincing your government of–how did you describe it?–the seriousness of the crisis?"

"Well, as Mr. Mayhew was saying, we've both sent very blunt messages to our governments, and–"

"Blunt messages?"

David nodded. "I explained that the military solution they propose is not feasible, that the only realistic options are outside intervention or negotiation."

"Negotiation?" The king glowered, sat forward on his throne. "With the rebels? But I've never talked about negotiations. Has someone in my government talked to you about negotiations?"

David took a quick glance around the room; all the ministers were looking at him with the same dark stare, as if in mimic of the king. "No, Your Majesty. My point in mentioning it was, again, to convey the severity of the situation, to explain that the solution they propose is unworkable and there needs to be a reappraisal of policy."

The king gazed at David for a long time before slowly sitting back, apparently mollified. "And you think this will have an effect?"

"I'm certainly hopeful it will."

King Rahman gave a caustic chuckle. "Well that's fine, Mr. Richards, but I think my people would like something a bit more substantial than your hopefulness."

David looked down at his intertwined hands in his lap. Maybe it was as simple as feeling under the scrutiny of everyone in that room, or maybe it was more than that, some reservoir of faith that still lay in a corner of his heart, but David found himself looking up, staring directly into the king's eyes.

"I have every confidence, Your Majesty," he said in a strong, assured voice, "that my government's policy here will change very soon." He saw that doubt still clouded the king's face, it lingered in the air of the chamber, and he felt compelled to add: "In fact, I am absolutely certain of it."

After another long silence, staring at David, the king began to nod. He turned to his ministers. "Well, I suppose we have no choice but to trust in that." He now offered David a conciliatory smile. "No offense, Mr. Richards, it's not a lot to carry us, but if it's all we have . . ."

When King Rahman abruptly got to his feet, everyone else in the chamber hurried to do likewise. "So, to better news next week," he said, and strode quickly toward a side exit.

To forestall the worst rumors likely to spread in Laradan from the *Esmeralda*'s return—because as giddily hopeful as those rumors had been before, it could be predicted they would now turn exceedingly dark—the king delivered a radio address that same evening. To his subjects, he struck an encouraging tone, offering that the United States and Great Britain were assessing their response to the shelling of the city, while their plight was drawing official attention in a number of European capitals, as well as at the United Nations in New York. If the king's characterization of the Anglo-American expressions of concern was highly creative, his account of developments elsewhere was barely less so; from what David had ascertained, most of Kutar's envoys in Europe had only managed to arrange noncommittal chats with mid-level foreign ministry officials, while the strenuous appeals of its U.N. representative to address the full General Assembly had instead won the promise of an appearance before a minor subcommittee in some two weeks' time. In any event, whatever heartening King Rahman's radio address might have given the populace was greatly undermined by the start of another intense bombardment from the ridge within moments of its conclusion.

Certainly most of the Moonlight residents shared a sense of gloom that evening. For them, however, it stemmed less from the effects of the bombardment, or even from their inside knowledge that most everything the king had said was a fiction. Rather, with their greater degree of worldliness, it was borne of the recognition that, in the modern era, if a first atrocity in war goes unpunished, so in all likelihood will any that follow, that, if history was any judge, their best hope for rescue had already passed.

Curiously it was the hotel resident who had always professed the least optimism about their situation, whose every comment on the topic had been laced with cynicism, who now seemed the most broken at being proven right. That night, Stewart McBride stretched out on his bed and forced himself to read again and again the telex that had been handed him off the *Esmeralda*.

The first part consisted of the full text of his article, as it had appeared in a number of American and European newspapers. The dispatch he'd sent out had run to nearly six thousand words, and he had mentally prepared himself for an edited length of less than half that; instead, the end product, as distilled by his desk editor in New York, ran to precisely 160 words.

A mere 160 words to tell of a city being murdered. To chronicle the deaths of two thousand people, the wounding of five thousand more. In fact, it was worse than that, because the entire second paragraph– seventy-two words, Stewart knew the number by heart–consisted of the same backgrounder on Kutar that had been attached to all his previous reports.

Below the text was a list of those newspapers which had carried the 160 words–some of the larger American newspapers, another dozen or so across Europe–followed by a postscript from the New York desk editor: "Might place more prominent if readers given context of why Kutar important, why should care. Keep to around 50 words. Stay safe."

No matter how many times he reread it, the postscript still made Stewart laugh. On his bed, he tossed the telex to one side, took his cigarettes from the nightstand.

Fifty words. In their generosity, they were giving him fifty words to make readers care about a place most had never heard of, a people they didn't know.

He lit a cigarette, blew a cloud of smoke toward the ceiling. As if only to put himself in an even darker mood, he lay there for some minutes and toyed with different possibilities.

How about, "People should care because innocent people are being slaughtered for no apparent reason, and to stand by and do nothing reflects badly on all of humanity"? No, Stewart thought to himself, too preachy. How about, "People should care because, according to one informed source, it was the United States and Western Europe that got Kutar into this fucked-up mess in the first place"? Or maybe the more direct "you," as in, "You should care, dear reader, because, in the opinion of one disgruntled observer, the day is coming when all the Kutarans of the world, all the poor wretches who have toiled their whole lives for nothing, who have been shot and tortured and spit on while you did nothing, are going to rise up and take revenge on you, and you won't see it coming because you could never be bothered to notice them in the first place." A bit wordy, Stewart reflected, probably well over fifty words, but he did rather like the tone.

But the longer he lay on his bed, the sound of that night's bombardment reaching him as a series of distant rumbles and cracks, the more Stewart understood that he wasn't truly as cynical as all this, that it was, in fact, some inextinguishable ember of optimism or naïveté he carried that had made the disappointment of this day so crushing. And he also came to understand that it was precisely this inextinguishable thing which had caused him to stay on in Kutar, that as much as he might profess otherwise, he still did believe he might make a difference, make people care, and as he lay there, he recalled moments in history where journalists had done exactly that. Photographs of children dying amid a famine. Accounts of horrific or pointless battles that had helped turn a people against a war. It was capricious, nothing was a given, it depended largely on what was happening—or more accurately, not happening—in other parts of the world at the time, but there had been those occasions when, against all odds, journalists had galvanized people to care and to act.

And as his thoughts turned in this way, Stewart was revisited by a singular memory. It was of the night the rebels had launched their surprise assault on the ridge, that panicked flight he had made with the Kutaran army and the other journalists across the desert from Zulfiqar. In his mind's eye, he still saw that fiery cascade of tracers and artillery shells and mortar rounds over Gowarshad Pass as they had approached the capital, and he remembered just where he had been on that highway when the images of the battle ahead began to take on sound—a low rumble at first, growing to a yawning roar. Everyone caught up in that desperate journey had known that reaching safety meant getting over that mountain, passing through that storm of explosions and fire, and as they started up the pass, Stewart had trembled with both fear and a kind of rapture, because he had never felt such terror, he had never felt so alive, and now, in his room in the Moonlight Hotel, it was as if he were reliving that whole ghastly, thrilling night.

And the combination of these things—the faith he had never fully lost, the memory he could not dispel—led him inexorably toward one thought. He could not make the world care if he stayed where he was, simply continued to chronicle the slow death of this city in his two-paragraph dispatches. The awful rapture he had known on the slopes of Gowarshad Pass would not revisit him at the Moonlight Hotel. The only path left was to go over the ridge.

When all this unfolded to him, Stewart was gazing at the small chandelier over his bed. To a degree he had never experienced in his short life, he was amazed just then by how dangerous the wandering mind could be, the truths it might discover and then refuse to let go.

———

They stood at the pool's edge, and for a long time, David merely stared at the journalist. "Are you out of your mind?" he inquired at last.

Stewart seemed to anticipate this response; he sighed. "Think about it. I'm not talking about taking off this afternoon, but just think about it. If I can get into KPLA territory and find out what's happening up there—not these bullshit rumors we're hearing down here—but what's really going on, maybe the outside'll finally take notice."

David stared into the pool. Whether due to a lack of guests or restrictions imposed by the city, Arkadi Hafizullah had recently shut off its intake valves, and the water had already dropped a foot or so under the harsh sun, was beginning to cloud. As he considered Stewart's idea, his thoughts naturally turned to the CIA report he had tucked away in his room, that he had only ever shared with Nigel. "And what if it isn't bullshit? What if they really are massacring people?"

"Then the outside has to respond, doesn't it?" Stewart said. "They can't just sit back and watch another genocide happen."

"I wouldn't count on that. I'd say the world's become pretty comfortable with genocide. More to the point, what happens to you? If they're doing massacres up there, I can't see the KPLA letting you interview people, take pictures."

Stewart shrugged. "It's the chance I take. We've got to do something here, David. We can't just let this go on."

David studied the journalist. He appreciated, more than he ever had before, that despite all his hard-earned cynicism, there remained about Stewart McBride the trace of the seminarian. "We're not just letting it go on," he replied. "We have to wait a bit longer, that's all."

"For what? For the American government to change its mind?" Stewart gave a bitter laugh. "For Christ's sake, you really think that's going to happen? Why? Because of your report?"

It triggered an irritation in David. "Yes, I do think that's going to happen." He looked into Stewart's eyes. "No one writes to the Undersecretary of State the way I did yesterday. I put my career on the line. I may not even have a job after yesterday. Well, who gives a shit? The important thing is that if you call them out on their lies, you put it to paper, they can't come back with their same bullshit platitudes. You rub their nose in it, they have to respond."

Stewart nodded, chastened. "Well, I hope you're right. And I'm sorry. I know you're doing what you can."

Through the patio doors, David saw that Nigel was waiting for him; it was Saturday morning, nearly time for their usual appointment with the rebel messenger up on Gowarshad Pass. "I have to go, but we can talk more about this later, okay?"

He had started across the patio when Stewart called after him: "It's kind of a competition, isn't it?"

David turned. The journalist was smiling at him, but it was a forlorn smile.

"To see which of us is more deluded," he explained, "you with your reports, me with my dispatches."

David didn't reply, continued on toward the lobby doors.

There were some new adornments on the walls of Paolo's warehouse office. A small spread of color photographs had been taped alongside the desk. On the back wall, several oversize drawings by Paolo's children framed the outer window. One was a rendering of cars and airplanes in different colors of crayon, words written around the edges in a shaky child's hand.

"It's very curious, isn't it?" Paolo said.

In the folding chair, David looked over to see that his friend had finished skimming the photocopy of the note from the rebels, had set it to one side of his desk. "How so?"

"They always know precisely what we most need. Not just which foods, but the medicines, the plastic sheeting. It must mean they have spies everywhere, in all the ministries."

David nodded, gave a sardonic smile. "But maybe that's for the best. At least this way they're not sending us canned ham."

Paolo chuckled. "Or Baptist missionaries." He strummed his fingers on the desk surface. "And what of their messenger? Did he say anything this time?"

David shook his head. On Gowarshad Pass, he and Nigel had been met by the same young rebel as on their previous trips. As before, the man had not spoken, had given no indication that he even understood the questions they put to him.

"Very peculiar. I wonder what their idea is."

"Who knows?" David yawned. "Who the fuck knows?"

Paolo studied him, tilted his head in appraisal. "Something troubling you?"

David recounted his conversation with Stewart McBride by the pool that morning.

"But that's madness," Paolo said when he'd finished. "You told him that, didn't you?"

"Of course. I think he's just feeling a bit desperate about how to get people to pay attention. His last article didn't get much play, you know."

"But a dead journalist gets no play at all."

David nodded. "Anyway, it's not imminent. I pretty much got him to agree to wait until the next ship, see what news comes in."

The businessman's mouth curved into a gentle smile. "The next ship," he repeated. "Quite a lot depending on this next ship, isn't there?"

David looked around the room; he didn't want to talk about the ship again, the mailbag, his report to Washington. He motioned to the drawing of cars and airplanes on the back wall. "From the older or younger one?"

Paolo swiveled in his chair to see. "The younger one, Fabrizio, the four-year-old. He's obsessed with airplanes."

"And what's it say?"

The businessman pointed to the different messages across the paper. "I love you. We all miss you. Please come home soon." He lowered his hand, but continued to stare at the drawing, his smile lingering. "My little darlings. How I miss them."

David stepped over to the photographs taped to the side wall. They were all of Paolo's wife and children; presumably they'd come in the last mail pouch. The boys were very cute and happy, beaming into the camera, but the anxiety on Andreina's face was plain. David remembered her being a gregarious, cheerful woman, but her smile looked forced, sickly, in those few photos where she managed it at all. He turned to see Paolo watching him, as if gauging his reaction. A kind of understanding passed between them and, without a word, David returned to his chair.

"You know what is interesting to me?" Paolo said quietly. "That even when we had the chance, when we knew how bad it would become and those last few fishing boats were still here, not one of us left. Myself, I can honestly say I didn't consider it for a moment. Why do you think that is?"

David pondered. "I suppose because we felt we could help in some way."

"So ego, then?"

David shrugged. "A kind of ego, I guess."

Paolo nodded, took his cigarettes from his shirt pocket. "Yes. Yes, I think you are right." He lit one, rolled it between his fingers. "For me, it seemed very simple at first—and, actually, it is still very simple." He waved a hand toward the inner window and the warehouse floor beyond. "All I'm doing is showing them how to store things properly, checking requisition forms, making sure it isn't all stolen, that there's some kind of system followed—the sort of job anyone can do." He gave a grim laugh. "But no, somewhere along the way, I convinced myself that only I could do it, only I was to be trusted. Ego, as you say. A very dangerous thing. It can make us believe we are important, and then we are trapped." He stared out at the warehouse for a time, still rolling his cigarette in his fingers.

"But for me, it is quite easy, not so much is being asked of me. For you, it's much more difficult, no? Everyone looking to you for answers, for the solution, waiting for what the next word will be."

"I volunteered," David muttered flatly. "No one forced me to do this."

All at once, Paolo seemed to appreciate that David didn't want to have this conversation. "No. No, of course, that is true." He abruptly rose. "Come: I would like to show you a place."

David followed his friend out of the warehouse and they started down the long expanse of Pier 4. It was a bit unnerving to be on that broad, exposed span, and David wondered how many binoculars on the ridge were trained on them at that moment. "This your idea of a leisurely stroll?"

Paolo laughed. "We have a destination. I think it is important at times like this to have a kind of refuge, you know? A place to be alone for a time." He pointed to a two-story building—a pilothouse, from the looks of it—at the far end of the pier.

The building was empty, and they climbed the stairs to the second floor, its banks of windows affording sweeping views of the entire harbor. On a table in the center of the room, a large sketch pad lay open to a very accomplished ink drawing of a busy waterfront: freighters at berth, stevedores and cranes unloading cargo, fishing dhows setting out to sea. David picked up the pad to study the drawing.

"This is wonderful. You did it?"

Paolo flipped a dismissive hand. "Just scratches. Of course, the pens I have to work with aren't the best."

David slowly turned the pages. There were five or six other drawings there, all finely rendered, all depicting different hectic maritime scenes. "I had no idea you were such an artist."

Paolo grinned. "My youthful ambition, just like Hitler. But then I was seduced by the glamour of the electrical-parts industry."

Carrying the pad to the windows, David found the different portions of Central Harbor that Paolo had chosen as his settings:

the small-boat marina, a section of Pier 3. "But you've taken some artistic license here, haven't you?" he said. "People? Boats?"

"Yes, well, I decided to draw it as I remembered," Paolo muttered, "the way it used to be." He stared out one of the windows. "It's something you should consider perhaps—to find a refuge, a place where you can forget things for a while. I think we will be here for a long time yet."

David returned the pad to the table. He thought of telling his friend about his chair on the Moonlight's roof, of the hours—sometimes, entire nights—he spent sitting there. But that chair was not a refuge, that view only haunted him.

After leaving Paolo at the warehouse, David experienced a momentary paralysis; he could not think of what to do or where to go. He decided that if he began walking, an idea would come to him, and so he set out for the main harbor gate and the diminishing city beyond.

The woman was about her age—maybe a young mother or a college student—and Amira could tell she had been quite pretty before this happened. Her cheek was cold and seemed to be growing colder, but Amira wasn't sure if this were true or her imagination.

She had seen the woman before, had even spoken with her briefly on a couple of occasions. She'd been brought to the field hospital in Independence Park three days ago, badly cut up from glass and shrapnel after a bombardment in the northern suburbs, but she had appeared to be recovering well until this. Amira had been outside tending to the children when she'd heard the commotion in the main tent, and by the time she went in, the young woman was already on the operating table, her gown torn open as the doctors massaged her chest. With all the doctors and nurses hovering over her torso—she'd gone into cardiac arrest, from the looks of things—Amira had stepped to the far end and begun caressing her cheek for want of anything more useful to do.

It had all become quite mechanical and removed to Amira, and this was something that, if she'd stopped to think about it, would have shocked her, that she never would have believed possible. But thinking about it was the one thing she couldn't allow herself to do, none of them could.

Instead, she viewed it as simply doing a job, a strangely repetitive one, because this was the only way her mind could process how hideously ugly the human body can become in the blink of an eye, how easily it can be torn and ripped and punctured just like anything else in the world. And so when she felt her thoughts slipping toward sorrow over what she was seeing or touching, she would imagine being in a butcher shop, she would think of sides of beef and legs of lamb or those odd cuts of meat she had passed in grocery stores but had never bothered to identify. When this didn't work, when they looked at her with eyes dulled by shock or pain, eyes that wouldn't turn away, she would think of living animals, of the glassy stare of fish or goats or certain large dogs. Mostly, though, she tried not to think at all, to drift off into a place of her own creation and to stay there.

But none of this worked with the young woman on the operating table. Perhaps it was because she had obviously been very pretty once, or because they appeared to be so close in age. Amira gazed over her naked body, past the thick, red-rimmed stitches crisscrossing her chest, to the pale skin of her belly.

She had been in enough situations like this by now to have noticed what that small patch of hairless skin below the navel might reveal about the dying–how it turned a yellowish brown on those with dark complexions, a marble gray on the lighter ones. It was very difficult to tell with this woman's belly, though; like the coolness of her cheek, Amira suspected she might be inventing both the good and the bad signs.

She thought of David. He had been at the edge of the medical area, leaning against his tree, when she had rushed inside. She thought of him out there now, waiting for her to return, and she drew some comfort from this.

There was a sudden whoop from the other end of the operating table, and when Amira turned she saw that the doctors and nurses were laughing, hugging, patting each other on the back. Looking down, she saw that the woman's chest was heaving, thrashing crazily from side to side, her fingers were scratching at the air.

"We did it," one of the doctors shouted. "We saved her."

Stepping away from the young woman, Amira joined in the celebration, laughing and embracing the others, accepting their embraces of congratulation in return. An ambulance waited outside, and the medical team shifted the woman onto a gurney, wheeled her from the tent for the trip to the hospital. Amira trailed along behind, watched until the ambulance pulled away. Only then did she turn toward the grove of trees with a smile of happiness, of triumph even, only to find that David was no longer there.

The room had the musty, slightly sour smell of old books—appropriately enough, since these were its main feature: the leather-bound volumes ascended from the floor nearly to the ceiling along all four walls.

David had never ventured into the Moonlight's library before, and he strongly suspected none of the other guests had either. The place had the feel of a perfectly preserved Victorian reading room—along with the books were half a dozen leather armchairs, reading lamps, an enormous standing globe beside a long table—and as he advanced inside, David wouldn't have been terribly surprised to find an old man slumped in one of those oversized chairs, forgotten and mummified decades ago.

From glancing over the titles, it appeared much of the reading material tended to the obscure—extending to nearly three shelves on one wall was a set of the British government's 1930 census of India—but in one corner he found an assortment of more recent paperback novels, probably left behind over the years by Moonlight guests. On an end table nearby was an oversize pictorial book commemorating the seventy-fifth anniversary of the hotel's opening, and as David absently flipped through it—photographs of the Moonlight under construction, a number of group shots of black-suited, stiff-looking men posing for the camera—he came across an old promotional brochure for the hotel that had been tucked between its pages.

Judging from the clothes and hairstyles, the brochure dated from the early 1970s. David glanced through it, was amused by the staged, poorly reproduced photos, the somewhat tortured phrasing of the captions—and then he came to a photograph of the Contessa. She was quite a bit younger, not nearly so thin as now, but it was unmistakably her, sitting haughtily in an armchair, one hand raised, as she expounded to half a dozen or so Western tourists gathered in rapt attention.

"Long a favorite retreat of Hollywood celebrities and the international jet set," the caption read, "the Moonlight Hotel is also the home in exile of the Baroness von Würtemstein, who can be found most evenings chatting in a friendly manner with other guests in the lobby."

———

Arkadi Hafizullah was behind the receptionist desk reading a newspaper, but instantly affected a smile at David's approach. "Good afternoon, Mr. Richards. Can I be of some service?"

"Afternoon, Arkadi." David leaned against the counter. "Yeah, I'm a little curious about something, I thought you might be able to help. The Contessa—just when was she promoted?"

The hotel manager frowned in puzzlement. "Promoted, sir?"

"Well, that's probably not the right word, but according to this"—David brought the brochure up—"she's a baroness." He flipped through the pages until he found her photograph, held it across to Arkadi. "See? I'm guessing this was printed—what, ten, twelve years ago?—and back then, she was the Baroness von Würtemstein."

The manager gravely studied the photograph for a moment, began to chew a corner of his lip. "Perhaps it's a typo," he offered finally.

"Ah, I hadn't thought of that." David set the pamphlet on the counter, gave Arkadi an indulgent grin. "But why don't you tell me the real story."

The hotel manager sat back in his chair, exhaled heavily. "I told her not to become a contessa. Baronesses, they're quite common, but contessas are much rarer. Besides, all our literature"—he nodded toward the brochure—"had her that way. But she insisted. She's a very forceful personality, as I'm sure you know."

David nodded. "So is she even a baroness?"

Arkadi shook his head. "Originally a showgirl from Stuttgart, from what I understand. At least, that's what the police said."

David rubbed at his temple. "You've kind of lost me here, Arkadi."

"Yes, it's a confusing story." The manager half rose from his chair to peer about the lobby, as if making sure no one else was within earshot. "Apparently they were impostors, she and the baron. They had traveled all over Europe for years pretending to be royalty, staying in the best hotels, going into expensive jewelry stores—well, you know how it works: 'I will take this diamond now, put those three in the vault for me, and my secretary will come tomorrow with the money to collect them.' I gather they were very convincing, and when people started to ask questions, demanded to be paid, they would move on to the next place, until finally I think there was no place left in Europe for them to go. That's when they came here. They had been here maybe a month when the men from Interpol came, but Luigi must have been warned, because he disappeared just before they arrived."

"Wait–who's Luigi?"

"The baron," Arkadi explained. "Luigi something–I don't re-member now. According to the Interpol men, he was actually a tour guide from Naples. He took all the money and fled, just left the baroness stranded here."

David gazed off. All at once, the Contessa's animus for Ital-ians made a lot more sense. "So what happened? They didn't ar-rest her?"

"They wanted to, but I think the king–the former king–was quite charmed by her and refused to let them. If she goes back to Europe, she will be in trouble, but as long as she stays here . . ." The manager trailed off with a shrug.

"So she's just been living here all this time for free?"

"Well, yes, free, but in return for certain services." Arkadi took another nervous glance about the lobby. "You see, I began to think that it might be good for the hotel to have a royal person living here, that maybe this would be attractive to tourists. So I told her, 'No swindles, no borrowing money from the other guests, but you can stay here and be the baroness for our customers.' And it has worked very well–she has that regal manner, you know–and I have to say, the guests adore her. At one time, I was concerned be-cause she had become very insulting, I was worried people would be offended, but instead it made them like her even more–espe-cially the Americans, for some reason. We had one American couple come back every year just to be insulted by her."

"It's certainly her strong suit," David said.

The manager nodded. "Yes, she's very good. But, as I said, I was very much opposed to the move up to contessa; it seemed un-necessary." He looked to David with an earnest expression. "But the problem, Mr. Richards, is I think she has lived this role so long that she might actually believe it now. I don't know what would happen to her if she were unmasked, if someone confronted her. I think it might destroy her."

"Somehow, I doubt that," David said. "I think the old broad

could survive just about anything." He gave Arkadi a reassuring look. "But don't worry. I won't do that."

———————

She found him where she knew she would, in his chair on the roof.

"Talk or silence?"

"Talk." David smiled up at her. "Just as long as it's not about the ship, what the Americans are likely to do."

"It's a promise." Amira settled into the other chair. It was a quiet night, with a three-quarter moon that gave the mountains a chalky glow. From somewhere beyond the hotel walls came the insistent bark of a dog.

"So have you finished reading all your letters?" he asked.

Amira smiled. "Finally. I'm not sure what it is about knowing someone living under siege, but it seems all my friends suddenly want to tell me their life stories, their intimate secrets. Regular Prousts, they've become. Maybe they think I've a lot of time on my hands, or that it's safe to confide in me because . . ." She stopped as the obvious answer came to her, came to both of them.

"They're concerned about you," David supplied. "They're probably not sure how to express it."

"Yes, I suppose that's it."

"And what of your boyfriend? He must be worried."

"Kenneth? Yes, I imagine he is. He hides it, though. 'Do hope you're enjoying your holiday in the sun,' that sort of thing. He's a sweet man, really, but there's this insistence on turning everything into humor."

But Amira didn't want to talk about Kenneth; the world was becoming crowded with things to not talk about. She gazed up at the palm trees. In the moonlight, their fronds shone silver, as if laid with a frost. The dog still barked, and from behind, the night's surf breaking on the shallows sounded almost like laughter. "Tell me about your development projects."

He turned to her with a questioning look.

"Your development projects here. Tell me about your favorite one."

David considered for a moment, finally settled on the water diversion scheme in the Bejah valley, in the far north. The project had been started by his predecessor but completed during David's first year in Kutar, and it had involved putting a pumping station on a river up in the mountains, laying eight miles of pipe to bring it down to the Bejah. He told Amira how the water had come on line just in time for spring planting, that the transformation in the valley had been astounding.

"All of a sudden, these people who'd been subsistence goat-herders for centuries, they're farmers—and rather rich farmers, at that. You see, the Bejah had been so poor for so long that it had a very small population—about seven hundred—because goatherding just couldn't support any more than that. So now, when they start farming, they don't have the land pressures, they can all work big enough plots to make a nice living. It's really quite amazing. You look at photographs from just two years ago and now, and the houses are bigger, the kids are healthier, they have better clothes, equipment—tractors, some of them—and it's all because they got water on the land."

David had grown quite animated in the telling of this, more animated than he'd been in a long time, and it only occurred to him when he was finished that he'd spoken in the present tense, how inappropriate that was now.

"Well," he added, "that's what it was like last time I was there, before all this."

They fell into silence again. This was something else about war that David hadn't foreseen, the way it constantly floated in the shadows of everything, the way it could rise up in one's mind or words without warning. It instilled a unique kind of oppression.

"Why did you leave the park today?" Amira asked after a time.

David wasn't sure how to answer, he stared out over the railing. The dog had stopped barking at last, and now there was only the low rumble of a truck moving somewhere in the dark.

"You knew there was an emergency, didn't you? By the way we all rushed into the tent?"

"I guess I didn't want to face any more sadness just then."

Amira nodded. "But we saved her. Well, they saved her, the doctors—all I did was wipe her forehead. She was young, about my age. She'd gone into cardiac arrest from her wounds and I thought she was going to die. But she didn't. When I came outside, I wanted to tell you, but you were gone."

David rested his head against the chairback. "I'm sorry," he said. "I wish I'd been there. I would've liked to have been there."

"It's something to keep in mind, you know. They don't always die. Sometimes we can save them."

The days passed with their usual rhythms. The tides followed their course. The sun rose and it became hot, then hotter still, before the gradual cooling of late afternoon. The birds sang early in the morning, and then again toward evening; who knew what they did in midday.

There were, naturally, the normal small variations. On some days, the sea was choppy and whitecapped. On others, it lay smooth as glass. On some mornings there was a cool ocean-borne breeze, and on others the air was still. It all served to remind David that there was a constancy to the world that even war couldn't disrupt.

Yet in this city and at this particular time there was another rhythm, another way to mark off time—the sailings of the *Esmeralda*—and over the course of that long week of waiting, perhaps none felt it more acutely than David. This was not at all a pleasant sensation, however. Rather, with each passing day, the ship's return drawing that much closer, he experienced a deepening sense of claustrophobia, a slow smothering under the weight of others' expectations.

He had promised so much. To the king, to Stewart, by extension to all of them. Not least to himself. So many promises riding on the power of words hastily scrawled at a shipping clerk's desk to turn hearts and governments.

And yet having started with the promises, David felt incapable of tempering them. To the contrary, it was as if he were keeping his own doubts at bay by believing that much more adamantly. Like a man sitting at a roulette table, drunk from losing, he had put everything on the next spin of the wheel, and it was only on Thursday evening, on the eve of the *Esmeralda*'s return, the wheel already spinning, that he first seriously entertained the possibility that he could lose, when he first pondered where that might leave him.

This occurred to him while he stood on the front steps of the Moonlight Hotel, as the embassy car which had delivered him from his last meeting in the city passed down the gravel drive. Staring at the stilled fountain, David tried to think of how he might prepare for what tomorrow could bring, of who could possibly advise him.

———

Swinging the door open, a look of relief instantly rose on Nigel's face. "Ah, Richards, excellent timing." Leading the way into the room, he pointed to a thick book, open and facedown, on his bedspread. "I've been trying to get with that new Churchill biography, but I've hit rather a dull patch; afraid I'm just not that interested in who his mother might have slept with. She was an American, you know. Quite the tart, by all accounts."

David smiled. "So I've heard."

The First Secretary crossed to his dresser, lifted a decanter. "A sherry?"

"No thanks."

"Mind?"

"Not at all."

"So how did your talk with the emergency operations chap go?" Nigel called over his shoulder as he poured himself a glass. "Did he see the light, as it were?" He chuckled at his own joke.

That afternoon, David had met with the chief of the emergency operations office of the Interior Ministry to discuss the system of rolling electrical blackouts in the capital. As every Laradani had observed by now, the shutdowns were mainly falling on the working-class hillside neighborhoods, while other enclaves—most notably, Baktiar Hill, home to the city's wealthy—were not being affected at all. Added to everything else, this inequity was fueling a growing—and to David's mind, easily defused—anger among the poorer residents.

"He seemed to get it," David replied. "He said they'll initiate a new routing schedule within a day or two."

In fact, the meeting had been a maddening ordeal in which the middle-aged functionary had first tried to convince David that the blackout controversy was "a fiction of the popular imagination," then that the wealthier neighborhoods operated on their own independent transmission lines. It was only when David made it clear that he knew a thing or two about electrical grids, and was prepared to take the matter up with the interior minister himself, that the flustered man suddenly agreed there was an urgent problem that needed to be addressed at once.

Glass in hand, Nigel came back across the room, motioned David toward the two armchairs by the desk. "It's really quite remarkable, isn't it, how they listen to us." He settled into one of the chairs with a sigh. "I remember one of the chaps at the embassy a few years back saying that if we came up with a halfway plausible reason and just pressed hard enough, we could get them to repaint the country: 'Enough with all this white, let's go with red.' A joke, of course, but he was probably right."

David nodded. "It's especially remarkable now."

"Yes, especially now." Nigel sipped his sherry, scrutinized David with an unusual solemnity. "I take it you're concerned about the ship tomorrow."

David managed a weak smile. "Terrified might be more accurate. I kind of promised the moon and stars here, so if there isn't a clear sign that things are changing . . ." He looked around the room.

Nigel was extremely neat when it came to his personal possessions—his four pairs of dress shoes were precisely lined up along the far wall, his five identical navy-blue suits hung in the closet—but much less so with his voluminous papers. Reports and correspondence formed irregular mounds on his desk, while across the floor, high stacks of books and file folders teetered precariously.

David turned back. "What do you think they'll say? The State Department, I mean."

The First Secretary gave a slow shrug. "Why, I really wouldn't know, old boy. I should think you'd have a much better idea of that than me."

David shook his head. "Except I don't. I feel like I can't figure out what my government is doing anymore at all."

Setting his sherry glass on the desk, Nigel folded his hands in his lap and stared up at the small chandelier on his ceiling. From outside there came an occasional low thump, but in the closed room it was impossible to know if the sound was that of far-off shelling or of waves striking the promenade wall.

"Let me put a little riddle to you, Richards," he said at last. "It's one that was put to me . . . Lord, it's been almost forty years ago now, but it's always stayed with me." He looked down to David. "It was right after the war, when I was stationed in Berlin—my first foreign posting, very junior diplomat, mainly dealing with refugees and reconstruction and so forth. It was still the time of the Four Powers arrangement, so we mixed quite easily with the Soviets, and I became friendly with this Russian chap in the office, Sergei Malenkovsky his name was. Secret police, of course—I rather imagine all the Russians in Berlin at that time were—but a decent enough fellow. Anyway, one night we were out together, a bit into our cups, and Sergei proceeded to tell me a story of when he had been a police chief in some town outside Moscow back before the war. He told it to me as a kind of riddle.

"It seemed that a champion athlete lived in this town—a shot-putter, I think it was, or maybe the discus—in any event, one of the very best in Russia. Until one day, this chap was denounced. Apparently he was about to head off to some athletic competition in Western Europe somewhere, and once there, so the denunciation went, he intended to defect. So Sergei brought him in for questioning. Of course, the man denied everything—'I only want to win gold medals for the glory of the state,' all the usual business—and he was so convincing that, by the end of the interrogation, Sergei wasn't sure whether to believe him or the informant. Well, not a problem in normal circumstances—throw them both in prison, that's how they did things under Stalin—but this was a unique case. Obviously if Sergei put the athlete in prison and it cost them a medal at this competition—and remember, even back then the Russians were obsessed with sport, all that rot about building the new Soviet man—then it would be Sergei's head in the noose. But if he approved the chap to travel abroad and he defected, it would be his head again. So what to do? This is the riddle, how Sergei presented it to me. 'If you were in my position,' he asked me, 'what would you have done?'"

By Nigel's silence, David saw that the riddle had now been put to him. He considered for a time, but couldn't come up with an answer. His confounding caused Nigel to smile.

"No, you see, you can't solve it. Nor could I. But for Sergei, it was very simple, the most obvious thing. He brought the athlete back in for more interrogation, except this time he only asked him one question: 'Are you right- or left-handed?' When the chap said right-handed, Sergei had his officers hold him down, they stretched his right hand across a table, and then Sergei smashed it to pieces with a hammer."

Quite unconsciously, Nigel unfolded his hands in his lap, began to knead his fingers.

"You see how that works? 'An accident has occurred; our champion athlete has crippled his hand.' Now there is no reason to let him go abroad, he has no opportunity to defect, and if Russia loses out on a medal because of it—well, accidents happen, no one is to blame. You see? Problem solved."

He reached for his glass of sherry, took another sip.

"But the key point here, the reason I brought it up, is that you couldn't solve the riddle. Why is that? Because you're not a coward. And because you're not a coward, you're incapable of thinking in a cowardly way. Very laudable at normal times, but in the current situation it puts you at the distinct disadvantage of not being able to foresee what might be coming."

David arched an eyebrow. "Because my government is cowardly?"

"Not just yours, all governments. By their very nature, all governments are cowardly. Naturally it can take any number of forms—it might mean slaughtering their own people or someone else's, it might mean simply doing nothing and calling it a policy—but ultimately they're all cowardly. But this is the thing about cowardice: to survive by it, you also must be very clever. Like my friend Sergei. So, you see, here is the problem. You can never over-estimate the sheer ingenuity that cowards are capable of bringing to a task. If it's important enough to them, they can outsmart you every time."

There was a quiet in the room, finally broken by Nigel leaning forward to pat David's knee in a consoling way. "I'm not saying that's what will happen tomorrow—maybe we'll be in for a pleasant surprise. I just want you to be prepared. That's all."

———

On the eastern flank of the ridge, a single mortar lobbed shells down on the New City at intervals of every forty-five seconds or so. Whenever the gun fired, a brief flash of yellowish orange lit up that corner of the ridge, and then David's eye was inexorably drawn to the white contrail arcing into the sky. At a certain point, the contrail fizzled out while the shell kept rising, lost in the blackness. It always took a surprisingly long time for the shell to come down, so long it was almost possible to imagine that maybe this one had continued on up into space, leaving behind only its trail, a white streamer to join all the other white streamers hung against the night. But then, from some corner of the New City there would come the flash and that peculiar sound a mortar makes when it explodes—a kind of liquidy crack, like breaking ice—and then a few seconds later, the equally distinctive *crump* it made when it was launched, and even though it was simple physics, the natural laws of sound traveling over distance, David could never get used to the idea that the awful first sound he was hearing had been caused by the second.

In his lap lay his photo album. He had brought it up to the rooftop with the intention of looking through it, but in the hours he had sat there, he had yet to open it.

He wasn't sure why he had carried it with him all this time, through all his foreign postings, why he hadn't just left it at his parents' home in Cleveland ages ago, because the truth was, he had only ever looked at it once and that had been thirteen years ago, on the day after Eddie's funeral when his aunt had given it to him. His aunt had spent hours in his parents' den going through the old photographs, picking out the best ones of the two boys together, carefully pasting them in chronological order in the album. She had meant it as a gift, a way for David to remember his brother, and out of politeness, he had sat beside her on the couch and looked at the photographs.

A burst of white light refracted off the taller commercial buildings of downtown, followed immediately by a red glow. Just as the first wisps of black smoke curled over the rooftops, the ice-cracking sound, and then from far away—only audible because David was listening for it—the soft *crump* that had started it all.

He felt very alone up there, suspended between his conversation with Nigel and the *Esmeralda*'s return. Part of him wished that Amira would choose this night to make one of her visits to the rooftop, but another part of him didn't want that at all. In any event, it was very late—from the position of the moon, David estimated two or three—and Amira had long since gone to sleep. He stared at the white contrails draping the northern sky, their gentle twisting, their slow drift into nothingness, and it reminded him of the tentacles of a jellyfish.

On the day when he had first taken the old chairs from the rooftop utility shed, David had noticed a narrow cot set against one wall, the resting quarters of some long-ago workman. When at last he tired of watching over the city that night, he went and lay upon it. He closed his eyes, tried to will sleep on, but through his mind floated images from the photo album beside him. But not really images: sounds, moments, entire conversations, all those remembrances that refuse to leave no matter how hard one tries to banish them.

———

The first bad sign was that the satellite telephone wasn't there. It had been two weeks since David had requested it, and as the mail pouch was emptied he watched for a parcel slightly larger than a shoe box, but there was nothing like that for him.

The second bad sign was the signature on his letter from the State Department. Not the Secretary's, not even the Undersecretary's of the previous week, but rather of someone with the title of Deputy Assistant Undersecretary for Trans-Oceanic Regional Affairs. As soon as he saw that signature, David slid the letter back into the manila envelope and set his face in as placid an expression as he could muster.

The harbormaster's office wasn't quite as crowded as the week before–the various government officials numbered perhaps two dozen or so–but the effect of all their hopeful stares in David's direction was the same. He leaned to Nigel.

"I'm going to read it outside."

The First Secretary glanced up from his reading, gave a quick nod. "I'll join you in a moment."

This time David didn't stop at the stairwell but continued on down to the empty clerks' office on the second floor. Stepping to the large picture window, he briefly gazed out at the activity along Pier 4, as if to forestall knowing for just a short while longer. Then he slid the letter out.

> *Dear Mr. Richards:*
>
> *I wish to thank you for your report of November 17, as well as for your very frank addendum of November 18, regarding the current situation in Kingdom of Kutar. As you are no doubt aware, this administration has long held that the frank and candid exchange of differing viewpoints within governmental agencies is essential to the proper functioning of democracy, and we greatly value your contribution in this regard.*
>
> *In response to specific issues raised in your report of November 17 and addendum of November 18, I am pleased to report that the adverse state of affairs in Kingdom of Kutar you have so ably described has served to foster a renewed sense of commitment throughout all levels of this administration to the principle that the indiscriminate use of force and/or violence against a civilian population by governmental and/or nongovernmental armed forces is unacceptable. In testament to this commitment, please find enclosed personal communications from the Secretary to His Majesty King Abdul Rahman II, in which the Secretary unequivocally expresses the administration's deep concern over the current situation in Kingdom of Kutar, as well as our firm belief that a successful ces-*

sation of hostilities is the course of action most likely to lead to this situation's improvement.

Pursuant to this, I must add that we are deeply concerned by a possibly inadvertent statement contained in your addendum of November 18, in which you suggested that Government of Kutar (GOK) might be contemplating negotiations with the Kutaran People's Liberation Army (KPLA). As you are no doubt aware, the KPLA has recently been placed on the State Department Terrorism Index (SDTI), Probationary Status, which explicitly bars the United States government or the governments of any allied nations from negotiating with said entities. As a result—and as the Secretary makes clear in his personal communications to His Majesty King Abdul Rahman II—it is our firm position that a resolution of the conflict in Kingdom of Kutar precludes negotiation of any kind between GOK and KPLA, and I would urge you to further impress upon GOK the very serious ramifications that a violation of this stricture would likely occasion.

On related matters, I am pleased to report that, in recognition of the great importance placed on your mission in Kingdom of Kutar, the Office of Mission Security, Communications, and Intelligence is continuing its review of your request for a telephonic "scrambler." I am further pleased to report that the contribution of the United States government to the ongoing relief effort for the city of Laradan now totals in excess of $9 million, complementing some $24 million from private American donor organizations, a level of assistance that exemplifies the long-standing American tradition of generosity to those in need, and which I am sure will convey to the Kutaran people our very strong commitment to their cause and continuing welfare.

Once again, I thank you for your efforts to keep us apprised of developments in Kingdom of Kutar, and hope you derive comfort at this difficult juncture in knowing that both the current situation in Kingdom of Kutar and your personal welfare are sources of deep concern to a great many of us here. I would also like to take this op-

portunity to wish you and any other Americans still residing in Kingdom of Kutar a most enjoyable Thanksgiving.

In the clerks' office, David slowly set the letter on a desk. It was only then he noticed Nigel Mayhew leaning against a nearby wall, watching him.

"Not good, is it?" the older man said quietly.

David shook his head. Nigel came to take up the letter. As he read, David stared out at the pier, the *Esmeralda*'s crane still hoisting pallets from her hold, but his eyes didn't focus on anything in particular. Behind his back, he heard Nigel's soft whistle.

"No negotiations but no assistance either," the First Secretary said. "Not exactly what one wants to hear when your city is being bombed to rubble, is it?"

David turned to him. "What do I do, Nigel? What the fuck do I do?" He tried to smile. "Another frank addendum?"

"If you like."

David shook his head. "I don't think I have the stomach for it."

"No." Nigel looked at his watch. "I'll go on up and seal the pouch. Easy enough to run interference for you with the chaps up there, but I'm afraid the king wants to see both of us right away."

At the mention, David groaned. "Oh, Christ. What the hell do I tell the king?"

Nigel scuffed his shoe along the floor, thinking, then looked up. "To borrow an expression popular with you Americans, fuck him. If he'd gone into negotiations when he had the chance, if he hadn't listened to Munn and his generals, all this could have been avoided. He's only himself to blame."

David grinned in spite of the situation. "You want me to say that to the king?"

"If you don't, I will. Not going to see you beaten up in there again, old boy."

For a long moment, David stared at the First Secretary and,

to his surprise, he felt tears welling up. "You're a good man, Mayhew," he whispered. "A good friend."

"Ach." Nigel flicked a dismissive hand in the air. "Let's not get all modern here, Richards. Just don't like seeing a white man getting knocked about in these parts—sets a bad precedent." He smiled. "I'll run up and seal the pouch. You want to wait here?"

David nodded. "I'd appreciate that." He watched the older man start away, but then called after him. "By the way, I think that's the first Americanism you've got right: 'fuck him.' Every other one you've mangled beyond recognition."

Nigel frowned, appeared genuinely surprised by this news. "Surely you jest. I've always rather prided myself on a facility for idioms."

"I jest you not. When it comes to idioms, you blow chunks."

The First Secretary's frown deepened. "Blow chunks?"

David grinned. "Okay, so now you have two."

———

A cool breeze was coming in off the water, and they decided to walk the mile or so to the palace. The streets were largely deserted at that early-afternoon hour, but the few people they passed stared into the faces of these two foreign men in their midst, as if trying to read what news they might harbor. To these looks, David and Nigel averted their eyes, held their expressions so as to reveal nothing, and each Laradani they passed was too polite, too deferential, to press their curiosity with words.

As they walked, David tried to think of questions he might put to Nigel, to draw on the older man's experience, but only one kept coming to him, and he finally gave it voice: "What do we do now?"

"We persevere," Nigel replied quickly, as if he'd been pondering the same question but had already found an answer. "We carry on. We do what we can. That's all anyone can ask of us now."

David nodded, fell silent again.

Across the city rang the occasional gunshot. This was always the case now, at all hours of the day and night, and David probably only took notice of them that afternoon because they sounded a bit different: louder, but at the same time muffled, not the clean pops and cracks he had grown accustomed to. He looked at the sky and saw a filmy haze that hadn't been there the day before–the first harbinger of the clouds of winter–and assumed it was this thickening that was altering the sound of the gunshots, simultaneously amplifying and dulling their echoes.

As they turned onto the wide boulevard that led to the palace gates, he contemplated the ordeal that lay before them in the chamber hall. He again tried to think of something to ask Nigel, some bit of advice, but nothing occurred to him.

So engrossed was David in his thoughts that it took him some time to notice the quieting around him, that the only footsteps he was now hearing were his own. He stopped, turned around.

Nigel was sitting in the road perhaps fifty feet back, his legs stretched straight out before him, his hands held to his chest, and David's first incongruous thought was that he looked very much like a man performing sit-ups.

"Nigel?" he called, still too puzzled by the sight to do anything but stare.

And then David saw the strange movement of Nigel's lips beneath his mustache. He was working them furiously, biting them, licking them, as if something were stuck in his mouth or he was trying to form words.

"Nigel?" David started back toward him.

And he now saw that Nigel's hands were not held to his chest, but rather clutching at his shirt, pulling it away from his skin, as if the red spot that was spreading there, over his heart, was a stain he didn't want to have touch his flesh.

"Nigel!" David shouted, and began racing the last short distance to him, but before he got there, Nigel pitched and slowly rolled to the side, his hands not breaking his fall, his fingers still clutching at his shirt, and even before he reached him, David knew by the flop of his head, the low settling of his body on the stones, that he was already too late, that Nigel was already gone.

Ten

David did not feel any of his customary nervousness. He did not look out at the view or the road ahead, only at the ground just beyond his feet. Without Nigel, it was a difficult journey.

The rebel messenger waited for him at the usual meeting place, beside the rocky escarpment just past the third hairpin. On this day, he didn't wear his cocky smile, he watched David's approach with a certain somberness.

David stopped with about three feet between them. He saw the envelope containing that week's instructions tucked into the young man's shirt pocket, and motioned for it. Instead the man extended his right hand as if to shake David's.

"My name is Rustam," he said in English, in a surprisingly soft and gentle voice. "I was very sorry to hear about Mr. Mayhew. We all were. I can assure you that it was a . . ." He glanced off, as if searching for the right phrase. "An inadvertent action."

In different circumstances, David might have reacted with amazement; these were the first words the rebel messenger had uttered in any language over the course of their meetings on

Gowarshad Pass. On that day, though, less than twenty-four hours after Nigel's death, David merely stared at him.

"And the other five thousand you've killed," he said finally, "have they all been inadvertent actions?"

The young man seemed taken aback and slowly lowered his outstretched arm. When David again motioned for the envelope, he brought it from his pocket with an air of embarrassment.

With the envelope in his hand, David looked into Rustam's eyes. They were dark brown and appeared wounded, and David was struck by the thought that the man had been expecting some sort of absolution.

"Fuck you," he said, and turned and started back toward the city.

———

Arkadi had mentioned the existence of an old foreigners' cemetery up on Baktiar Hill. That same afternoon David went to look it over.

The walled compound had fallen into disrepair and no one had been interred there since the days of the British Empire, but David felt Nigel would have approved of the site, of being placed there alongside his long-departed countrymen. Early the next morning, he and all the other residents of the hotel, guests and employees alike, went up to the cemetery to cut away the weeds, and when the locals saw the activity and learned its purpose, many of them joined in as well.

As Nigel's funeral cortege passed through the streets of Laradan that Sunday afternoon, thousands lined the sidewalks to pay their respects, and the rebel guns on the ridge remained silent. At the graveside ceremony, the king's representative read a eulogy in which Nigel Mayhew was described as Kutar's most loyal and dedicated Western friend. Since the First Secretary had left no instructions in the event of his death, had never indicated any religious preference, it was left to each of his fellow Moonlight residents to say whatever they felt appropriate: remembrances, tributes, bits of recalled prayers. By the ceremony's end, a spectacular sunset was spreading over the western mountains, the early clouds of winter were lit a fiery red, and it seemed a terribly sad thing to leave Nigel up there alone.

And it was as if something had snapped, had broken in all of them. Across Laradan in the following days, Nigel Mayhew's death cast a pall that, while quite different from that which had accompanied the first great bombardment, may have been even more keenly felt. For fourteen years, the British First Secretary had been the face of the West in Kutar: steadfast, principled, a tad condescending, perhaps, but a man with a genuine affection for the kingdom and its people. Western ambassadors and attachés and development officers had come and gone, but Nigel Mayhew had always remained, and his sudden passing now was such an obvious metaphor to the city's inhabitants that it required no explication, no words.

Naturally his Moonlight colleagues were the most profoundly affected, and over those subsequent days each struggled in his or her own way with that paradox common to mourners: a sense of utter aloneness, for grief is too intimate an emotion to truly share, conjoined by an urgent need for companionship, to not be left alone with one's thoughts for too long. Paolo no longer spent countless hours at his warehouse office or with his sketches in the Pier 4 pilothouse. Amira limited her time at the Independence Park medical tent, Stewart his journalistic expeditions through the city. Instead, each morning and again in the evenings, all lingered at the table in the hotel lobby, and at that table they spoke gently, with solicitousness of one another. Even the Contessa endeavored to be kind.

And for David, sorrow mingled with a kind of guilt. Not about the particulars of what had happened that day–after all, it had been Nigel's idea to walk to the palace–but rather a guilt over what the city had lost and what it had been left with. On that day, a bullet had come and it had found Nigel and it had not found him, it had found the capable man and not the other, and if this was a random and blameless thing, it was a further indication of this city's terrible luck, that it was truly a place of the damned.

But this depth of mourning cannot be sustained indefinitely, it has to break, and it was Stewart McBride who finally broke it.

In the silence, the Contessa gazed along the lobby table.

"As you all know, I'm not one given to easy judgment," she said at last. "Live and let live, that's always been my motto. Nevertheless, I must point out that this idea is the height of idiocy." She leaned in Stewart's direction. "This wait is trying on all of us, young man, but, good Lord, this is no time to panic."

He laughed. "I'm not panicking. I'm a journalist, remember?"

"But you don't even speak the language, Stewart," Amira said. "The first time someone speaks to you up there–"

"I have a good fixer who'll go with me. He's from the north, speaks four or five dialects. He thinks there won't be any problem."

"Well of course he doesn't." Amira threw up her hands. "What do you pay a fixer for something like this? A hundred dollars a day? Two hundred? And if you don't go, he doesn't get paid. Of course he doesn't think there'll be a problem."

Stewart sighed, sat back in frustration.

It had been nearly two weeks since he'd first told David of his intention to cross into rebel territory, but Stewart had agreed to hold off then in hopes of better news coming on the *Esmeralda*. With that news only further disappointment, he'd resolved to set off at once–but then Nigel had been killed. Out of a kind of respect for him and a concern for the others at the hotel, Stewart had delayed his departure once again, but now, the fifth day after the First Secretary's death, the futility of staying on in Laradan was becoming intolerable. He'd chosen to tell the others over breakfast that morning, but so far the idea had met with a cold reception.

"When would you leave?" Paolo asked.

"Soon," Stewart said. "Maybe as early as tonight. Everything's arranged." This drew dismayed looks around the table, which Stewart tried to dispel with a grin. "Come on. Aren't any of you curious to find out what's happening up there?"

"Of course," Paolo replied, "but not curious enough to be killed for it."

"Bravo, signore, bravo," the Contessa cried, "for once, you talk some sense."

"What do you think, David?" Amira asked.

One by one, the others focused on him. Of all those at the table, only he had yet to voice an opinion; this was because he could think of no argument they hadn't already tried. Still, it was required of him to say something. "I think you should wait."

"What for this time?"

"Well, the ship's coming back in two days and—"

"Oh, Christ," Stewart cut him off, "not with the ship again. You know as well as I do, David—hell, better than I do—there won't be anything in that goddamned mail pouch."

"But how can you be sure?" Paolo interceded. "Maybe this time—"

"Look." The journalist sat forward abruptly, his frustration sliding into anger. "I don't know what you all are telling yourselves, but what I can tell you is that no one is coming in here, there will be no rescue. Once the Alliance pulled out, that was it. Up until then, maybe this was a crusade to defend democracy or to protect a strategic ally or whatever other bullshit they came up with, but that didn't work out, so now it's back to them being a bunch of savages killing each other just like they always have." He gave a bitter chuckle. "For Christ's sake, they even put it in my dispatches. 'A former British colony,'" he recited from memory, "'the Kingdom of Kutar has long been wracked by internecine violence between its northern population, primarily tribal clans, and the more prosperous south.' That's the backgrounder they tack on to every one of my stories out of here. You see how that works, the message it sends? They're a bunch of savages again, gone back to their killing ways, it's not our fault. We'll do the relief-ship thing because, after all, we're compassionate, we're humanitarians, we can all feel good about helping out, but any more than that? It's their problem, let them sort it out."

He slumped back, wearily shook a cigarette from his packet on the table.

"Well, if all that's true," Amira said, "how does your going over the ridge change anything?"

Stewart shrugged. "Maybe it doesn't. But it's the only thing I can see that might." He peered around at the others. "Unless someone has a better idea."

No one spoke. As he watched the journalist, though, David saw that perhaps he had one last line of argument.

He watched Stewart read through the first pages, waited for him to reach the highlighted passages on page six. When he did, the reaction was nearly identical to what David remembered seeing on Nigel's face: the dropped mouth, the stunned look.

"Jesus Christ," Stewart whispered. "They're talking about genocide."

David nodded. "At least the possibility of it."

After the gathering in the lobby, he had taken Stewart aside and asked him up to his room. There, he had retrieved the CIA analysis on the rebels and pressed it into the journalist's hand.

In the chair by the desk, Stewart skimmed through the rest of the report, then returned to the highlighted sections. When he finished, he slowly looked up, fixed David with a frown. "So how long have you had this?"

"Since just before the evacuation. The ambassador insisted I read it before agreeing to stay here."

"And you've just sat on it all this time? For fuck's sake, David, this is huge. This is the smoking gun."

For the briefest moment, a pulse of doubt passed through David's mind. But then he remembered what was written on those pages—he had them practically memorized. "What do you mean? There's no smoking gun there."

"No?" Stewart became animated, waved the papers in his hand. "For Christ's sake, they're comparing the KPLA to the Khmer Rouge, they raise the specter of genocide. No one's done that before, and here you've got the CIA doing it. You don't see how that's important, how that's newsworthy? Right after we've learned what the Khmer Rouge did in Cambodia?"

David stifled a sigh, replied in a calming voice: "First off, you seem to have edited out all their weasel words. Look back through it, Stewart; there's a 'perhaps' or 'maybe' in front of every statement they make. And second, that's a preliminary analysis, which means that everything in it is to be taken as speculative, uncorroborated."

But this didn't chasten Stewart at all. "Who gives a fuck? If we're talking about changing what's happening here, what difference does it make?" He fixed David with an imploring look. "Let me use it. You've got to let me use it."

This was not going as David had planned, he quickly shook his head. "You know I can't do that; it's a top-secret document."

"Then what the hell did you show it to me for?"

"To dissuade you from going up there. To show you what you might be up against. Forget genocide, Stewart. Forget the Khmer Rouge. The point is that if they're even 20 percent accurate—let's just say the KPLA are doing massacres here and there—then they'll kill you, too."

The journalist's fervor seemed to drain all at once; he sat back, gazed around the room with a meditative air.

"Let's walk through this," he said finally. "The administration wants to wash their hands of this place without appearing to do so, right? So they talk about deep concern and dangle the vague promise of aid at some point in the future. But they also don't want the Kutarans to negotiate with the KPLA, so they put the KPLA on the terrorism list. The problem there, though, is that if they're terrorists, the administration has to actually do something. But not if they're given probationary status. 'Needs more study.' Perfect. All bases covered." He turned to David. "But the one thing they forgot about was this report. At the very least, they'll have to explain why, with their own intelligence agency warning of genocide, the KPLA isn't a full-fledged member of the terrorism list. They won't be able to explain that, the KPLA will have to go on the list without any strings, and when that happens, all of a sudden they're going to have to act. Don't you see? This could be the thing that finally messes up their chessboard, that gets people to sit up and take notice."

In the silence between them, David studied the journalist.

Stewart McBride was a constant surprise to him, a bedrock cynic on one hand, but then a man made naïve by his enthusiasms on the other. For starters, David had a hard time seeing how people might suddenly be galvanized over a CIA report that posited the theory of unknown people being killed somewhere in an unknown countryside, when the verifiable fact that a civilian population center was being shelled into dust didn't seem to faze them at all. For another, he had firsthand experience with the glacial pace with which Washington moved; even if the CIA disclosure caused a mini-scandal, it could be months of hearings and conferences before the KPLA's terror-list status was changed, many more months before this translated into anything material.

But then again, maybe not so naïve. Maybe Stewart McBride actually understood better than David what might capture the world's attention. Certainly there had been times in the recent past when a news report, well timed, had sparked an overwhelming popular reaction, had swept aside all the usual roadblocks to action.

In fact, though, it was something quite different that caused David to consider Stewart's entreaty. Upon becoming a Foreign Service officer, he had taken an oath. He fully knew that passing top-secret documents to a journalist was not only a violation of that oath, but a fireable offense—perhaps a criminal one as well. But against this was both a growing anger at his government's lack of honor toward Kutar and the realization that, with the CIA report, he held a lever that might save a life—at least temporarily. In this equation it was very clear to David what he must choose.

"I'll make a deal with you," he said. "You can use the report on two conditions. First, no attribution. Second, you don't go over the ridge until we hear back, until we see what the reaction to it is."

Stewart winced at this. "You mean waiting until the ship comes back again?"

David nodded.

"But Christ, that'd mean me sitting around here for nine more days."

David shrugged. "That's the deal. Take it or leave it."

The journalist turned, stared out the window at the sunstruck sea as he pondered.

———

"So what did you say to change Stewart's mind?" Amira asked.

David smiled. "Nothing in particular. Just force of personality, I suppose."

She laughed lightly. "Well, that was my first guess, of course, but I think there's probably more to it than that. He's quite upbeat all of a sudden, he's actually looking forward to the *Esmeralda* coming tomorrow."

She searched his face, as if for a clue to what he was withholding, and it caused David to finally turn away.

So many secrets, more than seemed conceivable among such a small group living in such isolation. But the CIA report was one secret he couldn't share with Amira—especially with her relatives still trapped somewhere over that mountain range. "I'm sorry," he muttered. "I can't."

Amira nodded, looked back out over the rooftop railing. It was a calm night, just a couple of guns at the farthest end of the ridge firing down on the city, the clouds absorbing all but the slightest sound of them.

She was constantly amazed at how difficult it was to find something to talk about now. She would have expected just the opposite, that under the circumstances they would all talk themselves silly if only for the distraction. The problem, though, was in finding a topic that didn't suddenly bump against something that couldn't be discussed or that would propel them back into desolation. To discuss Nigel, how they missed him? Her day at the medical tent, or David's latest round of pointless meetings? About what their lives had once been like, what they hoped to return to? Confronted with this maze, it was easier to share the quiet.

After a while, a topic came to her; it seemed a safe one. "You live in there, don't you?"

David saw she was pointing at the rooftop utility shed.

"I came up this afternoon looking for you and happened to peek in." Amira smiled again. "You've done it up quite nicely."

Another secret, but her expression relaxed him. In fact, it had been more than a week since David had asked Amin's help in cleaning out the room. They'd stacked the shovels and rakes and bags of cement along the outer wall, and then Amin had swept and mopped, put clean sheets on the cot. It was like a tiny little home now.

"Thank you," he said, "but it was mostly Amin's doing. And I wouldn't say I live there. I mean, sometimes if I can't sleep, I'll come up, watch the city for a while. But it's kind of a vicious circle, because then I'll get drowsy and I know if I slog back downstairs it'll wake me up again, so I'll just go in there, stretch out."

She chuckled. "And how often does that happen?"

David looked over at the shed. The sacks of cement were white, their lettering had faded over the years, and in the night glow, they looked like so many pillows heaped there. "Well," he said quietly, "I guess it's pretty much every night."

And now Amira saw that even this topic threatened to slide them back. She fell silent, stared up at the clouds. They were like a comforter over the sleeping city. She listened for the sound of the surf behind them, but the bay had been placid for several days now, not even its whisper reached the rooftop.

"Tell me about your village," he said. "Something you haven't told me before."

Amira settled against the chairback and thought for a time, grateful for the diversion; it came to her, she laughed out loud. "Oh, I know! What my grandfather did for my eighth birthday; you'll absolutely love this." She glanced over. "On second thought, maybe I shouldn't; it'll just provide new ammunition for one of your anti-oligarchy rants."

David grinned. "Excellent, tell me."

She propped her chin on a hand. "First you need to know the background—otherwise, it doesn't make any sense—but all through my grandfather's growing up, Chalasan was extremely poor, the poorest village in the valley. That's because the British, when they finally defeated our clan in the warlord rebellions, they decided to make an example of it, to show everyone the cost of insurrection, so they imposed this special tax just on Chalasan, and warned all the other villages in the Altafaram to have nothing to do with us or the same would happen to them. The story my grandfather tells is that, when he was young, the worst insult you could say to someone in the valley was to call them a Chalasani. So he grew up very bitter—you know, this proud clan, now completely humiliated—and when he left for England, he vowed that one day he would get his revenge. He planned it for when I was living there, on my eighth birthday.

"What he did was to build this enormous hydroelectric generator down by the river—I don't know the technical numbers, but big enough to give electricity to the entire Altafaram—because, back then, there was no power anywhere except in the cities. It was a huge project, and while one work team was building the plant, another wired all the villages for electricity. Everyone was so excited—I remember people talking about it constantly—and he arranged it so that it would all be finished for my eighth birthday, just before I was to go back to England. My whole family came out when it was time, and my grandfather organized this great party, a feast in the main square. He waited until it was dark, of course, and then he led me over to this big metal box with this switch—you know, making a big ceremony out of it—and when I pulled the switch, all at once, all over Chalasan, the lights came on. Everyone just went mad." Amira laughed at the memory. "But then, and this is the part you're going to like, because then we went up to the main house—to the top of the round tower, you know?—and I could see that all Chalasan was lit up. But looking down the valley at the other villages, there was nothing, just darkness like always. So I said to my grandfather, 'But, Papa, what about all the other villages, where are their lights?' And he kind of peered down at me—he's a very imposing man—and he said, 'What, you want them to have lights?' And I said, 'Yes, yes, I want them to have lights.' And he became very serious. 'Amira, I want you to consider this very carefully, because these people, they have been very bad to us and they don't deserve to have lights. I want you to think about that and, if after some time, you still feel the same way, then maybe we'll give them lights.'" She laughed again, more forcefully than before. "You see, for most people, revenge would have been to only wire Chalasan. But no, my grandfather, he'd wired the whole valley, so that all during the construction, everyone was thinking,

'Oh, what a wonderful thing Mr. Hamid is doing for us, we were so wrong about the Chalasanis, they really are very good people,' and it was all so he could then turn around and taunt them."

"Jesus." David joined in her laughter. "I'm beginning to understand his success in business now."

"But wait, it gets better. Because then I started to cry. I was so upset that he was being mean, and my grandfather just didn't know what to do. Here he had spent all this money, he had obviously been planning his revenge for years, and now he'd made his granddaughter cry on her birthday. And I remember he knelt down to my level, trying to calm me, but also kind of pleading. 'Amira, why don't we wait a few days; please, just a few days?' And I said, 'No, Papa, I want them to have lights right now,' and I'll never forget, he got this very sad look, and he turned to one of his workers, 'Okay, turn them on.' And then—poof—the other lights came on, all the way down the valley, as far as you could see. I was so glad and I looked up at my grandfather to thank him, but I don't think I've ever seen him so miserable." Her laughter died away into a contented sigh, she wiped tears from her eyes. "Well, it's all so medieval, isn't it?"

David smiled. "But impressive. Amira, the bringer of light. I think for my eighth birthday, I got a box of crayons."

"You see? I knew I shouldn't have told you. You're going to torment me with this forever, aren't you?"

"Forever and ever."

They settled into silence again, a happier one than before. From somewhere close by, a dog began barking insistently, and David wondered if it was the same one as on the earlier night. He listened for a time, finally decided it was different.

Lost in his own thoughts, it was as if he'd forgotten Amira was still there, was somewhat startled when she yawned.

"Well, I'm sorry for your insomnia," she said, rising from the chair, "but I'm exhausted. I'll see you in the morning, okay?"

And maybe he had been thinking about it for a while now, or

maybe it was because he'd spent much of that afternoon struggling
to compose a letter to Sarah, Nigel's wife—now his widow—to go
out on tomorrow's ship, but David looked up to her then in a beseeching way. "Can I ask you something? Kind of a favor?"

Amira stopped, settled back into the chair.

"There's something I want to make sure gets back to my parents," he said. "I mean, if anything happens to me here."

A week ago, Amira might have made a dismissive gesture at
this, she might have said, "Don't be silly, nothing's going to happen to you." On that night, she said, "Of course."

David nodded, looked back out over the city. The obvious
question lingered between them, unspoken, but then all at once he
decided, rose, and started across the roof toward the utility shed.

He returned carrying a large, beige photo album. The sight
caused Amira to grin. "Family pictures?"

He came to stand before her, held the album close to his side.
"Kind of."

"May I see them?" She held out a hand. "I'd love to see what
you were like as a boy."

He stared off for a moment, into the night, debating one
last time.

"There's something I haven't mentioned before because . . ."
He turned back to her, tried for a smile. "Well, because I don't usually mention it." He placed the album in her outstretched hands. "I
had a brother. Edward. We called him Eddie."

The number of officials gathered in the harbormaster's office had
again declined from the Friday before—perhaps just fifteen or so
now—and gone altogether was the note of suspense that had accompanied the prior openings of the mail pouch. This time, David
didn't bother leaving the room to read his memorandum from the
State Department, because now there were no anxious gazes in his

direction, he was just one more man standing there reading words of little consequence.

To judge by the signature, Kutar had dropped yet another rung in State's list of foreign policy concerns—the previous week's Deputy Assistant Undersecretary had relegated letter-writing duties to his deputy assistant—but other than this and a few date changes, the memo was a faithful replication of the last one: disappointment over the continuing violence; peace best achieved by victory; no negotiations with the KPLA. At least this week there was an accompanying note from the Office of Mission Security, Communications, and Intelligence:

> *Dear Mr. Richards:*
>
> *This is in reference to your request for the delivery of a secure telephonic communication apparatus (i.e., "scrambler") with satellite capability for use in your present mission in Kingdom of Kutar. As you are no doubt aware, requests of this nature normally undergo a very thorough interdepartmental review at State, a process which can be time-consuming, but in light of the high-priority status given your mission, I am pleased to report this office has initiated and completed its review of your application in record time.*
>
> *That said, I must unfortunately inform you that we have determined Kingdom of Kutar to be an unsuitable environment for a secure telephonic communication apparatus at this time. Given what we understand to be the current unsettled state of affairs in Kingdom of Kutar, we have very deep concerns—which I am sure, upon further reflection, you can appreciate—that this technology, if provided, could conceivably fall into the hands of individuals or groups of individuals whose interests are inimical to those of the United States, and thereby compromise the integrity of the Department of State's secure telephonic communication system throughout the region.*

I regret we were unable to look upon your request more favorably at this time. Should you wish to appeal this determination, or if you feel there is other pertinent information that may cause us to reconsider, please do not hesitate to contact this office at your earliest convenience.

David chuckled, handed the letter off to Stewart McBride, standing alongside. "Here, I think you'll enjoy this."

The journalist had come down to the harbor that morning in high spirits. He had spent much of the previous two days holed up in his room, feverishly composing a long article on the issues raised in the CIA report, but he shook his head in dismay as he read.

"Jesus, I remember now who we're dealing with," he said when he'd finished. "I never should've agreed to this fucking deal."

David smiled. "Too late now."

"Anyway, I think I've got you beat." Stewart handed him a scroll of telex paper. "Read the note from my editor, that last bit."

David glanced over the edited version of Stewart's dispatch–still a mere two paragraphs, still only a news brief buried in the back pages of newspapers–and found the editor's comments at the bottom:

Still having trouble getting much space due to subject matter, constant focus on the negative. What about trying something more human interest/uplifting along the lines of "hope endures among the ashes" or, best, a kind of Romeo and Juliet "young love transcends the battlelines"? Give it some thought; could really help to give this country the attention it deserves.

They shared a low, bitter laugh, much to the bafflement of the Kutaran officials standing nearby.

"Well, in lieu of Romeo and Juliet," Stewart said, "let's hope genocide gives them a stiffie."

Dimitrios Terezios, the *Esmeralda*'s captain, was lounging in the harbormaster's swivel chair, his feet propped on the desk, but he slid them to the floor at David's approach. "Hey, sorry to hear about the British guy," he said. "He seemed okay for . . . well, for a British guy."

David nodded, suspected this passed for deep empathy in Dimitrios's world. "Thanks. He was okay. He was very okay."

"What do you want to do with his stuff?" Dimitrios motioned with his chin.

At the far end of the desk, someone had divided out the mail for the Moonlight residents, made a neat short stack for each. David found Nigel's: a manila envelope from the British Foreign Ministry, three letters from Sarah, several others from friends or colleagues.

"I don't know," he said. "Send it back, I guess."

As the one o'clock hour approached, David cinched up the outgoing mailbag, tied its cord in a knot; inside was his report detailing the death of Nigel Mayhew, and Stewart's dispatch entitled "The Next Cambodia?" He was stepping away when a Kutaran official came to his side with a worried expression.

"Aren't you going to seal it? You know, with the piece of metal?"

David looked around to see that others were watching him with concern as well. "Mr. Mayhew did that," he replied. "I don't have the metal press to do that."

The disappointment in the room was palpable.

———————

Late that evening, David returned to the harbor, but found Paolo was away from his office. The warehouse guards motioned down Pier 4 in the direction of the little pilothouse.

The businessman was at the desk on the second floor, working on one of his sketches. The windowed room was like an artist's studio now, his finished drawings tacked haphazardly across the walls, the floor littered with discarded efforts and cigarette butts. David leaned over Paolo's shoulder to examine his current effort: a busy dockside scene, a freighter being unloaded.

"Very nice. Is it the *Esmeralda*?"

Paolo smiled. "Except without the rust. I don't have the proper pens to draw rust, so maybe it will be the *Esmeralda* of twenty years ago."

"And where's Dimitrios?"

"No Dimitrios. I try to keep my scenes pleasant, like your Norman Rockwell."

David chuckled, strolled to the far end of the room. There was no other chair, so he sat on the floor, rested his back against the wall.

Paolo glanced up from his sketch. "You look very tired."

David had just finished with his usual round of Friday meetings, all those which accompanied each return of the *Esmeralda*: at the palace; at the Foreign and Interior ministries; with the military high command at their headquarters up on Baktiar Hill. The ones that day had been unusually tedious and protracted; he hadn't finished with the generals until nearly nine o'clock.

"I think I'm just getting worn out by the futility of it all," he said. "These endless meetings, all these ministers and generals asking me to decipher what the American directives mean, when we're going to do something. What do I tell them? I've run out of things to tell them. What I want to tell them is, 'Stop looking to the Americans,' but they're incapable of that." He wearily shook his head. "You know, Nigel said to me a while back that the Kutarans are like children, always looking to their father figure for answers. I thought it was ridiculous at the time—typical Brit condescension—but I understand what he meant now."

Paolo set his pen down, folded his arms over his middle. "But you must admit, your government is doing all it can to promote that."

David nodded. In the report he had sent out on the *Esmer-*

alda that day, he had included yet another long disquisition on the absurdity–"cruelty" was the word he'd used–of the American policy. Spurred by the tenuous prospect of American assistance at some future date, he had pointed out, the Kutaran government was continuing to wage a war it could not possibly win on its own. At the same time, since that theoretical American assistance was contingent on the palace spurning negotiations with the rebels, the policy meant a perpetuation of the bloody stalemate, the people of Laradan condemned to be shelled until the city collapsed or the Americans finally chose to become involved.

"No, you're right, of course," David said. "We've maneuvered them into this trap, the trap of hoping. If they would just give that up, if they stopped looking to the outside for rescue, they would see things much more realistically. The problem is, I'm not the person who can tell them that."

"Who is the person?"

David thought for a moment. "Nigel."

Paolo gave a weak smile, reached for his packet of cigarettes on the desk. "But maybe it is not so grim as you think. This CIA report about genocide, it will have an effect, no?" He turned back to David with a start. "Sorry. Stewart mentioned it to me, but he didn't say how he obtained it."

Against the wall, David nodded, gazed about the room. Until a few hours earlier, he, too, had been buoyed by that notion, caught up by Stewart's optimism, but it had drained away over the course of his meetings. "Yeah, maybe that changes everything. Or maybe that along with my report, the news that Nigel's been killed. That's what I've been telling myself." He looked back to his friend with an ironic expression. "Or maybe it'll be in a month from now, when the KPLA starts impaling kids on pitchforks. Or maybe not. Actually, I can already see the letter on that one: 'As you are no doubt aware, this administration has long discouraged the impaling of children on farming implements.'"

David leaned his head against the wall, closed his eyes. He listened to the calls of the seabirds outside and it soothed him.

"But whatever happens," Paolo said gently, "you can't blame yourself. You do understand that, don't you? This is all being decided in Washington. It's not your doing."

David opened his eyes to see that his friend was watching him with an air of concern. He smiled. "Well, thank you, Paolo, but you're wrong. Because I'm their salesman. That's my job. I'm the one who keeps the charade going, who keeps hope alive."

When he finally left the pilothouse, David decided to walk back to the hotel along the promenade. It was quite late by then, past midnight, and the refugees who lived on the grass fringe had long since put out their little campfires; they resembled so many odd-shaped bundles scattered there as they slept. The pretty wrought-iron streetlamps along the seawall had been shut off for some time now, either as a conservation move or to impede the work of the rebel artillery spotters at night, and with the fog coming in off the water, the walk was cast in a murky gloom. Occasionally David made out the figure of another person moving in this gloom—they leaned against the railing or were pacing over the stones—and after a number of such sightings, it occurred to him that they were all men, men like him who could not sleep.

He was avoiding Amira. In the two days since he had shown her his photo album on the roof, he had not visited her at the field hospital in Independence Park, he had stayed away from the table in the Moonlight lobby altogether. On both mornings, he had left the hotel very early, and found any excuse—such as visiting Paolo at the harbor—to stay out until late, only returning when he was quite certain she would be asleep.

He was not exactly sure why he was doing this, except that he felt a kind of embarrassment over their conversation, an embarrassment that was growing worse as time went on. Without really intending to, he had talked about Eddie in some detail, had told her things he'd never told anyone: about the two of them growing up, about what had taken him to Vietnam and what had happened there. All this from someone for whom even hearing the word "brother" still caused a tightening in his chest, who had virtually excised the word from his vocabulary for the pain it evoked, and the experience of breaking with that had left him feeling both astonished and ashamed. This shame he could not explain either, but it was as if he had transgressed in some way. Against Amira? Against Eddie? He didn't know. Instead, he was only left with the feeling and a deepening reluctance to face her.

As he walked, David tried to busy himself by thinking of tomorrow's roster of meetings and appointments.

At noon, the rebel messenger on Gowarshad Pass. After that, another session with the king's senior advisers at the palace, then on to the Interior Ministry, then back to army headquarters again. The next day, more appointments, more conferences, more meaningless discussions, and then another round the day after that, a routine that would keep all of them occupied through the week, carry them along until the next voyage of the *Esmeralda*, when the cycle would start over at the beginning.

While Rome burned, David thought to himself, Nero had fiddled; in the face of disaster in the modern age, meetings were held.

Approaching the Moonlight's back gate, a voice suddenly barked out from somewhere in the darkness, commanding him to stop. David froze as a powerful light swept the fog, finally found his face. The light was quickly extinguished and one of the soldiers posted at the gate called out an apology, ushered him forward.

The fog seemed much thicker on the hotel grounds, as if clinging to the bushes and trees, and his progress up the gentle rise was guided only by memory and the faint glow of the lobby lights in the distance.

"Hello," she called softly.

The sound caused David to jump and he peered into the murk, made out the shape of Amira amid the arches of the gazebo.

"Jesus, what is this," he called back, "scare-the-shit-out-of-the-American night?"

He heard her laugh. "Sorry. Did I startle you?"

"Hell, yes. I didn't think this place could get any creepier, but I'd forgotten about the fog."

As she came down the lawn toward him, David saw she wore an amused expression. She gazed up at the trees. "Rather like England, isn't it? It means winter is coming. That and the clouds, they're always the first signs." She turned to him, her mouth still set in a smile. "I've barely seen you the past couple of days. If I didn't know better, I would think you're avoiding me."

David looked at the ground, scratched at the back of his neck. "Yeah, well, just really busy, you know? All these damned meetings, and then with the *Esmeralda* coming in today . . ."

Amira waited until he had looked up. "We never have to talk about him again, David. If you want to–anytime you want to–we can, but if you don't, that's fine, too. I'll never ask you to."

David nodded, felt his throat abruptly tighten. "Thank you," he managed.

She reached out to pat his arm in an almost collegial way. "In the meantime, I miss you. Why don't you come to the park tomorrow, after your meeting on the pass? We can have lunch together."

He smiled, as much in gratitude as in amusement at the suggestion. "Lunch? People still eat lunch in this city?"

"Well, gruel. Maybe I can get my hands on some glucose solution for dessert."

David laughed. He would be down off Gowarshad Pass by 12:30; his first meeting at the palace wasn't until 3:00. "Okay. That would be nice."

"You promise?"

"I promise," he said.

They walked together toward the lights of the hotel.

———

The air was rent by the call of thousands of birds. They swirled in the sky in great flocks, flitted between the branches of every tree. The number of birds in that section of Independence Park had seemed to grow steadily over the past days, but Amira had never seen so many as on that afternoon, and it suddenly occurred to her that it was because they were losing their perches elsewhere. In Independence Park, as throughout the city, the trees were disappearing, cut down by the refugees for their campfires, and that corner of the park by the field hospital had probably only been spared thus far by the presence of soldiers and the medical staff. Amira stood for a while to watch the birds.

She heard the splash of running water, and turned to see that Sister Evangeline had emerged from the main surgical tent, was washing her hands at the water tank by the entrance. Amira strolled in her direction.

"Hello. How are you today?" she called.

The nun straightened with a broad smile, flicked water from her fingers. "Good. Very good." She motioned toward the surgical tent. "It's quiet in there today."

Evangeline was a few years older than Amira, possessed of that statuesque beauty which marked so many Kutaran women from the far north, and she had long since traded in her religious habit for the green hospital scrubs of the other nurses, her faith only discernible by the large gold crucifix which hung from her neck. Amira was fond of her; Evangeline had gone out of her way to make her feel welcome and appreciated over these past weeks.

Reaching into a side pocket, the nun brought out a pack of cigarettes, automatically handed one to Amira and took another for herself.

"That new doctor has banned them from the operating room," Evangeline explained, bringing out a lighter. "He believes they are bad for the patients." She said this with a lilt to her voice, as if she considered the man poorly informed.

They strolled together through what passed for the pediatric section of the field clinic. By observing Evangeline during these walk-arounds, Amira had become quite proficient at detecting the telltale signs on the skin or in the eyes which signaled the primary stages of infection or disease. The task was complicated in the pediatric section, however, by the red tarpaulins overhead. They had been put there as protection against the sun—and now, against the dew that settled at night—but they tended to cast the children and their mothers in a deceptively healthy-looking russet glow.

"This one is about ready to go home," the nun said, stopping to indicate a little girl in front of them, squirming and climbing in her mother's lap.

"Wherever that might be," Amira replied. "I get the feeling a lot of the mothers prefer staying here. At least they know their children will eat regularly."

Evangeline chuckled, puffed on her cigarette. "I'm sure that is true. We have a lot of malingerers."

She had told Amira that she was from a farming village near the provincial town of Ezzam, in the far northeastern corner of the country. It was an area where Catholic missionaries had made inroads at some point in the past, before giving up or being run out, and they had left behind a small but devout community of the faithful. Amira hadn't asked Evangeline the status of her family, if they had fled to the city or remained behind rebel lines, and the nun had never volunteered the information.

Amira peeked beneath the bandage on a young girl's arm—no discoloration around the stitching, the wound was healing—and straightened, continued on their stroll.

"Why did you become a nun?"

Evangeline seemed puzzled by the question. "Well, I felt called, I suppose."

Amira nodded, but the answer was less than satisfying. She was still not used to the idea that deep rumination over one's life and work was a largely Western phenomenon, that in most of the world, people simply did what was available to them.

"You were never curious about . . . ?" From Evangeline's stolid expression, Amira knew she wouldn't get any help with this one. "You know, being with a man?" She regretted the words as soon as they left her. "I'm sorry, that's very rude. Probably no one has asked you that before."

Evangeline giggled. "I think every nun has been asked this many times." She looked around her, at the rows of sick and injured children, at the patch of grass beyond the canopy, lit by the afternoon sun. "Of course, I've thought about it. But I tell myself that to be with God, to know that I am in His embrace, how can a man compare? Compared to that, how good can the pleasures of the flesh be?"

Amira thought of a reply, but decided against it.

———

David felt in a fine mood, better than he had in some time. What made this especially odd was that he'd just come from his meeting with Rustam, the KPLA liaison, on Gowarshad Pass, an event that normally cast him into a kind of directionless fury.

At the army base by the foot of the pass, he performed his usual ritual of handing off the rebel note to the officer in charge, waited a few minutes for his bad photocopies in exchange, then hurried for the idling embassy car.

"To Independence Park please, Musa," he told the driver. "To the field hospital."

Halfway there, though, an idea came to him. "Do you know of a wineshop on the way?"

In the rearview mirror, Musa gave him a confused look. "A wineshop, Mr. Richards?"

"Yes. You know, wine, for drinking."

The driver stared at the empty road in front of them, his

bewilderment only growing. "Well, maybe in the downtown district," he finally offered, "but I'm sure it will be closed."

David nodded. "But maybe we can find the owner."

———

They came to a quiet young boy, his chest wrapped in bandages, but his face lit up at the sight of Amira. She knelt beside him, stroked his hair. "There's my little man. How's my little man today?" She glanced up at Evangeline. "This is Ali. He's my favorite." She turned back to the boy, lightly tickled his neck, causing him to squeal with joy. "What a beautiful little guy. And so brave. You're very brave, aren't you, Ali?"

Evangeline watched this in silence, but a dark shadow settled over her face; she waited until they had moved on. "You shouldn't get so attached to them, Miss Amira," she said softly.

The comment stopped Amira in her tracks.

"You don't know what might happen to them," the nun explained, "to any of us here. You can't be loving them so much."

Amira felt a rush of anger, one that built as she stared at the woman's serene face, the shiny crucifix around her neck. "But isn't God watching over us, Evangeline?"

She said this in a caustic tone, intending to shame, but instead the nun slowly shook her head. "No," she muttered. "No, I don't believe He is."

Amira turned away from her, to the sunlit grass beyond the canopies, and there she saw David approaching. He carried something in his hand, and it was probably due to the incongruity of the setting that it took Amira a moment to recognize it was a bottle of wine. The sight instantly lifted her mood, caused her to laugh.

———

In his memory, it would always exist in three distinct parts. First, there was the pressure—on his cheeks, on his chest—a pressure so intense that David thought it must split open his skin. Then there was the burst of light, so hot and white that for a time there was no other color in the world. It was only after that light, quite separate, that there came the sound, and of this, David could never be certain whether he actually heard it or just knew it must have been there. And he would always know that these neat distinctions in his memory could not possibly be true, that all these things had occurred over such an infinitesimal span of time as to be beyond the ability of any human to discern, but his mind would never let go of the order he gave it.

He would not remember how long he stood there, staring into that cloud of dust and smoke where the tents and canopies had been, and he would not remember if he checked over his own body, to see if the blood on his face and shirt and arms belonged to him or to someone else. But he would remember going into that cloud, tripping over unseen things, groping with his hands in the chalky dark, and he would remember that for a very long time there was only silence, that, like a young child, this shrouded world had to wait for the scream to build in its throat.

He remembered to look for green hospital clothes, for a tall woman with long black hair, and that is how he found her. She stood where the children had been, where bits of the awning overhead now flapped like streamers, and her arms were extended out to either side in a helpless gesture.

"What happened?" Amira whispered. She was covered in their remnants—it speckled her chest and shoulders, it was in her hair—and some of it was torn from such deep places that the blood hadn't found a way to leave it yet. Her dark eyes looked into his, but it was as if she didn't see him. "What happened?" she asked again.

David didn't know what to do, so he put a hand over her eyes. The dust and smoke was thinning now, others were appearing in the murk, the scream had broken. Amira brought her hands in to make two trembling fists against her chest.

"What happened?" she screamed.

He kept his hand over her eyes, and whispered in her ear, "It's okay, it's okay," as he led her out, over torn blankets and cots and bodies, toward the fiery sunlight. When finally they emerged back into the day, everywhere people were running, shouting, bleeding. He became aware of a strange motion over the ground–he thought of hopping frogs or bubbling water–and he looked down to see that the grass was littered with hundreds of flopping, dying birds.

————

She still trembled uncontrollably, so David helped her undress, guided her into the shower. Amira stood under the spray, covered her face with her hands as she sobbed, and David watched the bloodwater run off her. Gathering up her clothes, he went out to the bedroom, to where Arkadi waited by the door.

"Is she all right?" the manager asked.

"She seems to be. I don't see any wounds on her." Blood dripped from the hospital scrubs to make little splashing sounds on the parquet floor; he wished he had thought to ask Arkadi for a plastic bag. "We should probably just burn these."

The manager nodded, pushed back the sleeves of his suit jacket to take the clothes from him. "The others have asked to see her. The Contessa–"

David nodded. "Not right now. Maybe in a while. I'll see what she wants."

With Arkadi gone, he returned to the bathroom. Amira hadn't moved from under the spray, her hands still clutched her face, but her trembling had subsided, the water running off her now was clean. Taking a hand towel from the washbasin rack, he mopped up the bathroom tiles, but despite several rinsings they retained a pinkish film. He turned off the shower, wrapped her in one of the large bath towels.

"Careful," he said as he helped her out. "The floor's still a little wet."

She sat on the edge of the bed, pulled the towel tightly around her. She stared at the wall in front of her. "Why'd they do it?" she whispered. "Why would they have done that?"

He sat beside her, stroked her back. "I don't know. I don't know."

With her calmed, David thought to check the bathroom again for any blood spots he might have missed. He had been quite thorough with the floor, but in the bathtub drain he noticed two small pinkish objects. Peering close, he saw they were bits of flesh. He experienced a moment of indecision—what was the proper way to dispose of such things?—but because he couldn't think of what else to do, he took them up in a wad of toilet paper and flushed them away.

When he returned to the bedroom, Amira was hunched forward, her elbows on her knees as she kneaded her hands. There was a peculiar energy to her now, a kind of sharp-eyed briskness.

"Do you think they've released a casualty list yet?"

"Probably not yet," David said. "But I can find out."

She nodded. "That would be good. Because there's a woman I'd like to find out about. The problem is, I don't know her actual name. She's a nun—Sister Evangeline—and I doubt they'd list her that way on the casualty list."

He watched her. "I can check."

Amira nodded again, but it wasn't clear she was listening to him, perhaps just nodding to the sound of his voice. "Anyway, it's not that important. I know she's dead. She knew it was going to happen. I don't mean she actually knew—she just had a kind of sense about it—because right before it happened, she said something to me that—" She was talking very fast, her words crunching together, but she abruptly stopped, looked up at him. "Oh, and somebody else. A little boy. His name is Ali. He's four. Or maybe five. I can't remember right now, but I'm pretty sure four. He's small for his age, very dark-skinned." What had made her eyes so beautiful was the light in them, the way they had reflected a certain serenity, but now those eyes reflected nothing; they were as dulled as clouded glass. "Anyway, his name is Ali. Ali . . . ? Damnit, what's his last name? Ali . . . ?" She was becoming a bit frantic now, her gaze flitting around the room as if the answer might be found there. "Why can't I remember?" She hit her knee hard with a fist. "Think. Ali . . ."

And then a great sob burst from her throat, her face crumpled under her anguish. David sat beside her again, leaned her into his shoulder. He made soft, soothing sounds as she sobbed, he stroked her wet hair. She felt warm and damp in his arms, like a baby.

It was evening when he came down. Arkadi and the others were at the lobby table and they watched, stone-faced, as he approached.

"How is she?" Paolo asked.

David sat, rubbed at his eyes. "Okay. No physical wounds, but pretty shattered. She's sleeping now."

The Contessa swiftly rose. "I'll go sit with her."

David turned, was about to protest, but there was such a plaintive, beseeching look on the old lady's face that he hesitated.

"I won't disturb her," she said. "Just to sit beside her, in case she wakes up."

"Okay." David nodded with a tired smile. "Yes, that would be nice."

The Contessa hurried for the staircase.

David glanced between the men. "She was asking for a casualty list."

Stewart sighed, took a folded piece of paper from his shirt pocket. "Still very early, but already it's fucking horrifying."

David unfolded the paper. "Jesus."

The list of the dead extended to two columns on the page. After about forty names, it continued with general physical descriptions: female juvenile, approximately ten, wearing white dress; torso of woman, probably middle-aged.

"Seventy-four by that count," Stewart said, "another two

hundred or so wounded. They're expecting quite a few more to die in the hospitals, and of course, there's probably some who were just, well . . ." He cleared his throat. "All in all, it's kind of a miracle she wasn't hit–seems like nearly everyone else there was."

David nodded distractedly as he looked down the list.

From the time he had spent outside the field hospital, he estimated that probably about a dozen doctors and nurses worked there. They had been grouped together on the death list–there were nine names there–but there was no reference to a Sister Evangeline. He scanned the page for a boy named Ali, and came to the notation: "Ali Farsawati, male, age 4."

"Do you think it was deliberate?" Paolo asked.

"Who knows?" David set the paper aside, rubbed his eyes again. "Who the fuck knows? Inadvertent. That's how the little shit up on the ridge will describe it. Another inadvertent action." He dropped his hands, rose from the table. "I should go back up."

The other men looked at him with something like pity.

"You should change your clothes, Mr. Richards," Arkadi said.

David turned to him, puzzled, but then glanced down; his shirt and trousers were blotched with smears of dried blood. "Yeah, I'll do that. I'll change."

––––––

Amira stirred in the dark. "Is that you?"

"Yes," David answered gently from his chair by the desk.

She settled back onto the pillow. "The Contessa was here before."

He nodded, even though he knew she couldn't see him. "She was concerned about you. They all are."

"That's nice. But they don't need to be." She was quiet for a time. "Did they release a casualty list?"

He scratched at a small cut on his hand. "No," he said. "Not yet."

It was a very dark night, so that all David could see was the vague outline of her in the bed. He had left the balcony door ajar, and the crash of the waves breaking on the promenade wall rose over the lawn and trees and came to where they were.

After a while, he heard the rustle of her, and then the bedside lamp came on. She was sitting up now, the sheet pulled over her chest as she stared across the room.

"What is it?" he asked.

She shook her head. "It's strange, but I can't actually remember it. I've been trying to, but I can't. I mean, I remember the feeling, this feeling of pressure, but then everything was just dark. Dark and dusty at the same time."

David nodded. "It happened very fast."

Amira shook her head again. "But it's more than that, I think. I think my mind must have . . ." She looked to him. "And then you came. You covered my eyes. I remember that, you covering my eyes. Why did you do that?"

"I don't know," he said. "Instinct, I guess."

"Instinct? Because you didn't want me to see? You wanted to protect me?"

"I guess so."

She watched him for a long moment, but David couldn't read the expression: thoughtful, appraising, but something else, too—fear, maybe, or sadness.

"What would you like to do?" she asked.

He didn't answer, wasn't sure what she meant.

"I want to make love," she said.

At first, he simply stared at her. He thought of her manic state of a few hours ago, her fragility, and wondered if this was really at all what she wanted. Then he looked down at his hands, twisted together in his lap, and he considered his own fragility, wondered if this was really something he wanted.

"I'm not dead yet, David," she said softly. "We're not dead yet."

He rose from the chair and started toward the bed.

———

By the following afternoon, the death toll from the Independence Park blast had climbed to more than one hundred. Among those killed by the lone heavy-ordnance artillery shell from the ridge were some forty-five children, as well as a medical team that included Kutar's most prominent pediatric surgeon.

Naturally news of the bombing traveled quickly through the city; it had been the single deadliest explosion in Laradan since the beginning of the siege, and lent added horror by the target it struck, the tender age of so many of its victims. While there was considerable speculation over whether the rebels had deliberately targeted the clinic, there could be no question, given their bird's-eye view of the city, that they knew exactly what their shell had caused. Any hopes this might inspire an act of contrition were soon dispelled, however; at 1:22 that afternoon, twenty-four hours to the minute after the blast, the KPLA batteries on the ridge opened up with the most ferocious and sustained bombardment in some time. Into the evening, and then into the night, shells rained down on every corner of Laradan.

By virtue of its neutral status, those living at the Moonlight were, of course, largely immune to this—but this was never truer than on that day. From morning to night, none ventured beyond the hotel grounds. Instead, all remained within their sanctuary and there they moved about on light feet, they spoke to one another in hushed tones, as if that great colossus had been converted into some vast convalescent home.

In a way, it had been. To have had Amira so improbably survive the Independence Park blast, coming after losing Nigel so capriciously, filled all of them with an indefinable gratitude, a sense that they needed to be caring, to tend to one another for as much time as any of them had left. Without conscious thought behind it, this manifested itself in an impulse to stay close to home, to move and speak softly.

As for the invalid around which all this revolved, Amira may not have had any clear memory of the bombing, but it appeared at least some tucked-away corner of her mind did. Almost that entire next day she slept, only occasionally stirring at the sound of one of the others peeking through the door to check on her. The Contessa, keeping vigil from an armchair beside her bed, kept these intrusions to a minimum before finally banning them altogether, turning back all who would enter with a baleful stare.

For David's part, the old lady's forbidding presence actually came as something of a relief, for he wasn't entirely sure what to make of the previous night. They had made love and he had stayed until Amira fell asleep, but then he had left, unable to decide whether staying in that bed, of waking up together in the morning or at some hour of the night, was something that either of them wanted. What he most feared was not that Amira would decide it had been a silly mistake—that would be easy enough to get past—but a mistake on the order that it might alter things between them, because David didn't think he could bear that kind of loneliness now, going back to sitting out on the rooftop alone. No doubt it was the apprehension of learning this that kept him from going up to her room all that day, but the old lady as her bedside sentry provided a handy excuse.

"You should see her," Paolo said.

David had been standing out on the pool terrace, staring up at the night, and he hadn't heard his friend come outside. He searched Paolo's face, tried to detect if there was a hidden inference in his words, but in the weak light spilling from the lobby, David couldn't tell much. He nodded. "But she's probably sleeping now. And the Contessa . . ."

Paolo shook his head. "She's awake. I was just up there." He smiled. "As for the old crone, just act like you can't hear her. That's what I do. It drives her mad."

David chuckled, started for the lobby. "Good advice. I'll do that."

He rapped gently on the door, opened it a few inches to poke his head through. Amira was sitting up in bed, looked to him with a wan smile, but the Contessa in her armchair was incensed.

"You, too?" the old lady spat. "I thought I made it clear we weren't to be disturbed. I just finished chasing off that little Italian."

Amira laughed lightly. "It's okay, Contessa. Come in, David."

He stepped through the door, pulled it closed behind him. "I wanted to see how you're doing," he said, approaching the foot of the bed.

"I'm fine."

"Finer still if she could get some rest," the Contessa chimed in. "Honestly, it's like Old Calcutta in here, the number of people tromping through."

David considered asking the Contessa to leave them alone for a minute, but that was to invite the very discussion he dreaded having. And anyway, unless Amira insisted, the old lady wasn't going to budge.

"So, how are you feeling?" he asked.

"Good," Amira said, still with the faint smile. "Tired. I can't imagine why. I've been sleeping all day."

David nodded, tried to read some sign on her face. He suddenly couldn't think of what more to say. "Well, I just wanted to check on you. I should let you sleep."

"Thank you. You, too."

He frowned slightly at this, not catching its meaning.

"Sleep," she explained. "You should sleep, too. You look exhausted."

He nodded again and turned, started for the door.

"And don't come back until I give the word," the Contessa called after him. "Perhaps tomorrow I'll post visiting hours."

David went up to the roof and stood against the railing. Shells were still falling across the city, so many explosions they produced a strobelike dance of red-and-white light against the low clouds.

Sleep, she had advised him. He couldn't imagine when he might sleep, only knew that it would not be for a very long time yet.

––––––––

He passed through those days as if sleepwalking. He went to his meetings, he sat across tables from men in business suits or military uniforms or white robes with gold stitching, and they all blended together. He watched their mouths move, the changing expressions on their faces, but he didn't really hear what they were saying–he didn't need to, they all were working off scripts now, long since memorized–and then he would recite his speaking lines with as much feeling as a bored actor or a sleepwalking man could manage. He wandered the city, but saw little of what passed before his eyes. He sat out on his roof, but whether it was a quiet night or a mad one, the city burning around him, he would not have been able to say afterward, so scantly did it register in his mind. And it was only when he lay on the cot in his rooftop home, as he stared up at that corrugated-tin ceiling, the burning candle casting it in neat, alternating ribbons of light and shadow, that he felt differently, that he felt as if he were truly awake, because, after all, what kind of sleepwalker dreams about wanting to sleep?

The source of it, he recognized, was Amira. He was now desperate to speak with her. Even to hear that their being together had been a tremendous blunder, that she might never come up to the roof again, even that would be welcome now. But it was as if she had become a sleepwalker, too, only going through the motions of conversation whenever he visited her room, their chats taken up with pleasantries and watched over by the Contessa, and it was only after enduring this for several days, after his irritation with her trivial talk and the old lady's constant presence had made David want to shake Amira, that he understood this was the way she wanted it—maybe more, needed it—as if his presence, what he might say, threatened to end her dreamy sleep, take her back to where she wasn't ready to return: to a sunny, bird-filled afternoon, to a bed they had shared in pained hunger.

A very quiet night, the low clouds over the city seeming to absorb all its sounds. This was not true, of course. Even on that night there came the occasional car horn or child's cry, the pounding of metal—for some reason unknown to David, there was always metal being pounded somewhere in this city—but the first sound he was conscious of was that of her approaching footsteps.

She touched his shoulder. "Hello."

He looked up to her with a guarded smile, hoped that neither his anxiety nor his relief showed. "Hello. And please don't ask if I'd prefer to be alone."

Amira laughed gently, moved toward the other armchair. "Do I ask that often?"

"Yes."

"I'm sorry. English politeness; it must be terribly annoying."

She sat, and he looked at her profile in the moonlight. She appeared to have grown thinner over these past few days, there was a new tautness around her cheekbones.

"How are you?"

She nodded. "Good. Better."

She looked out over the sleeping city, and wondered if he had this view memorized by now, if he would be able to point to places blindfolded. She couldn't comprehend the hours, the entire nights he spent watching over this dying valley, how he could endure it. This wasn't any of her business, though.

"It's odd how similar it is to being physically ill," she said instead. "Like having an injury or the flu, all you want to do is sleep. I wouldn't have predicted that." She smiled. "Of course, if I let the

Contessa have her way, I'd stay bedridden for the next month. I think I've rather become her hobby around here."

David nodded. "She does run a tight ship, would've made an excellent prison guard."

She watched him for a moment, and her smile slipped away. "I'm sorry, though. It must have been confusing to you, my not talking or coming up here."

"That's okay."

She looked down at her intertwined fingers. "I think I just needed time to process it all, you know? I don't mean about you or that night, but . . ." She picked at a fingernail, then spread her hands flat on her knees, stared out past the railing. "Because I do remember it. When I told you that night that I didn't, I don't know if I was lying or if it was really true then. Maybe it's come back to me in bits and pieces, or maybe I just wanted to pretend that night, that I thought if I tried hard enough, I could will it away. But I do remember it now. It's like a strip of film that constantly replays, that won't stop. Do you know what I mean?"

David nodded.

"I think I'm afraid it'll never go away. That wherever I am, whatever I'm doing, no matter how happy I am or . . . well, that it will still be there, that it will never leave my eyes. Do you know what I mean?"

David nodded again, remembered the little girl in the ruins of the Sarvanya orphanage.

She turned to him then. "So what do you do? Do you know? How do you get it to leave your eyes?"

For a long moment, they simply looked at each other. Then David rose from his chair and stepped over to Amira, reached for her hand, and she stood as well.

"I think you just go on, you just endure," he said. "I think that's all we can do."

And then he was brushing the hair from her face and he was caressing her cheek. And then he was kissing her lips, her jaw, he was placing a hand on her neck to keep her close, and he was feeling the pulse of her in his fingertips.

"How can you bear it, David?" she whispered, not even aware the words were slipping out. "How can you bear watching so much?"

"I'm so tired," he answered, so softly he wasn't sure he made any sound at all. "I'm so tired."

"I know you are," she whispered. "You need to sleep. You can sleep now."

He took her hand again and they went together to his little home on the roof. They lay down together on the narrow cot, and she stroked his face, kissed him again and again, and he kissed her back—her cheek, her mouth, her neck—and what he felt was tenderness and exhaustion and that magical way one body might yield to another. And then they were undressing each other, and they were moving together, looking into each other's eyes in the deep shadows of that small, forgotten room, and then she was clutching his head in her hands to keep him close, he was feeling the warmth of her against his skin, and they were breathing in the panted breath of each other, sharing the quickening beating of their hearts, and when it was over, when he lay back to stare up at that ceiling he had spent so many nights watching, she held him, she leaned over him to give delicate kisses to his eyes, bidding them closed, and she whispered to him, "Sleep, sleep, close your eyes, you can sleep now."

Dear Mr. Richards:

This letter is in reference to your report of December 1, regarding the current situation in Kingdom of Kutar and the death in that country of the British diplomatic representative, Mr. Nigel Mayhew. As you are no doubt aware, Great Britain has not only long enjoyed close political, social, and cultural ties with Kingdom of Kutar, but has also provided invaluable assistance to the United

States in forging our own close relations with the kingdom. For these reasons, we were all deeply saddened to learn of Mr. Mayhew's death.

In regard to specific issues raised in your report of December 1, I would like to say that your incisive analysis on what you perceive to be the potential shortcomings of American policy in Kingdom of Kutar was of profound interest; we were especially impressed by your discussion of the difficulties that have arisen as a result of the Kutaran People's Liberation Army (KPLA) being placed on the Terrorism Index, Probationary Status, and the ban on negotiations that this designation mandates. It is precisely this sort of keen analysis, formulated under what must be trying circumstances, that speaks to the professionalism and dedication of our Foreign Service Officers corps, and it is a contribution of which you should be justly proud.

On a related matter, I must unfortunately report that, in recent days, this office has received a number of media queries regarding an alleged CIA analysis, allegedly written several months ago, in which it was allegedly suggested that the KPLA might, under certain circumstances, be disposed toward genocidalist tendencies. While we have firmly denied the existence of this alleged report, our investigations have determined the author of these rumors to be a journalist, Stewart McBride, currently reporting from Kingdom of Kutar.

As you are no doubt aware, this administration has been a vigorous defender of the First Amendment, and of the news media's right to gather and disseminate information to the American public in a responsible and balanced manner. At the same time, it has strongly discouraged government officials from associating with those members of the news media whose reckless allegations of actions or inactions by the United States government are likely to provide aid and comfort to our domestic or foreign adversaries, and thereby pose a threat to national security. From our investigations, it appears that Mr. McBride's irresponsible assertions may have *stemmed from an inadvertent comment on your part, and for this reason, we strongly urge you to end all contact with Mr. McBride and to counsel Government of Kutar (GOK) to do likewise.*

On a more pleasant note, I am pleased to report that the contribution of the United States government to the ongoing relief effort for the city of Laradan now totals in excess of $22 million, complementing some $58 million from private American donor organizations, a level of assistance that exemplifies the long-standing American tradition of generosity to those in need, and which I am sure will convey to the Kutaran people our very strong commitment to their cause and continuing welfare.

Finally, you will no doubt be gratified to hear that your outstanding reports on the ongoing crisis in Kingdom of Kutar have served to foster a very deep and abiding sense of kinship with you and your ordeals among your colleagues here at State, a sense of close personal connection which–I'm sure you will agree–is unfortunately all too rare in such a large and varied institution. For this reason, I know I speak for a great many of your colleagues when I wish you all continued progress in your mission in Kingdom of Kutar.

David looked up to see Stewart McBride standing over him. "So, what's the word?"

David shook his head, handed him the letter. The journalist didn't immediately turn to it, however, merely began to nod with a dull expression.

"I know. They didn't run it." He indicated the scroll of telex paper he held bunched in one hand. "Everyone denied it. State, the CIA, the NSA. They all just fucking stonewalled together." He gazed absently across the harbormaster's office. "I'm going across. You know that, right? We had a deal, but I'm going across now."

David nodded.

Musa eased the sedan past the gilded gates of the palace compound to merge with the scant traffic on Hamari Boulevard.

"Now to the Defense Ministry, Mr. Richards?" he asked.

The question was unnecessary, but in the backseat, David nodded; by now, Musa knew the Friday afternoon appointment schedule as well as he did.

As they headed up Baktiar Hill, David looked out at People's Struggle Boulevard. Here and there were reminders of where shells had landed—a crater in the road, a partially collapsed building—but in this prosperous section of the city, high walls and shrubbery obscured most of the damage.

They came to a break in the flank of walls, and David gazed out over the valley to see that the day was already ending, the whitewashed city taking on the first reddish hues of sunset. In the late brilliant light, the Moonlight Hotel on its promontory wore an unnatural sheen, its white marble glowing like glossed bone, its Indian sandstone turned a cotton-candy pink. From that distance, it looked like some great, garish dollhouse.

David glanced at his watch: nearly 5:00 PM. He knew Stewart was planning to set out just after dark—around 6:30 now with the shortening days—and he wanted to be back at the hotel before then, wanted to at least say goodbye to him.

He felt the sway of the car as they turned off the boulevard and into the circular drive of the Defense Ministry. David hunched down in the seat to peer up at the massive gray building and, at that moment, he suddenly recalled the expression on Stewart's face in the harbormaster's office, the uncertainty in his eyes when he had said he was going over the ridge. And then, an instant later, David was struck by another memory, this one of Eddie, on that afternoon in December, the two of them sitting at the kitchen table, the look in his brother's eyes.

"We're not stopping, Musa," he said.

But they already had. They were beneath the covered portico of the ministry's main entrance, the junior officer with his gold braid already coming down the steps to open David's door. From the driver's seat, Musa turned back to him.

"Pardon, sir?"

"We're not staying. We have to go." The junior officer opened David's door, waited for him to step out. "Tell him that. Tell him we'll reschedule for tomorrow."

David stared off as Musa explained this to the perplexed officer, waited for the door to be closed, for the car to start forward again. "Back to the hotel," he said then. "As quickly as you can."

––––––––––

At the threshold to his room, Stewart grinned. "Come to wish me luck?"

"Something like that," David replied.

He followed the journalist in. Stewart's meager possessions were spread over the bed, it appeared he was attempting to fit them into his rucksack with some degree of order, and other than these and the smell of cigarette smoke, there were few signs this had been his home for the past two months. David stood by the bed and watched him pack.

"Do you know how you'll go?"

Stewart cocked his head toward the balcony. "I'll show you."

His room was at the back end of the hotel, with a view of the city and mountains. On the balcony, Stewart pointed to the far western reaches of the coastal ridge, lit gold in the sun's last rays. "See that little cleft way down there? It's called the Salori Gap. The last few refugees who've made it down, they all came through there. It's just an old goat trail, so steep the KPLA isn't even bothering to guard it."

"You know that for sure?"

Stewart lowered his arm, gave David a scrutinizing gaze. "No. The last group of refugees came down—what was it, about a week ago—so it was open then, but . . . no, I don't know that for sure." He appeared about to say something more, but then abruptly led the way back into the room, resumed his packing. David leaned against the edge of the desk.

"What're you planning to do when you get across?"

Stewart hesitated, and David noticed the tremor in his fingers. "I don't know. The fixer says there's a couple of hill villages just the other side, so I guess the first thing is to take a look at them." He glanced over, tried to smile. "I haven't decided yet whether we should try to make contact with anyone still living over there or try to avoid them. I guess we'll figure that out when we see it."

David nodded. "I don't think you should do this."

The journalist stopped, stared down at his rucksack on the bed, and there was something in his posture that suggested he had been anticipating this, as if it were part of an argument he had been waging with himself. "And what's the alternative, David? To just watch this go on indefinitely? What's the alternative?"

David had no answer.

When they descended to the lobby, they found the other residents and the hotel staff had gathered to say goodbye. They huddled around Stewart to wish him luck, to urge him to be cautious. He accepted the worried embraces of Amira and the Contessa, kissed each of them on the cheek, and he placed an arm around Paolo as he thanked him for his help during those first difficult days of the siege.

David went with him out the front door and they started toward the front gate together, past the stilled fountain with its cherubs and egrets. In the twilight, the small white stones of the gravel drive gleamed like a path of snow.

They walked in silence down the tunnel of flanking palm trees, the crunch of their footsteps on the gravel sounding unusually loud in the stillness. The front gate came into view, and in the murk they could make out a lone figure standing on the far side.

"There's the fixer," Stewart said, picking up his pace.

But David clutched his arm, forced him to stop. "Don't go, Stewart. Don't do this."

The journalist searched his face in the dim light, then sighed, stared up into the fronds of the trees. For a moment, it appeared he might actually be reconsidering.

"I believe in God," he muttered finally. "I know that must seem weird—quite quaint and all in this day and age—but I do. And I truly believe that what I'm doing is so right—so right and important and necessary—that He will protect me." He turned to David with a vaguely contrite smile. "I know, fucking wacko, right? Like some fucking missionary in Borneo or something." The smile fell away. "But I've had thirty-seven years to come to this point. I can't turn my back on all that now."

They started down the drive again. As they walked, David stared at the young man waiting on the far side of the gate, his features beginning to take form in the lamplight. The crunching of the gravel sounded like machines working in the night.

But he had to try one last time. He again took Stewart's arm, again compelled him to stop. "Please, don't do it," he whispered in a voice gone hoarse. "I just have a very bad feeling about this. I think if you go up there . . ."

With an almost loving tenderness, Stewart reached out to touch David's face. "I have to," he said. "You know that." He patted David's cheek, tried to smile. "Don't worry. Everything will be all right. You'll be all right."

He then hurried on toward the gate and the man waiting for him there.

In the silence, Amira gazed up at the ceiling. The candlelight was casting the corrugated metal in alternating strips of brightness and shadow, and it reminded her of corduroy.

She turned into his side, ran her fingers lightly over his ribs. "You're worried about him, aren't you?"

David nodded. "He shouldn't have gone. I should have talked him out of it."

"But you tried. That's why you went out to the gate with him, wasn't it? And the only reason he delayed as long as he did, that was because of you. You did what you could."

She glanced up at his face—he was staring at the ceiling—and saw that he was unconvinced of this.

A strong breeze was coming in off the sea and it was causing the screen over the room's one window to puff every once in a while, the candle to flicker. From outside, the sound of the palm fronds brushing together sounded like tearing paper.

"He reminds me a little of Eddie," David muttered after a while. "The same impetuousness, the same temper. But also this kind of naïveté, you know? That was the thing about Eddie that was always so hard to figure out. There was this sweetness about him, this deeply trusting side, so whenever things went wrong or someone let him down, it came as this huge shock, a betrayal. I know it didn't seem that way to most people—I was always the good kid, he was the bad one—but I really think so many of his problems came from that, his basic sweetness, of just fundamentally not believing the world could be as cold as it is. So, a little lost. A little bit always looking to someone else to guide him. I think Stewart has some of that."

Nestled into his side, Amira lay very still. It was the first time David had mentioned his brother since that night with the photo album, but without seeing his face, she couldn't tell if he were truly talking to her or more to himself, and she didn't want to do or say anything that might intrude on his thoughts. At last, she gently nodded her head against his shoulder, she lay her hand flat on his chest; she didn't want to risk any more than that.

"I remember this conversation we had," he started again. "It was after he'd been in the bar fight, when the prosecutor offered him the deal of joining the army. I'd come home from college, and we were sitting at the kitchen table, just the two of us. Our dad was all for him taking the deal—he thought maybe a stint in the army would straighten him out, a helluva lot better than going to jail, having a criminal record—our mom was changing her mind every day, but sitting there in the kitchen, Eddie asked me what I thought he should do. And I'll never forget the look on his face sitting there. Kind of desperate—scared, I guess—but also really wanting to know. 'What do you think I should do?'

"And what I wanted to say to him was, 'Are you out of your fucking mind? They're going to send you to Vietnam. Plead out. You'll get a year, maybe eighteen months, but at least you won't go to Vietnam.' But I didn't say that. Because there was something in the way he looked, that question—'What do you think I should do?'—where all of a sudden I saw our whole life together, what it would be like. If he didn't stop looking to me or our father, if he didn't start deciding for himself, this was how it was always going to be. I would always be taking care of Eddie. I'd always be rushing home because he'd gotten into some kind of trouble. I'd always be bailing him out somehow. I'd always be the good son, and he'd never get out of that shadow unless he stood on his own, stopped looking to me. So I didn't say any of that. I said, 'You've got to make up your own mind.' And so . . . and so he did."

Now Amira rose up to look at him, to stroke his hair with her hand. "But you were right, David," she whispered. "It was the only thing you could do."

He clenched his jaw, shook his head. "I wasn't right. Christ, I'd give both my arms for the chance to bail Eddie out now. I wasn't right. And I vowed to never make that mistake again. To hell with getting people to stand on their own, making their own decisions. When you see them headed into a wall, you've got to do everything you can to stop them."

"Stewart," Amira whispered again, and David nodded.

And on that night, some twenty miles from where they lay, Stewart McBride suddenly had occasion to recall a gaudy religious print that had hung in the hallway of his Catholic boyhood home.

It was of Jesus stepping forth to surrender to the Romans, his hands outstretched, his downcast face a study in sorrow and pity, and even though he had not laid eyes on that painting in fifteen years, at that moment of remembrance, Stewart believed he could recall its every brushstroke, as if every rock and spear and awestruck face on that canvas had been etched onto his still-believing heart.

This remembrance came to him as he walked through an empty village just over the coastal range from the sea, at that instant when he and his guide turned onto a moonlit street to find three men waiting in the lane before them. And, yes, there was a bolt of shock, a spasm of grief that Stewart felt course through his entire body, because it was so hard to accept that it should end this way, when he had only just begun, but then this passed, it all passed, all the hopes and fears that had stalked him these past days and, just like that, a memory from his boyhood rose up before his eyes to comfort him, and he walked toward the waiting men with outstretched hands, with sorrow and pity for all of them.

———

Rustam sat on a rock beside the road, and he watched David's approach with a bemused expression. When finally he rose, it was with an exaggerated sigh.

"It's much easier for you, Mr. Richards," he called. "You only have to walk three turns of this road. For me, it's eight." He waited until David stopped in front of him. "Still, all for a good cause, I suppose."

David didn't answer, didn't acknowledge the young man's existence in any way other than to hold out his hand for the envelope. Rustam placed it there, but continued to fix David with an indulgent smile.

"You know, you're a rather peculiar choice for a diplomat. I think most diplomats in this situation would try to take advantage of the opportunity to talk, to maybe find out what the other side is thinking." He gave a theatrical shrug. "But maybe it's my fault. Maybe I got things off on the wrong foot by not speaking, and by the time I saw the error of my ways, I'd already offended you." He paused, arched an eyebrow. "But even now, there's nothing you'd like to ask me, to say?"

The only words that came to David were the same ones as before: "Fuck you."

Rustam laughed at this. "Oh, Mr. Richards, you really are incorrigible, aren't you? But that's all right. In fact, it has a certain charm. Well, until next time."

He turned to go, but had only taken two or three steps when he abruptly stopped, wheeled around. "Oh, amid all the pleasantries, I almost forgot."

Drawing a small blue booklet from his shirt pocket, he came back toward David, placed it into his hand.

It was an American passport. David quickly flipped to the information page. The photograph had been carefully removed with a penknife, but just below were the vital statistics—the name, birth date, and place of birth—of Stewart Henry McBride.

"Where is he?" David stepped toward Rustam. "What have you done with him?"

The messenger got his bemused grin. "Oh, so now you want to talk."

"Goddamnit, what have you done with him?" David lunged for the man, took hold of the front of his shirt, but then froze at the sound of clicking guns. Looking up, he saw that three other young rebels stood on the rocks above, their guns raised and aimed at his head.

Rustam yanked his shirt free from David's clutch, took a step back to appraise him. The look in his eyes went beyond anger; it was utter fury.

"Don't you remember, Mr. Richards?" he shouted. "I offered you my hand in friendship, but you rejected it. Don't you remember?"

With that, the messenger turned and started up the road, leaving David to stare after him in numb disbelief.

————

It was Amira who at last broke the quiet. "Maybe they're holding him prisoner. That's possible, isn't it?"

"Yes," Paolo said, "quite possible–probable, in fact. It would be very stupid of them to have harmed him in some way."

This eased the somberness that had settled over the lobby table, and David carefully studied each of them there, the relief now coming into their faces.

"He's dead," he muttered.

The others looked at him as if stricken.

Paolo jumped in: "Well, I don't know that we can conclude that, David. In any event, one must always hold out hope at times like this that–"

"No." David cut him off. "One mustn't always hold out hope. That's where you're wrong, where we've all been wrong since this started. Stewart is dead. We all know that."

In the silence, Paolo settled back in his chair. After a time, he gently cleared his throat. "Well," he said, "perhaps a prayer, then."

At the far end of the table, the Contessa began to cry, softly and to herself.

————

Dear Mr. Richards:

I am in receipt of your report of December 15, regarding the current crisis in Kingdom of Kutar, and of the murder and/or abduction in that country of American journalist Stewart McBride. As you are no doubt aware, Mr. McBride has not only long enjoyed a reputation for veracity, balance, and fair-mindedness in the very best traditions of American journalism, but through his work in the lesser-developed nations of the transoceanic region, has served as an inspiration to the many who recognize that a free and unfettered

press forms the very cornerstone of democratic society. For these rea-
sons, we are all deeply saddened to learn of Mr. McBride's murder
and/or abduction.

On a more pleasant note, I would like to take this opportunity
to wish you a happy holiday season, and do trust you will ex-
tend these wishes to all of our very good friends in Kingdom of
Kutar . . .

Part Three

Eleven

It was called the *ajira tokharan*, or "time of blindness." It came every winter to Laradan.

According to a local explanation repeated over the centuries, it occurred when the clouds that had been building along the coast for weeks could finally build no more, when they lay overhead as solid and unmoving as if a gray shroud had been thrown over that strip of land between the mountains and the sea. Then, and by a mechanism that could only be attributed to a kind of magic, the clouds simply collapsed, fell to earth, leaving the residents to wake up one morning to discover that the clear, dry air in which they normally dwelt had vanished, replaced by a fog so thick it blocked out all but the intimation of the sun, by a rain so light it was barely felt on the skin. The *ajira tokharan* normally only lasted a few weeks before ending as swiftly as it had come, and though the scant moisture it provided was what had originally made that coast habitable, it had always been considered an ill-omened time in Laradan, a bad-moon period when sane men went mad or animals died for no reason, when the most inexplicable events were liable to take place.

In fact, the phenomenon had a fairly simple meteorological

explanation–the cool and moisture-laden air off the southern ocean colliding with the desert-heated winds from the north–but that year, whether one ascribed it to science or legend, the time of blindness brought a ghastly new dimension to life in the city.

In the gloom, the firing of the artillery guns on the ridge could no longer be seen, only heard, and the same was true of the explosions they caused. And while it had always been difficult to gauge the direction or proximity of these things by sound alone, distorted as they were by the echo effect of buildings, the fog rendered this utterly impossible. Instead of the shrill scream the traveling missiles had made in the desert-dry air, they now passed overhead with a low and diffuse rumble, rather like thunder. And where before the concussions of their explosions had radiated only a relatively short distance and aboveground, had been felt mostly in the chest, they now seemed to travel through the earth and farther, were felt in the ankles and knees as well. Along with this were the strange tricks common to fog everywhere, its ability to smother sounds from the opposite side of a street, for example, while simultaneously delivering crystal-clear snippets–a gunshot, a person's scream, a child's laughter–from some distant neighborhood. What all this meant to the residents of Laradan was that no longer could any of those sounds they had come to associate with danger be dismissed as remote, as part of someone else's misfortune; in the *ajira tokharan*, nothing felt remote, anything might be close by.

It also made life in that small city exponentially smaller. Without the benefit of seeing any distance or trusting in one's hearing, an individual wanting to learn what was occurring a few blocks away either had to constantly monitor the rumors on the streets or conduct a personal reconnaissance. If choosing the former, it meant remaining in a constant state of doubt, for so many of both the best and the worst rumors were unreliable now. If choosing the latter, it meant risking a journey into the fog, a fog that might, at any moment, fill with shrapnel, or that might cloak some awful scene until one came to stand in the very midst of it.

Then there were the everyday and tangible signs of the war's steady worsening. With the siege now entering its fourth month, the government's evermore-severe austerity measures left most residents with electricity and water for only a few hours each day—not at all if an explosion or fire had destroyed the local lines. In those grocery stores and markets still operating, whatever food was available was rapidly passing beyond the means of all but the wealthiest to buy; for everyone else, sustenance increasingly came from those basic staples—semolina, rice, beans—being distributed from government stockpiles or off the *Esmeralda*. Against the chill of the misting rain, there was only the warmth that the burning of furniture or books and magazines could provide, the last small supplies of coal or firewood now as expensive as food. And then there were the graves. With the hillside cemeteries either filled to capacity or too dangerous to enter, impromptu ones were sprouting up in the corners of parks, in vacant lots, on that wide median concourse of People's Struggle Boulevard once intended for restaurants and coffeehouses.

Yet the effect of all these hardships was probably not at all what an outsider, suddenly dropped into Laradan, might expect. Rather than a terrified and panicked populace, they would have instead found one that appeared to be adapting to their ever-straitening circumstances with pluck. To the degree that it was possible or applicable, the residents of Laradan still went to jobs, still organized their days around familiar routines. They visited friends and relatives, they celebrated birthdays, they still talked and joked and argued and made love. On those occasions when the war's thrall could not be denied—when, for instance, someone close to them died—they tended to respond with remarkable poise. Children were buried by dry-eyed parents, parents by stoic children, while passersby to an atrocity might briefly linger over it, but with the same mild interest they may have once shown at the sight of a man changing a flat tire.

But if in observing this an outsider came to a new appreciation of man's essential nobility in the face of suffering–all the time-worn clichés about the resiliency of the human spirit, and here it was on naked display–they would have misinterpreted the situation. Rather than nobility or even stoicism, what they were observing was a people steadily moving beyond fear, beyond hope, beyond all but a kind of pretense of human emotion, and toward a place of stone-hard indifference. The residents of Laradan laughed and joked and played with their children and made love to their spouses because these were the last instincts they clung to, these were the flickering memories they carried of what it meant to be human. What they desired–to the degree they could muster the will to desire anything–was simply to survive, and in this most elemental urge, they increasingly had less in common with normal people in a normal city, than with a colony of carpenter ants jittering about their kicked-in home, programmed by biology to think only of what tasks lay immediately ahead, really to not think at all. Resilience, certainly, but not one to be confused with defiance–because along with the physical battlefield of war, there is the spiritual, and on this battlefield, too, the residents of Laradan were gradually expiring.

Naturally that handful of people remaining within the preserve of the Moonlight Hotel were spared the worst of these ravages. This was due not only to their comparative safety and comfort, but to their ability to still imagine a future. In this, even the weekly disappointments delivered in the *Esmeralda* mail pouch were crucial; after all, disappointment itself was an emotion increasingly beyond the grasp of the others.

In smaller ways, however, these most fortunate of Laradan inhabitants did experience its deprivations. Meat and vegetables had largely disappeared from their dinner table, just as they had largely disappeared from the markets. As in the rest of the city, the austerity restrictions meant the hotel only had water and electricity for short periods, while the elaborate irrigation system over its grounds had been shut down completely, leaving the lawn and flower beds to wither and die before their eyes. In their physically weakening states, the residents' coughs lingered, cuts refused to heal.

And if in subtler form, those at the Moonlight were, in fact, beginning to be afflicted by the same apathy that had already taken such hold of those around them. It had been just a month since Stewart's death, not quite two since Nigel's, and yet those remaining at the hotel found they only occasionally thought about their lost colleagues. When traversing the city in times of shelling, they now barely reacted to sights and sounds that previously might have caused them to recoil or hurry for cover. There was no meeting of such importance that it required strict punctuality or a freshly pressed shirt on David's part, no sufficiently dire crisis at the harbor warehouse to lead Paolo to forget that tomorrow it would be supplanted by another. Amira, unable to face the prospect of another Independence Park bombing, had begun working in the refugee administration office, securely within the Interior Ministry building, but increasingly there were moments when she could think back on that bombing, her reaction to it, and be somewhat startled at the person she had been then, how differently she might react to it now.

But perhaps much of this was borne of simple exhaustion, the tremendous effort it took to endure the time of blindness. In the fog and misting rain, one felt tired all the time. In the fog, it was easy to live inside a very small and private place, to believe that nothing would ever change, to stop trying to even imagine it.

———

It was Friday morning, the day of the *Esmeralda*'s return, and when David came down to the lobby, he found the Contessa at the table playing a game of solitaire.

"Ah, excellent, the functionary," she called at his approach. "Just the man I was looking for."

"And good morning to you, Contessa." He poured himself a coffee from the side table. "Functionary. That's meant to be insulting, isn't it?"

"Not at all. Why in some circles, it's even considered a term of respect."

David sipped from his coffee, looked at her game. It was a form of solitaire she played often—all the cards were faceup and spread out in four equal rows—but he'd never been sufficiently interested to ask its rules. He glanced up to see the old lady watching him. "Something on your mind?"

"As a matter of fact, yes." She sat back, folded her hands on the table. "I have to say I'm becoming a bit alarmed by the esprit de corps around here. Perhaps I'm overly sensitive, but I feel a certain . . . ennui is setting in."

"Really?" David arched an eyebrow. "Do you think it could have anything to do with the city being bombed to dust, people dying in the streets?"

The Contessa nodded brightly. "That would be my guess. In any event, I think we should host a party."

"What?" David gave an incredulous laugh. "A party?"

"Precisely. I think it would do wonders for everyone, get their minds off things. As it is, everything is 'the war this, the war that'— really rather tedious, don't you find?"

Still chuckling, David shook his head in amazement. "Tell you what; there's still some booze in the bar here, so how about one night after dinner, we all go in and get drunk. How's that?"

The old lady gave a suffering sigh. "I'm talking about a real party, a gala. We'll invite the king. It will be an event."

But David was already tiring of this joke. "Look, it's a crazy idea—I'll give you that—but given the situation, I really don't think it's the appropriate time to—"

"No," she cut him off, "it's the most appropriate time. Everyone needs a little pageantry in their lives, and especially at times like this. It shows that, no matter what, life goes on."

David stared off across the room. He wasn't in the mood for an argument, he just wanted to have his coffee in peace and go about his day. "Fine," he said, "whatever."

"Splendid." The Contessa beamed. "I'll work up a list of things for you to do."

"What? You expect me to help you?"

"Well, naturally. There's a lot of work involved with something like this—and it's not as if you're doing anything more important around here."

Unable to find a reply—because, truth was, the old bat had a point—David took up his coffee and made for the French doors to the poolside terrace.

For a time, he stood on the flagstones and peered into the gray, felt the mist settle on his arms and face. In breaks in the fog, he could make out the bare branches of trees overhead, leaf-shorn shrubs, and fallow flower beds, and so long as he forgot about the temperature, it was easy to imagine he was gazing upon a truly wintered scene rather than upon a place that was dying of thirst. It struck him as poignant, cruel in the way nature could be cruel, that this should be happening now, just when the air was so heavy with water.

When he returned to the lobby, he saw that Amira and Paolo had joined the Contessa at the table. From their bemused expressions and the old lady's animated gestures, her topic of conversation was obvious even from a distance.

"So, what do you think?" she asked them as David approached. "The functionary here thinks it's a grand idea."

"First of all, I'm not a functionary," he said. "Second, I said it was a crazy idea. Crazy, as in absurd. As in stupid."

The old lady gave a dismissive sniff, focused on the others.

"Well, it's an amusing thought," Paolo said, "but I'm concerned—"

"Thank you, signore," the Contessa jumped in. "As a member of the Latin races, I knew you'd approve."

"But I'm concerned over how the rebels would react. After all, we must be careful—"

But the old lady sprang forward. "No! I say we have to stop being so careful." She looked along the table, briefly fixed each of them with her steely gaze. "Let me tell you a story from Romania. In July 1944, there was planned to be a great party at the royal palace. It was to celebrate Prince Nikolai's engagement, and it was to be the social event of the year. But by then, the country was in absolute chaos—the Reds were closing in, Bucharest was being bombed every night, people were fleeing for their lives—so how could the party possibly go on, you ask?" She gave a dramatic pause. "But it did go on. And it was fabulous. The orchestra played, the champagne flowed, we danced until dawn. And what message did it send? It said to the world, 'We may have lost, this may be the end of us, but at least we know how to live, at least we go out with dignity.' And so it is with us. Whatever is to happen here, we must show them that we still know how to live."

For a while, the others merely stared at her. David had long since told both Amira and Paolo the old lady's true story, and there was something rather impressive about hearing such an impassioned and vivid speech from someone who was not actually Romanian royalty—nor even Romanian, for that matter. To David's surprise, it also seemed to stir a thoughtfulness in the others, a pondering that devolved into a kind of mischievous expectancy.

"I rather like the idea," Amira said at last.

Paolo nodded. "Me, too."

They looked at David. Even he, as much as he wished otherwise, was starting to see the proposition in a new light. "Well, I suppose it can't make things any worse." He turned to the Contessa. "So when do you want to have this party?"

"Three weeks from today," she replied promptly.

"Three weeks?" He grimaced. "Christ, Contessa, who knows if the city will even be standing then? Why not next weekend?"

"Out of the question." The old lady vehemently shook her head. "An event of this sort requires a great deal of planning. Besides, if we're to have the king, he needs to be invited well ahead of time; anything less than three weeks is gauche."

David stifled a sigh. "I'm pretty sure his social calendar is wide open, but okay." Glancing at his watch, he saw it was nearly nine; provided Dimitrios had successfully maneuvered in the fog, the *Esmeralda* was approaching the harbor. He looked to Paolo. "We should probably get going."

"Oh, yes, of course, the ship." The businessman jumped up. "I'd almost forgotten."

So jaded had he become to the State Department memorandums, their turgid turns of phrase, that David had skimmed well into the body of the letter before its significance even began to register. Bolting upright in his chair in the harbormaster's office, he raced back through the text until he found the pivotal phrase:

> *. . . a redaction that allows for a bold new approach toward ending the conflict in Kingdom of Kutar.*
>
> *As you are no doubt aware, the compiling of the State Department Terrorism Index (SDTI) is a highly refined process in which a great number of factors are thoroughly weighed and analyzed by an array of interagency specialists before any final determinations are made. If laborious, this comprehensive approach enables us to designate the placement of a suspected terrorist organization and/or political movement and/or national government along the spectrum of SDTI's color-coded ranking system with a very high degree of accuracy. For this reason, it is a source of deep concern that, through an inadvertent clerical error, it now appears the*

Kutaran People's Liberation Army (KPLA) was improperly des-
ignated "mauve" (Probationary Status: Evildoers Ascendant)
rather than its proper coding of "taupe" (Cleared, But No Student
Visas: Indigenous Malcontents). While a fact-finding committee
has been appointed to determine how this oversight may have oc-
curred, we do trust you will extend our apologies to the Govern-
ment of Kutar (GOK) for any inconvenience this may have
caused.

On a more positive note, the reclassification of the KPLA on the
SDTI has provided the basis for a broad reappraisal of American
policy in Kingdom of Kutar and, after extensive interdepartmental
discussions, it has been concluded that an advancement of desired
political, social, and economic goals might best be achieved by
KPLA and GOK entering into a dialogue of national reconcilia-
tion (DNR). In furtherance of this, please find enclosed personal
communications from the Secretary to His Majesty King Abdul
Rahman II, as well as to the (name not furnished) commander in
chief of the KPLA, which we ask you to present to the addressees
at your earliest convenience. Needless to say, we are all extremely
pleased at this opportunity for the United States to play an even
greater role in bringing the ongoing crisis in Kingdom of Kutar to a
peaceful resolution.

After reading through the letter half a dozen times, David
slumped back in his chair, stared off across the room.

"A dialogue of national reconciliation." He wasn't sure
whether to be elated or furious.

———

"So an inadvertent clerical error, hmm?" General Kalima asked
this with a pleasant lilt to his voice, as if finding amusement in the
situation.

"That's what they say, General," David replied.

"And you believe them?"

David looked steadily at the bald, middle-aged man in his field uniform on the other side of the conference table. "I've no reason not to, sir. As you know, I've no way to communicate with Washington directly, so I have to take them at their word."

The general nodded at this, one corner of his mouth turning into a wry smile.

If David had been unsure how to react to the new directive from the State Department, no such uncertainty had been evident among the Kutaran officials he'd met with during that very long day. At the palace, the news that the KPLA had been removed from the Terrorism Index had sparked outrage from the king on down, and the further suggestion that it was now time for peace negotiations had only intensified it. If less heated, the response had been the same among the bureaucrats at the Interior and Foreign Affairs ministries. David could hardly blame them. For more than three months, and through some fourteen thousand deaths by latest count, the Kutaran government had been repeatedly advised— more, ordered–by the State Department to spurn all negotiations, only now to be told by the same agency that negotiations might save them.

David had been braced for more of the same in his meeting with General Kalima, the army chief of staff, but so far, it hadn't worked out that way. Instead, and even as the other three generals in the Defense Ministry conference room glowered in fury, Kalima had greeted him warmly, had spent the first minutes of their meeting asking after the health and welfare of the other foreigners at the Moonlight Hotel.

"And tell me, this business of peace talks," the general now asked with the same lazy lilt, "this dialogue of national reconciliation, are we to understand that the United States would act as guarantor?"

"As guarantor, sir?"

"Yes. To assume the role of sponsor, if you will. A commitment of assistance if the dialogue breaks down, or if one side violates the terms."

David glanced at the other three men in the room—if looks could kill, he'd have been in his grave a long time ago—then back to the chief of staff. "Of that I'm not certain, sir. I wasn't given any instructions independent of that." He indicated the papers Kalima held in his hands, a copy of the Secretary of State's letter to the king. "My sense is that this is something of an evolving initiative."

General Kalima grinned broadly, showed two perfectly straight rows of white teeth; with his bald head and intense dark eyes, it gave him a decidedly feral look. "Evolving initiative," he repeated. "I like that." With a chuckle, he turned and said something in the local language to the other generals but, by all evidence, they didn't grasp the humor. In the ensuing silence, Kalima carefully reached into the inside pocket of his uniform jacket to bring out a pipe, then a small silver tin, then a gold lighter, arranged them neatly on the conference table.

David had rarely dealt with the chief of staff—the Friday afternoon meetings at the Defense Ministry were usually handled by his underlings—and he felt a deepening wariness as he watched Kalima methodically measure out a pinch of tobacco from the tin and tamp it into the pipe bowl. He was reminded of a cat toying with his prey, waiting for the moment to strike.

"And tell me," Kalima said, not looking up, still tamping, "what was the response of the king, his councilors, to this proposal?" Again the languid, vaguely amused tone, as if the answer didn't really much concern him, as if he were asking out of a kind of politeness.

But a peculiar question, David thought to himself—surely the general didn't need him to ascertain the palace's reaction—and he debated how to reply. "I think it might be best for you to take that up with them, General. I'm not sure it's my place to—"

"Quite right." Kalima looked at him then with another grin.

"You're absolutely right, I'll take it up with them." With the gold lighter, he lit the pipe, let a few puffs of smoke escape from the corner of his mouth. Lolling back in his chair, he watched the smoke curl and float toward the ceiling as if they had all the time in the world. "And this letter from the Secretary of State to the KPLA, the one asking for peace talks, you intend to deliver it?"

And here it was, David thought, the moment when the mask of languor fell away, when the cat pounced.

"It's my duty to, General," he said. "I've no choice in the matter."

But David was wrong, the mask stayed in place. Instead, General Kalima fixed him with a pleasant smile, took another thoughtful puff on his pipe. "Yes," he said. "Yes, that's right."

With startling abruptness, Kalima rose, extended his hand across the table. "Well, thank you so much for coming by, Mr. Richards. I imagine you must be very tired; this has been a long day for you."

————

"Why do you like being up here so much?" She was nestled into his side, gazing at the metal ceiling.

David, staring at the same place, considered for a moment. "I don't know that it's a matter of liking, really. I think I just feel better—safer—being up high, seeing out."

Amira reared up to smile at him. "Except with the fog there's nothing to see. And as for safety, it's probably just the opposite, you know. Because if a shell does hit the hotel, the odds are it will land up here."

David laughed lightly. "I didn't say it was logical; that's your hang-up." He brushed the hair from her face, grew more serious. "But if it makes you nervous, we can sleep downstairs."

She shook her head, settled back.

There remained a mustiness to the room that no amount of cleaning could fully dispel. It was alleviated somewhat by the window in the eastern wall, the cool breeze that passed through, but Amira imagined that if she were alone, she would find that smell and the room's small size—it was maybe fifteen-by-twelve feet—claustrophobic. Instead, the combination of having David beside her and the enfolding fog made it cozy, like an oasis set up in the clouds.

She traced a finger over his chest. "So do you think the peace talks will actually happen?"

He grinned. "You mean, the 'dialogue of national reconciliation'?" He couldn't help it; every time David thought of the insipid phrase, it made him want to laugh.

As he had shuttled between his meetings that day, news of the change in American policy had raced through the city. In contrast to the pure rage of most of the government officials he had met, the reaction in the streets had been more nuanced, even contradictory: rage, too, but one mixed with a kind of quiet elation at the idea that their ordeal might soon end. For the moment, the mood in the streets didn't much matter—they weren't the people with guns—and David suspected the true test would come tomorrow, when he made his weekly pilgrimage up Gowarshad Pass, this time with a letter to the rebel leadership from the Secretary of State.

"I think the KPLA will have to make the first move," he answered her. "I don't see the king budging just yet."

"Just yet?"

"Well, eventually he'll have to. Right now, he's just so furious about the KPLA being taken off the terror list that I don't think he even sees the corner he's been painted into. Everyone in the city knows about the negotiation plan, they want peace, obviously, so the longer he holds out, the more that's going to eat away at his support. And since it's an American proposal, he has to figure there's no way we're coming to his aid if he doesn't play along."

Amira slowly shook her head. "Christ, it's really quite Machiavellian, isn't it?"

David pondered this. "No," he said at last, "not Machiavellian. That's actually the worst of it. I don't think enough thought went into any of this to qualify as Machiavellian. Just clumsiness. Incompetence." He recalled a conversation he'd had with Nigel. "Or cowardice. Of just wanting to be rid of a problem in a way that doesn't look like you caused it."

There was a long quiet between them, before Amira whispered: "So, the talks will happen, then. There will be peace."

He nodded. "As long as the rebels aren't stupid. As long as they realize all they have to do is make the first overture."

At various times in that very hectic day, David had occasionally felt the tug of another emotion in response to the State Department letter: along with both anger and relief, a strange undercurrent of foreboding. Lying in the narrow bed with Amira just then, he felt this emotion grow, push away the others.

This was coming to an end. One way or another, this was ending soon, and the suddenness with which David could now imagine the future—not just the future of this war, this place, but the real future, what lay beyond that—was something he wasn't at all prepared for. What a bizarre thought, so perverse he could scarcely acknowledge it to himself, that after all these weeks and months of dwelling in this dying land, there was now a part of him that wished to remain in that awful limbo for a while longer, that dreaded the prospect of seeing it end.

He tried to comprehend the source of this. Had he so gone past the point of being shocked by war as to become addicted to it? Or was it that he feared what he might discover in its aftermath, that this experience had so scarred him there was no returning to his old life?

But as he lay there that night, David came to understand that, most of all, it had to do with the woman beside him, that along with the horror and sadness of these past months, there had also been laughter, there had been love, there had been the sharedness of gazing out at the city and the fog in their armchairs, of lying

in their bed in their tiny rooftop home. All that, too, was going to
end, one way or another, and when this realization came to him,
David recalled the last words she had said—"There will be peace"—
and in the soft, almost mournful way she had spoken them, he
wondered if the same understanding had come to her.

David reflexively reached a hand to stay Rustam. "No," he said,
"it's addressed to your commander in chief."

The rebel liaison looked up with a bright smile. "Yes, I see
that, Mr. Richards, thank you. But we're very informal in the
KPLA, not too concerned with protocol." He continued tearing
open the manila envelope, and slid the letter out. When he saw the
signature, he lifted an eyebrow in surprise. "From the Secretary of
State? Is this really his signature?"

"That's really his signature."

As Rustam read, David glanced at the rocks above them. He
couldn't see the liaison's coterie, the three men who had once
trained their guns on him, but he assumed they were there somewhere, watching. His attention was drawn back by Rustam's
snicker.

"Dialogue of national reconciliation." The young man tapped
the letter with a finger. "I like that. That's very good."

"Yeah, I know, everybody likes it."

With a pleasured sigh, Rustam slid the letter back into the
envelope. "Well, it's all very interesting, isn't it, Mr. Richards? I'll
pass it along." He turned to go.

"But wait," David called after him. "If there's a reply . . . ?"

Rustam got his bemused grin again, looked David up and
down. "My, suddenly you can't get enough of me." He tapped the
envelope against his leg. "Don't worry; if there's a reply beforehand, I'll make sure it gets to you. Otherwise, I'll see you next Saturday." He turned again, sauntered up the road.

But that very night, there came from the ridge the sustained crackling of gunfire–not of the usual siege artillery, but of lighter weapons: machine guns, rifles, grenade launchers. In the fog, it was quite impossible to determine what was taking place, but by midnight, rumors were reaching the Moonlight that government troops had launched a surprise ground assault, that a pitched battle was being waged atop Gowarshad Pass. Through the early-morning hours, these rumors multiplied and became more incredible–the army had broken through the rebel lines in several places, the KPLA was in full rout–and all Laradan, it seemed, was awake and joining in the celebration–from everywhere in the fog came the honking of horns, shouts of jubilation–but what didn't change was David's inability to establish the truth of any of it. Several times and by a variety of routes, he tried to reach the army base at the foot of Gowarshad in his embassy car, only to be turned back at army roadblocks. He had no better luck in making for the palace or the Defense Ministry; the entire city was locked down, nothing was moving from one district to another except the rumors.

Then, just after dawn, the gunfire on the pass abruptly stopped. A short time later, an army officer strode into the lobby of the Moonlight Hotel, there to escort David to an urgent meeting with the army chief of staff, General Hassan Kalima.

———————

Urgency was the last thing General Kalima's manner conveyed. Leaning far back in the swivel chair, he clasped his hands behind his head, propped his boots on the desk, as if settling in for a long, leisurely chat.

"So I gather you're anxious to learn what has happened." He grinned at David. "I've had reports from all over Laradan of you trying to get past the checkpoints."

David gave a sheepish shrug. "Sorry about that, but it's kind of my job."

"Hmm."

Rather than to the Defense Ministry, the army squad car had

brought David to the same military base he had spent much of the night trying to reach, the regimental headquarters at the foot of Gowarshad Pass. There had been a great deal of activity in the courtyard when they pulled in, soldiers excitedly dashing to and fro, but his officer escort had immediately led David into the administration building and to the office where General Kalima was waiting.

"Well, not as spectacular as the best rumors you've probably heard, unfortunately," the chief of staff muttered, looking around the small, drab room. "No great breakthrough, the rebels still control the ridge, but something of a success nonetheless." He fixed David with an appraising stare. "Were you ever in the military, Mr. Richards?"

David shook his head.

Kalima nodded. "I ask because I think civilians and soldiers probably experience a siege quite differently, what is the worst aspect of it for them. For a civilian—well, I don't know for a civilian, but I imagine it must be a feeling of helplessness—but for a soldier, it's quite different, not what most people would probably expect. It's not the shelling, or the living in trenches and foxholes, all those other things one thinks about. No, the worst aspect is never seeing your enemy. It's not knowing if they suffer at all on the other side. When you see only your side, it's very easy—natural—to start thinking you are the only ones suffering, the only ones dying. On the other side, life is good. They have nice tents and beer and women, this is all a great holiday for them. So this is why I launched the assault, so that my men could finally see their enemy. A limited operation, not meant to break the siege or take the ridge, just to accomplish this one small thing, you see?"

He waited for David to nod.

"In practical terms, in terms of casualties, one might say it wasn't worth it. We appear to have lost somewhere in the range of two hundred men up there"—he motioned toward the windows behind him, in the direction of the pass—"and for that we took forty-seven prisoners, maybe killed about the same number. But war is never about these kinds of numbers. It's about psychology, morale, and measured in this way, the assault was a victory, because now, for the first time, my men are able to see their enemy, these prisoners we have taken. Do you understand this?"

David nodded again, slower than before. As in their last meeting, he sensed something slippery and cunning about the man. He also sensed there was a subtext to this conversation that Kalima was deliberately keeping beyond his grasp, and that the only way to uncover it was to be blunt.

"I do understand, General," he replied, "but I also question the timing. After all, you've had nearly four months to launch this assault. Why now, just when the subject of peace talks has come up?"

To his surprise, Kalima reared back and laughed uproariously. "Ah, the plainspoken American," he said amid his laughter. "That's excellent, Mr. Richards, right to the point. I often feel we Kutarans should try to be more like you Americans; it would save everyone so much time." With a happy sigh, he rolled his feet off the desk, sat forward. "But surely you know, even without being a military man, that these sorts of actions are a long tradition just before peace talks. It's called playing for advantage, to go into negotiations from a position of strength. All armies do it—even your own—and no one takes offense."

This was, of course, one explanation, but in Kalima's toying manner, David was convinced it wasn't the real one, the subtext remained hidden.

"Come," the general said, leaping to his feet as swiftly as at their previous meeting. "I would like to show you something."

He led the way from the room and out of the building, started across the courtyard.

In the misting fog, David saw they were approaching a large cluster of soldiers—scores, perhaps hundreds of them—packed tightly together and facing inward, like an enormous football huddle. As they neared, he heard angry shouts from the crowd, hoots of laughter, and floating above this, a high-pitched wail.

At the sight of General Kalima and David, the soldiers quickly separated to create a path into the circle for them, and all at once David found himself at its hollow center, standing over four bound and terror-stricken men. They were rebel prisoners, obviously, and just as obviously, they had been beaten and kicked and spat upon, their faces already swollen from the blows they had taken, blood dripping into the dirt from where their binding ropes had cut into flesh.

"For Christ's sake, General," David whispered, "what are you doing?"

"What?" Kalima turned to him in mock puzzlement. "What's wrong, Mr. Richards?"

"You can't do this." David's voice was more forceful. "Does the king know you're doing this?"

"The king? What about the king?" Still with the mocking frown. "What, you think this might jeopardize the peace talks? That if the KPLA finds out we've mistreated their men they won't want to talk? Is that what you think?"

One of the prisoners was a young man—a boy, really, perhaps fifteen or sixteen—and he trembled violently from either shock or fear. The general stepped to the boy's side, unholstered his pistol.

"For God's sake, Kalima," David shouted, "don't! Don't do this."

The general pointed the gun at the kneeling boy's head; the boy began to wail, to keen out a prayer or a plea.

"As I mentioned, we took forty-seven prisoners," Kalima said calmly. "I've sent a few to each of the garrisons, because I want all my men to have the opportunity to see their enemy. First to see them alive, and then . . ."

The single shot to his head sent the boy sprawling in the dirt. His mouth gulped for air, the toes of his bound, bare feet wiggled in their death reflexes, but if he made any sound it was lost amid the roaring cheer of the surrounding soldiers. After watching the still-twitching boy for a moment, General Kalima turned back to David.

"What do you think, Mr. Richards? Do you think if we kill them all, it will hurt the chances for peace talks, for this dialogue of national reconciliation of yours? Do you think if we kill them, maybe our American friends won't come to our aid? Please tell me. I'm always open to suggestions, different viewpoints." He stepped to another of the prisoners, raised his pistol again. "Would you like to try your luck with this one?"

But David turned and pushed his way out through the circle of soldiers, pressing in closer now as the spectacle moved toward its conclusion.

———————

Perhaps it was the play of light or the particular angle from which he was viewing him, but at that moment, Paolo Alfani looked a wholly different man than the one David had known. Surely his friend had not turned haggard and gaunt overnight, but it seemed that way. Behind his little metal desk in the warehouse office, his once-round cheeks had become drawn, wattles of flaccid skin hung from his throat; even his white suit, now yellowed and mottled with stains, sagged everywhere on him, as if several sizes too large. He was like a melting man sitting there, and it made David wonder if, viewed from a particular angle, others might be shocked by the changes in his own appearance.

"So, no dialogue?"

Under Paolo's somber gaze, David took the metal chair across the desk, shook his head. He had just come from a meeting on Gowarshad Pass, where Rustam had given him an "emergency" missive from the rebel high command. In response to the army assault and the execution of the KPLA prisoners two days earlier, peace talks were now out of the question, the KPLA's terms for settlement were the same as they had always been: total and unconditional surrender of the royal government.

"Just as Kalima intended it," David said. "He's clever. If nothing else, you have to give him that."

Paolo nodded. "And the king, do you think he approved the attack? That's what everyone is asking."

David shrugged. "Who knows? Who knows what's really going on here anymore? Was the palace in on it, or did the generals do it to fuck the palace, to freeze out the moderates?" He wearily shook his head. "Who knows? I suspect we'll never know. In the meantime, on with the war. Onward to victory."

He gazed over the walls of the office, saw that his friend had tacked up more family photographs, more children's drawings.

"I keep thinking about this conversation I had with Nigel just before he died. He was talking about cowardice, the ingenuity that cowards are capable of at times like this. I know what he means now, but I think it's more than that. Even more than the cowards, it's the killers, the thugs. Because once a place like this starts to rip apart, you're always going to have men like Kalima who want to rip it more, who have nothing to gain by putting it back together."

Paolo gave a wry smile. "The meek shall inherit the earth, just not anytime soon." He looked out the inner window to the warehouse floor. "I see that even here, you know? The men working here, all my guards, this war is the best thing that has ever happened to them. They all have their little smuggling operations off the *Esmeralda*, they're becoming rich from it. If peace comes, that's over for them."

David frowned. "You mean they're pilfering?"

The businessman feigned offense, reared back in his seat. "What? Please, there is no pilfering here. I run a very tight operation." He shook his head. "No, no, it's much more sophisticated than that, it's far beyond pilfering. Each of them, they arrange to have their own small cargoes come in: whiskey, drugs, toothpaste, anything you can imagine. If you watch the unloading, you see how it works. The big pallets come in, they're brought down to here"–he waved a hand at the warehouse floor–"and then all the other small pallets come off and they continue on to"–he fluttered the hand in the direction of the city–"well, to who knows where."

David had never really thought about the possibility of smuggling before–certainly Paolo had never mentioned it. If David had, he probably would have assumed a few things were slipping in–that was only logical–but nothing on the order that his friend was describing. "But how does it work? Doesn't the KPLA watch what goes on board in Palumbo?"

"Of course," Paolo said, "but they're in on it, too. They're becoming rich from it, too. The same with Dimitrios and his crew. They're all in it together, like a mafia." His eyes narrowed as he scrutinized David. "You're surprised by this? But this is the way it is in war, in any war. There are always those who become rich from it. Myself, I could be a millionaire many times over in this position, but instead"–he grinned, ran his fingers along the lapels of his coat in self-mockery–"the model of Italian rectitude."

David didn't share in his humor. In fact, the more he considered this news, the more he felt a rankling. "But why haven't you mentioned this before, Paolo?"

The businessman shrugged. "And to what purpose? Do you want it to be stopped? If you tried to stop it, they'd kill you in an instant. Me, too, my own men. War is one thing, there can be a mercy, but to go against the business of war, the mafia . . ." He gave David a sympathetic, almost fatherly look. "You see? This is how it happens. When we decided to stay, it was very simple–the killers on one side, the victims on the other–the morality was clear. But now we have men like Kalima, like my guards here–as you say, the thugs. But the worst is what will come after, because when this war does end, however it ends, it will be these kind of men who run things, the ones with the money and power. The decent people who used to have it–the engineers and doctors and businessmen–

they're already finished, they traded it away for bread and firewood. So when a place like this tears, there is no mending it, there is no going back to the way it was."

He stared out at the warehouse floor again, his expression grew grim. "Well, maybe it's good that none of us will be here to see it. Either we'll be dead or we can go back to our lives, we can have our nostalgia."

"The Contessa's really taken to this party planning, hasn't she?" Amira said.

In their bed, David smiled. Of all the bizarre aspects to living in Laradan now, the Contessa's gala preparations were quickly becoming among the most surreal. Initially she had attempted to press-gang the Moonlight staff into running errands for her, but when David put a stop to that, she had hired several personal assistants. Most every morning, this unhappy band could be seen trooping into the lobby to receive their day's instructions—the old lady wanted fresh flowers, an orchestra, elaborate decorations—only to face her wrath in the evenings when they returned empty-handed.

"It's a shame the king didn't make *her* army chief of staff," he said. "She'd have this war over by now."

Amira giggled. "Except she would have executed the prisoners, too."

"That's true. If she even bothered taking prisoners."

In most every other way, however, Laradan had returned to its deadened torpor. The spasm of euphoria that had erupted at the prospect of peace talks had all but passed from memory, a collective drunken fit best forgotten. For the city's inhabitants, it was now simply back to waiting, to counting off the shells coming down from the ridge, the days until the *ajira tokharan* might end. The time of blindness was lasting much longer than normal that year and, naturally, everyone took this as an omen.

In the bed, David groped for something to say. He thought of asking Amira to tell another story about her village in the north, or some anecdote from England, but even telling these stories had become an effort, they left a sad longing at their end.

"So how are things at the refugee office?" he tried at last.

"Okay." She smiled. "How are things in the diplomatic corps?"

He chuckled. "Okay."

A light whistling rose in the room. It was from the mesh screen over the window, bowing inward with the night's stiffening breeze. The candle beside them flickered.

"It means the *ajira* is going to end soon," Amira said. "It's always the first sign, the wind."

"I hope you're right. I don't know how much more of this fog I can take."

But just then there came a thump on the roof, and then a scratching of something slowly dragging across the metal sheets. Amira sat up in alarm. "What is that?"

"I don't know." David sat up as well. "A cat maybe?" Although he knew it wasn't a cat.

A moment later, another thump, another scratching.

"Stay here," he said, and slid from the bed, took up his trousers from the floor. As quietly as he could manage, David pushed open the shed door, stepped out. The fog was thinner than it had been earlier that night, dispersed by the growing ocean breeze, and across the whitewashed expanse of the roof, he saw perhaps a dozen palm fronds scattered. He heard a crackling above him, and looked up to see another frond floating down out of the mist, coming to rest on the shed roof with a slight thump before beginning its slide off.

"What is it?" Amira called from inside.

"It's the trees."

She came outside then, a blanket wrapped around her, but drew up in bewilderment at the littering across the roof. "But I didn't think palm trees lost their fronds."

"Occasionally they do," David said, "but not like this. They're dying."

She turned to him. "But not the entire trees, right? You mean just the fronds, right?"

In the sad searching of her eyes, he felt an urge to lie, but then decided against it—the time for protective lies was over—and shook his head. "They were transplanted here, put down on bedrock, so they don't have taproots. This little mist isn't enough. Without irrigation, they die."

With hesitant steps, as if not really wishing to see but drawn anyway, they crossed to the rooftop railing. Through the thinning mist, they saw that the hotel lawn was covered with hundreds of shorn fronds, that still more were cascading down from the sky. They came down to earth as if in slow motion—thrashing, gliding, performing peculiar zigzag patterns in the night—like so many severed wings struggling to find flight.

———————

Dear Mr. Richards:

This letter is in reference to your report of February 2 regarding the current situation in Kingdom of Kutar. Naturally, we were very disappointed to learn of the mistreatment and execution of prisoners of war at the hands of the Army of Kutar (AOK), and of the adverse impact this action appears to have had on the prospects for a dialogue of national reconciliation (DNR). As you are no doubt aware, this administration has long been a champion of the principle that the mistreatment and/or extrajudicial execution of prisoners of war is, in most circumstances, an inappropriate standard of conduct for both governmental and nongovernmental military forces.

On a more positive note, in light of the conditions outlined in your report of February 2, and the clear indication that Government of Kutar (GOK) is currently unwilling to enter into a DNR, we now feel it is morally incumbent upon the United States to as-

sume an even greater leadership role in bringing this crisis to a peaceful resolution. After extensive consultations with other Alliance members, it has been concluded that the optimal approach toward effecting such a resolution is to provide for a temporary departure of limited duration from Kingdom of Kutar of His Majesty King Abdul Rahman II, to be immediately followed by a DNR between GOK and KPLA representatives.

As you are no doubt aware, this initiative represents a significant advance from our previous policy, but we are now in strong agreement with the Department of Defense (DOD) that such an initiative affords the best hope for a just and lasting peace in Kingdom of Kutar, as outlined in the accompanying DOD report, "Optimizationalization of Kutar Situation." To this end, please find enclosed personal correspondence from the Secretary to His Majesty King Abdul Rahman II, which I ask you to personally present to His Majesty at the earliest opportunity. In support of the proposal outlined by the Secretary, I urge you in your meeting with His Majesty to stress that this course of action is only being recommended in the firm belief that it will create an optimizationalized atmosphere in which to further build on the peace process. Should His Majesty concur with our appraisal, we will, of course, assume responsibility of effecting the Royal Family's temporary departure of limited duration from Laradan, and of ensuring their privacy, comfort, and security during their temporary residence of limited duration abroad.

With the letter, David rose from his chair in the harbormaster's office and quietly made for the clerks' room on the second floor. There he took the same desk where he had sat that afternoon many months earlier with Nigel. Just as on that afternoon, he stared down at the blank sheet of paper before him and tried to form a reply.

Different thoughts came to him. He thought of asking the State Department precisely how removing the king might advance peace talks, when this was something the KPLA themselves had never asked for. He thought of telling them that the king was the only figure capable of keeping this country together at all, that removing him would not mean peace but only a continued standoff between the hardest warriors of both sides. He thought of telling them that the very notion of a dialogue of national reconciliation was now such an absurdity as to constitute a lie, that the United States couldn't shirk its responsibility to this country by merely perpetuating a fantasy.

But he had already told them all this in so many words and so many times before—in anger, in pleading, in the dry language of the bureaucrat—and at a certain point, the constant retelling simply made him a party to the lie, the role he performed in it. And so, when finally he picked up his pen, he wrote on the paper a single sentence.

———

The king stared at him with an unsettling smile. "So now my good American friends want me to go into exile, hmm?"

In his chair at the foot of the royal carpet, David gently shook his head. "Not exile, Your Majesty. As I believe the Secretary states in his letter, what is envisioned is just a brief stay abroad."

"And yet this is something the rebels have never asked for. So I'm curious why the Americans think this might somehow lead them into peace talks."

It was the same question that had stumped David, and while he'd anticipated the king raising it, he'd been unable to form a very satisfying reply. "I think the idea, Your Majesty, is to try to create an environment, a calming, that might induce them to do so."

The king chuckled. "I see. A calming. Remove the king from the picture and suddenly everyone will grow calm, everyone will remember that they love one another." He looked around at his ministers with an edgy grin. "What do you think? Do I excite people too much? Do they need a break from me, a chance to calm down?"

The ministers seemed unsure how to respond to his sarcasm; some smiled tentatively back, others fidgeted, but no one said a word. When the king's gaze returned to David, the irony was gone, his eyes were hard, angry. "And what of you, Mr. Richards? What do you think?"

David had anticipated this question, as well. "Please understand, Your Majesty, that I don't formulate my government's policy. My duty is only to report back on what I see here, and—"

"I understand that; I'm not asking you to formulate policy. I'm asking your opinion."

David took a steadying breath. "My opinion is immaterial, Your Majesty. It's not my role to have an opinion. My role is to deliver the Secretary's letter, and to—"

The king cut him off with a scornful laugh. "So you're a messenger boy, in other words."

David shrugged. "If that's how Your Majesty wishes to characterize it, then yes, I'm a messenger boy."

Abdul Rahman lurched forward in his throne; for an instant, David thought he might come down the carpet for him. "But you're still a man, Mr. Richards. A man who has been here, with us, through all this. So now I'm asking your opinion as a man. Not as the American representative, not as their messenger boy, but as a man."

In the heavy, waiting silence of the royal chamber, David stared down at the carpet in front of his feet. After a long moment, he decided, looked up to the king.

"Your Majesty, I submitted my resignation today. Technically, I'm not supposed to announce that until my superiors are informed but"—he allowed a thin smile—"you've kind of forced my hand."

Around the chamber were hushed whispers. The king sat slowly back, shock on his face. "You resigned?"

David nodded. "Both as American representative here, and from the Foreign Service. But until the *Esmeralda* reaches Palumbo tomorrow, until my superiors are informed, I'm required to continue to fulfill my official duties. So if you really care to hear my opinion, I'm afraid you'll have to invite me to come back then."

As he stared at David, the king's expression began to change, astonishment giving way to appraisal, then to something very much like admiration. Finally he looked to the courtier on his right, the official scribe of council proceedings, and muttered something; the man flipped the page of a large ledger book. The king turned back to David.

"So, Mr. Richards, it is now officially tomorrow."

David grinned. "Okay. I guess as a king you can do that." He grew more serious. "My opinion is that you should stay. My opinion is that it would be disastrous for this country if you left."

But the time of blindness did not end. It continued on for far longer than anyone could remember, longer than most any other recorded in the history books, days bleeding into nights, nights into days, their only differentiation the density of the gray. There were more bombardments—some fierce and sustained, others half-hearted—but for those still alive in the city, they seemed to blend together to form a dull, throbbing continuum at the periphery of their existence. Those at the Moonlight stayed busy: the Contessa with her party plans, Amira at the refugee office, Paolo down at the harbor. David kept himself occupied for several days by cutting down those trees on the hotel grounds that had died from lack of water, borrowing a chain saw from the gardener who was too bereft to do the job himself.

He discovered that it was a tremendous relief to finally be free of the endless meetings, of those faces staring into his, waiting for answers he could not give them, of being a participant in the farce. The following Friday, he returned to the harbormaster's office, but only to collect his personal mail and that of the others at the hotel; his packet from the State Department he handed, unopened, to a minor palace official, to do with as the palace saw fit. His loyalty now was to those of them there–at the Moonlight, in the city–and he felt his last obligation was to endure as they did, to stand vigil over all their slow wasting. To the degree that he found comfort, it was in their company: in the small acts of humanity–laughter and compassion–that still played in Laradan's streets and ruins; in the stories of disobedient Italian children or fictitious Romanian princes told over the lobby table; in the touch of her, the feel of her skin, as they lay in their rooftop home. Even amid the fog, there was spreading over the city a collective sense that they were nearing the last days now, and a certain peace was settling in.

But in Kutar, nothing ever happened in a predictable way.

The first change David noticed was the band of bright light that spread beneath the utility shed door. The second was the multitude of voices–excited, happy–rising from the distance. Sliding his arm from under Amira, he rolled out of the bed.

"What is it?" she asked sleepily.

When he opened the door, the brilliant light momentarily blinded David, he saw nothing but a shimmering whiteness.

"It's over," he shouted. "The *ajira* is over."

Shielding his eyes against the brightness, he tentatively crossed the rooftop in the direction of the voices, to the side that overlooked the promenade. When his eyes had adjusted, he saw that thousands of people were gathered there–they filled the stone walk as far as he could see–and they all appeared to be laughing, dancing, shouting with joy. Amira came alongside him.

"They're going absolutely nuts," he grinned. "I've seen them celebrate the end of *ajira*, but it's never been like this before."

But it was Amira who first noticed something odd about the crowd: they were all pressing as close as possible to the seawall railing, their attention was focused out to the bay. Her gaze traveled slowly over the water and then it stopped, the sight took her breath away. "Look." She urgently pointed. "Look."

And then David saw: far out in Serenity Bay, fairly sparkling in the radiant morning light, an American warship lay at anchor.

Rushing back to the hut, they frantically dressed and made for the rooftop stairs, raced down the long staircase to the lobby. No sooner had they reached it, however, than the main entrance door swung open and a lone figure appeared in the halo of harsh light. Then, striding briskly toward them, came the diminutive and rotund figure of Colonel Allen B. Munn.

Twelve

From the flagstone terrace, Munn took a long look around the Moonlight grounds—its dead shrubs, the stumps of felled trees, the open pit of the swimming pool—and gave a low whistle. "Man, they've really let this place go, haven't they?" He turned in his chair to David. "And you're not looking so great either, Richards: You been eating?"

"Don't call me Richards," David said. "It reminds me of someone else, and he's dead now."

"Oh, right. That Mayhew guy, right?" Munn shook his head with a sigh. "Yeah, that was a damned shame—martyr in the cause of freedom."

David observed there was no actual sentiment behind these words, just one of those easy phrases that rolled off Munn's tongue from long memorization.

The American destroyer was moored some five miles offshore, well out of the range of the rebels' guns, and Munn had come in on a high-speed launch. In the lobby, he'd immediately led David out to one of the wrought-iron tables on the terrace.

"So, what've I missed around here?" he asked.

David had never fully decided if Munn's blitheness stemmed

from stupidity or was a by-product of his down-home act; either way, he detested the man.

"Gee, quite a bit, Colonel. I'm sure you saw the improvements on your way in. We got rid of most of those slums in the Old City, all those trees cluttering up the parks. And you probably noticed how everyone's slimmed down; they call it the Colonel Munn Diet, in honor of the guy who came up with it."

Munn stared evenly at him, appeared to be struggling in his effort to keep things pleasant. "Actually, it's General now. General Munn." He pointed to the single silver star on his uniform collar. "Came through about three weeks ago." His finger trailed down to his left breast. A great array of medals and ribbons were pinned there, but he indicated the three medallions at the bottom. "These are new, too. Service medals." His finger went down the line. "Operations Kindred Spirit, Stalwart Friend, and Resolute Ally. Personally, I thought it was kind of overkill—could've just had one award for all three—but hell, it's not like the Medals Committee is gonna listen to a one-star general, now, is it?" He pointedly gazed over David's plain white shirt. "The point being that apparently someone up the chain of command appreciates my efforts here, even if an FS-9 development officer doesn't."

David grinned. "Still, you'd think the Medals Committee could be a little more considerate; pretty quick here you're going to have to grow a bigger chest just to hang them all." He watched the muscles in Munn's jaw flex, was pleased his baiting was having an effect. "And so what's this operation called?" David raised a quick hand. "Wait, wait, let me guess. Let's see, could it be . . . Operation Bosom Buddy?" He shook his head. "No, bosom's probably a bit risqué for the Pentagon. How about Operation . . . Faithful Friend." He shook his head again. "No, you've already used up 'friend' . . ."

"You enjoying yourself, Richards?"

"Maybe . . . Partners in Peace?" He saw the general's eyebrow lift slightly in surprise. "Jesus, that's it, isn't it? It's Operation Partners in Peace." David slumped against the chairback in his laughter. "Unbelievable. You sons of bitches are just unbelievable."

With growing irritation, Munn reached down for the brief-case at his feet, swung it onto the table. "All right, enough bullshit; we gotta get to work." He undid the clasps, flipped up the lid.

David leaned toward him. "Actually, you know what, Munn? We don't. Maybe you haven't heard, but I resigned from the State Department. So, in fact, I don't have to do anything. I don't even have to sit here and talk to you."

A sly grin spread across the general's face. "Yeah, well, maybe that's the first thing we should go over." From his briefcase, he pulled out a letter-sized envelope, tossed it in front of David. "Read it."

The letter was on heavy bond and signed by the Chief Legal Counsel of the Department of State:

Dear Mr. Richards:

Under the emergency provisions provided for in Chapter 7, Article 23, Clause 3 of the Foreign Service Code, revised 1958, your tender of resignation from the Foreign Service has been de-nied. Consequently, you are hereby notified that you remain under employment as interim representative of the United States of Amer-ica in Kingdom of Kutar, and remain subject to all rights, respon-sibilities, and obligations your continuing service entails.

David looked up to see Munn watching him with obvious glee. "What the hell is this?"

"Yeah, didn't figure you for the type who'd actually read the Foreign Service Code." Munn pointed to his briefcase. "I got a pho-tocopy of the relevant pages in there somewhere, but let me give a quick rundown. Turns out that in certain emergency situations–and what we got going on here has been deemed as such–the fed-eral government has the authority to order any employee to stay at their post for up to ninety days whether they like it or not.

Sounds Communist as hell, I know, but there you have it. Anyway, what it boils down to is that, during this emergency period, that employee is legally required to fulfill any and all duties of their position, and failure to do so makes them liable to criminal prosecution. Those charges can range from dereliction of duty on up to . . ." He trailed off, savoring the moment. "Well, you like guessing games so much, how about you guess what the charges can go up to? Give you a hint; it starts with a *t*."

David merely stared at the man.

"You got it, pardner: treason. And guess what? Failure to carry out your official duties in a foreign country during wartime? A foreign country that the United States has deemed vital to our national security interests? That's right, that's treason." The general sat back. "So what's all this got to do with you? Well now, I'm gonna tell you. For some reason, it seems you've managed to get the ear of the government here, and since you've chosen to advise them contrary to American policy initiatives, that's a problem. At 1600 hours today, we—you and I—have an appointment with the king and his grand council. At that meeting, I intend to advise the king in no uncertain terms that any hopes for peace depend on his temporary departure of limited duration from Kutar. I further intend to advise him that this temporary departure is to be initialized pronto, as in tonight, that at 2200 hours he and the royal family are gonna come down to the harbor and get on that launch, and they're gonna go out to that destroyer, from whence they're gonna depart for a temporary period of time. And you know what you're gonna do at this meeting, Richards? You're gonna sit there and nod along. And if the king or anyone else in that room asks your opinion, you're gonna say, 'General Munn is absolutely right,' you're gonna say, 'Operation Partners in Peace, now that's the plan for me.' Are we all clear on that?"

David still didn't speak, just stared back.

"And let me tell you something else, Richards—I can call you Richards, can't I?—that if you step out on this, if you so much as sneeze funny in there, I will make it my eternal and godly mission to see you brought up on treason charges, to see that you are convicted on all counts, and fifty years from now, when they dump your bones in the potter's field outside Leavenworth, I'm gonna make sure I'm still alive just so I can come on up there and piss on your grave."

He reached into his briefcase and brought out another sealed envelope, tossed it in front of David; this one bore the stencil "Top Secret" in bold red letters.

"Read it, destroy it," Munn instructed. "Word leaks out, I'll see if I can't get you an enhancement on the treason charge, send you to the electric chair." He snapped the briefcase shut, rose to his feet. "Well, got to get to my other meetings. I'll meet you at the main palace entrance at 1530 hours. In the meantime, I suggest you get yourself spruced up, find a clean shirt. You're representing the United States of America here, son; the least you can do is look presentable." He started for the lobby.

"General, can I ask you a question?"

Munn stopped, turned around. "Sure. As long as it's not a stupid one."

"Exactly why are we doing this? Why are we trying to get the king to leave?"

Munn shook his head. "Aw, you suckered me on that one; shoulda known it would be stupid." He briefly gazed over the dead lawn. "Same reason we do anything, Richards: to see if it's gonna work."

"Completely out of the question." The Contessa flipped a dismissive hand in the air. "The gala is tonight and the king's attendance is mandatory. You did explain that to this Munn fellow, didn't you?"

At the lobby table, David turned to the others.

"But what will you do?" Paolo asked.

David shrugged. "Not much I can do; it turns out I'm still the official representative here, so I'm required to follow policy." He gave a sardonic smile. "Guess I should've read the fine print when I joined up."

"And what happens if the king agrees to leave?" Amira asked. "Will the Americans send in peacekeeping troops?"

David began to answer, but was cut off by the Contessa.

"This is all quite fascinating, but can we please get back to the matter at hand?" She glared at David. "Let me repeat: it is simply unacceptable that this should happen today. Good Lord, for months you Americans have been dicking around here—if I'm using that expression correctly—so why the rush now?"

David didn't bother with a reply, turned back to Amira. "To answer your question: no, there's no plan to bring in peacekeepers right away. I'm sure Munn will dangle that as a possibility, make vague promises, but the plan as far as it's been worked out is to take the king out and form some kind of provisional government that'll negotiate with the KPLA. Exactly how that happens, though, the Kutarans are going to have to figure out on their own."

"But that's madness," Paolo cried. "If there's no foreign soldiers here to force them, the KPLA will never agree to negotiations."

David nodded. "And, in all likelihood, neither will the interim government. Whichever figurehead they appoint, the real power brokers will be Kalima and his generals, and I don't see any way they'll go into peace talks."

"So it will go on," Amira muttered.

Paolo leaned over the table, fixed David with a beseeching look. "You must explain this to the king, David. You must. You can't just let this happen."

David felt a surge of anger, but toward who or what, he wasn't altogether sure. "I can't, Paolo; I told you that." He took a calming breath, glanced at the three of them. "The more immediate issue is, with or without the king, that ship sails tonight. I think you should get on it. All of you. It's a chance we didn't know we would have, but it's the very last one. After this, there won't be another."

The silence around the table was broken by the Contessa's disgusted sigh. "Well, I'm certainly not running—not after all the hard work I've put in around here."

David was aware of Amira's gaze on him, but resisted looking in her direction.

"And what about you?" she asked softly. "You've been ordered to stay, haven't you?"

He had known the question would come from one of them, that they wouldn't simply pack up and go on his advice. The problem was David couldn't answer without telling the truth—and that meant revealing the contents of the top-secret directive that Munn had handed him. Yet it was inconceivable that he would keep it from them, after all they'd endured together. He turned to Amira.

"No. In fact, I've been ordered to leave." He took in their shocked expressions. "Whatever the king decides, it doesn't matter. As of tonight, the American presence here officially ends."

Paolo slowly sank back in his seat. "So they're truly washing their hands of it," he muttered. "The betrayal is complete."

David nodded. "The betrayal is complete."

———

He decided to walk to the palace. The crowd along the promenade had thinned greatly since that morning, but the seawall railing was still lined two or three deep with people staring out at the gray battleship on the horizon, there was still an excitement in their voices and faces. Clearly, the famed Laradan rumor mill had not yet caught wind of that ship's true mission.

As he walked, David thought of the king, of how completely alone and helpless he was now. It was one of the pitfalls of being an absolute ruler, of surrounding oneself with sycophants. It all worked very nicely when times were good, when the biggest decision to be made was whether to name the new airport for yourself or your father, but when things went bad, who did you turn to, who could you trust? The clan chieftains whose loyalty you'd won over through patronage or threats, who'd always dreamed of being kings themselves? The palace courtiers who had dutifully agreed with your every utterance, but who now saw your power slipping away by the day? The generals? The technocrats? No, you were on your own now, and your blood was in the water. And, if only to add insult to injury, the agent of your destruction was going to be a corpulent little Texan who had come to smile to your face and tell you he was there to help, even as he shuttled among your aspirants and bought up their support with promises, reassurances, lies.

David noticed an open space along the seawall railing and decided to stop there briefly, to gaze out at the sea.

At one time, that bay would have been studded with the white sails and brightly painted hulls of fishing boats, but now it was just a flat expanse of clouded blue, broken only by the gray tower and guns of the American destroyer lying at anchor in the distance.

He remembered that day he had gone sailing with Paolo and Nicky, how from out on the water, the city had looked like some wedding-cake creation. He wondered how different it might look now. Not much, he decided. Despite all the devastation visited upon it, Laradan would probably look much the same from out there, its scars muted by the scrim of haze, its blackened patches softened by the surrounding walls of whitewash. It was another of those small surprises that war revealed, how much work it actually took to destroy a city. Not as much as building one, but it still required patience, doggedness.

He felt the presence of someone beside him, and turned to see it was Amira.

"I followed you," she said. "I hope that's all right. I thought maybe you could use some moral support."

He gave a bitter chuckle. "'Moral.' Funny choice of words."

But then he took her hand and they continued along the walk together, in the direction of the palace.

"Are you a boxing man, Mr. President?" General Munn called.

In his seat alongside, David leaned over to whisper: "It's 'Your Majesty.'"

"Oh, right." Munn turned back to the tiny man seated on the throne at the far end of the room. "Are you a boxing man, Your Majesty?"

The revised question drew no response, either. From his perch, Abdul Rahman II continued to glare at the two men seated at the base of the royal carpet.

Thus far, the grand council meeting did not appear to be going at all well for General Munn. His ten-minute presentation on Operation Partners in Peace had been delivered to absolute silence, had elicited no response other than stony stares from the ministers and generals gathered there.

Yet this may have been an illusion, for what had immediately struck David was how radically different the mood in that chamber was from the other times he had been there. Gone was Abdul Rahman's haughtiness, his sneering sarcasm, replaced by a kind of nervous petulance, and David noticed that the king looked at his courtiers far more often than on previous occasions. Not to take in their dutiful nods and approving smiles, however; on this day, there were few of these. Instead, it was as if the king were searching the faces in that room to find which allies he had left, who had been turned, and in the number of perfectly impassive expressions he found there, in the way so many avoided meeting his eye, he could not have been reassured.

"The reason I ask," Munn continued, "is because maybe there's an easier way to illustrate all this. You see, sometimes war is a lot like a boxing match. You know, you get into a clinch with the other guy and you're wrapped up"—and here Munn actually raised his arms, made two fists in front of his chest–"you can't get a good swing in and, meanwhile, the other guy's working the jab. In a nutshell, that's what we've got going on here. You're caught up in a clinch with these guys, you're wrapped up, and they're just keeping on with the body shots. So seems to me what you've got to do–same as in boxing–you've got to come up with a new strategy, get out of the clinch, step back where you can play the long game, unload the roundhouse on him. Are you following me here, sir?"

From his expression, it appeared the king thought Munn an imbecile, albeit a particularly dangerous one. "And just how do you propose I'm to throw this roundhouse if I'm not even here?"

Munn frowned. "Well, I was kind of using the boxing thing there for explanatory purposes, Mr. President, not to be taken literally per se."

"I understand that, General; I went to Cambridge, I understand analogies, even bad ones. But it still begs the question of what role I'm supposed to play if I'm in exile."

"Well, you see, there again, sir, I think we're experiencing a bit of a communicational lapse. Because no one's talking about exile here. What we're talking about is a temporary leave of limited duration, a way to kind of step back from the situation, let the dust settle, come in with a counter-initiative."

"That counter-initiative being this dialogue of national reconciliation of yours?"

Munn beamed. "Absolutely right. You got it now, sir."

The king sighed. "And what steps will the United States take to ensure this dialogue actually takes place?"

Munn scratched at his ear. "Uh, steps, sir?"

"Yes, steps. Does it intend to act as intermediary in the talks, bring in troops to stabilize the situation?"

The general scratched at his ear more forcefully. "Well, I'd say both those scenarios are certainly options we'd give serious consideration to if there were indications they might be optimal approaches from the standpoint of objective achievement at some particular point in time; absolutely. 'Course, we'd hate to impose our will on the situation, like to see the Kutarans settle this thing themselves." He tried an ingratiating grin.

The king leaned back in his throne, gave another deep sigh. "Let me ask you a question, General."

"Shoot."

"Can you tell me why I should have faith in anything you propose, when everything you've done here, every bit of advice you've given and every military operation you've conducted, has been a complete failure?"

Munn blinked hard, shifted in his chair. "Well, believe me, Mr. President, I can appreciate your frustration with the slow pace of progress. But let me just say as a military man, that when you're dealing with something as complex as military operations, I'm not sure how helpful it is to try and simplify things down into terms of success or failure. I really think you've got to take what I like to call a macro view on this stuff, and if we do that here, I think we can agree that the situation we've got going on is not a completely non-positive one."

The king leaned forward in anger, gripped the edges of his throne chair with both hands. "Really? We've buried eighteen thousand of our people, General. One quarter of this city has been burned to the ground. My people are surviving on one-half emergency food rations. What part of all that constitutes progress in your eyes?"

General Munn cleared his throat. "Well, you see, here again, that's precisely the point I'm trying to make, Mr. President. Okay, no question about it, we've hit some suboptimals, but the point is, let's learn from that. Let's try a new approach, get out of this clinch"—he raised his fists again—"let's go for the roundhouse."

Abdul Rahman II looked away from him, cast a long, sweeping gaze over the row of ministers and generals seated to his right, then did the same with those on his left. But his courtiers were a study in inscrutability, their faces revealed nothing. The king turned to Munn once more.

"Excuse my bluntness, General, but it comes back to the same thing: Why should we listen to you? After everything that has happened, after the Americans and everyone else just walked out of here, what possible reason do we have to trust in anything you say now?"

David had expected another bout of nervous ear-scratching from Munn. Instead, the question appeared to inspire him; he sat up very straight, his chest expanded, and he looked directly, boldly, into the king's eyes.

"I'm very glad you asked me that, Mr. President." As the king had done, Munn gazed along the rows of ministers and military men. "If I may, I'd like to tell you gentlemen just a little bit about how we, in the United States Marine Corps, go about choosing the names for our operations. With each one, we try to capture the spirit—the very essence, if you will—of that operation's objective. We have elite units of soldiers—some of the finest men and women in the Corps—who do nothing else but select those names, who dedicate their professional lives to that task. And let me tell you gentlemen, that for every Marine, no matter his race, creed, or color, it is considered both an honor and a privilege to be chosen to serve on the Operational Appellationizing Task Force." Munn's chest expanded even farther as he turned back to the king. "The name of this operation, Mr. President, is Operation Partners in Peace. If I may, I'd ask you to cogitate on that for just a moment: Partners in Peace. Because let me assure you"—and here Munn actually managed to work a slight tremble into his voice—"speaking for myself and all the fine young men and women who have worked so hard in putting this together, that no name could be more appropriate, none more fitting, for the mission that lies before us."

David glanced around the chamber, tried to gauge if anyone

was buying this. When he looked back to the front, he saw the king watching him with a curious smile.

"And what of you, Mr. Richards? Last time we spoke, you had a rather different opinion."

Before David could speak, Munn jumped in.

"Very glad you brought that up, Mr. President. Because what's come through loud and clear in my discussions with Mr. Richards here is that whatever initial reservations he may have had on this thing, they've now been fully satisfied. As a matter of fact–"

"Thank you, General," the king raised his hand, "but it would really be more effective to hear that from him. Mr. Richards?"

Every man in the room turned to David. At his side, he felt Munn's waiting stare. He glanced along the right side of the room until he found General Kalima. The chief of staff was gazing back at him placidly, opaque, a hesitant smile working at his lips.

On his walk to the palace, David had pondered the king's utter isolation, his sudden solitude; now, sitting in the grand council room, he felt it was a status they shared.

But what David also felt was a sense of duty, an obligation he could not shirk. He looked to the king.

"My opinion hasn't changed, Your Majesty. I think you should stay. I implore you to stay. And, with all due respect, I can't imagine why you would believe anything the American government might tell you now."

———

The gilded front gates of the palace swung open. Amira was waiting for him on the other side.

"So is he going to leave?" she asked.

"I don't know. I don't think so."

She took his hand, and as they walked down the boulevard together, David told her what he had said in the royal chamber. It didn't seem to surprise Amira; it almost seemed she had expected it.

"What does it mean for you?"

He shrugged, forced a smile. "Well, it sure makes getting on that ship a lot less attractive. Munn's vowing to throw me in irons and have me brought up on treason charges." He saw her worried look. "That won't happen—probably malfeasance in office, interfering with government operations, something like that—but not even that if things work out here."

"Work out how?"

"If the king stays on. If he manages to come to some settlement with the KPLA. The Americans just care about results, so if that happens, all will be forgiven."

They walked in silence for a while.

"So you're staying on?" she asked.

"I don't see that I've a choice. I have to see this through to the end."

"Me, too."

David drew up on the walk, wheeled to face her. "No, Amira. You have to go. You can't stay just because I'm—"

"It's not because of you. I'd already decided, no matter what you did. Paolo, too. We're all staying." Her expression softened as she looked into his eyes. "And by the way, I knew you would stay. I never thought for a moment you'd go along with Munn's plan."

He leaned down to kiss her. "I guess you know me better than I do, then."

They continued along until they came to a spot on the boulevard that David remembered, a particular pattern in the asphalt. He stopped again, let his hand fall from Amira's as he stared at it.

"What is it?" she asked. "What's wrong?"

"Nothing." He took up her hand once more, clutched it tightly. "Nothing." They walked on.

The first guests began to arrive shortly after eight, but the Contessa, already fuming at the lackluster performance of her assistants, could not have been at all heartened by their pedigree. David had invited those former embassy staffers he'd been able to locate, Amira her co-workers at the refugee office, but by nine o'clock, the only near-notables in the lobby of the Moonlight were a couple of fifth cousins of the king–at least, so they claimed–and the minister of tourism. There, they nibbled on soda crackers and Bulgarian sausage, the closest approximations to canapés the assistants had managed to find in the city, and politely listened to the same ukulele quartet that had made its debut at the German embassy reception several months ago and which, by all evidence, had spent little of the interim in practice. Even so, David found the sound of music echoing off the walls a pleasing change from the silence which had so long held that vast room, and was quite enjoying catching up with his old colleagues from the embassy. As was to be expected, these conversations tended to quickly turn to the topic of the American warship in the harbor, of what it foretold, and there was always a somewhat awkward moment when David had to feign ignorance and shift the discussion elsewhere.

He was chatting with the tourism minister when the Contessa, clad in an extravagant gown and bedecked in a large percentage of her jewelry, sashayed to their side. She fixed the minister with a radiant smile.

"So honored you could find time in your busy schedule to join us this evening, sir, but if you'll forgive me, I simply must borrow Mr. Richards for a moment."

Once they'd retreated to a secluded corner, the old lady's manner abruptly changed. "I'm holding you personally responsible for this." She furiously jabbed a finger at David. "Where is that damned king?!"

The Contessa had sent an ornately designed invitation to the king weeks earlier, and David was supposed to have followed up with reminders during his meetings at the palace. This had not happened. "Relax, Contessa. Maybe he'll still make it, but there's rather a lot going on in the city tonight, you know?" He nodded toward the terrace doors, in the general direction of the warship.

"Exactly," she spat. "An American ship. Which is why I hold you responsible."

He tried to cajole her with a smile. "But even if the king doesn't show, it's still a fine party. Aren't you having a good time?"

At this, the old lady fairly trembled with rage, David thought she might actually strike him. But then some minor princeling entered the lobby and the Contessa instantly affected her glowing smile as she hurried in his direction.

It was just before ten o'clock when Arkadi Hafizullah came alongside to whisper in David's ear.

"The king is on the radio. He's addressing the nation."

"What's he saying?"

"I think we'd better turn it on."

Within moments, news of the broadcast had spread through the lobby. The ukuleles fell silent, conversations stopped, and all gathered before the radio Arkadi had placed on the reception desk counter. As the king's soft voice carried through the room, it was clear they had missed most of his address, but not its most crucial detail.

"For all these reasons," Abdul Rahman II said, "I believe that the best hope for peace might come with my temporary departure from the kingdom. As a result, this evening I have briefly transferred full governmental authority to the first minister, and I shall now leave for a stay abroad. Please be assured that this is not an abdication. This is not the end of the Rahman monarchy. Rather it is a brief departure from the normal state of affairs in the interests of peace. So now, I take my leave of you, my dear people, but your loyalty and devotion and courage of these past months will stay with me, as the very best part of me shall remain here with you. And so, until the better days that surely lie ahead for our nation, I bid you all happiness and health and strong hearts. Goodbye, and may God bless each of you."

The radio transmission filled with static, and was then cut off. From the back of the crowd, someone let up a shout, and there began a mass exodus out the French doors to the poolside terrace.

From the far end of Serenity Bay, the lights of a fast-moving boat could be seen cutting across the darkened water, heading out to sea. From the growing throng pressing against the promenade railing below, there arose a great sound, part prayer, part wail, and it rose until it seemed to envelop the entire city.

And then this sound mixed with that of the low thumps from the guns on the ridge, and then Laradan was wreathed in plumes of white dust and red flames by the explosions that were everywhere in its midst.

Watching the ferocious bombardment from the stern of the high-speed launch, General Munn slowly shook his head. "Well I'll be damned," he muttered. He turned to the sailor manning the boat's tiller. "You ever wonder why these people can't just get along?"

Thirteen

Rustam sat on a flat rock above the road, and he watched David's approach with a smile that could only be described as affectionate.

"It's good to see you again, Mr. Richards," he called. "It hasn't been the same up here these past few weeks." The rebel liaison stood off the rock, climbed down to the road. "In your absence, they were sending up some poor fellow from the Interior Ministry, but he was absolutely terrified the entire time." He stopped in front of David. "But I'm a little confused; does this mean you're the American representative again?"

David smiled despite the situation. "I'm not really sure. It was all left a bit vague." He raised the thick manila envelope in his hand. "But the president's office asked if I would deliver this, and I agreed."

"Oh, that's right," Rustam said, chuckling, "Laradan has a president now, doesn't it? What kind of man is he, this Mr. Nassiri? The opinion of most everyone up here is that he's a front man for General Kalima, but maybe that's not correct. Certainly some of his cabinet choices have been interesting—one could even say conciliatory."

David had been through enough of these meetings with Rustam to know his questions were designed less to gather information than to show that the KPLA knew everything that transpired in the city; it had been just a day and a half since the king had left on the American destroyer, and Abdur Nassiri, the colorless first minister who was now acting head of state, had named his new cabinet only that morning. David pressed the envelope into Rustam's hand. "They want to talk, to negotiate."

The liaison took the packet with a doubtful expression. "Well, I'll pass it along but, between us, I don't see much chance of that." He motioned up the hill, toward the top of the pass. "They're just not a very talkative bunch, and they have a special problem with Kalima."

"Kalima's not running things," David replied. "Nassiri is."

Rustam gave a weary nod, as if to indicate this fiction had already become tiresome, and looked to the city with a meditative air. A breeze was coming up the hill, and it rustled his dark hair, fluttered the collar of his shirt.

"It might seem strange to say this," he muttered, "but part of me envies you. In its own way, these past months, it must have been fascinating to be down there." He turned to David. "I don't know if I've mentioned this before, but my major at Harvard was clinical psychology–Harvard has a very good psychology department–so for a person of my interests, the chance to observe what takes place at such a time, the strategies people devise, well, it would have been fascinating. 'Maybe we should attack, maybe we should surrender, maybe if we send the king away.'" Rustam smiled. "Now that was a strange one, all the commanders were very puzzled by that, because it's not something we ever asked for. But not so strange, really, if you know the psychology of these things. When people are frightened, they'll do most anything to satisfy their torturers, they'll even come up with ideas of their own. 'Would you like me to dance?' 'Would you like me to sing?' It's actually rather basic, isn't it?"

"I wouldn't know," David said. "I didn't go to Harvard." He saw the envelope in Rustam's shirt pocket, held out his hand. "You want to give me the note?"

Instead, the young man cocked his head to the side, studied David in that smug way of his. "And you, too, I find fascinating. For example, I can't imagine you had any particular affection for the king, and yet you urged him to stay, you destroyed your career for him. You hate coming up here, you know it doesn't accomplish anything, but even now, betrayed by the king and your own government, you come anyway. Some would almost think you a masochist."

"Going for your master's here, Rustam?" David impatiently motioned with his hand. "Why don't you just give me the note."

"But no, I don't think a masochist at all. I think probably more it's that you feel trapped by the situation. You've been given this role to perform, and you must keep performing it in the small hope that maybe it will help one day. Hope against hope. That's it, isn't it?"

The liaison paused, as if for a response. When none was forthcoming, he sighed, took the note from his shirt pocket. "All right, Mr. Richards, have it your way. I must say, though, that if I have one constant criticism of you, it's your uncommunicativeness."

David reached for the envelope, but Rustam didn't release his grip on it, waited for David to look up.

"There won't be peace talks," he said. "I tell you this man to man. And there won't be many more sailings of the relief ship. This has to end now. For all our sakes, it's time to end this." He let go of the envelope. "I just want you to be prepared, Mr. Richards."

─────────

"What will it mean for the city?" Paolo repeated David's question. Folding his arms over his chest, the businessman stared up at his office ceiling, shrugged. "To be honest, not very much."

"But how can you say that? If they cut off the ship, Laradan can't survive."

David's bewilderment at Paolo's statement was just a continuation of what he'd felt ever since stepping into the warehouse office. He'd come there immediately after his meeting with Rustam on Gowarshad Pass, but throughout his recounting of that conversation, the businessman had remained profoundly unstirred, could have been watching a show on television for all the reaction he displayed.

"What's going on, Paolo? Something's up with you."

Paolo exhaled heavily, unfolded his arms. "I was planning to talk with you about this in a few days, when I have a final accounting, but maybe we should do it now." Taking a key from his shirt pocket, he leaned down to unlock one of his desk drawers, brought out a small black notebook. "Understand that this is quite preliminary—I'm still waiting for numbers from the Interior Ministry—but I've been making some calculations."

"Calculations?"

Paolo set the notebook on the desk, opened the cover. "On food supplies."

David sank back in his chair, watched as his friend flipped through pages filled with notes written in a small concise hand.

"We can say that, before the war, about 70 percent of Kutar's population lived along the coast here," Paolo explained, "so with the refugees now, maybe 75 percent—roughly, 3 to 3.2 million, yes? The problem is, the coast only grows about 40 percent of the food; all the rest is either grown in the north or imported." He came to a page in the notebook, tapped at it. "Ah, here we are."

David saw that a long series of equations had been written there; Paolo's finger trailed down the column.

"I've made an inventory of what we have stored here, and the ministry is doing the same at the mills and private warehouses, any sources they can think of." His finger stopped, he looked up. "But even if they find quite a lot and we do everything perfectly—perfect distribution, no hoarding, no waste—we will hit a threshold in probably six, at most eight, weeks."

"What do you mean, a threshold?"

Paolo's gaze slid away from David, out the window to the warehouse, and then it slowly slid back. "Famine."

David stared into his friend's eyes. Although he had sensed where they were going the moment Paolo brought out the notebook, he still couldn't quite process the news, looked for loopholes. "But you said the Interior Ministry hasn't finished their inventory. Maybe there's a lot more . . . ?"

The businessman shook his head. "They won't find much. The way prices are, any substantial stores would have been in the markets or looted by now."

"And the *Esmeralda*?"

Paolo continued to shake his head. "She makes very little difference. We need two or three *Esmeralda*s every day, not one a week. If the rebels cut it off, it means we reach the threshold a bit sooner, that's all." He took a glance at his calculations. "Actually, it's worse than that, because this is a statistical model, it doesn't take into account economic disparities. If we're eight weeks away from a statistical famine, it means the poor people, the refugees, will be affected much sooner. And even before they start dying . . ."

"Riots," David supplied the answer. "Panic."

Paolo nodded. "That's always the way. And once the panic starts, it becomes unstoppable, everything comes apart very quickly."

For as long as he could, David put off asking the question, just stared into space. "So the panic," he finally said, "when does that start?"

Paolo looked down at his notebook, thoughtfully bobbled his head. "Being optimistic on what the ministry finds, and taking into account the general apathy among the population—a good thing in this situation—let's say . . . two weeks, maybe three."

"So, it's over then," David whispered.

By way of answering, Paolo closed his book.

But when David left the warehouse that afternoon, he found an army squad car waiting for him at the harbor gate. He recognized the junior officer standing alongside as the same one who had escorted him to his meeting with General Kalima several weeks ago.

———

The general was by one of his office windows, gazing up at the ridgeline, but he turned in welcome when David was ushered through the door.

"Ah, Mr. Richards, thank you so much for coming." He strode toward his desk, motioned to the metal armchair before it. "Please, have a seat. May I get you a tea or a coffee—perhaps something stronger?"

"I'm fine." David took the chair.

He had never been in the chief of staff's personal office before, and one glance was enough to tell him that Kalima wasn't a desk general. Other than an enormous aerial map of Laradan on one wall, the room had the feel of a disorganized storage shed in an army barracks: along the edges were stacks of boxes, an assortment of helmets and rifles. The desk itself was of gray metal and bare save for a few orderly stacks of papers.

Taking the swivel chair on its opposite side, the general leaned back to swing his boots onto the desktop, fixed David with a friendly grin. "And how are things at the Moonlight? Everyone in good spirits? I understand you had a little party the other night."

"Everyone's fine." While David had seen Kalima on several occasions, most recently in the palace council room during that last audience with the king, they hadn't spoken since the day of the prisoner executions at Gowarshad barracks. David had been keen to keep it that way, saw no reason to mask his contempt for the man now.

Still smiling, the general picked at a fingernail. "Ah, but I'm sensing maybe you're still upset with me over that business with the prisoners. Is that so?"

David returned his gaze. "It's a war crime to execute prisoners, General. I'm sure you know that."

Kalima's grin broadened. "Yes, I remember some mention of that during my training at Fort Bragg. But you know what is strange to me? Why is something like that a war crime, when bombing a city isn't? It's odd, don't you think, an inconsistency? But whether it's Laradan or Hanoi or Tokyo, no one seems to have a problem with that. I killed forty-seven combatants, men who'd had a hand in killing thousands, and I get criticized for it. When the Americans firebombed Tokyo, they killed ninety thousand civilians in one night, and they got medals for it. Strange, no?" He raised the palms of both hands. "Well, who are we to judge? This is all worked out by lawyers." He swung his legs down, leaned forward on the desk. "In any event, I didn't ask you here to discuss ethics, Mr. Richards, so how about I apologize–sincerely apologize–and we move on to other things?" That was the apology, apparently, because Kalima immediately continued. "You see, I'm curious to get your opinion on a rather important matter. One could even say the future of the country depends on it and, as the American representative, I think you might be able to give us some guidance."

David chuckled. "Then shouldn't I have this conversation with Mr. Nassiri?"

Kalima briefly looked puzzled, but then his expression cleared. "Oh, yes, of course, the president. Well, as you can imagine, President Nassiri is a very busy man, so he's asked me to assist him where I can. And since this matter is more of a military nature than a political one–"

"Except I'm not a military man, General. I thought I already told you that."

But Kalima was determined to ignore David's hostility; he gave a quick nod, reached for a manila folder atop one of his paper stacks. "Yes, but this is actually a very simple business, not complicated at all. Even just as a man of the world, I think your opinion might be helpful."

He opened the manila folder, and David saw that inside were a number of magazines—or more accurately, judging from the cover of the first one, weaponry catalogs. Kalima drew this one out, idly flipped through its pages.

"First off," he said, "I'd like to ask you a question. In our assault of a few weeks ago, do you know why we went directly up the Gowarshad Pass road?"

"I haven't a clue."

"Because, you see, every textbook—even common sense—argues against attacking in this way. It means your soldiers are bunched together in a small area so they are easy to kill. Also, passes are always low points on a ridge, so even if you reach the summit, the enemy still controls the high ground above you." Kalima glanced up. "Of course, you know part of the reason—this was a limited operation, not meant to break the siege but to make a quick strike, take prisoners—but I'm curious if you understand the tactical reason behind it."

David sighed with impatience. "General, I'm a busy man, as I'm sure you are. If you have something to say, rather than waste time with these questions you know I can't answer, I suggest you just say it."

Kalima laughed merrily at this. "Oh yes, I'd forgotten how annoyed you get with that. Fast, fast, the American way. Very well." He leaned back in his chair. "We stayed to the road because that's the only place along the front where we could be certain there were no mines. Maybe heavy mines to blow up vehicles, but not antipersonnel ones, because the rebels go up and down that road all the time. Every place else on the line, the no-man's-land between us is filled with mines, theirs and ours. That is why we have this stalemate: two armies dug in, facing each other across a strip of earth that, because of the mines, it is impossible to get across.

Rather like the trench warfare of World War I but, unfortunately for us, a stalemate where all the advantages lie with the enemy: they have the heights, the artillery, they have the time. You see?"

He paused, as if for some acknowledgment, but David didn't give him one. A cool light came into the general's eyes.

"Except this is not 1917. For modern armies, there is now a weapon—well, more a device, I suppose—that makes this kind of warfare obsolete." Leaning forward again, he took the catalog he had been leafing through and turned it to face David.

Almost against his will, David looked down. Across both open pages were photographs and technical drawings of a squat metal cylinder that looked rather like a portable propane tank with a number of wires attached.

"The Eagle Freedom Deathstar ultra-low-frequency concussion grenade," Kalima explained, "manufactured in Valdosta, Georgia. They just finished development on it last year, an absolutely ingenious device. It's fired at close range from a shoulder launcher, a sensor triggers the grenade to burst just above ground, and the low-frequency concussion detonates any land mines in a fifty-meter radius. With just twenty-five of these Deathstars, we could win this war." He motioned toward the aerial map of Laradan on the far wall. "With twenty-five, we could clear out a large enough section of no-man's-land to send a division across and, within two or three minutes, before the rebels could react, we would be in their trenches. When that happens, they're finished. Their line is cut in two and their artillery is sitting just above, completely unprotected and useless to them at that close range. We pour more men into the breach, we send some up to take or destroy the artillery, while others fight their way down the trench line in both directions, making the breach bigger. Now they are the ones trapped, stuck on top of a ridge with nowhere to go." He raised a finger. "But very bloody. A lot of men killed on both sides—there's no getting around that—but one quick, coordinated strike and it's done, the siege is over." He slowly lowered his hand. "So what do you think?"

David shrugged. "I'm thinking you should have mentioned it to Munn when he was in town; I'm sure he'd have given you enough of these Deathstars to blow up half the country." But then a thought occurred to him; he gave a wry smile. "But, of course, you couldn't do it then, could you? You needed to get the king out of the picture first."

Kalima chuckled. "Hmm, interesting theory, Mr. Richards." He folded his hands together, propped them under his chin. "Actually, I suspect even Munn would have a hard time helping us with this. You see, the Deathstar is extremely advanced technology—I understand the Pentagon spent $28 billion on its development—so they guard it closely, they will only sell it to their closest Alliance allies. Even then, it's very expensive; just for the small number we need, in the neighborhood of $30 million."

David felt a new surge of impatience. "Then what's the point of all this, General?"

His jaw still perched on his hands, Kalima smiled. "The point is that the Red Chinese have pirated an exact copy: the People's Red Lantern of Defensive Fury, or something like that. According to people who've tested it, it's just as good as the Deathstar—maybe even better. It's also one-third the cost, so for what we need here, maybe $9 million. Naturally, we want to uphold international patent laws, but at those prices . . ."

"So maybe you should cozy up to the Red Chinese."

Kalima's smile eased away. His face settled into the same hardness as that day at the regimental barracks, and David knew that, at long last, the general's hand was about to be revealed.

"We already have," he said. "And we have twenty-five Red Lanterns waiting for us right now in Palumbo, waiting to come here on the *Esmeralda*. What we don't have is the $9 million in cash to pay for them. That's why I asked you here."

David was too startled to even articulate a reply.

Kalima continued: "Put succinctly–because I know that is your preference–we have cash-flow problems. When the rich people fled from here, they took almost all the hard currency out with them. And because of the communications shutdown, we can't access any of the government's hard-currency accounts overseas. By going into every vault and reserve account in Laradan, the central bank has managed to find about five million dollars–American dollars–in cash. But what they also found was this."

Reaching to a different stack of papers, Kalima took the top folder and opened it, slid it in David's direction. Stapled together was a sheaf of papers giving an accounting of the American embassy's operational fund as reported to the Kutaran central bank: a $7 million cash deposit in July, several large currency exchanges through October, and then nothing after that, a static balance of $4,213,778.

And now David understood precisely; he looked to the chief of staff, slowly shook his head. "Not a chance, Kalima. Not a fucking chance."

"But why not? You're still the American representative here. All it requires is for you to go to the embassy and take the money out. We could do it ourselves but, since the embassy is technically American soil, the politics of that get quite complicated." He grinned. "Plus, I understand from our intelligence people that your vault is very sophisticated, nearly impossible to break into."

David's amazement only deepened as he stared into the general's serene face. "Are you out of your mind? Even if I thought it could work–which I don't–do you have any idea how many laws I'd be violating?"

The general gave a lazy shrug. "Which laws? Certainly not ours. International laws? But the Americans don't pay attention to those anyway. As for your own laws, you know they won't matter if this works. If we win, all will be forgiven."

David looked away from Kalima then, stared vacantly across

the office, and as much as he thought the idea was ludicrous, as much as he detested the man he sat across from, he felt an undeniable stirring of something inside, something crazy and thrilling and defiant and desperate, and it was taking an increasing effort to tamp it down.

"Anyway," he muttered finally, "it's too late."

"How's that?"

He turned back to Kalima. "It's too late. The KPLA are about to cut off the relief ship. Their messenger told me this morning."

"But, as I said, the Red Lanterns are already in Palumbo. If we can organize this quickly, work out an arrangement with the *Esmeralda*'s captain this next Friday, they can be here the following week. So, you see, we only need two more sailings."

But the more he had time to think about it, the more David grasped a change in himself. It stemmed from his conversation with Paolo earlier that day, in learning of the coming famine. Maybe if Kalima had gotten to him before that, maybe then . . . but now it was as if the last small reservoir of hope or resistance had been drained from him, there was no fight left in him, and all David could think of now was how to end this as quickly and bloodlessly as possible. He shook his head.

"I'm sorry, General. It's too late. I can't do it. And I can't be party to something that's going to kill thousands more people. It just has to end now." He rose, started for the door. He had almost reached it when Kalima called after him.

"Just one more question, please, Mr. Richards."

David stopped, turned around.

"I understand from the Interior Ministry that Mr. Alfani is making an inventory of food supplies in Laradan. Tell me, what has he learned so far?"

"That we're heading into a famine."

"Is that so? How soon?"

"Maybe six weeks."

The general frowned, chewed his lip with apparent concern.

"And that's based on how much food there is? On how long it can feed three million people?"

David shrugged; the answer was self-evident.

"But I think maybe Mr. Alfani has made an error in his calculations. Because you see, in my experience, civilians starve; soldiers don't. So maybe we should ask Mr. Alfani to make a new calculation, not based on food for three million people, but on food for forty thousand soldiers." He arched an eyebrow. "Actually, that's a very simple equation, isn't it? We could probably calculate it right now."

David gaped at him in disbelief. "You're saying you'd let the city starve?"

The coldness returned to Kalima's eyes. "We won't give up, Mr. Richards. If we have to fight to the last man and the last bullet, that is what we will do. But the rest of the city will die before us. That's what happens in war, to the people without guns. It's happened before, and I'm ready to let it happen here." His manner abruptly changed; he jauntily waved a hand in the air. "But you decide. I don't want to influence your decision. It's really your choice."

———

Two sets of images, almost like spools of film. Try as he might, David could not be rid of them.

One, a whitewashed city ablaze with thousands of lights viewed from some removed vantage point—perhaps from the sea or the veranda of a hilltop home—and then those lights blinking off one at a time, each light a life, a family, a neighborhood, until all those lights were gone and what was left were faint orange glows in the shadows, the cigarette glows of the hard men who still lived and waited and could survive anything.

The other, explosions along a ridgeline, a mass of men, tiny as ants, racing up into a cloud of brown dust and black smoke, and then nothing but silence, stillness, never again the thump of artillery, the crack of gunshots, a city returned to the land of the living.

Amira slept beside him. Several times David thought to wake her, to tell her what he was seeing, because he knew he was being seduced by one set of these images—who wouldn't be seduced?—and he didn't trust his judgment about anything anymore. But he didn't wake her. Instead, he let her sleep, stared up at the ceiling and let the images play, rewind, play again, as if this were a kind of penance to be paid for his thoughts.

"I think it's a splendid idea," the Contessa announced. "Bravo, Mr. Richards: Finally, you show some initiative around here."

"First off, it's not my initiative," David said. "And second, I haven't said I'm doing it." He glanced between Paolo and Amira. "I'd like to hear what you think."

Paolo exhaled heavily. "From the standpoint of logistics? It might work. If these devices are as small as you say, they can probably be packed in among the rest of the smuggled cargo. Of course, it will all depend on Dimitrios, if he agrees to it." He paused. "But the other question is what this might do to you. Surely this is illegal in some way?"

David grinned. "Let's see: embezzling four million dollars from the American government to smuggle pirated Red Chinese weapons in on a Red Cross ship. Yeah, I'm no lawyer, but I imagine there's some kind of illegality in there. It could go well with my treason charge, though." He grew more serious. "But what about from a standpoint of . . . I don't know, morality? To know you'd be doing something that means the killing will continue, that you're helping a guy like Kalima take over."

But Paolo slowly shook his head. "On morality, I don't know what to say. I think I'm too tired—maybe just too hungry—to think about morality anymore." He gave a wan smile. "To bring in weapons to stop a city from starving—that seems easy enough—but to then give them to a man who's willing to let that city starve for his own power, that's more difficult, isn't it? I'm sorry. These questions are too much, they give me a headache."

David turned to Amira. She hadn't said a word since he'd told them of Kalima's scheme, had merely watched him from across the lobby table with an unreadable expression.

"I don't know what to say," she whispered.

He tried to coax her with a smile. "Well, try. Something, anything . . ."

But Amira shook her head. "No. We're not the ones who'll have to live with the consequences—the consequences either way. Only you will. So I don't think it's even right for us to give our opinions. I think you have to decide this on your own."

"Oh, nonsense," the Contessa jumped in. "If he didn't want to be told what to do, he wouldn't be asking, now would he?" She wheeled to David. "I say, let them have it. Smash those hooligans up there to pieces, and then, if it's truly peace you're after, go to their home districts and lay waste, burn them to the root. It's what we used to do in Romania, and it always worked."

Amira roused from her sleep to find David sitting on the edge of the bed, fully dressed. She reached a hand out for him, touched his back.

"What is it?" Although she knew what it was.

"I don't know what to do," he whispered. "Every time I think it's clear, that I've decided, I see the other side."

Still stroking his back, Amira looked around the darkened room. Out the window, the sky was taking on the dark-blue tinge of approaching dawn.

He rose quickly, read his wristwatch: nearly 6:00 AM, the curfew was about to end. "I think I'll take a walk." He turned to her then, and she was so beautiful lying there in the soft blue light, peering up at him with her dark eyes, that his doubts only deep-ened. "I won't be long."

She nodded. "Would you like me to come with you?"

He considered this, ran a hand through his hair. "Yes," he de-cided. "Yes, I think I'd like that."

They went out into the paling blue light, through the city that still slept. The streets they walked were empty, smoky, as if this were a place that had already died.

They came to a spot Amira remembered. It was on the tree-lined boulevard leading away from the palace, the spot where David had suddenly stopped that day after his meeting with the king to stare at the ground. On this morning, he did so again.

"This is where Nigel died." He ran his shoe over a pattern of cracks in the asphalt. "Right here." He pointed down the road toward the palace. "I was there, maybe fifty, sixty feet away. When I first turned around, I didn't know what had happened. He was just sitting in the middle of the road, his legs out in front of him, and I couldn't figure out what . . ." He lowered his arm. "I miss him. I miss him all the time, but never more than right now. He was a much better man than me."

"He wasn't a better man than you, David," Amira said softly.

But he nodded. "He would have told Kalima to go to hell, he wouldn't have entertained this for a minute. It would have been very clear to him." He stared down at the cracks in the road. "He died before I got to him. I don't know if I told you that. It was a high-caliber bullet and it went through his heart, clean through and, just like that, before I could even get to him . . . Just like Eddie. It was the same way with Eddie."

He looked at Amira then.

"You know, they don't tell you the circumstances, the details, the American army. It's just, 'died in the line of duty,' 'died in the service of his country.' But when I started working for the govern-ment, I had a friend at the Pentagon pull up Eddie's file and he told me. He was hit in the head, in the right temple. I don't know why, really, but I wanted to know. I asked three different doctors about it. They all told me that, from where he got shot, the caliber of the bullet, he would have died instantly, he never would have felt anything. I'm not sure why, but it was important for me to know that. I guess I wanted to be sure that he didn't suffer, that he didn't linger. And I was comforted by that, I was always comforted by that. But after Nigel, I don't know anymore. Because I wish I'd gotten to him, you know? To talk to him a little, to tell him it was going to be okay. I think that would've been better."

He sighed and turned to the sky, to the stately old trees lining the boulevard. "I guess what I'm trying to say is that we forget about people. We use them and then we abandon them. It's our worst sin. Other empires, they never knew when to leave, but we never know when to stay, we leave all the time. Friends are only friends for as long as they're useful, as long as we've decided they're important, but then they're not anymore and we forget all about them. That's the American sin. It's only been eight years since the end of Vietnam. Sixty thousand Americans, a million Vietnamese, but how many Americans think about it at all now, what we left behind? Or these wars in Central America now. Vital to our national security, just like Vietnam, but eight years from now, whatever happens there, do you think most Americans will remember, that they'll even be able to find El Salvador or Nicaragua on a map?"

He fluttered a hand in the air, toward the trees. "And this place. What the hell was this place? It was a war game. It was a chance for Munn and a bunch of military advisers to win some service medals. It was a chance for the Alliance to see how well they worked together in a live-fire but low-risk, no-consequence landscape. That's all it was. And what is it now? 'Kutar? Where the fuck is Kutar?' It wasn't even around long enough for people to forget about it."

He turned to Amira.

"But Nigel didn't die in vain. I can't accept that." And then David heard his father's words and it was as if they were suddenly reunited, joined together by the rage that had stood between them for thirteen years. "Eddie didn't die in vain. All the people here, they haven't died for nothing. I refuse to believe that. I fucking refuse to believe that." As if stricken, he looked down to the street again, its memorized pattern of cracks. "He was a better man than me—I'll always know that—but I can't do what he would have done. Our sins are different. And I can't stand by and watch this happen again."

————————

They led Dimitrios to the empty clerks' office on the second floor. As they carefully laid out the plan, the *Esmeralda*'s captain listened with utter impassivity, could have been a statue save for the gentle heaving of his potbelly as he breathed and the way his beady eyes darted between them.

"So I realize it's a hell of a thing to drop on you all at once," David said in conclusion, "but what do you think?"

If Dimitrios pondered the enormity of what was being asked of him, the process took milliseconds; he gave a quick lift of his shoulders. "Sure."

David and Paolo looked at each other. They had anticipated all kinds of potential objections from the captain and spent hours compiling a point-by-point list of assurances. That none of it was necessary came as something of an anticlimax.

"Sure?" David said. "Just like that?"

Dimitrios shrugged again. "Sure. I like you guys. Hell, if the money's right, I'll bring you an atom bomb, I don't give a shit."

David and Paolo glanced at each other again, for they'd always known this would be their biggest hurdle.

Paolo shifted in his chair. "On the money, I'm afraid it's not very much. You see, this weapon system comes as a complete unit and—"

But Dimitrios stopped him with a raised hand. "Save me the speech. When you say not much, exactly how not much are you talking about?"

"Two hundred thousand," Paolo replied.

"For me?"

"For everything."

"What?" The captain lurched forward in outrage. "Are you out of your fucking minds? Two hundred grand for something like this? I'm gonna spend that just tipping out my crew and those KPLA fucks in Palumbo."

"But that's all there is," Paolo protested. "The government has scraped up every dollar left in Laradan and—"

"Let me just get this straight." Dimitrios pointed a menacing finger at them. "You guys want me to smuggle in weapons under a Red Cross flag, violating the most sacred law of the seas, you want me to endanger my ship and the lives of my entire crew—most of whom, I should add, have wives and young children—and in return, I get bupkes? Just what kind of sick individuals are you?"

David saw that it was time; he took the envelope from his shirt pocket, placed it on the desk in front of him.

"The rebels are about to stop the relief shipments," he said quietly. "It may be next week or three weeks from now, but they're cutting it off. That'll mean the end of whatever you're making off the smuggling rackets and—"

"Smuggling rackets?" Dimitrios feigned indignation. "Now wait just a goddamned minute, I don't know what you're trying to imply here, but—"

It was David who now raised a hand for silence. "If this plan with the Red Lanterns works, it means the war is over. When that happens, there's going to be a huge amount of reconstruction work here, all kinds of materials being shipped in." He slid the envelope in Dimitrios's direction. "That's from General Kalima, the guy running the show here now. It's an official letter designating

you the sole shipping agent for all maritime commerce in and out
of Kutar for the next six months."

Dimitrios stared at the envelope, then peered suspiciously at
David. "Sole, as in exclusive?"

"As in exclusive."

The captain sat back and looked into space for a time. At last
he gave a heavy sigh. "I'm a soft touch. That's always been my
problem. So where's the money?"

David pointed to a mailbag in the corner. "If you think carrying two mailbags out might arouse suspicions, the other one stays
behind." He motioned toward the ceiling, the harbormaster's office
overhead. "When I seal that one up, I'll bring it down here and we
can switch them."

It wasn't clear whether Dimitrios was absorbing any of this;
as he stared at the mailbag containing $9 million a few feet away,
he uncontrollably licked his lips, seemed lost in a distant reverie. It
reminded David of one other detail.

"Another thing," he said. "Kalima's got people in Palumbo
and every other port in the region. If, for any reason, that money
doesn't get there, it would go very badly for the person responsible. For that matter, I wouldn't want to get on the wrong side of
the Red Chinese when it comes to money."

This brought the captain back with a start; his beady eyes
burned into David's. "I find that fucking offensive. Here I am on a
fucking humanitarian mission, trying to help you guys out, and
you're fucking threatening me?" He shook his head in disgust.
"Well, I'm gonna pretend that didn't happen. I'm gonna put that
down to stress."

———

David had anticipated that a sense of relief—maybe even euphoria—
would settle over him and the others at the Moonlight during those
days of waiting for the *Esmeralda*'s next return, the deliverance

from their ordeal this would herald. Instead, there was a burdensome quality to that time. It was as if each of them now saw this city and their hotel home through a new prism, as a place from which they would soon be physically freed, but cast into an outer world they might no longer recognize. There was also the burden of carrying such a profound secret, of never being able to say to the loss-shattered refugee staring out from his tent or to the hotel cleaning girl fraught with concern: "Don't worry: It will be better soon."

Something else, too, the strain of terrible suspense, because the other great secret being kept in that city—the approaching famine—was becoming less of a secret every day. Its revealing didn't require the famous Laradan rumor mill; the inhabitants saw it in the empty marketplaces, the incremental reduction in their food rations, they felt it in the dull hunger that never quite left them. In fact, on this topic the rumor mill was completely silent, no one said a thing; the people of Laradan were still human enough, still scheming enough, to imagine that perhaps they were realizing something before the others, that keeping this knowledge to themselves might somehow play to their advantage.

But this quiet would not last long, for if there is nothing so docile as a hungry man, there is nothing so volatile as a starving one, and the flash point comes in the blink of an eye, in the slightest turn of the stomach, and when it comes, it sweeps everything else away.

To David and the others at the Moonlight, it seemed a particularly odd choice of words for such a slow and broken place, but all grasped that they were in a race now, a race between the *Esmeralda*'s return on the one hand, and biology on the other.

He found her standing against the rooftop railing, gripping it with both hands. Watching her from behind, David was reminded of a woman standing at the prow of a ship looking over a moonlit sea, an image he carried from a book he had read, or a movie he had seen, or maybe the last wisp of a memory that had grown obscure to him. He came alongside, leaned next to her.

"What do you see?"

Amira shook her head. "I feel like I've committed this view to memory, every last building and tree. But then the odd thing is, when one of them goes, I find I actually don't remember it at all. Isn't that strange? Like just there, in the downtown"—she pointed to the commercial zone of the New City—"didn't there used to be another tall building, seven or eight stories? There was, wasn't there?"

David nodded. About a week ago, the seven-story Kutar Commercial Bank had come down from a direct hit with a heavy bomb.

"But now I have only the vaguest recollection of it," she said, "no idea what color it was, what its windows looked like. So it makes me wonder what I'll remember of all this when . . ." She leaned forward to stare down at the hotel grounds. Directly below, the still water of the entranceway fountain gleamed like an enormous turquoise pendant. "What if the weapons don't get here, David? Or if Kalima's plan doesn't work?"

"Then the city falls."

"And what about you? You'll go to prison, won't you?"

Prison had actually become one of David's lesser worries. If the rebels took the city and learned what he had done, it would probably take a strenuous effort by the American government to keep him from the gallows—not a high-percentage play when Washington already regarded him as a traitor. He wasn't going to tell Amira this, though. "Maybe for a little while."

She smiled at him, a sad smile. "You could change your name, hide out in England."

"And what would I do in England?"

"We'd find something. I'd support you."

David smiled. "Great, and what's the headline on that story?

'Foreign Service Officer destroys career on moral grounds, becomes houseboy to oligarch princess.'"

Amira laughed. "Maybe night watchman; let's play to your strengths."

They stared out at the darkened city for a while. There was a nearly full moon and it gave the whitewashed buildings a spectral quality. David could never remember Laradan looking so haunting and ancient. It was Thursday night; the *Esmeralda* would be docking in less than twelve hours.

"I remember this incident when Zahra came to visit us in England," Amira said softly. "That's my great-aunt, the one I lived with here when I was a girl. It was two or three years after I left, so I must have been ten or eleven. I was so excited to have her meet my friends, to show her London—you know, all those things you do when someone visits. But I remember the second or third day she was there, we walked into town to buy something, just the two of us. We were walking along, I was chattering away to her and, all of a sudden, Zahra wasn't there. I turned around and she was standing on the sidewalk, frozen, just completely overcome by it all. You know, this peasant woman who a few days earlier had been tending goats, who had probably never been more than twenty miles from her village before, and there she was, in the middle of an English high street. And I felt so sorry for her. She was so overwhelmed, so out of place. I'll never forget that look on her face."

Gripping the rail with both hands, Amira leaned back to stare up at the sky.

"Christ, David, how do we ever go back home from this? How are we ever going to walk into a fancy boutique or watch a stupid movie or read about some celebrity? How do we ever care about that stuff again? I used to feel that I lived between two worlds, my life here and there, but now I feel I've lost both of them. I don't know how I stay or go back to either one of them."

He found it difficult to watch her, how pretty and alone she appeared in the moonlight, and he looked back at the view. "I think it will take time," he said. "Spending time with your family, your friends, Kenneth." When he turned, he saw that she was staring at him, bewildered. "But that's his name, isn't it? Your boyfriend?"

She blinked rapidly, as if he had wounded her in some way. "You're not going to die here, David," she whispered. "And you won't go to prison."

He tried to smile. "Okay."

"Do you promise?"

"I promise."

They had worked out a simple code with Dimitrios. If the Red Lanterns were on board, he was to start along the pier and then draw up, brush at his neck with a handkerchief as if wiping away perspiration.

The captain had apparently forgotten all this in the intervening week. Stopping in full view at the top of the gangway, he turned in the direction of the harbormaster's office and raised both hands high in the air to give an exuberant thumbs-up signal. In case David and Paolo had somehow missed the gesture, he repeated it several more times.

General Kalima beamed broadly as David stepped into the office, and it was only then that some of David's elation at the day's events began to dissolve, when he remembered its chief beneficiary.

"Well done, Mr. Richards, well done." The chief of staff warmly clasped his hand. "The people of Kutar shall be forever in your gratitude."

David forced a smile. "At the very least, you should be."

Kalima laughed. "Yes, yes, myself, as well."

The general had been standing by the large aerial map on his wall; David motioned to it. "Have you decided where you're going to launch?"

"Yes. I will show you." He led the way across the room, pointed to an area near the center of the map. "Fatikh. Do you know it?"

David did; it was one of the working-class hillside neighborhoods, a warren of three- and four-story apartment buildings and narrow streets.

"It's very close to the front," Kalima explained, "and because of the tall buildings, the attack force can assemble without being seen from the ridge."

David nodded, and his gaze traveled up the map to the crest of the mountain, found the tiny square that had once been his home. "And when is it going to be?"

A hesitation in Kalima, he studied David. "You do understand that very few people know about this still, yes? Even the soldiers in the assault force, they won't know until the last minute. So please, not a word to anyone, even the others at the hotel."

"Of course."

The general turned to the map. "At 6:15 Sunday morning, just at the end of curfew. That's also when the KPLA change their gunner crews, so their reaction will be slow."

David was startled. "But that's in less than thirty-six hours. Isn't that a little quick to organize everything?"

Kalima shook his head with a confident grin. "The Red Lantern is a very easy weapon to use—two hours with the manual and even a child could do it. The Americans should be extremely proud." He tapped at the map. "We'll bring them up to the forward trench tomorrow night, my engineers will work out the coordinates while the assault force assembles, and then at 6:15 . . ." When he looked at David, his face settled into a more thoughtful expression. "But I think it's best if you're not in the area, Mr. Richards. I'm sure you'd like to be but, as I said before, there will be a lot of shooting, a lot of random gunfire, especially from the rebel side. I think it's best you stay at the hotel until it's over, yes?"

David nodded.

"You will promise me? You will stay at the hotel?"

David gave a sardonic smile. "This sudden concern for human life, it's not at all like you, Kalima."

The general laughed, slapped David on the back. "Ah, you're thinking of my threat to let the city starve, aren't you? I suppose it's safe to tell you now, that was just a bluff. How could I ever do such a thing, starve my own people? Just a bluff, like in a poker game, you know?"

David wasn't quite buying it, but saw no reason to argue the point now. "Well, you've got a good poker face, then."

"Yes, I've been told that. And you? Do you play poker?"

"No," David replied.

Kalima nodded. "Maybe for the best."

———

Rustam met him at their usual place, sighed at the sight of the large manila envelope in David's hand.

"Still they persist, no?" he said. "Is it more of the same? Pleas for negotiations? Talk of a unity government?"

David handed him the envelope. "Most of it, I suspect. I don't read all of it."

Rustam shook his head. "Well, I suppose one can't blame them. In some ways, it's almost endearing, isn't it? How they refuse to give up hope." He reached into his shirt pocket and brought out his own, much smaller envelope. "Maybe you should open it here, just in case you have any questions."

David tore open the envelope, unfolded the single slip of paper inside, only to discover it was blank.

"It's over, Mr. Richards," Rustam said. "The ship yesterday, that was the last one. If it tries to return, we will destroy it." He gazed out at the city. "It's time now to end this. I imagine that's something we can both agree on."

But David, thinking of what had come in on that last ship, of what was to happen the next morning, struggled mightily to not smile.

Rustam turned back to him, extended his hand. "And since there'll be no more notes from us, I imagine this will be the last time we see each other. I know we got off to a rocky start, Mr. Richards, but I'd like to think that, if not a friendship, at least we developed a certain rapport."

David didn't reply, but this time, he shook the young man's hand.

It began very much as he had envisioned it. A series of white flashes on the barren hills just above the Fatikh neighborhood, and then an instantaneous blanket of black-and-gray smoke and plumes of dirt over a wide swath of no-man's-land, and only after that the sound, a series of pops rather like far-off firecrackers.

In the small park just off People's Struggle Boulevard, David leaped to his feet. Training his binoculars on the lower edge of that wreath of smoke and dust, he scanned back and forth along the government trench line. From what he could make out, the soldiers hadn't started up the hill yet.

He had, of course, broken his promise to General Kalima—at least part of it. While he'd kept quiet about the timing of the attack, he had never seriously entertained the notion of staying at the Moonlight to watch it from a distance. Instead, slipping from Amira's sleeping embrace at about 4:00 AM, he had descended through the hotel and with a couple of packs of American cigarettes had bribed the guards at the promenade gate into letting him break curfew. From there, he had begun the five- or six-mile walk up to the little park on Baktiar Hill with its panoramic view of the city and of the Fatikh neighborhood, perhaps a mile or so inland. He had been tempted to move even closer, but had finally decided that no other vantage point would give him this bird's-eye view, and so he had sat in the obscuring shadow of a large shrub and anxiously counted off the minutes, the seconds, until 6:15.

Now there came the clatter of machine guns, the whoosh of grenade launchers, bursts of red and orange were everywhere in the blanket of smoke over no-man's-land, but still David could see no soldiers starting up from the trenches.

"Where are they?" he whispered to himself. "Where the fuck are they?"

And then finally he saw them, hundreds of antlike figures emerging out of the smoke, clambering over the broken ground, and the sight came as such a profound relief, such a precise replication of the images that had played in his mind, that it took him several seconds to realize it was all wrong. The soldiers were running in the wrong direction. They were coming down the hill, not going up, they were appearing out of the smoke just in front of the government trenches. And now they were in those trenches, and now they were past them, in the streets of Fatikh, and everywhere antlike figures were running, scattering, going down, and up the hill hundreds more were coming on, a whole hillside of them coming on.

"Jesus Christ," David muttered in shock, and then there was no more time for shock, he sprinted back through the park to People's Struggle Boulevard. Already people were running, cars honking and careening around them, and everyone was going in the same direction, downhill, toward the sea, and someone shouted, "The rebels have broken through, they're in the city," and the air was rent by a wail of car horns and human voices and in-coming rockets. And all David could think was to join in the stampede down the hill, to get back to the hotel, back to Amira.

Time froze, time fast-forwarded, everything was just a series of jarred, out-of-focus images as he ran. Above his own rasping, ragged breath, David heard the gunfire growing louder, closer, the rebels pouring down into the city like a tide, like lava off a mountain, and the nearest thing to a strategy he could devise was to keep as much distance from them as possible, to try and cross over the last place that tide would reach, and so he raced for the promenade. Others were already there, thousands of them, and they were pressing tightly against the seawall railing, as if hoping that somehow the tide of war wouldn't reach this farthest point, more pressing in all the time, so many that surely the railing would collapse and spill them into the bay. David stayed to the clear, inland side of the walk, kept running, collided and caromed off those running the other way. Just a mile or so to the Moonlight now, its white walls and red domes bouncing and jarring before his eyes.

And as he ran, it came to David why he hadn't seen the army assault force forming in the streets of Fatikh, why it had been the rebels who had seized the initiative. Because there had never been an assault force. Because instead, Kalima had cut a deal with the KPLA. And then something else occurred to him, how Kalima had arranged it. Through him. Through all those packets of letters he had carried up to Rustam on Gowarshad Pass.

In the path ahead, a group of men stripping out of their clothes, some already down to their underwear, clothes and boots and guns scattered on the stones around them, and as he approaches, David realizes that they are government soldiers trying to become civilians again. They spot him coming on, they look at him with faces contorted with fear and helplessness and rage, and here is a danger that David hadn't anticipated, and he just gets his hand up in a placating gesture, is still thinking of the right words to say when, out of the corner of his eye, he sees the rifle butt swinging in—almost as if in slow motion, almost as if he is watching the climactic moment of a baseball movie—and then he sees an explosion of little white lights against a blackness, he hears the blow to his head more than feels it, a crack, and then he is on his hands and knees on the stones and the soldiers who want to be civilians are standing over him.

Something metallic and gummy in his mouth, a smell like iron in his nose, and David feels the blood running down his cheek, sees it dripping off him to spatter on the stones, but more than this, he feels their shadows above him, and so he summons his last strength to lift his face to them, eyes already starting to flutter closed, and through the blood filling his mouth, he tries to smile or say something they might like to hear.

Fourteen

He marked the days by their dawns. With each, he found he had lost a bit more of her during the night.

First to leave was the touch of her: the feel of her hand, the way she tousled his hair, kissed the nape of his neck. After this, it was her scent: the perfume she wore, the breath of her. By the fourth morning, he began to lose the sight of her. He tried to forestall this by concentrating on specific moments when they had been together but, try as he might, her likeness grew steadily more indistinct, a ghost floating ever farther away, and then, not even a ghost, just an absence where she had been. In this way, he lost her smile, the shape of her eyes, he lost the memory of the hopefulness with which she had gazed out at the world.

What stayed was her sound—her laugh, her sigh, the quiet way she sneezed—and it was a great comfort during those long days of waiting to still have these, to hear her again whenever he wished. But then even these started to go, one by one, drowned out by the other sounds in his mind or those coming from beyond the walls of his cell: the shuffling footsteps of the guards in the corridor, a distant car horn, the bang upon his door, upon his ears and teeth, from the firing squad in the courtyard.

By dawn of the seventh day, he found she was gone completely, that he had nothing left of her to lose, and it occurred to him that this had not happened in the sleep of his nights, but rather in all those hours he had spent watching that gap beneath his door, in all those other sounds he had listened to.

This realization came to him at that moment when his cell door was suddenly cast open, and there stood Rustam. He stared down at David with his wry smile, gripping a strip of white cloth the way a cook might grip a dishrag.

"So at last I find you, Mr. Richards," the young man said in that soft, gentle voice of his. As he came across the room, he raised the blindfold. "I'm sorry."

Two men leading him, their hands clutching his bound arms just above the elbows. Down four flights of stairs and through a cool, noisy hallway, and then out into the sunshine of the courtyard, a brightness that even the blindfold couldn't keep out.

Not the rhythmic tromping of feet, not the firing squad commander's death song. Just the two men beside him, gripping David's arms as they walked. The heat and bright of the courtyard left abruptly, and then they were in another place of cool shadow.

The idling of a car engine, one of its doors being opened, and David was guided into it. With the fingers of his tied hands, he felt the texture of the seat–vinyl–and between that and the tinny whir of the engine he decided he was in a small sedan. The car's other doors opening and closing, different weights settling in, and David believed there were three others in there with him–the two who had led him, a driver–and he confirmed this by isolating the different cadences of their breathing.

The sedan started forward, went only a short distance before stopping. A whispered exchange between the man sitting in the front passenger seat–Rustam, David was quite certain–and someone outside. The sound of a heavy gate opening, and the car went forward again, passed over some kind of metal grate. Different sounds then—truck horns, music, a child shouting—sounds of the city. Somewhere far off, the blare of martial music, the rhythmic beating of drums.

A journey of ten seconds at most and then another stop. The car doors opening, the weight of its passengers lifting, and now David was being taken out, guided along a paved street, only one hand holding his arm.

Another idling car engine—a deeper, richer hum than the first—another door being opened, David helped into the backseat, joined by the man guiding him. This car was air-conditioned, its seat was of plush fabric, but something odd: on the air, the powerful scent of mint, and from the front seat, a soft crunching sound, the smacking of lips.

Fingers tugging on his wrists, untying the rope, and then the blindfold was pulled from his eyes. David blinked against the abrupt brightness, looked to the man beside him: Rustam, as he had suspected. He turned to the smacking sound coming from the front passenger seat and there, clutching a small box of candy and wearing a happy grin, was General Allen B. Munn.

"Junior Mint?" Munn held the box toward him. When David didn't respond, he brought the candy back to his side, popped another in his mouth. "I gotta tell you, Mr. Richards," the general said with a slow shake of his head, "you're a sight for sore eyes. You've had me worried half to death here."

"So I gather you two are already acquainted." Munn motioned to Rustam as the Mercedes pulled through the gates of the Moonlight Hotel. "Rusty here's the new minister of social welfare—gonna be a hell of an asset to the new administration."

In the lobby milled dozens of armed Kutaran men, some in street clothes, others in various patchworks of camouflage, and they quickly parted as General Munn led the way to the mahogany table. Drawing up at its head, he set his briefcase atop, glanced between David and Rustam.

"Have a seat, Mr. Richards, we've got a lot to go over. And Rusty, you wanna kinda move everyone back away from here–got some kinda sensitive stuff to go over with Mr. Richards here."

Rustam moved off, began shooing the clusters of men across the room.

"Helluva kid," Munn said, settling into his chair. "Went to Harvard, you know?"

David took the seat alongside, gazed around the lobby. In contrast to the emaciated and haggard look of many of the government soldiers in recent weeks, the rebels appeared well fed and rested, were clearly enjoying their opulent surroundings.

"Now first off," Munn said, "I do hope there's no hard feelings over that whole episode with the king. Suspect we were both feeling a bit suboptimal at that point in time, probably both verbalized some things we regret–sure know I did."

David watched as Munn rummaged through his open briefcase. He noticed a second silver star on the general's collar, and a new service medal–presumably for Operation Partners in Peace–on his chest.

David had barely said a word since his blindfold had been removed, figured the less said until he could figure out what was going on, the better. On one matter, though, he could hold back no longer. "Where are the others?"

Munn glanced up from his rummaging. "How's that?"

"The others who were staying here."

"Oh, right. Yeah, the empress and the Italian guy got flown out a couple days ago."

"The empress?"

"You know, the old lady, the empress of Slavonia." Munn shook his head in awe. "What a woman–real class–but the poor thing, she couldn't access her bank accounts due to the communications breakdown and she needed to get to the Cayman Islands right away. Had to lend her the money out of my own pocket."

"What about Amira? Amira Chalasani."

A flicker of wariness came into the general's eyes. "Her? Yeah, well, my understanding is that they've got her residing down at some kind of ladies facility."

"Ladies facility?"

Munn shifted in his chair. "Prison, as it were. Some business about her being a counter-revolutionary or something."

David lunged forward. "But that's absurd! She wasn't involved in anything."

"Yeah, well, the problem we got there is, turns out she's a dual citizen, so we're gonna have to step pretty carefully. Kinda have to respect the independence of their judicial system, if you know what I mean."

But if David still hadn't a clue of what was happening, he certainly knew that Munn's attitude toward him had undergone a profound transformation—and that Munn seemed to have a lot of clout with the rebels. "I want to see her," he said. "She didn't do anything but help with the refugees here. She has to be released."

The general eyed him, a brief test of wills. "Tell you what, Mr. Richards, why don't we get through our work, and then we'll see if we can't work something out—appeal to the authorities, so to speak. In the meantime, don't worry, nothing's gonna happen to her. I've got a personal assurance on that from the vice president himself."

David frowned. "But Kutar doesn't have a vice president."

"It does now: General Kalima. He's the one who picked you up, too. Apparently he was worried you might want to verbalize certain aspects of your interpersonal dealings in a non-positive mode, but once I assured him that wasn't gonna happen, it was all smooth sailing—don't see any reason we can't work the same deal with this Chalasani gal." Munn chuckled, shook his head in amusement. "Ole Kally, he's really something, isn't he? A master strategist. Gonna be a hell of an asset to the new administration. Bit rough around the edges, 'course–might want to run him through one of those democracy workshops that USIA puts on." He turned back to shuffling through his briefcase. "Ah, here we go."

The general carefully brought out an oversize, embossed envelope, handed it to David as if it were something fragile and precious. "You got some pretty heavy-hitting people behind you, Mr. Richards," he said with an ingratiating smile. "Hell, you might outrank me before this is all over."

The letter was from the Secretary of State, and it had been written on his personal stationery:

> *Dear Mr. Richards:*
>
> *In light of your outstanding and meritorious service under extraordinarily difficult circumstances in the Kingdom of Kutar, I very much look forward to the opportunity to meet with you personally in the near future, and to discuss your future career options here at State. You may also be flattered to learn that I cited your case at this week's Cabinet meeting as a sterling example of the selflessness and courage of our Foreign Service Officer corps. As the President so eloquently verbalized at that meeting, your heroism in the face of such adversity personifies the very values and ideals of liberty, democracy, and economic opportunity that have made our nation a beacon of freedom throughout the world, and he joins me in the hope that we might find an even more prominent position for you in this administration from which to promote said values and ideals.*

David set the letter down, more bewildered than ever. Here he had thought he would be going back to the States in shackles; instead, the Secretary was supposedly talking him up to the President.

His pondering was broken by Munn's perfunctory cough;

the general had retrieved a manila folder from the briefcase, had folded his hands atop it.

"Now, next thing we need to go over," he said, lowering his voice a little, "is the whole monetizational aspects of this situation."

"Monetizational?"

"As in money. As in four-point-two million dollars of money missing out of the embassy."

So now it all turns, David thought to himself. He came slowly forward in his chair. "Right, well–"

But General Munn cut him off with a raised hand. "Why don't you just hold off there for a minute, Mr. Richards, because I got some textual data of an explanatory nature here that might help clarify the situation." He flipped open the folder. From what David could make out, the top page was an affidavit of some sort: a short paragraph followed by several blank signature lines. "Now, this gets a little complicated, but near as I can determine, what happened was, that money was transferred from State over to a Defense Department account at some point in time for some kinda unspecified fiduciary purpose. 'Course, DOD is gonna replace those funds at some point, but the upshot of it all is that, because of this transfer, that missing money is currently a DOD concern, not a State Department one. You following me here, Mr. Richards?"

David shook his head. "Not really. I never heard anything about this transfer."

Munn turned the affidavit around to face David, set a pen atop it. "Yeah, well, that's because we're just finalizing it right now. But retroactively to the beginning of the fiscal year. Just as soon as you slap your John Hancock on this puppy."

But David merely stared at the general in confusion. With a sigh, Munn reached into his coat pocket for his box of mints, popped another in his mouth.

"All right: Let's see if I can't explain this in layman's terms." He stared across the lobby as he chewed. "First off, now that we've got regime change here, State naturally wants to patch things up with the new boys as quick as possible—let bygones be bygones, right? But that's kinda tough if it comes out that their man here dropped four million bucks trying to get them whacked. And it will come out if State can't explain where that money went. I mean, that's big bucks for you people. You're talking the General Accounting Office all over your ass, maybe congressional hearings, just one helluva mess. Now for illustrative purposes, you got any idea how much money went missing from the Pentagon budget last year? Ballpark figure, try right around seven billion. So that's the reason for the transfer: move the loss over to the guys with the proven ability to handle it. I mean, hell, four million"—Munn chuckled again—"you get five or six generals together, we can spend that on lunch."

It was beginning to make sense to David now. "So by covering the four million, you're basically buying State's silence on all this. And to make sure I go along with it, they give me a big promotion instead of putting me on trial."

Munn grinned. "We're a forgiving nation, Mr. Richards; everyone deserves a second chance. One thing I do want to caution you on, though: some of the boys back in procurement are pretty PO'd you went with the Red Chinese knock-offs on this thing. You ever find yourself in this situation again, make sure you buy American." He reached into the open folder, brought out half a dozen more affidavits. "Now, most of this stuff is just kinda pro forma—that you weren't mistreated in prison, that, based on your experience, the KPLA embraces the democratic lifestyle, stuff like that—but it's all gotta be signed, too."

At that moment, Rustam approached the table. "The foreign minister is here to see you, General."

Munn nodded. "Thanks, Rusty. You mind telling him I'll be a few more minutes? Just want to finish up with Mr. Richards here."

Rustam nodded, started to go, but then noticed David

staring up at him. He returned the gaze with a smile, but it was guarded, hesitant, it had none of the smugness so often displayed on Gowarshad Pass.

"Tell me, General," David said, "what are we calling them now?"

"How's that?"

David pointed to Rustam. "Rusty here and his pals. What are we calling them now?"

Munn riffled through his briefcase with a slight frown. "Well, I'd have to double-check the mission statement, but I'm pretty sure we got 'em down as the liberation forces."

David laughed lightly. "Liberation forces. That's great. From tribals to terrorists to liberators in less than six months, that's some real progress." He turned to the general. "So when did the fix go in? I mean, I can't really believe that you and Kalima were in on it from the very beginning, so I'm thinking it was right around the time you decided to get rid of the king. You come back in here, you take him out of the picture, and then it's just a matter of getting Kalima to cut a deal with the KPLA. Is that how it worked?"

Munn was stunned into silence, didn't take his eyes off David, didn't blink. At last, he began to slowly shake his head. "Son, I don't know what the hell you were smoking in that prison, but . . ." But now his shock was giving way to irritation; he leaned close to David. "You actually think we'd bother to plan something like this? For what? You think anyone cares enough about this cat box of a country to want to overthrow the government, that we give a rat's ass enough to pick sides?" He suddenly remembered Rustam was still standing alongside, turned in his direction. "No offense, Rusty. I'm just speaking, uh, metaphorically here." He wheeled back to David. "You State Department types just don't get it, do you? We don't need to pick sides. I mean, sure, maybe for a little while we tilt to one, try to help 'em out, but if they can't get their act together and the other side is rolling, well, get with guys with the mojo. That's the way we do it, and that's what makes us the greatest nation on earth. Because we're supple. Because we're adroit. Because we can change with the times. Because whatever happens, at the end of the day, we can be friends with anybody." He looked to Rustan again. "Isn't that right, Rusty?"

The young man gave a wary nod.

"They're killers, General," David said. "They sat up on that ridge for five months and they pounded this city into rubble." He turned to Rustam. "What's the body count, *Rusty*? You have any idea? Twenty, twenty-five thousand? Maybe a couple thousand more, the ones still buried under all the ruins you guys created?"

"Let me remind you, Richards," Munn said through clenched teeth, "that you are speaking to a government minister here, an ally that—"

"And they're still killing people, General. Every morning at the prison, the firing squad comes out. Some mornings it goes on for hours. Did you know that? Did you know that your new pals here are still murdering people?"

Munn had gone from florid to white with rage, the muscles in his jaw rhythmically flexed. "Maybe you'd better leave us, Rusty," he said in a hard, low voice. "Looks like me and Mr. Richards are hitting a conversational mode here."

The young man retreated from the table. In the heavy silence between them, Munn stared out the lobby windows to the swimming pool terrace. David watched as the grinding of his jaw slowed, the color gradually returned to his face.

"You know what the difference is between you and me, Richards?" he asked finally, still staring off. "I'm an optimist. I believe in the essential goodness of people, and I believe in redemption. And when you believe in those things, you don't pass judgment on others, you recognize that we all have our failings."

"I really hope you're not talking about the KPLA here, General," David said.

Munn turned to him then. "Oh, but I am. And about Kalima, too. That's exactly who I'm talking about. Now, no question there've been some unfortunate excesses here—some instances of irrational exuberance, if you will—and I think guys like Kalima and Rusty would be the first to admit that. But I also think we gotta play fair. Fact of the matter is, building democracy, it's a messy business, and I'm not sure any of us can be so high-and-mighty as to tell others there's one right way to do it. I mean, hell, even look at the United States—we had that whole slavery thing, there's been some criticism of how we treated the Indians—so I don't know that any of us should be getting up on our high horse and passing judgment here. The important thing is that the Kutarans now have a chance to start over, to begin a new chapter. They've broken with the past and, sure, that's always tough, that's always messy, but out of that, they can build something new, better than it was before. And you know who they owe it all to? Kalima. The one guy who saw how things were going and decided it was time for a change, who had the courage to extend a hand of reconciliation across the divide, to become a warrior for peace. Sure, maybe this played out different than we'd anticipated—Kalima pulled a pretty innovative move there—but it's all kinda worked out, hasn't it? The war's over, the new government's setting up, people are coming home, getting back to work, looking to the future." His anger was long gone, replaced by a kind of misty-eyed thoughtfulness. "And you know what all that reminds me of? It reminds me of America. The courage to break with the past, to boldly march toward something new, to adapt, to endlessly adapt. Maybe you think that's naïve. Maybe you think I'm just some kind of hopeless romantic here, but I love my country too much to stop believing in freedom now. We are a light unto the world, Mr. Richards, which is why, a week ago, these guys"—he waved a hand at the lobby—"they thought they hated America, they thought we were the enemy, and now they're our friends. What does that tell you? It tells me that, even here, people yearn for freedom, they yearn for democracy. It tells me that everyone is capable of redemption."

"Democracy," David repeated with a bitter chuckle. "It's just one of those words that rolls off your tongue, isn't it, General? Democracy. Freedom. Ally. And none of them mean a thing. In six months, we'll have forgotten all about this place again. It'll just fall away, back into oblivion."

Munn watched him with a smirk, a slow shake of his head. "I don't know what happened to make you such a cynic, son, but you're wrong. And seeing as how you're so highly regarded back in Washington, I'll tell you why you're wrong." He leaned close. "You remember that geologist team that was out here last year? Well, they're on their way back. Somebody at the Geological Survey finally thought to give those maps of the northern mountains a closer look, and you know what he found? One hundred percent perfect conditions for titanium. And not just a little. All indications are we could be looking at the largest titanium deposit anywhere in the world." He sat back with an air of triumph. "That plays out, this country becomes . . . I don't know, the Switzerland of the region, a vital American ally. It means our commitment to this country is just beginning."

David stared at Munn. Then he laughed. "Nineteen seventy-two, General."

"How's that?"

"That's the last time they decided there was titanium here—1972. They sent a huge team over, mapped the entire highlands. You know what they found? Nothing. Not a goddamned thing."

With a look of consternation, Munn reached into his pocket for another candy, slipped it between his lips. As he chewed, he gazed over the lobby. "Oh, well." He noticed the affidavits on the table between them, tapped them with a finger. "So, why don't you sign these things, we can both go on about our day."

David looked down at the papers, shook his head. "No.

Sorry, but I'm not going to be part of this whitewash, General. You want to go back to the way it was before, bring me up on charges, that's fine, but I'm not going to be a party to this."

General Munn let out a weary sigh. For the briefest instant, David thought he might have flummoxed the man, but then Munn turned to call across the lobby: "Hey, Rusty, is that justice minister still around here?"

Presently a young, severe-looking man approached the table, introduced himself as Walid Ardeshir, the new justice minister.

"Good to meet ya, Wally," Munn said. "Just got a quick question on this Chalasani gal you got down at the ladies facility. What charges is she facing again?"

"Enemy of the people," the man muttered.

Munn whistled through his teeth. "Ouch, sounds serious: I'm not even gonna ask what the penalty is for something like that." He looked at David. "So what do you think, Richards? Think there might be something we can do to help her situation?"

For a long moment, David stared into the general's placid face. Then he took up the pen and signed the sheaf of documents before him, one after the other. When he was done, Munn gathered them up, double-checked that they'd been signed in all the right places.

"All right, Wally. Looks like Miss Chalasani's case just got adjudicated. How about sending someone down to the ladies facility and bring her on up here?"

The new justice minister shifted uneasily on his feet. "But we can't do that, sir. She's a dual citizen and the charges against her are very—"

"Yeah, yeah, that's terrific"—Munn waved a hand—"just go get her."

As the young man left, the general gave David a sheepish grin. "They're kinda green on the whole speedy-justice thing, pretty steep learning curve." Sliding the affidavits back into his briefcase, he snapped it shut, got to his feet. "Well, let me go wrangle with the foreign minister. They're talking about changing the name to the People's Republic of Kutar, and I'm trying to tell 'em the 'people's' bit is a big non-positive. Just sounds commie, you know?" With his briefcase, Munn started purposefully away.

———————

He waited for her at the foot of the entrance stairs, just across from the fountain. After a time, he heard someone coming down the marble steps and turned to see it was Rustam. The young man stopped at his side.

"I'm sorry, Mr. Richards," he said. "Not for how it turned out, of course, but . . . well, for you, I guess."

David nodded, looked at the stumps of the palm trees that had once lined the hotel drive. "So what was it all for, Rustam? The great war of liberation, getting rid of the Americans, the old regime, and now you're right back in bed with them: Kalima, Munn. What was it all for?"

There was a quiet as Rustam considered the question. "It got away from us," he said at last. "I tell you this as one man to another. It got away from us. All we wanted at the beginning was for the regime to leave us northerners alone, self-rule or autonomy or . . . But we kept winning. The old regime just kept falling apart, and so we kept on. What else could we do?"

David looked at him then. "You could have accepted Nigel Mayhew's peace deal. That would have given you everything you wanted. All this could have been avoided."

Rustam smiled as he stared over the dead lawn, a small, private smile. "Why did we keep on?" he said softly, as if to himself. "You know, I think it's the same answer I found when I was at Harvard. For my senior paper, I decided to write about the psychology of war, why young men are attracted to it." He laughed gently. "Big mistake. I read so many books on the subject, all these different theories—it's biology, it's social conditioning, it's peer pressure—but you know what I concluded? Men go to war because they can.

That's all I could come up with. Well, a pretty short paper—I ended up writing about compulsive hand washers or something—but I think the answer to your question is the same. Why did we keep on? Because we could. Why did we destroy this city? Because we could. I don't think there was a lot of thought behind it. I think it just kind of . . . happened."

A sedan came up the gravel drive, and David moved away from Rustam in anticipation. As it circled around the fountain, the passenger door was flung open and Amira leaped out, ran to him. For a long time, they didn't kiss or even look at each other, just embraced, held on.

"I thought you had died," she whispered, her voice muffled against his chest.

He rubbed her back. "I promised I wouldn't, remember?"

Amira broke from their embrace then, hurried back to the car, and when she returned, she held his photo album in her hands. The sight made him laugh, brought tears to his eyes.

"And I made a promise, too," she said.

———————

They walked in the direction of Independence Park, slowly, hand in hand. For a long while, they barely spoke. In a peculiar way, there was very little to be said.

As they walked, the martial music and beating drums that had carried for hours on the air grew steadily louder until, on the wide avenue fronting the park, they discovered a victory parade was under way. As the sunken-faced residents of Laradan lined the sidewalks to watch, there passed a steady procession of military trucks, rebels still toting their rifles. Interspersed with these were clusters of much healthier-looking civilians—presumably northerners bussed down to the city for the occasion—and they clutched small Kutaran and American flags as they waved to the onlookers.

Amira suddenly gripped David's arm. "My God, there's Zahra!"

And sure enough, there was her great-aunt, looking precisely as Amira had described her, and she was leading her village's contingent down the avenue, smiling, waving to the crowd, fluttering her little Kutaran and American flags in the air.

Taking David's hand, Amira began to press forward, maneuvering through the crowd toward her great-aunt. But then she stopped. Going no farther, she just stood there, at the edge of the parade, and watched the old lady pass, watched all the others she knew from Chalasan—her cousins, her childhood friends—pass. Then she turned and started out from the crowd, away from the sight.

———

General Munn was doing paperwork at the lobby table when one of the rebels excitedly approached; he carried a bundle under his arm.

"What you got there, fella?"

The young man held the bundle out. "One of the men found it up on the roof, in a little shed up there."

The general set his pen down in amazement, stared at the American flag folded in its plastic sheath. "Well I'll be goddamned; it's the embassy flag." He took it with both hands, gave a merry laugh. "That's an omen of freedom right there, son, an omen of freedom."

———

David and Amira walked to the end of Pier 4, and there they sat. Through that long afternoon they stayed there, watching the ships coming into port, bringing back those people who had once found refuge in foreign lands, bringing in those things that might be needed to rebuild a ruined city. Through that afternoon they stayed there, watching the ships, reading the names of their home ports, imagining that eventually one might come that could take them to a place they didn't know.

"A mystery story, straight out of a plot from a novel by John Le Carré."
—The New York Times Book Review

THE MAN WHO TRIED TO SAVE THE WORLD

A swashbuckling Texan, a teller of tall tales, a womanizer, and a renegade, Fred Cuny spent his life in countries rent by war, famine, and natural disasters, saving many thousands of lives through his innovative and sometimes controversial methods of relief work. Cuny earned his nickname "Master of Disaster" for his exploits in Kurdistan, Somalia, and Bosnia. But when he arrived in the rogue Russian republic of Chechnya in the spring of 1995, eager to put his ample funds from George Soros to good use, he found himself in the midst of an unimaginably savage war of independence, unlike any he had ever before encountered. Shortly thereafter, he disappeared in the war-rocked highlands, never to be seen again. Who was Cuny really working for? Was he a CIA spy? Who killed him, and why? In search of the answers, Scott Anderson traveled to Chechnya on a hazardous journey that started as as a magazine assignment and ended as a personal mission. The result is a galvanizing adventure story and a tour de force of literary journalism.

Nonfiction/Adventure/978-0-385-48666-8